BOUND TO HAPPEN

BOUND

BOOK TWO

ANNIE R MCEWEN

BOUND TO HAPPEN

ISBN: 978-1-963705-07-2

Cover design: Clarissa Kezen ckbookcoverdesigns.com

Published in the United States of America by Harbor Lane Books, LLC.

www.harborlanebooks.com

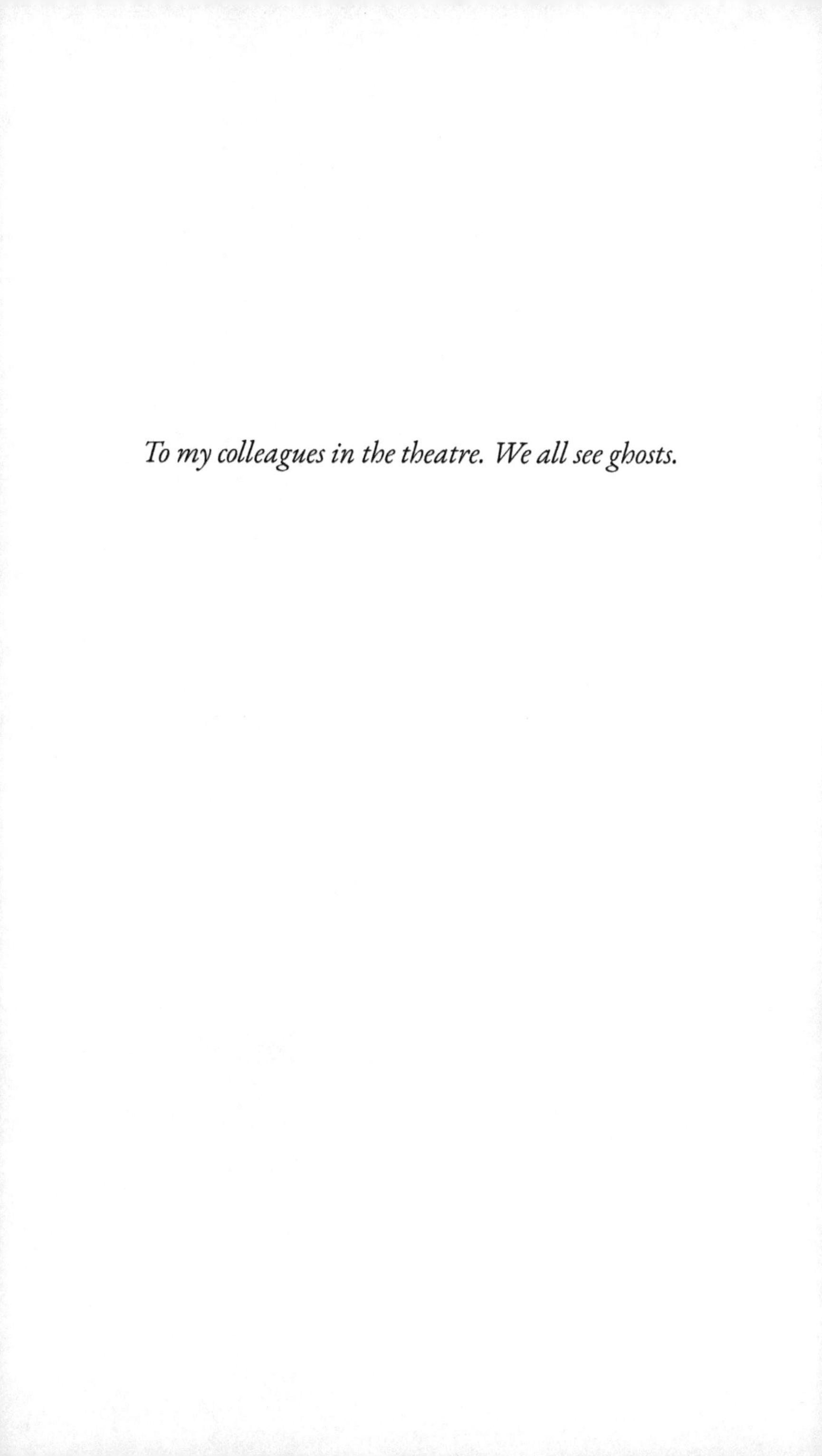

To my colleagues in the theatre. We all see ghosts.

ONE

"Shakespeare's dead."

"He was really old, Fee."

"Mice live a long time."

"Parrots live a long time." The pulsing vein in Abeni's forehead said she was fighting an eyeroll. "Mice live one to two years, on average. You got Shakespeare after you came to London on the NEH grant. Two and a half years ago, Fee."

"Three."

"Oh, right, I forgot. You're one of the Illuminati who got their grant renewed. Twice."

The garden at the back of their Victorian-mansion-now-flats had been eroded by a century and a half of shifting property lines. What remained was a fifteen-by-thirty rectangle that only caught the sun on one side. It was where the climbing roses grew, forgotten for decades but improbably thriving against the brick wall—new leaves here, a cluster of buds there. Despite the neighbor-hood's name, it was astounding that anything at all bloomed amid the tightly packed buildings of Bloomsbury.

Shakespeare's small white corpse lay across Fee's open hands, on a blue handkerchief. She spoke without lifting her eyes from it. "Did you dig the hole?"

Abeni pointed to a cavity in the dark earth, under the roses. The clustered blossoms overhung the spot in clumps, their faces turned down as though in mourning. Fee forced herself to look into the hole. It seemed deep enough. Mouse times five or six. There was a layer of scarlet petals at the bottom, making Fee tear up.

"Thank you for the flowers."

"He was a grand little mouse, Fee. He deserves orchids, but roses are all the garden offers."

The two of them stood there for a bit, staring at the hole. The finality of it was somehow worse than Shakespeare's dying. He'd gone so quickly. One minute up and scurrying, pink nose wrinkling and whiskers a-quiver. Next, he was down, with hardly a twitch to mark the end. So fast it seemed impossible, as though he might jump up squeaking and run along her arm. *"Ha ha! Fooled you!"*

People liked to say, *it's a blessing he didn't linger*. Fee wasn't sure it was true with mice or humans. At least a long illness gave you a chance to brace yourself. Though, with her parents...

"Fee." Abeni's voice was kind but firm. The voice of the coroner before the sheet was pulled back from the body. "You ready?"

Abeni probably had a lecture to get to. It wasn't fair to make her late. Graduate teaching assistants were held to high standards at the Slade. "I'm ready. Let's do this."

She knelt on the soggy ground by the hole, not caring if her jeans got soaked. Carefully wrapping Shakespeare in her hanky, like a little burrito, she lowered him into the hole. She stayed on her knees for a minute, wanting to say something but not wanting to look like a complete fool in front of her flat mate. Finally, she softly recited a few lines from Christina Rossetti, a poet who'd lived deep in Death's shadow and died in Torrington Square just a few blocks away.

"Be the green grass above me,
With showers and dewdrops wet;
And if thou wilt, remember,
And if thou wilt, forget."

"Amen," Abeni said. Fee stood and they hugged, long and comforting. Abeni pulled away, holding her friend by the shoulders. "Aoife Gowdie, you were the best mouse mum ever. Shakespeare had a wonderful life." Abeni picked up her shoulder bag from the lawn where she'd dropped it to dig the grave. "You look like you could use a cuppa and some food."

"I've got work to do at the British Library."

"And I've got a gaggle of first-years to flog for their crimes. Tea later?"

"Sure, but not too early. Five o'clock?"

"King's Café. Chin up, pet." Abeni left, heading for the street and the Slade.

Fee stayed where she was, staring at the dark cavity

with her blue-swaddled mouse in it. She bent and picked up the trowel Abeni had used. It was a fancy one she'd bought at Marks & Spencer in better times, when she had visions of backyard horticulture. Carefully, she filled in the hole and tamped down the top. Then, she stood by the mound of dirt while a single shaft of sunlight muscled its way through autumnal London clouds to shine on the grave.

———

"Come on, Fee, you need to get out more. You've been buried in the Libe for months. Is that a stipulation of your grant?" Abeni leaned forward, elbows on the table, and lowered her voice to a sepulchral drone. "To retain funding, the recipient must crawl between the pages of old books and stay there until she grows mold."

"Results, Abeni. Gotta get 'em, and that takes work."

"Crikey, I forgot! Me not having a stipend to study clog dancing novelists in the Jacobean Era."

"Ha bloody ha. It's lesser-known poets and play-wrights and where they—"

"Lived and worked, yeah, I got that. You, on the other hand, are working and not living." Abeni pointed to Fee's untouched plate. "You don't even eat."

"I eat." She looked guiltily around the King's Library Café. It was six o'clock, closing time, and the waitstaff were staring at her meaningfully. She'd spent most of the last hour on her laptop while Abeni mowed through a ham sandwich, a salad, a slice of apple tart, and two mugs of cocoa.

Her flat mate rapped her knuckles on the table to get Fee's attention. "Come out with the Club tonight."

The London Underground Club, LUCIES—Abeni and a dozen mad mates who called themselves "urban explorers." What they mainly did was bribe, cajole, and sometimes crowbar their way into the hundreds of below-ground features the city offered. Tunnels, crypts, buried streets, lost rivers, WWII bunkers, defunct railways. Fee didn't understand the lure of metropolitan spelunking, but the LUCIES...they were one cellar shy of being addicts.

"Come *on*, Fee." The way Abeni stuck to a topic made leeches seem flighty. "You had fun at the holy well."

True. The after-hours visit to the ancient spring in the basement of the Australian embassy delivered just the right balance of trespass and wonder. "That was great, yeah. Because the Club didn't have to pry open any windows or pick any locks. What would they have done if your girlfriend Sarah didn't know an assistant to the Royal Air Force advisor? An assistant with a key and an alarm code."

Abeni lifted one shoulder and both dark eyebrows at the same time. "There's always a way in." She leaned toward Fee and grinned, displaying white teeth, full lips, coffee-colored skin, and eyes as big and honest as a child's. "If a place wants you inside, it *opens*."

"Right, the sexy burglar motto." The waiter headed their way with eviction on his face, and Fee closed her laptop. "Okay, but this is the last time. What are the LUCIES breaking and entering tonight?" She and Abeni both stood, gathering their various bags and jackets.

"No breaking and entering. Ben from the LUCIES, his husband's brother is the commercial real estate agent, so Ben got the key. You'll love this place. Most of it's not even underground. And it's in the neighborhood you're studying, where all those old poets and playwrights were kickin' it. Maybe it'll be haunted by their ghosts."

God forbid. "It's in Covent Garden?" Curiosity tiptoed up Fee's spine. "Is it a house?"

"Better. It's a theatre."

Two

"Christ, Abeni, it's the mansion from *Dark Shadows*." Fee let her head fall back. She could just make out faded lettering across the building's façade, near the top. *The Olympiad.*

Abeni's answer was a short bark of laughter, followed by, "Naw, it's a theatre, like I said."

"Looks more like an abandoned train station." Fee waved a hand at the looming four-story structure facing Drury Lane. Stone quoins wrapped the corners and brick chimneys rose from the steeply pitched roof. Dormer windows stuck out at irregular intervals, their sectioned glass panes reflecting the streetlights. "St. Pancras's sister, the one locked in the attic."

"No shade, Fee, but you do fight having a good time. Come on, then." Abeni grabbed Fee's arm and dragged her around the corner of the building to a door—the stage door?—a few steps up from an alley. The LUCIES were milling restlessly around the steps while Ben, cursing, fumbled with a chunky key ring. Holding her huge, mountaineer-type backpack in front of her, Abeni bullied her way up the steps to Ben's side. The second he got the door open, she pushed through and dragged Fee with her.

Inside, it was dark. Very, eerily, stomach-dropping dark. Fee had just enough time to think about cutting and running when the rest of the LUCIES tumbled in, waving their flashlights, shoving and cackling like a flock of geese. Several of them yelled about light and there was a heavy *thunk*, followed immediately by applause as a row of filthy and decrepit-looking wall sconces marching around the perimeter of the room flickered to life. It was a miracle they illuminated anything; the space was high and deep as a barn.

Fee blinked like a lemur as she blundered forward. Her flat mate hadn't been kidding. "Jesus, Abeni, you're right. It *is* a theatre." Abeni had walked ahead and Fee, gawking at the ceiling about a mile overhead, ran into her from behind. They both laughed.

Abeni grabbed Fee's shoulder. "Told tha, din't I, hen? It's like Grand Theatre back home."

Home for Abeni being Doncaster, Southern York-shire. In the U.K. since age three, Abeni had lost the accents of her Ghanaian homeland, while grad school in London had schooled away most of the North Country speech. But when she got excited, her r's came out as "*ahr*'s" and words like "tha" poked through.

"The Grand in Doncaster," Fee mused. "Nineteenth century?"

"Aye, built in 1899. Been done over."

Fee let her eyes roam the Stygian interior of the

LUCIES' latest discovery. It looked pretty bad, but from her point of view, "done over" wasn't always an improvement. It was tough to recover anything historic from a building when most of it had been replaced. "Why hasn't this place been done over?"

"Costs a bloody mint is why." Abeni burrowed into her backpack and came up with a miner's light on a head strap. "Investors are finally sniffing around. The biggest one wants to pull down the place to build luxury flats. Ben's husband's brother is doing handsprings."

Back, front, and one-handed handsprings, no doubt. The commission on the sale of an ideally situated parcel in Covent Garden would enable the CRE to drive clients around in a Mercedes. With mink seat covers.

Fee squinted into the barely illuminated theatre. "I'm surprised the power's on. Should we even have lights? What if somebody sees them from outside?"

Abeni had gone back to squirreling through her backpack. Pulling out a battery lantern, she flicked the switch and it glowed reassuringly. "Most of the windows are boarded over, at least on the lower floors. And nobody ever looks up. Power's on because the seller turned it on. Or maybe Ben's brother-in-law. Nobody wants a potential buyer breaking a leg in here." Another battery lantern came out of the backpack and Abeni handed it to Fee. "You'll need this. Not all the lights work."

Fee took the lantern and switched it on. The other LUCIES were switching on their own, one by one. Drifting dust sparkled in the weak light from the ancient wall sconces, and the battery lanterns bobbed and traveled in the LUCIES' hands as the group fanned out. The auditorium looked like an underwater scene, phosphorescent fish darting in the depths.

"Does this theatre have a history?" she asked Abeni.

"That'll be your patch, Ms. Theatre Historian, not mine." Abeni turned and grinned, teeth pearly in the gloom. "Maybe you can research it, since you have *a grant.*"

Right, sure, Abeni, I'll do that. She lifted her lantern and moved it in a slow arc, trying to see into the depths of the auditorium. The Olympiad wasn't the biggest theatre she'd ever been in, but it wasn't a bijou playhouse, either. Mid-sized, she'd call it. The floor was gently raked, higher at the back, lower toward the stage, the slope giving better visibility to patrons in the rear. One mezzanine at the back sagged dangerously in the middle, but there was no dress circle or other levels higher up. Despite its imposing exterior, the Olympiad was clearly not intended for large crowds or wealthy patrons.

The LUCIES, including Abeni, had scattered. *Guess I'm on my own. Lone Safari to Theatreland.* Holding her lantern high, she took a few cautious steps, shuffling to avoid tripping over something or falling through a hole in the floor.

There was plenty of risky footing. The auditorium looked more than a little like a war zone. Rows and rows of parallel holes in the floor showed where the lowest level seats—what Brits called the stalls—had been bolted to the planks and then ripped up. Carried away for salvage, probably, but some seats never made it that far and were in pieces here and there. A few rows close to the stage were miraculously still in place. She made her careful way to the end of the front row and ran her hand over a cast iron armrest. Like even the most utilitarian Victorian items, the armrest and seat supports were nicely cast in curling forms. Pretty.

The seat bottom was flipped up. Unlike the slatted seat back, it was solid and looked like oak. She desperately wanted to sit in it, just for a minute or two. Just to feel what it was like to be in the audience for a play or variety show in the horse-and-carriage era.

She pressed the seat down as gently as she could, but the hinges screamed, and she yanked back her hand. Her fingers came away black and gritty with decades of dirt, so she decided against the Theatre Seat Immersive Experience. Fee was relieved she'd worn grubby clothes: her faded black Bonobos jeans and a knit henley that'd seen better days.

Turning toward the stage, she hoisted her lantern again and scrutinized the proscenium the best she could in the stingy light. If she were a painter, she'd call the pale arch *Still Life: A Study of Death in Progress.* The top part of the arch was intact, a plaster scroll anchoring the middle. Inside the scroll, incised, black-painted numbers read 1881. Abeni's Doncaster Grand was the younger sister, then, by eighteen years.

Sadly, the bottom eight or ten feet of plaster on both sides of the proscenium arch were missing altogether. The underlying wood frame was exposed and somehow embarrassed, like a Gaslight Era lady whose skirts had blown up and shown her knickers. *Poor old girl,* Fee thought, *your frillies are gone.*

Above the ruined part, intact decorative plaster rose china-white and undamaged. The motif, blooming tulips, was charming.

The old theatre tugged at Fee's heart. The historian in her accepted its slide toward oblivion, but the theatre lover was offended. Was she naïve to cling to the belief that actors practiced their art in a sacred space, worthy of preservation? Oh, yeah, probably. But it was hard not to feel pity for the once-treasured, now-trashed Olympiad. It seemed so wrong that—

Fee's shoulders jerked at a small but distinctive noise from somewhere close. A dry rustling or scrabbling, familiar, unmistakable. Abeni had moved far enough away that Fee had to raise her voice to a yell. "Oi, Abeni! I thought you said there were no rats in here."

"Oi, yourself," Abeni yelled back. "What I said was that when the agent gave Ben's husband the key, he said the building was rat free."

And a realtor would never misrepresent a property, Abeni. Fee heard the faint scrabble again, closer. She hadn't kept a pet mouse for years to not recognize rodent claws when she heard them. Frowning, she shifted her feet uncomfortably and peered down at them.

Ben, key holder and de facto headman of the night's safari, was already at the far side of the auditorium. He shouted as he pointed to some wonky-looking balconies on either side of the crumbling proscenium, "I'm going up there. Who's with me?"

Everyone except Fee whooped assent. A few even jumped up and down, yelping like beagles on caffeine.

Fee, the single, well-behaved cocker spaniel,

demurred. "Uh, I've got some issues with heights, so I'll hang out on the ground floor. Don't forget to drive your pitons in deep and keep those carabiners buckled."

Laughter and a few mocking chicken clucks were flung her way as the group ambled into the murk.

Abeni lagged behind. "All right, then, Fee?"

"Perfect, tickety boo. I just want to explore the stage. Go play with the other kiddies."

"Give a shout if you—"

"I will." She made a shooing motion. "Go!"

Abeni waved, then turned and sprinted after the LUCIES, dodging rubble. Fee waited until the sound of combat boots faded. She closed her eyes and breathed.

The smell of a theatre. Even through dust, damp, and the stale tang of human occupancy, an old theatre had a scent like no other building. It was made up of all the everyday elements of the actor's craft. Sand, bags of it for counterweights on the curtains, buckets of it backstage in case of fire. Scorched dust, the faint burnt caramel smell of it when heated to the combustion point by footlight bulbs. Resin, from the wings, where dancers dragged their shoes in it so they wouldn't slip.

Stage make-up. That smell really took Fee back. Back to her undergrad days when she'd wanted so fervently to be an actor. She'd worn commercial stage make-up, then. Pancake foundation and heavy eyeliner, waterproof mascara on top of fake lashes, three graded layers of blush.

In the glory days of this theatre—Victoria on the throne and bustles on bums—actors wore greasepaint, lard blended with powdered calcimine. They mixed their own raw pigments into it: blue, pink, yellow. Pure carmine for lips. Sometimes antimony, a deadly poison, for shadows under cheekbones, in the creases alongside the mouth. She saw those long-dead, painted players moving behind her eyelids, as on a silent movie screen. Sarah Bernhardt as Cleopatra, long-nosed and long-limbed, her gaze kohl-lined and brazen, her fingertips hennaed. William Terriss as Henry VIII, his face bristling with fake whiskers and his hair dyed orange.

Her eyes snapped open and her shoulders twitched. That scrabbling noise again! It was close, *very* close, and if it wasn't a rodent she'd eat her hat. If she had a hat. Maybe she should've worn one, a hard hat. She dropped her head back and examined the ceiling. It was mostly broad patches of visible lathing, the plaster not where it should be but on the floor in water-stained lumps.

Up in the balcony, one of the LUCIES yelled something and a mixed chorus of laughter followed. Ben's shrieking tenor, Abeni's husky guffaw, the German guy whose name she hadn't gotten. He had a reverse donkey laugh. *Hah-eee. Hah-eee.* The laughter and shouts faded as the group was drawn away by something else. Dressing rooms, maybe, or the manager's office.

Fee picked her way carefully across the space in front of the orchestra pit, toward stage left. It was left only in theatrical terms, since everything was defined from the perspective of the actor facing outward. If she knew her theatres, there would be a door with steps behind it. The steps would lead onto the stage.

She found them, and they did. A half dozen wooden and surprisingly solid steps clunked hollowly under her feet as she climbed them. At the top, she took a deep breath of the familiar-but-strange air and held it for a count of five. Exhaling through her lips, she walked gingerly out and across the cupped and uneven boards of the stage, alert for any loud creaks or cracks that said *Warning! Rotten boards! You'll fall into the trap room and break your leg!*

In a play, disaster would have struck as she approached stage center. In boring real life, nothing happened. The theatre was old and made ugly by surface damage, but surprisingly well-built. The boards barely made a sound as she crossed them. At stage center, she halted. After a moment's thought, she traveled downstage and examined the row of antiquated footlights on the lip of the proscenium. Electric, since they had lightbulbs in them. Some lightbulbs, at least, more or less every other socket. There was probably a switch for them somewhere, but it would be a balmy weekend in Hell before Fee started an electrical fire in a historic building by flipping it.

Leaving her lantern just behind the empty middle footlight socket, Fee backed up to stage center. Sighing, she lifted her head. If she were an actor, she'd give herself a long moment before she delivered her first line, using it to look into the audience and get its measure.

Regret stabbed her again, sharp and unwelcome as a thorn. She was sure—fairly sure, anyway—that she'd made the right choice to put aside an acting career. That didn't mean it didn't still hurt. The most painful part, at the very center of the hurt, was admitting she didn't have enough talent for an actor's life. At least, that's what her professors in UNC's Department of Theatre had told her. They would know, wouldn't they?

They weren't in this theatre, though, on this night, this stage. What harm could it do to gaze beyond the dead footlights as though she belonged here? She could almost sense the patrons who filled the auditorium. Ladies with hats on their heads, gents with them on their laps. Smells of perfume and powder, tobacco and damp wool, rising from the stalls. A cough here, a murmur there. Then, a hush as she, the actor she might have been, held them breathless and expectant.

Idly, she used her toes to trace an invisible X on the dusty boards just in front of where she stood. Her mark, in theatre parlance. The stage manager called "Places, please!" and she hastened to it. The curtain slid open, making a dignified shush on its metal rings, the sound of a gown sweeping across a ballroom floor. The warmth from the footlights swelled to greet her like a lover's smile. Every face in the audience turned up to hers.

What play had she given them? Had they come to laugh themselves silly at *Charley's Aunt*? Or to see Nora in *A Doll's House*, so warm and beautiful, so sly and vain? Were their tickets bought just so they could weep with poor, doomed Ophelia?

Ophelia. The name ached like a bruise. At the end of her sophomore year at UNC, the Theatre Department produced *Hamlet*. She'd been shattered when the director hadn't cast her as Ophelia. He'd probably made the right decision, and it was certainly his to make. *Don't be a sore loser*, she'd told herself afterward. There were students with more roles under their belt and probably more talent, too.

But even now, she wondered if her lingering French speech—thirteen years of life in Paris with her family had left her with an Eiffel Tower-sized accent—had something to do with the casting decision the director *had* made for her.

Gertrude, Hamlet's mother, painted by Shakespeare as an out and out tramp.

It was grossly unfair if her Frenchiness influenced the casting, but Fee didn't dare raise objections. The raising might have required an explanation of why she sounded not just like a Parisian but one from the year 1774, the year she'd left France in order to slip through time to the 21st century and university life in North Carolina, USA.

Only Fee, her great-aunts in Savannah, and a handful of witches in Wales knew the why and how of *that*.

Her accent had faded away by the time she graduated, but the memory of Gertrude the Whore and her seventy lines in *Hamlet* hung on, still jabbing at her ego. If she'd just had that one chance, that one dream role, she could've binned her acting ambitions and gone with a gladder heart into the academic end of theatre.

Specifically, Theatre History. Even more specifically, London Theatre of the 1600s. Her life and work, now. Her change of major so late in the game threw the timetable for her degrees off, but that wasn't the problem.

The problem was the other thing, the acting thing. It still had its hooks in her. Changing her major hadn't changed her first love.

Well, I've got a stage totally to myself, now. She pressed and swiveled her toes a little, one foot at a time, into the gritty boards. *Your cue, Ms. Gowdie.*

With no one to see, hear, or judge, she lifted her voice in Ophelia's monologue, childishly happy to give the words to an empty theatre since she'd lost her one chance to give them to a full one.

"And I, of ladies most deject and wretched,
That sucked the honey of his music vows,
Now see that noble and most sovereign reason
Like sweet bells jangled, out of tune and harsh—"

She took in breath for the long last lines, but before they left her lips, she heard them from stage right. The words unfurled from a male voice, deep and exquisitely English, but with an underlying hoarseness, an edge she felt in her bones.

"Blasted with ecstasy. Oh, woe is me,
T'have seen what I have seen, see what I see!"

Fee whirled toward the sound, peering into the deeply shadowed stage right wings. "Who's there?" Five tense seconds ticked by. She spoke again, louder. "Show yourself!"

After fifteen more seconds of staring into the dark, she shrugged. Just what she needed in a group of people she barely knew, to be caught looking like the wannabe thespian she was.

And a phantom voice from the gloom—really? One

of the LUCIES, of course, taking the piss out of the American. The newest member of any group always got the practical jokes, the hazing. Who cared? She wouldn't be joining the LUCIES for any more of their troglodyte parties, so they could take their initiation and sod right off with it.

No more words issued spectrally from the wings, so the joker must've lost interest. Pivoting her toes on the stage again, she arranged her arms in a graceful arc, then executed a *sauté* and *changement* combination, low ballet jumps in first, second, and third positions. The near silence of her landings amazed her. Despite its age and decades of neglect, the stage was sound and solid. It would've been a joy to act, to dance, on a stage like this.

Her UNC Theatre Department turned up its nose at musicals, but she'd done a run of *Sweet Charity* with a local community theatre in Chapel Hill.

"*I always get what I aim for, and your heart and soul's what I came for.*" She lustily sang the verse in a voice *The Chapel Hill Herald* called "not bad at all," and followed it with *chaine* turns to the right. Ending in a sultry pose, she belted, "*Whatever Lola wants, Lo-la gets!*" Hip cocked and chin lifted, she pouted at the mezzanine.

Damn it! She whipped around to face the stage right wings. That offstage male voice was back. Was he *chuckling?*

"Wanker!" she shouted into the dark recess. Still no response. *Coward.*

She crossed downstage and picked up her battery lantern, plotting her next hour. She wasn't at all sure she wanted to catch up with the LUCIES, but she wouldn't mind striking off for a little urban exploring of her own. She was even grudgingly glad she'd come. Abeni was right, she needed to get out more. And the building *was* in Covent Garden, the focus of her study. Two centuries past the end date of her thesis, true, but maybe something interesting, something theatrical, even, had been on the site before the Olympiad was built. Theatres in London had an almost comical habit of being built, destroyed, and rebuilt on the same spot, like Florida beach houses after hurricanes. While she was here, she might as well look around.

She raised her lantern to negotiate the backstage area. With any luck, she'd find the stairs that led to the dressing rooms.

———

"Abeni, this was great." Fee pulled Abeni aside. They could barely hear each other in the gabble of the LUCIES, loosely gathered in the auditorium after a two-hour rummage through the premises. Everyone was tired but still energized, nobody more so than Abeni.

"You had fun, yeah?"

"Uh, yeah. I need to come back."

"Back—*here*?" When Fee nodded, Abeni went on dubiously. "We don't usually visit a place twice, Fee. Repeated visits might, you know, draw attention."

"I can see how that might be a problem. But when I was exploring the—well, I guess you'd call it the basement—"

"Cellar."

"Right. Well, in the cellar, I found some evidence of a much earlier structure."

"You mean, like, *under* this one?" Abeni narrowed her eyes suspiciously at the floor, as though she expected a building to rise between her feet.

"Maybe. It looks that way, though I can't be sure without a closer look. And better light."

"Isn't there somebody you can just tell about it? I mean, you've got connections with the National Trust."

"They're not the kind of connections who would drop everything and rush over here to share a speculation. *If* there's even something to speculate about, which I can't begin to say without another look."

Abeni went quiet, which was rare for her, but she was obviously thinking. That was good. And she wasn't dismissing her flat mate's proposition as complete rubbish—even better.

Fee gave it a push. "I'm not saying there's another theatre under this one. But London theatres had a repurposing ethic that makes shabby chic look lame. Sometimes, three or four operated serially over the course of a few hundred years, all in the same spot." She put her hand on Abeni's arm, cross-training hard under the sleeve of her vintage British Army field jacket. "Please, Abeni. Can I get back in?"

Abeni shifted so her back was to the other LUCIES. "I can't believe I'm doing this." She jerked her chin at Ben's overloaded key ring, lying atop a stack of broken theatre seats a few feet away. "It's the blue key. Ben doesn't need it to secure the door, it just pulls to and locks. Knowing our Benjamin, he'll go home and hand the keys to his husband without even looking at them. Nick will forget about them until he sees his brother next, and by then, he'll have forgotten which key it even was. Space agents, the lot of them."

Abeni winked, then strode over to Ben and started a high-volume discussion about where the club was going for drinks and food. Her venue suggestion was met with loud groans and objections, and in seconds the group was totally absorbed in bickering.

With a mental apology to Mom and Papa who'd raised her to be unerringly honest, Fee sidled, quick and silent as a wraith, to the boxes and wrenched the blue key off the ring.

THREE

Gil watched from the shadows as the whole squawking gaggle prepared to depart the theatre. He only truly had eyes for the black-haired, breeches-wearing woman, and, because of that, he saw her lift the key. It was a neat piece of work; no St. Giles cutpurse could've managed it better. Hope surged within him.

She'd come back, she must. In all his long exile, none but she had heard his voice. How his heart soared when she startled at the sound of it! And she'd cursed him when he laughed, the pretty shrew. If she only knew he'd stand for hours while she heaped foul invective on him, just to watch her expression as she—heard—him—laugh.

'Struth, if she could hear him, dare he hope that she might see him? The irony was not wasted upon him. In life, he had done so much, so often, to avoid being seen, as every sharper skirting the law does. Now, he was desperate for just one pair of eyes to light upon his dusty frame and know it for what it was. A man, adrift on an ocean of unfathomable loneliness.

There. The outer door thudded in its frame as the last of the lantern-waving jackanapes went out, and the woman with them. Gil ambled to the middle of the stage, for no particular reason other than to place his feet where hers had been. The mouse scuttled after him and settled a few feet away, grooming its whiskers with its paws.

"Have ye no mouse affairs requiring your attention?" he asked, and the mouse paid him no heed. Just craving company, Gil supposed. Despite urging it away, Gil surprised himself by craving the mouse's company, too.

There was no argument that the vilest thing about his exile between the living and the dead was the solitude. Even so, Gil could not remember, among the thousands of prayers he'd sent to everyone from Osiris to the Virgin Mary, even once asking for a mouse.

He must try to be exact. A dead white pet ghost mouse. Dead? That was obvious. They were sharing a world, were they not? A ghost? He'd rubbed shoulders with enough ghosts to recognize one, though the mouse was the first four-legged example in his experience. A pet? The creature had almost turned somersaults of joy when the comely woman entered the theatre. It had singled her out of the twittering mob and flown to her side like an arrow, even though—if it was her mouse, and it appeared to be—it must have met its end somewhere else. Ghosts could do that. Turn up here or there, tethered to loved ones by bonds that even death could not sever.

Unlike him. He was tethered not to a person but a

thing, a theatre. Not even that. A hollow shell. A moldering monument to a moment, his death.

Look ye on the bright side, Gil. He tried, but after so many years, a merry outlook wasn't easy. Forsooth, death had some things to recommend it. If he'd stayed in the world of the living, what could he have looked forward to? Discovery as the undesirable author of plays appearing under desirable playwrights' names. Getting cup-shot every night with other undesirables. Penury, since fear of discovery made him loath to demand what his work was worth. Falling to the plague.

Or, angels forfend, he might have gotten the pox. It was better to die than lose his nose to it like Will Davenant. Willie might have been a rich and popular writer, but it was hard to look past the nose. At least Gil still had all his parts, not that he'd had occasion to use them in over three hundred years.

He did remember how his parts worked. They certainly worked well enough when the woman was capering around the stage, her breasts jouncing in a fashion guaranteed to stiffen a man's member like a tree. Then, she'd gone off exploring the theatre's nether parts, while he and the mouse slid from shadow to shadow behind her. Gil had never envied a rodent, but when the mouse darted out, nosed under his mistress' pantaloon hem, and crawled up her leg...

Gadsbobs, if he were a manly mouse, that's just what he'd do.

The woman had given a little shriek and shaken out her breeches, ghost mouse and all. Gil stiffened again, recalling it. When she lifted her leg and shook it like a tambourine, the jiggle of her buttocks had made him clutch himself in desperation. Perchance he could train the mouse to do the trick on command.

They—mouse, woman, him—were in the lower regions of the house at the time, the damp and airless parts euphemistically dubbed "artistes' wardrobing."

Wardrobing be buggered. Theatre was more honest in his day. Players stripped, if required, behind the scenery. Admittedly, there were no scene changes. If the play started in front of a painted Renaissance Florence, it ended there. There'd been no women on the stage, either.

The fine-arsed woman in breeches...before she'd started capering and singing, she'd delivered a few of the mad virgin's lines from *Hamlet* to an audience even less visible than him and the mouse. Good strong voice. Odd inflection, almost foreign. Perfect diction, no dropped aitches or slurred vowels. He hated slurred vowels. And her pitch, the silken female quality of it, the way it stroked him just as surely as if she'd had a hand on his—

Hell's mouth, what he felt around the woman was all new. Or new again, since in the far reaches of his mind he recalled a time when existence meant life and life meant his senses, all five, at riotous work upon his body. To hear, to see, to taste, to smell, to *feel*...

When was the last time he'd felt anything? Charles the First still had his head upon his shoulders, so more than three centuries. In all the time since then, he'd had not a groatsworth of sensation in any part of himself. Now, he felt a buzz in his limbs, the crawling of a hundred tiny legs attached to a dozen invisible insects, not the verminous, but the rare and priceless kind. Cochineal beetles, perhaps, or azure-winged butterflies. What did it mean?

He could say only that the pricking of his flesh began at his first sight of the woman who'd entered the theatre like a summer storm and too soon departed, leaving him in utter disarray. Suddenly restless, he began pacing the stage aimlessly, like the veriest amateur who'd forgotten his lines.

Women. That woman. All women. He wasn't quite so dead he'd forgotten how he adored them.

To be sure, women in the theatre was the subject of many a tap-shackled sermon he'd delivered to his friends when the mood took him to reform theatre. It only made sense. Putting aside the visibly false bosoms and padded hips of a thirteen-year-old boy actor, a screechy falsetto wasn't even close to a woman's voice.

Especially the woman who'd been declaiming Ophelia while he, in the wings, sank helplessly into the sound and sight of her like a sailor lost to the sea.

He stopped pacing in stage center again, scratching his jaw. There was a lilt to that phrase. Sailor and sea and sight. *So, in the sloshing, sightless*—no. *So, in the swells, the sailor, sightless*—not that, either. He'd work it out when he found wherever he'd mislaid his quill.

By the Cross, she was a comely thing, the woman, with shapely limbs shown off in those breeches and a curling muchness of hair on her head. The hair had the color and sheen of the India ink he'd stolen pots of through the years, so many that clerks in the Olympiad's office grumbled about an "ink pixie." The woman's hair was madly disordered by her dance. If he touched it, it would feel like a bird's nest made of silk.

And tall, the woman was, for her sex. He would look her straight in the eye when she came to his arms.

To his arms in his bloodstained sleeves. To his chest in a bloodstained shirt.

Hope dribbled away like the last drops from an upended tankard. He sank down in a rumpled heap, still on the spot where the woman had stood. Impossibly, the spot felt warm. Sitting tailor-legged, he curled his fists on his thighs and brooded. Never had it felt so hard to be so dead.

The dimmest donkey in London could tell him the bloodstains would put the woman right off, despite the irritating truth that more than half the blood on his shirt wasn't his.

Most of the blood was hers, the earl's whore. Everyone's whore, really, Polly Makepence, but a good-hearted trollop and his friend. She hadn't deserved a rapier in the lungs from a drunken noble. Gil had held her in his arms while she drowned in her blood and her brown eyes dulled. They'd gone wild with fear, those eyes, before the light fled them. 'Twas that made him lay her gently down, fist his own dagger, and lunge at Earl Bandon.

Which hadn't ended well for either of them.

Bandon's rapier had aimed for his throat but slewed to the side when Gil charged him. Just a rent in the flesh, the sword made, a wound that elsewhere on his body would have healed in a fortnight. But it had opened the great vein in Gil's neck, and he'd fallen, bleeding out upon the floor as neatly as a hen being drained for the stewpot.

It was doubly irritating that of the three of them who died that night, Gil was the only one still loitering around. Polly, bless her generous loins, was dead and gone; he wished her a full jug of gin and one of those frowsy red petticoats she liked. If there was justice under Heaven, the Earl was roasting like a turnip in the ashes of Hell. While Gil—

"What ails ye, mouse?" The creature was back at his side. It sat on its haunches, studying him, one tiny, long-fingered paw resting on Gil's foot. "Come ye on, then," he instructed. The mouse climbed up Gil's thigh to his fist, nosing at it until it opened. Crawling into his cupped palm, the mouse curled into a ball, tucked its tail around itself, and slept.

Sighing, Gil let his eyelids droop, his head with them. Why not follow the mouse's example? He'd slept away whole decades. What was one more night? Maybe he'd dream of the woman in breeches.

FOUR

Overnight, Fee's resolve hardened and took shape. She'd spent three years chasing her book's thesis: that the whereabouts of lesser-known seventeenth century poets and playwrights in London could be discovered and mapped. While the NEH didn't demand results when it handed over grant money, the pursuit of fairies was discouraged. So far, she hadn't even produced gossamer wings, much less playwrights and poets.

This morning, though, having seen the cellar under the Olympiad, she finally felt she was on to something. The evidence of an older—much older—building beneath the 1881 theatre wasn't proof positive, wasn't the Grave Circle at Mycenae or Leakey's skull. But it excited her more than anything she'd stumbled across in three years. It might turn out to be nothing...

No. As her Francophile great-aunts in Savannah would say, the evidence was *"plus que rien,"* more than nothing.

Stealing the key gave her some qualms. After the theatre rout, Fee had gone straight to Bloomsbury from Drury Lane, but the LUCIES had made a night of it in pubs and clubs. At ten the next morning, when she inspected a frowsy, eyes-half-shut Abeni across the breakfast table, Fee decided not to mention the key until her flat mate's metabolism caught up to the hour. By eleven, Abeni had inhaled two mugs of tea and some paracetamol. She looked capable of coherent speech. Fee braced herself and dove in.

"I had a really good time with the LUCIES."

Abeni made a noise into her mug. It might have been assent. Might have been a prelude to hurling.

"I did some Internet research after I got home. The Olympiad was active from 1881 to about 1948." One webpage—" (the iffy www.secretsofoldlondon.co.uk, only two hundred views since it went up nine years ago) "—said it was built over some demolished earlier structures."

Abeni's eyes had closed. One elbow was parked on the table, hand supporting her head. Was she even awake?

Fee soldiered on. "The Olympiad started out as a legitimate house, a serious theatre. Then, it slid into cabaret. Magic acts, dancing girls, poodles through hoops. It took some bomb damage during the Blitz. It was repaired, but it never really got going again. You know, changing tastes, the end of the era, television."

Still nothing from her flat mate, but Fee stuck to her guns. "I, uh, listen, Abeni, about the key. Will Ben's husband's brother be mad?"

Abeni sat upright with a snort. "You Yanks. Three

years in the U.K. and you still say mad when you mean bothered. Arsed. Hacked off."

"You Brits. Still using 60s slang. Tell me, will Ben's brother-in-law be hacked off? About the key?"

Abeni stretched a hand to Fee's plate and nicked a piece of toast. "Doubtful. Estate agents have bins of keys, copies of all of them. And the brother-in-law knows Ben is a numbskull, so he'll just figure he lost it somewhere."

"Won't the—what's his name, anyway? I have his key, I can't keep calling him 'the brother-in-law.'"

"Javier. Javier Almeida of Glenfall, Cole, and Abernathy, commercial realty agents. Not as posh as they sound, believe me."

"But won't Javier want to change the lock? I mean, if he thinks the key is lost, he might be afraid somebody will find it and burgle the place."

"It's a falling-down Victorian theatre, Fee, not the Bank of England." Abeni frowned at Fee's plate, empty of toast, and got up, groaning, to put more bread in the retro toaster. "What would thieves be after? Dust?" Two slices went in the toaster and Abeni slammed down the lever. "Gargh. Tea is not up to my head. I need coffee."

Quietly, to spare Abeni's hangover, Fee collected her breakfast dishes and put them in the sink. On the way to her room, she considered what to wear to do more digging around in the Olympiad. A raggedy pair of jeans, her faded, sky blue UNC Women's Lacrosse hoodie, a pair of worn-out hiking boots she'd been meaning to toss —those would do. She'd take a backpack with her cellphone, water bottle, towel, notebook, and some plastic baggies in case she found—what did archeologists call them? Sherds. Maybe she should pack a sandwich, too, or at least a protein bar.

And the Marks & Spencer trowel.

FIVE

"If she returns today," Gil told the mouse, "I will show myself. And have speech of her, God willing." *If she doesn't shriek and run, only to return with a pitchfork.*

He must look his best. When he'd been a proud young cock so long ago, he'd swaggered. Now, there was but one unbroken looking glass left in the theatre, and that, he averred, was one too many. He remembered the day a hopeful ingenue had used her shoe to drive a nail into the wall of the bare dressing room allotted to four supernumeraries. On the nail, she'd hung a plate-sized piece of glass in a cheapjack frame. Gil had salvaged it a decade later.

The ingenue was long gone by then, having decamped without ever attaining a principal role. She'd left behind the mirror and a single shoe, perhaps the one she'd used to drive the nail. He wondered about that. Who left a shoe behind?

She and a few of her fellow players were the last of the

tenants—the live ones—at the old Coronet Theatre for a while. The scuttling rats and the stray cats who dined on them were—save him—the house's only permanent residents in the interval before it was consigned to oblivion. He'd been on the verge of breaking long custom to converse with the handful of spirits who drifted in and out of the place, when the world exploded.

In truth, it was more like a dusty sigh. The Coronet was barely standing when it was pulled down in 1869. Gil was rendered homeless for a time, and it was most unsettling. He slept through most of it.

The Olympiad went up on the rotted bones of the Coronet. When the new theatre opened its doors, Gil went through them with everyone else. Players came and went, dramas and comedies good, bad, and indifferent were staged. It was comforting to be in a theatre again. Though it wasn't the Coronet, it wasn't the same.

Not long afterward, Wych Street where it joined Drury Lane fell under the hammers and machines of a wrecking crew, and for some years a great roar of work filled the ancient quarter. From the new theatre's roof, he watched the district being pounded to rubble, the rubble hauled away, and a monstrous roadway replacing it. Then came the giant underground tunnel and the roaring coaches in it. Above, buildings tall as the Dover cliffs went up. Old Covent Garden, the place he'd known for good and ill, in hard and harder times, was as gone as a mayfly in December.

He shook himself. Needs must set memory aside; he should fix his mind upon the future. The ingenue's mirror, now in his attic lodging, was a window into that future, by troth. A crooked sort of window, since the glass hung awry. For a gold guinea, he couldn't straighten it. The concussions of the mechanical carriages around the theatre jarred everything loose.

His reflection wasn't so bad from the shoulders up. Hair fell to his collarbone, dark as a chestnut hull. Combing it through with his fingers, he tied it back with a bright red ribbon he'd taken from what he called his Cabinet of Curiosities. It was his fancy to harvest bits and pieces from every era he'd suffered through in the theatre's long and double tenancy. He'd made a home in a wooden chest for his relics. Bits of cloth. Worthless jewelry. An umbrella—a clever tool, that. A selection of unmatched shoes. Some ladies' stockings, he blushed to admit.

Turning his head side to side, he examined his face in the mirror. With a scowl, he scratched the dark stubble of his chin. He'd not cared for the widespread fashion for beards in his day. Just his luck that he'd needed a shave on the day of his death and so, it appeared, he would need one for eternity.

Thom Heywood, that too-lucky playwright, was drunk one night and announced to the tavern in general that Gilbert Sorley of Kent possessed a lynx's face, but he wasn't referring to facial fur. And who was his fellow forger to burble about lynxes, when he'd never set eyes upon one? A cat was what he'd meant, one of the legion that prowled Drury Lane. Just as Thom had prowled it until he shed his Lincolnshire accent, became a favorite of Charles First, and started signing plays with his own name.

It was more than possible Thom had been calling Gil a sneak thief. *Pot, thou didst call the kettle black.* Thom and Gil were both dead now, so no point in chasing the insult to ground.

He turned his body one direction, then the other, trying to see himself the way Thom had seen him, the way the woman in breeches might see him. Gil would own to a cat's eyes. Slender, upturning over sharp cheekbones, the irises gray-blue in some lights, hard blue in others. Hard enough that the rabble in St. Giles feared him. Blue enough that the wenches in Covent Garden favored him.

Neither wenches nor anyone else favored his skin, alas. In life, he'd paid little enough heed to the hide that covered his bones, until those times when the glass of a window brought him up short and he gawped as though at a stranger. Dusky in low light, ochre in bright, his accursed skin gave up what he was as surely as if he'd shouted it from the rooftops.

Gil dragged his hand down his face, scratching again at the bristle on his jaw and upper lip. It added to the swarthiness of his mien. A good look for Othello, he considered, though that was beyond his touch in his acting days. He'd been hidden among a motley of trifling characters. Townsman. Messenger. Third soldier from the right. But a principal role? Even the lowliest apprentice knew it was safer to fashion a Moor from face paint than to put one who might *be* a Moor on the stage in such a visible part.

For the breeches-clad woman no less than the stage, his skin might present a problem. But 'twould be the blood-painted shirt that truly damned him. He came to that reckoning even without the cheeping of the creature who watched with mousely disdain from the floor.

"Have you nothing better to do than vex me?" he asked it. The mouse gave a single loud squeak and Gil opened his mouth for a riposte, then pressed it shut. Nails of the Cross, he must stop conversing, not to mention arguing, with the thing.

Still, the mouse was right, a plague on its hairy little balls. The woman would take one look at his bloody besmirchment and flee for her life, thinking a rogue had followed her into the building. Even though the rogue had been there long before she entered.

He sighed dispiritedly. Perhaps, if he shed the shirt... he pulled it roughly over his head, keeping his breeches. They were only lightly spattered, and one did not appear before a strange woman unbreeched unless she was the sort to expect coin and vigorous activity. His hose had seen better centuries, but he'd moved the worst parts to the back of his leg. Since he'd not done much hill walking in the past three hundred years, his shoes did him credit. He'd shined them with a bit of hardened grease he found backstage.

He twisted this way and that before the glass. What he saw without his shirt did not grievously affect him. There was something to be said for having died young and hale, not to mention impermeable to decay. He bared his teeth—all there. Flexed his arms, still carven like stone. His belly was flat and partitioned with muscle.

He should do penance for it, but he was vain about his chest. Many a trollop and even a few decent women had admired it. His shoulders were wide, his arms muscled like a stonemason's, and—he turned his back to the mirror and looked over his shoulder—a woman would find a handful of taut arse should she discover herself in a position to appreciate it.

He turned again to the glass and stilled, considering his masculine allure. No more boastful than the next man, he could still say he was, in a word, fine. To a certain class of woman, he'd been very taking in his day.

His day. Which even the most-broadminded observer would say was between 1630, when he'd more or less grown to manhood, and 1642, when his days as a living man had run out. All the beauties that had winked and smirked and postured at him during that span...he'd known what to do with them and had done it with enthusiasm.

But this woman? Forgetting his hair was bound, he raked his fingers through it and cursed at the mess he made. Tearing out the ribbon, he began again to smooth the dark pelt and tie it back. With a sigh, he pulled on his shirt and tucked it into his breeches.

Hark, there were noises below. The mouse chittered excitedly and made for the door. With a last glance in the glass, Gil followed.

The woman was back.

———

The square pit below the ground floor of the Olympiad appeared less like an open grave with a lantern and a woman in it. Gil crept, silent as a monk, into a patch of shadow just inside the door. Sound would betray him faster than sight, and he had to bite his cheek to keep mute. What he spied from his hiding place was enough to make any man, dead or alive, groan aloud.

The woman was crouched on her hands and knees, digging like a badger in a corner of the packed-earth cellar floor, her arse in the air. It was an arse intended by God to inflame any man who was lucky enough to view it. Gil, at the best of times in his life, was tenuously clothed in honor. At the sight before him, he came unstitched at once and was flooded by dishonorable urges.

While the vision of the digging woman was one he'd give a half crown for, he did have to wonder if his breeches-clad pretty might be a bit thin in her reason. She had a spade, too small to be more than a child's toy, all-over painted with flowers and butterflies. Was she, in her poor addled mind, planting a garden?

Addled or not, he would speak with her. To that end, he'd done all he could to present himself as a gentleman of worth. If she overlooked the deadness, of course.

Tucked into his lightless corner, he watched her dig for a span of minutes while he pondered what to say first when she saw him. *If* she saw him. Hearing him above, on the stage, made seeing him by no means a certainty. He'd be wroth to have gone to all this trouble if she did not, though some gut-deep conviction—arising from lunacy or Eros, he couldn't say—made him certain that she would.

Perhaps, he'd begin with a bit of verse. Milton might do. "*In naked beauty, more adorn'd...*" No, best not start with offing the clothes. Old Milton was a prig, anyway.

There was Dryden, "*Beauty is nothing else but a just accord and mutual harmony of the members, animated by a healthful constitution.*" God wot, Dryden sneezed out gales of words and what did they mean, anyway? A woman would be numb with boredom by the time a man finished that speech.

Ah, Edmund Spenser. He'd had a most agile pen. "*To whom I mean it most, whose fair immortal beam, hath darted fire into my feeble ghost.*" Couldn't ask for nicer than that. Ned even squeezed in a ghost at the end.

Gil tugged at his threadbare cuffs and counseled himself to calm. He was as well-fettled as any man could be, in his condition. It still rankled that on the day of his death he'd left a nearly new suit in the clothes press of Polly's room at the Boar. It had assuredly been robbed before his body had cooled.

Give ear, the woman was rising. One of her knees gave a little crack and Gil thought it the dearest sound he'd ever heard. Still bending over, she brushed dirt from her breeches. In a thrice, she would turn, raise her eyes, look into his, and, if his brain didn't entirely melt from fear, he would greet her.

She straightened and turned. Now or never. *Tempus fugit, carpe diem, strike while the iron is hot.*

The woman's eyes lifted, not to his face but somewhat lower, then widened into blue-green saucers. She shrieked like a parrot. "*Shakespeare!*"

God damn that mouse. The creature was so weightless, Gil had not even marked its presence on his shoulder.

She shrieked again, louder, and thrust out her hands. "Shakespeare, *Shakespeare!*"

'Swounds, that over-rated scribbler from Stratford-upon-Avon never got calls of *Author, Author* so fervent, and why was she screeching for him, anyway? Predictably, and before Gil could stop it, the mouse responded by making a mighty leap from his shoulder to the woman. It landed on her shirt front and clung like a burr by its claws. Sobbing with joy and shock, the woman cupped her hands around the rodent and—

Her fingers passed right through its body. Her whole body stiffened, and she jerked her hands away as though she'd grabbed a pot straight from the fire.

Throwing his script to the wind, Gil improvised. "Shades and spirits possess no corporeal mass," he began, trying for a smile and knowing it probably came out as a grimace. "You cannot harm the creature, mistress. 'Tis no more than a dandelion puff in your hands."

At last, at *last,* she met his eyes. Hers—like ocean under sky—were blank with wonder and fear, and her voice trembled. "Shakespeare's *dead.*"

"I know, I was at the funeral." At his remark, her pale face lost even more color. He feared she might swoon. "Hold! You speak of the mouse. Well, yes, if he is a ghost, he is dead. Ipso facto."

The woman dropped her eyes to her breast. Again, carefully, she cupped her hands below the mouse, who settled in apparent contentment. Raising her nested pet to her lips, she kissed the air just above the animal's head. The slow tear coursing down her cheek cleaved Gil's heart in twain.

"Fear not for its comfort," he offered hastily. "Whatever ills beset us in life, we are, at the end, released from all. The mouse remembers you, is that not marvelous? Memory is the salve of its condition, and yours." Oh, for the love of Thomas à Becket, he sounded like a priest.

She nodded gravely and he took heart. Apart from the screams, she was taking Act One of *The Apparition in the Cellar* remarkably well. No fainting, no running about in circles. It was almost as though she'd spoken with the dead before, and that boded well for the rest of their little play. Still, he must tread carefully. The mood of the public could change in an instant, as any actor who's taken a rotten egg in the face will attest.

The woman looked up at him again, her eyes still bright with tears but—flinty. Her words bore the same sharp tone. "Just who the holy fucking hell are *you*?"

A profane observation, but it wasn't as though he hadn't known she had a mouth like Stew Quay at low tide. Time for Act Two, Scene I.

Gil's salutation might have graced Whitehall. "Most fair and gracious mistress, I am Gilbert Sorley, of Kent and Drury Lane. Poet, playwright, actor. Late of the Coronet Theatre. Your most humble and obedient servant." He followed with the most florid bow of which he was capable. A courtier's bow, a Cavalier's.

She shifted one hand from the mouse—not that it needed holding, since it was merely floating above her palms—and *Iesu Cristo!* she cautiously but decisively reached out and touched him. The poke of her forefinger into his chest sent a bolt of excitement directly to his loins, and his whole body shivered.

The woman's astounding eyes narrowed. Her expression became, if possible, flintier. "You're not like Shakespeare. You're solid."

If not completely solid, part of him was assuredly on its way. That part hadn't responded with such alacrity in a very, very long time.

The woman took a step back, cradling the mouse to her bosom again. "No one but me can see you, right?"

Ah, the spoken English of moderns, so imprecise. "Do I correctly understand you to say that none save you are *permitted* to see me?"

She shook her head, black curls bouncing in a girlish way that softened his heart, while the other part grew harder. "That's *not* what I meant." She shaped her words painstakingly, like a tutor addressing a thick pupil. "Is it true—that I am the only person—to whom you are —visible?"

She was riddling him! He adored riddles. After a moment's thought, he replied, "If any other besides your fair self has seen me or sees me now, it defies my experience of the nearly four hundred years in which I've done nothing to conceal—" he swept a hand across his body, "—this manly form." *Well done, me.* Circumlocution of a positively Oxfordian sort *and* he'd directed her eyes to his well-knit limbs.

Alack, the woman did not seem impressed. Even as he watched, her eyes performed a fickle English sky. Clear at matins, cloudy at noon, coldly dark at vespers with a silver streak of lightning, foretelling storms. Her next comment said *cold rain*.

"Mister—Sorley, is it? Tell me *exactly* when you were born."

He'd rather hoped she'd say something more convivial. *Well, met, good sir. I am Mistress Fairfine of Manyriches Hall. Utterly charmed to make your acquaintance.*

No matter. He would obey her command if she asked him to walk on his hands. "I came to light, mistress, one cold January morn in the year of Our Lord, 1616."

She pulled her head back sharply, as though he'd thrown something in her face. Then, dismayingly, she gave him one word, as sharp and cold as an icicle falling from a roof.

"No." Still clutching her mouse, she spun around and strode briskly away. At the last instant before the door to the stairs, the mouse vaulted from her arms, scurried across the floor, and ran up Gil's body to his shoulder where it sat, chittering.

The woman skidded to a halt and turned. Her face was both furious and hurt, tear tracks catching in the lantern light.

"*No,*" she repeated, icier than before. Then, she plunged through the doorway and out.

He heard her feet thudding on the stairs and a fair amount of cursing, since she'd forgotten her lantern and the stairs were unlighted. A few seconds later, there was the scrape and squeal of the stage door opening, followed by a very eloquent crash as the door slammed so hard in its frame Gil fancied the building shuddered. He knew he did.

The cellar lapsed into silence again. Shakespeare Not the Bard rubbed its nose against Gil's jaw. "None of that, mate. This is *your* fault. From what clodpate did you learn to throw yourself on a woman like that? A gentleman holds himself back, mouse. Holds. Himself. Back."

Gil blew out a sigh that went all the way to his shoes. He picked up the woman's lantern, holding it high to illumine the hole she'd dug. No point to it that he could see; it revealed nothing but ancient, dirt-caked cobbles. He placed the lantern back on the floor, next to the small trowel. "She'll have to return," he told the mouse. "She's left her tools behind."

And her pet, which was interesting. The mouse could have followed its mistress back to wherever she resided, just as it had—for reasons Gil could not fathom —found its way from the place of its death to the theatre. Instead, it stayed with Gil when the woman departed. Something profound abided in that. Something possibly hopeful, his mind told him, but his heart was too full of frustrated desire to think it through.

He trudged up the cellar stairs to the floor above. The rodent squeaked in his ear until he lifted it from his shoulder and put it in the first dressing room he came to. "Kindly spare me your glowing portents, Nostrada-mouse. In fact, be off. Chew a nice hole in the base-boards. I shall be occupied for some time, penning verses to Despair."

Six

Fee stomped home. She actually took the Line 243 bus, but even sitting, her posture had a stomping quality to it. And the ride was far too short for her feelings to subside. Confusion. Shock. Anger.

Fear. For the block and half walk from the bus to the flat, she felt—pursued. Not by a person, but a thing. *Her* thing, her history.

Damn, damn, damn. She'd gone into the Olympiad in a bright state of mind—excited, full of hope for her book. She'd left with her mind as dark and disordered as the cellar.

It didn't help that the Bloomsbury flat didn't feel like home. As she unlocked the door and toed off her shoes, it occurred to her for, oh, the thousandth time since she'd "come back"—her euphemism for the snapped temporal rubber band that sent her from 1770s Paris to 21st century U.K.—that she didn't feel at home anywhere.

Maybe, for now, home was where the electric kettle was. She was in the kitchen just long enough for it to boil when her cellphone sounded. *The Sorcerer's Apprentice*, the ringtone she'd set for Jana Smithbury-Tewkes, her witch-aunt in Wales.

"*Now* what are you doing?" the caller barked before Fee even said hello.

Good old Jana. Blunt as a mallet. "Making tea," Fee answered. "Other than that, I'm contributing my two pence to the history of British drama. And how are you today, Auntie?" The Welsh witch wasn't a blood relation, but Fee had called Jana and her coven sisters aunts all her life.

"I'm just fine," Jana said tersely, "for a witch whose expensively educated niece doesn't know how to use her mobile, or her email, or her—"

"Don't you follow me on Insta? I post all the time."

"I follow you in the Tarot, Fee. Spit it out. What just happened?"

That's a really good question, Auntie Jana. Fee put the call on speaker so she could rummage in the kitchen cupboards for her V&A Museum mug. "My mouse died."

"He was elderly, Fee."

"So people say." Rather than share her afterlife encounter with Shakespeare, Fee moved to the other weird current event. It was no use prevaricating. Aunt Jana had a remarkable gift for divination. Once she saw something in the cards, it was as good as on the front page of the *Times*. "I, uh, met a man."

A pause long enough to ride a broom halfway from coastal Wales to London followed. Jana broke it. "I'm guessing this wasn't a speed date."

"Nobody does speed dating anymore, Jana. But no, it wasn't a date of any sort."

"Was there a sign?"

"You mean, was he holding up a placard like a tour guide at an airport? Souler Party This Way?"

"Don't be cheeky. You know what I mean."

"I do, unfortunately. No sign, Jana. No tingle, no buzz, no aura, no parade of pixies chanting and pointing." Just his assertion that he'd been born in 1616 and was, therefore, extremely dead. And he'd somehow made a pet of the mouse she'd buried the day before. "I was doing some impromptu archeology in an old building, and he surprised me, that's all. He's just a man."

"You think?" Jana's sarcasm was so serrated it could've pruned the roses over Shakespeare's grave. "Just a man. Well, if that's all he is, I won't see him in the cards again. But if I do, or *you* do, and you don't tell me—"

"I know, you'll send a squad of tap-dancing gnomes over here to keep me awake nights until I come clean." Time for a topic change. "How's Rumpel?" Short for Rumpelstiltskin, Jana's color-changing cat and successor to No Name, the cat Fee fondly remembered from childhood. No Name's best color had been cerise.

"Rumpel's fine. He's added a new shade. Mulberry, I think, though your Aunt Poppy calls it puce."

Poppy, the Irish widow witch. Jana, the magickal goods shop owner. Morgana, the potions-maker. Wren and Rowan, the couple who owned Basil and Bee, an organic farm. Selene, elder witch, gifted seer and small as a twelve-year-old but great in wisdom—she had passed away while Fee was an undergraduate. Together, they were the League of Extraordinary Women who had watched over Fee since she was born.

As dear as the witches were, thoughts of them dropped Fee onto a battlefield of emotions. They weren't just part of her past, they'd help put her *in* the past, when she was four. They'd helped haul her out of it, too, when after thirteen years she'd appeared again in the Welsh stone circle where the witches were observing what they called Samhain and the rest of the Western world called Halloween.

Jana was still passing on local news. Fee forced herself back into the flow. "They're raising alpacas, now?"

"You know Wren and Rowan. Mostly Rowan. Wren's happy with her goats and her bees, but Rowan likes exotic livestock."

As opposed to Jana's color-shifting cats. "Please give them my fond regards. Not the alpacas. Just Wren and Rowan and the rest of the group."

Another long pause ate up time. While Jana was apparently thinking, Fee hunted for the tin of lavender-mint tea bags; Abeni never put them away in the same place twice. Fee was sure that any second Jana would return to the man, the Tarot, and what they meant, but instead, her auntie went aunt-y.

"You said you'd visit at Lughnasadh, but you didn't."

Fee mentally spun the Wheel of the Year, the calendar of witches' Sabbats, until she got to August first, Lughnasadh. "I've been working like crazy. My grant's running out and I really have to show some results." Results, results, her all-purpose excuse.

Jana hummed disapprovingly. "It was different when

you were at university in North Carolina, Fee. Not to belabor the obvious, but you live on the same land mass, now. Maybe you can make Samhain. That's October thirty-first, in case you've forgotten."

"I didn't forget." How could she? It was her preferred date to jump centuries.

"You've got time to plan, it's just now the first of September."

"I'll try, Jana, I really will."

"And listen, Fee." *Here it comes, the souler warning.* "If something happens with that man—"

"Signs and portents, I know."

"Signs, portents, earth elementals oozing through the floor, anything at all. Contact me immediately."

Earth elementals? Fee found the lavender-mint tea in the fridge. The tin seemed light; time to restock. Holding it in one hand, she used the other to salute her phone. "Right-o, Wing Commander Jana."

The call ended. Jana wasn't one for goodbyes.

The water had gone cold in the kettle for the second time. Fee switched it on, then stood at the kitchen table a few feet away so she wouldn't forget again. While the kettle hissed, she stared out the double-glass French doors into the garden. The flat being on the ground floor, the patch of green was right outside. She couldn't see Shakespeare's grave; a drooping rose branch masked it. So late in the year, there weren't many blooms and even the leaves were yellowing. When the last of them dropped, she'd see Shakespeare's little mound of dirt every time she looked outside.

The garden was full of birds today, as though every

avian in Bloomsbury had descended on it and its one spindly larch tree. The birds were all shouting at once, a chirpy William Tell Overture conducted by Aunt Jana. *It's a sign, it's a sign, it's a sign sign sign, it's a sign, it's a sign, it's a sign sign sign.*

She'd been dismissive with her witch-aunt, but Fee couldn't fool Jana or herself. The man in the cellar wasn't just a sign. He was *the* sign. The irksome, unwanted herald and proof of who she was, yapping at her. *You're a souler! It's starting!*

It wasn't like her mother hadn't warned her a hundred times what to look for. Fee had even listened for the first twenty, each of which began with Mom's disclaimer.

"You might not have inherited the souler gene, or whatever it is. It skipped your great-grandmother, Louise. But your grandmother and I had it. You did the drawings, just like us, so you should be prepared."

The drawings. The pictures she'd drawn from age three until she and Mom had gone through time to join Fee's leathling father, a soul trapped—then rescued—from exile between death and life. Fee's drawings, crude at first and then more and more detailed, were of a building, always the same one. Steep roof, three stories, a projecting gable at the front with a small round window. How could there be any connection to the Olympiad? Her drawings didn't have the faintest resemblance to it. Was it too much to hope the souler gene had skipped her, like Great-grandma Louise?

"The surest sign is that you'll feel something in the presence of your leathling," Mom always added after the disclaimer. "A tingle, a creepy, crawly, buzzy thing. A burning under your skin."

From the jump, she'd batted away her mother's warning with jokes and denial. "*Quel horreur!*" She clapped her hands to her cheeks. "*Comme les framboises!*"

Mom hadn't been amused by the comparison of their shared souler heritage to a strawberry allergy. "Not funny, Aoife. If there's anyone who ought to take this seriously, it's the little girl who crossed a few centuries holding my hand."

Crossed them twice, Mom. The second time was when Fee was seventeen and the sensations under her skin burned so fiercely she thought she might burst into flames. Consumed with waking dreams of people and places she didn't recognize, she finally admitted to her parents what was happening.

That was when her souler heritage became horribly real—on All Hallows' Eve in the Dordogne, at the inter-section of ley lines where her parents brought her and she'd stood, swaying drunkenly. She could barely stand upright under the weight of her woolen cape, thick gold strips sewn into the hem. "For c-college tuition," her mother had explained brokenly. "Your great-aunts shouldn't h-have to pay."

Weeping too hard to speak after that, she'd pressed a handkerchief, old Irish linen with shamrocks embroi-dered in the corner, into Fee's hands. Papa wept, too, as he had on the day she'd first met him in the Tuileries Garden. "*Tá mo chroí istigh ionat,*" he said over and over, "My heart is within you."

Then, in the flash of the setting sun, everything she cherished became two hundred-fifty years in the past.

Afterward, she'd engaged in some delusional gymnastics and convinced herself nothing had really changed. She'd gone away, but her parents were still and impossibly alive in Paris. Their daughter was just their daughter, not a souler. Her supernatural inheritance? That went into a dark cell of her mind, and she threw away the key.

Until today. The kettle snapped off and Fee crossed to the counter to drop a tea bag in her mug, then poured in boiling water and took the mug to the table.

If the man she'd met in the Olympiad's cellar was a leathling—and she wasn't quite ready to cave on that point—why hadn't she felt the tingle when he appeared? There'd been nothing. No twitch, no buzz, no burn. No warning.

Just *him*. Gilbert DOB 1616 Sorley. *If* he was what he said he was, he might not be anything special to her, but she'd have to admit she'd encountered a creature of the extramundane.

Two of them, if she counted Shakespeare. At the time, she'd held herself together, but now the image from a couple days earlier rushed painfully back. Her, putting her mouse's cold little body in the ground.

Rushing in after that image, the one from today. Her, holding some white ball of nothing that had Shakespeare's fur and Shakespeare's squeak, but couldn't possibly be her lively, warm, loyal...

Her eyes filled. She buckled at the knees, crumpling into a kitchen chair, elbows on the table. "Oh, Shakespeare, my baby. My poor little baby." She crossed her arms and dropped her head onto them, sobbing.

The tears went on for a while. She finally, wearily, picked up her mug. The tea had gone cold. Not bothering to remove the teabag, she took a gulp, then wiped her face on one of the linen napkins stacked in front of her. Abeni wanted paper, the gaudier the better. Fee, who'd grown up with real napkins and hated paper, argued for cloth and won.

Her laptop was on the table, along with the other files and books they both dumped there between meals. She pulled it to her and flipped it open. Maybe she could lose herself in work for a while.

Except, there it is, my idiotic screensaver. A thumbnail of my life with the not-quite-alive.

She stared glumly at the photo of St. Rhydian's Castle in Wales, where her mother had met her father. The man Fee called Papa had waited between life and death for over two hundred-fifty years for Mom. She—a descendant of a famous witch—had inherited the ability and the mission to restore one soul. Like her mother before her, Mom was a souler.

Fee was all in favor of mixed relationships. But the ghostly love match of her parents had produced cataclysmic results. Progressive fading away in Mom. A wrenching separation to save her life. A pregnancy neither Mom nor her lover had expected. Four years in Savannah, Mom grieving the loss of her ghost, until a dream sent her and her child, Fee, to a place, Paris, and a time, 1761, where they could all be together and alive.

The series of events was so brutal that Fee had made up her mind *not* to repeat it.

To hell with the DNA. She took a swallow of tea, making a face. Was it really that bitter or were her memories turning it to vinegar? Maybe there was honey —no, the flat was out of that and other groceries. Both she and Abeni had been too busy lately to shop. Fee pulled over a scrap of notepaper and began a list. *Honey. Lavender-mint tea.* Mom loved lavender-mint tea, too. They'd had pots and pots of it in Paris. *Eighteenth-century* Paris.

If only she could've stayed there. She'd worshipped the city and her life in it from the moment she'd arrived with Mom, plonking down in the middle of the Tuileries Garden. Her wide, child's eyes taking in the people who looked like the illustrations in the *Perrault's Fairy Tales* book her Great-aunt Sophie had given her. The orderly landscaping, gardeners snipping away with shears. The tall, black-haired man leaping over hedges in his mad dash to reach her and Mom and crush them to his chest in a hug. *Papa, my Papa.*

He wasn't a garden variety ghost. Not a phantom, a spirit, a *boo-I'm-floating-past-your-window-in-a-sheet* thing. He was a leathling, from the Irish word *leath*, meaning "half." Neither dead and gone nor alive and present, a leathling might wait for hundreds of years for a special person—a souler like Mom—to sacrifice whatever was required, including themself, to redeem the leath-ling's soul and return it to the life from which it had been ripped before its time.

Oh, yeah, Papa was one of those. At least, that's what

she'd been told. Even now, knowing the truth, it seemed impossible.

She took another gulp of tea and grimaced again. Next time she shopped, she'd buy ginger-lemongrass.

The truth that Papa was a ghost had never seemed real because there wasn't anything ghostly about him. None of the adjectives—faint, transparent, illusory, insubstantial—applied.

Papa was manifestly substantial. Six feet and a few inches in height, he towered over the Frenchmen in 1700s Paris. His shoulders filled doorways, and he had the muscles of a dock worker. Precisely zero people mistook him for a ghost. He was *un tel gentilhomme*, a fine gentleman, who raked in money from import-export, or maybe smuggling; she'd never determined. Whichever it was, Mom partnered him in it. When she wasn't doing that or supervising the small army of servants who minded the family townhouse, or the slightly smaller army of her four children, Mom put her 21st century training to work as an 18th century historian. In college, Fee had even found an article Mom had penned in a microfiched journal. She'd memorized the citation: Gowdie Ó Loinsigh, Céleste. "Le Chateau de Vincennes and Hampton Court Palace: Some Comparative Aspects," *The Architect's Companion*, London; Vol. IV (1772).

While Fee was driving her *nounou*, her nanny, and later, her tutors, insane, Mom spent whole days in the *Bibliotheque du Roi*, not renamed the National Library until 1795. By then, of course, Fee had gone back to Savannah and Mom and Papa were...

Dead and gone. Fee's hand, still grasping the handle of her mug, started to wobble. She rose and went to the sink, dumping the tea and fishing out the tea bag to put in the compostables bin. Because she couldn't think of anything else to do, she went back to the table and sat, unfolding and refolding all the napkins.

Everything was dead and gone by the time she'd landed in Savannah. Her life in Paris. Her parents as she remembered them—Papa's hair going silver at the temples, Mom's eyes with fine lines at the corners. Her French-born brothers—Michael, a skinny twelve-year-old when she left, the twins Colum and Liam, just five. To save her sanity, she tried to think of them as seldom as possible.

Her great-aunts were the only fragment of her past still intact. Before she'd whooshed through time, they'd all been living in the house on Bull Street: her, Mom, and the four aunts. After a few years in the 1700s, she only clearly remembered her favorite, retired school-teacher Nicole, called Nikki. Mom never stopped telling her about all of them, though. Aunt Nikki, a fan of all things New Age. Aunt Sophie, the interior designer. Aunt Diane the realtor. Aunt Hélène, the oldest, a physician.

Only Hélène and Nikki lived in the Bull Street house now, but at least all four were still around, and that was some help in facing her losses.

Most of the Welsh witches were still around, too. She smiled wryly. *A mixed blessing.* When she was four, Jana had promised Mom she'd look after Fee if something went wrong and she and Mom didn't make it to Papa together. Clearly, Jana felt her looking-after duties were a lifelong commitment.

Her great-aunts and the witches. *Plus que rien*, as her Great-aunt Diane would say, more than nothing. And there were her mother's words in the Dordogne, which were supposed to comfort Fee but didn't, not really. "*You'll forget us, baby. Everyone is eventually dead and gone.*"

Everyone except the man she'd met in the cellar of the Olympiad Theatre. He was an implacable, impossible bookmark in her suppressed autobiography, *I Am a Souler*.

Even so, she wasn't sure she was ready to definitively say what Gilbert Sorley was. Mom had told her so many times that she would *know*. Know what? That he was a ghost, like her poor, dead mouse? A leathling, the special sort of ghost trapped between life and death? *Her* leathling?

Fee pushed herself up from the table. Her thoughts were driving her round the bend. She needed to do something simple and grounding, like laundry. She bundled the contents of the hamper in the bathroom and shoved them into the small washer-dryer combination. Where the hell was the soap? Rooting around in the bathroom closet, she found it behind a plastic tub of Epsom salts.

Set the temperature, set the timer. She managed it, but her brain kept throwing her back to the Olympiad's cellar. Once inside, she'd patted around the doorframe and found a light switch, an antiquated toggle in the center of a ceramic dome. Repeated jiggling did nothing. The single battery lantern she'd brought barely cut the gloom. All it did, when she waved it around, was make ominous hulks out of barrels and boxes heaped against the walls and throw glints of silver onto garlands of cobwebs. The lantern still gave enough illumination for her to dig, which she'd happily done for a half hour.

Then, *he'd* appeared. In the uncertain light, she hadn't been able to see all of Gilbert Sorley, but she'd seen enough. She'd seen his eyes.

There wasn't a name for those eyes. Smoky blue, startling in contrast to his dark, dark brown hair and dusky skin and beard. The expression in those eyes had reached out and stirred her. It was bold, hot, unnerving.

Attractive.

She put the laundry soap away and shook herself. Sure, Gilbert Sorley was attractive enough for a man she'd met in the Libe, or on one of the LUCIES' crackbrained excursions. But for a soul that might demand from her the kind of sacrifice her leathling father had pulled from Mom?

No man was attractive enough for that. Not today, not tomorrow, not ever. Mom and Papa had made sure Fee was forewarned. What Fee hadn't told her parents was that she was *forearmed*. Gilbert Sorley could be as attractive as any woman could want, but she wouldn't be his ticket out of wherever he was to wherever he wanted to be.

People had to accept it if they inherited diabetes or red hair. But souling? Fee didn't buy her mother's assertion that it was genetic. As far as Fee was concerned, it was an elective. If the man she'd met in the cellar of the

Olympiad was a leathling, he'd just have to wait for the next souler to come along, like a bus.

Her mother and grandmother let themselves fall in love with leathlings. That was on them. Women fell in love with gamblers, alcoholics, and womanizers. Fee was a different person than her mother and grandmother, a stronger one. Certainly, a more informed one.

She went back to the kitchen and opened her laptop again. Maybe she could manage a little research after all, on known theatres in and around what was called, in the 1600s, "Druary Lane." She could also search for unconfirmed but surmised theatres. By the time she went back to the Olympiad tomorrow, she'd be ready to dig and make notes.

Gilbert Sorley, if he was there? He could just stay out of her way.

SEVEN

"You fixed the light. Thank you."

She of the Fetching Arse didn't deign to turn and look at him when she spoke, just knelt on the cellar floor, digging away with her infant spade. Gil enjoyed the view no less than he had the day before. Shoeless saints, the woman's body made his mouth water like a plate of French macaroons.

"'Twas the work of a moment, for a man of my skills," he told her gaily. And a liar by omission, since he'd had not the slightest notion of what he'd done to the thing on the wall, though he'd known it was the master of the single lamp overhead. Thumping the adjacent wall a few times with his fist had brought a ceiling bulb to feeble life. Despite its glow, Gil remained in the shadows, not wanting to shock the woman more than he already had.

He fidgeted for a while. She dug for a while.

"You might as well come out," she finally tossed over her shoulder. "I'm not afraid of you."

He moved toward her cautiously, striving to seem unaffected in the slightest. *O ho, fa la, tra lee, 'tis nothing at all, 'tis naught to me.* "You left in a temper. I thought you might be disposed to violence. Might shout, throw things, curse. Whatever you do, when deranged."

"I am not deranged."

"I see. What are you, then?"

"Alive, for one thing."

That stung. "You wound me, mistress."

"Mr. Sorley—"

"Gil, please."

She swiveled on her knees to face him, her delectable mouth at the level of his thighs. The sight of her thusly positioned ordered all the hairs on his body to be upstanding, along with his pindle. He should have left his shirt untucked. It might be bloodstained, but it reached to his knees and covered a multitude of sins.

"Mister. Sorley." She was patient and slow, as if explaining London Bridge to a cat. "You need to understand that I grew up with a father who was trapped between life and death for over two hundred fifty years, and a mother who bore a child—me—to the aforesaid not-quite-alive man.

"When I was seventeen, my mother sent me to a powerful place in France, on All Hallows' Eve. I shut my eyes and presto change-o! I ended up almost three hundred years later in Savannah, Georgia, facing my four elderly great-aunts who, when I left Paris a week before, hadn't been born yet.

"My life has prepared me to accept spirits, ghosts," she swept her hand in a wide arc, and a lissome hand it was, "or—whatever. But, and I hope you won't take this personally, I believe your condition has *nothing* to do with me."

That rocked Gil back on his heels a bit. It was an extraordinary speech. For sincerity, it left behind the fragment of *Hamlet* she'd rattled from the stage as a racing horse would outrun a donkey cart. And yet, it omitted everything essential.

The way she'd felt throughout her life, the fear, the singularity, the loss, the anger. Watching her speak, he learned them all. Learned them from the flash of fire in her opal-green eyes. From her fists, balled at her sides. From her body—she was a terrifyingly beautiful woman —curving in and out at all the right places, but tense and straight as an arrow, poised to fly into space.

He smiled, lest he become the target. "You have an excellent voice for the stage, did you know? Your diction is superb. Odd accent, but if ever you crave a career upon the boards—"

"Please stop trying to ingratiate me. Just go on your way and—"

"Play in the lane like a good lad, is that what you're saying?"

"If the shoe fits, Mr. Sorley."

"Cloak. If the cloak fits. From the *Lawes of Ecclesiasticall Polite.* 'Which cloake sitteth no lesse fit on the backe of their cause, than of the Anabaptists.' The year 1593, if I mistake not."

"Oh, for the love of Pete—"

"Not among my acquaintances, alas. And I pray you, call me Gil. Your name is Aoife."

Her eyes sparked fire again. "How do you know my name?"

Gil pointed to her cloth sack, the neatly lettered tag on one strap: *Aoife G. Gowdie* with a string of numbers. "According to my old friend, Seamus O'Ruadh, the name means 'shining.'"

"Seamus. Is he one of your dead friends, Mr. Sorley?"

"Do please call me Gil. Since I knew Seamus in the reign of the Martyr King, I regret to say he is dead, as are all my friends. Except your shining self, of course."

She got to her feet. Front to front, Gil couldn't help but note that her breasts were as round and comely as her backside. His notice was a fraction too sustained, and her forehead creased in a scowl. He jerked his eyes upward.

"I'm not your friend," she snapped. "Where's Shakespeare?"

All the burning questions she might have asked, and she asked about *him*. Truly, the woman could whittle a man like a knife. "'Struth, lass, I've not seen him since the funeral, when my mother worked the gulling crowd. She had the enviable talent for diverting attention by holding my infant self to her uncovered breast, whilst using her free hand to cut a gentleman's purse from his side. I cannot say I remember the obsequies—"

"Not *that* Shakespeare, the other one."

"Do you mean the mouse?"

"He isn't 'the mouse.' He's *my* friend."

"Your dead friend. See, you already have one, why not another?" In the tense silence that followed, they both heard raindrops smacking puddles in the alley outside the cellar. *Splat. Splat.*

Steadfastly keeping his eyes on the woman's face, Gil spread a little balm over the moment. "I approve of the mouse's name."

"And that means the world to me."

An arid remark, but he was coming to know her style. Dry as the winds over Africa. "Curiosity compels me, though. Why name the creature after poor old Willy?"

"Poor old—do you mean the Western World's greatest playwright?"

"Please, don't believe everything you read in the broadsheets."

"'He never blotted a line,' that's what Ben Jonson wrote."

"'Would he had blotted a thousand,' is what he added."

"Jonson might have said that because he was jealous."

"*I* said it, Ben stole it. You're not wrong, though, Ben was jealous of everyone and everything. The man begrudged the sun that shone on the green when it could be illuminating his fat face."

"You're awfully bitter."

"Death does that to a person." Now, he was the dry one.

He took a steadying breath. Right before his eyes, it was all going wrong. Wrong and more wrong, as she finally spotted the age-blackened splotches on his shirt, the proof of Earl Bandon's bloody work. She didn't flee again, but he'd call the dawning expression on her face 'contained horror.' Fine, then, he hadn't died in a cleanly way; most people didn't. Gil's heart sank and his brain shouted, *Do something, you fool!*

It galled, but he brought the conversation back to the four-legged Bard. "I'm sure the m—Shakespeare is around here somewhere. He's perfectly safe. Her Virgin Majesty said, 'Fear not, we are of the nature of the lion, and cannot descend to the destruction of mice and such small beasts.'"

In the blank minute that justifiably followed his burst of pomposity, the water splish-splashing outside the theatre made up its mind to be a proper rain and roared down. Gil's heart lifted again. She couldn't leave the building in *that*. She must have realized it the second after he did, since she turned away and began wandering restively around the cellar, kicking at the dirt here and there, touching this wall and that support pier. After one circuit of the space, she stopped and fixed her eyes upward, on the ceiling timbers.

Gil followed her gaze. For a minute, the two of them admired cobwebs and wooden beams. Bemused by that among other things, Gil asked, "Why are you here, mistress?"

Without diverting her attention from the ceiling, the woman replied, "I have a grant from the National Endowment for the Humanities."

"Ah." He intoned it sagely, as though he comprehended what she said.

"I'm writing a book."

"Ah," he repeated, adding a slow nod to garnish his impression of sagacity. A few blank seconds tiptoed by, as well they might. "A book about...*cellll*-ars?"

He hadn't meant to drag the word out, but it left his lips reluctantly. Of books, he had no small knowledge, but not one about cellars came to mind. Perhaps, hers was the first. A noble undertaking. And scholars were wont to write odd things. He'd seen a book about worms, once, in a stall in Printers' Lane.

"Not about cellars." At last, the woman turned her face to him, and Gil nearly dropped from the impact. Her eyes, her skin, her lips. They drew him as a lodestone drew a pin, and he tightened all his muscles to keep from actually leaning in her direction.

"I'm writing a book," she repeated, unperturbed by his reaction, "about undiscovered Jacobean Era poets, playwrights, and theatres."

"Ah!" For variety, he said it exuberantly, and capped it with a short bow. "Fortune smiles upon you, mistress. You see before you an example of the first two things you seek. As to the third," he couldn't resist a little smirk as he drew a line with his toe in the hard earth of the cellar floor, "it lies beneath your feet."

As they had both stared at the ceiling, they stared at the floor. "There's another theatre..." she pointed at the shallow furrow his shoe had dug, "under this one?"

"Aye." He offered no more. He'd let her work a little for it.

She approached, the glint in her eyes less friendly than he might have liked, but he'd won over hostile audiences before. When she was a yard away, Gil got a good look at her shoes. Laced leather, very sturdy, more like a laborer's boots than a lady's. But then, the woman was in trousers.

"What can you tell me about it?" she asked him briskly.

"Which one?" He looked up from her feet and answered his own question. "There are three."

She pointed to the floor. "Three, here?"

He smiled. Smugly, he had to confess, but he *was* the only expert in the room. "The Hart, the Coronet, and the Olympiad."

"Three theatres." Skeptically uttered, as though Gil had suggested three dragons, or three goblins. Without further comment, she resumed her aimless tour of the chamber. The pilgrimage perplexed him. The cellar had no evident attractions unless one was looking for a spot to cache smuggled goods. Or root vegetables. Hide the odd murder victim or two.

He had a card up his sleeve and whipped it out with a flourish. "You'll find no trace of the Hart, I think. It was pulled apart when Elizabeth Tudor was young. Every scrap was used to build the Coronet, one of the first play-houses in London Town to be roofed." Gil assayed the cellar floor with a frown. "It's still here. Somewhere."

Still, the woman showed no more reaction than if he'd said the Thames was wet. Gil suspected she feigned nonchalance. Too proud to show interest, she would bide her time until she could summon the right response. The one that would say, with a yawn, *your disclosures are entirely of no interest and will probably bore me even more than you, but share them, if you must.*

Her subterfuge was useless; he sensed excitement building in her heart. It struck him with the sudden force of a fever that his heart would always know what transpired in hers. From this day onward, they would have no secrets, even if they tried.

She stopped her peregrination and faced him squarely. "How do I know you're not lying?"

Well played. She had deflected her excitement to his unreliability. "The same way you know I am dead."

"Speaking of that, and in your own words, please, what *are* you?"

"Brilliant? In my acting days, a broadsheet called me 'a Tyger upon the stage, the best of the roaring boys.' As to my verses, they themselves attest that I—"

"That's not what I mean, and you know it."

"Comely, then. Or at the very least, I do not pain the eyes." He lifted his chin and threw out his chest in a pose he'd learned from that smooth villain, Eliard Swanston, who always got sighs from the distaff public.

A veritable rat terrier, she kept at her quizzing. "You're not a ghost. Not a ghost-ghost, anyway, like Shakespeare. I can...*feel* you."

Oh, if she would but—his obstreperous organ twitched. In what he hoped was a casual gesture, Gil crossed his hands in front of his crotch, saying nothing.

Nor did she give voice, for a space. Perhaps, she ruminated about what he was. Or where, at this hour, she might find a priest and a flask of holy water.

"Maybe," she finally offered, "you're just displaced in time." The deduction seemed to please her, and she added, "A time traveler."

God's hat, she was a reader of fantasies and fables, like the ones that Wells fellow scribbled. An actor in Edward the Seventh's era had left a flimsy copy of *The*

Time Machine in one of the dressing rooms. Morlocks and Eloi and the like. The woman was decidedly sailing in the wrong direction if she thought he was one of those.

"Radiant mistress," he spoke carelessly, in light of what he was about to disclose, "I remember my death. Vividly. Even had it not been my own, it was an ugly sight." He brushed his hand across the rusty stains on his shirt.

Her sight went to them and then rapidly bounced away, as if it had struck something hard. Had there been a clock in the room, it would have ticked six times before her response. "You have a point," she conceded, and went back to circumnavigating the cellar without giving him another glance. "A flimsy one. It tells me what you're not, without telling me what you are."

A spirited wench. He liked that. When they got to the bedding part, there'd be a tussle for who was in charge. They could take turns. He'd like that, too.

But all that was in a future that might never happen if he didn't ensure it now. "You're digging in the wrong place, Aoife."

She faced him. Rigid with challenge, she bit out, "That's Ms. Gowdie to you, mister."

Acidity notwithstanding, her darting eyes gave away the nibble marks of curiosity. Mindful to show off his long frame and actor's stride, Gil sauntered to where she'd burrowed a few inches into the packed earth. He pointed. "Not here." Crossing to the opposite wall, he stamped his foot, making dust rise from the floor where the masonry joined it. "Here."

It took every mote of strength he had in his wretched soul, but he made a courteous bow, complete with a sweep of the hand that would have looked a lot better had he still had the ring on it that was nicked before his corpse had gone stiff. "Adieu, mistress," he intoned formally as he rose. Then, he strolled from the cellar, mounting the stairs with such a fine and heedless tread that no one would ever guess each footfall tore his heart.

His blithe comportment disguised the riskiest of hopes. The world hinged on whether or not she stayed and dug. If she dug, she would keep returning to the cellar, because treasure awaited the quest of her clever mind and poppet's spade. As he reached the dark stairs to the attic and climbed them, Gil, who hadn't invoked Papist idols since the Puritans made them dangerous, strenuously tried to remember the name of the patron saint of hope.

EIGHT

Fee thought the third day after Gilbert Sorley told her where to dig in the Olympiad's cellar would never arrive. When it did, bringing her a ten o'clock appointment at Heelis, the National Trust's Swindon headquarters, she wasn't pleased to be stalled in Reception for forty minutes. It was a bit like being in the waiting room of an exclusive vet, one of those TV vets who saved Muffin from the rare, life-threatening disease that other vets failed to spot. The long wait in the Trust's sleekly modern and aggressively green building was a tacit warning: the bag on her lap had better contain a really spectacular animal. The doctor wouldn't waste time on a budgie with the sniffles.

No budgie. The Tesco carrier on her lap held a small flat box, the size a jeweler might put a bracelet in. Inside the box were two layers of cotton she'd pulled out of a jumbo bottle of paracetamol. Between the cotton layers was a tiny clear plastic bag. And inside the plastic bag was a coin.

Smaller than a U.S. penny, the silver coin looked surprisingly new, considering the image on one side was Charles the First and the coin was in circulation from 1625 to 1642.

The Fields Specialist she'd talked to the day before at MOLA—the Museum of London Archeology—had nearly had a stroke over the condition of it.

"You *cleaned* it," Nazir Desai said bitterly. "What in blazes were you thinking?"

"I know, I know." She did know. While only the broadest view of academia would call Archeology an "allied" discipline to Theatre History, all historians, including Fee, knew that the dirt, tarnish, and grime on artifacts were also artifacts, rarely removed and then only by professionals. She'd been very careful, even looking up a webpage titled "Cleaning Ancient Coins", but she'd not been able to stop herself from taking her find back to mint condition.

Once the MOLA staffer stopped frothing at the mouth, he'd listened to her long and convoluted proposal. First, the decrepit Victorian building known as the Olympiad Theatre rested on a much earlier theatre, maybe two. Second, her research (a dig order from a ghost, not mentioned) and the coin (from a shattered ceramic box under nearly a foot of packed hazelnut shards, clay, and ash, all mentioned) suggested the buried building was a sixteenth or seventeenth century theatre. Third, the site should be designated an Unexpected Archeological Discovery. The label would halt plans to pull the Olympiad down until skilled excavation could take place, or at least until it was proved the site was or wasn't of archeological interest.

The whole time she talked, Desai's eyes stayed on the coin. He didn't touch it, even though he'd pulled on thin latex gloves at the start of their conversation.

At the end of Fee's spiel, he cautiously pushed the coin across the desk to her, then frowned as she picked it up barehanded and restored it to its baggie, box, and Tesco carrier.

"You'll have to submit all this to the National Trust," he said tersely. "We can't make a move until they ask us to." He made the appointment while she was still sitting at his desk.

And so there she was, two days later, cooling her Heelis at the Trust, *ha ha*.

Truthfully, she felt safer at the Trust than anywhere else. Ever since the start of her strange relationship with Gilbert Sorley, she'd felt like she was jumping out of her skin. At home in the flat, she restlessly paced all five hundred square feet, opening and closing her laptop, pulling the drapes open and shut, making tea and tea and more tea. When she went to the British Library for distraction, the vast reading rooms, even the spectacularly domed Round, seemed to shrink to the size of pill boxes; she was a single capsule clattering around in them. Fleeing to the King's Café for coffee and relief, the clatter of dishes and blabbering of students did nothing to drown the screams in her head. *"I met a leathling! He's handsome and magnetic and funny and dead dead dead!"*

She shifted, trying to get comfortable in the vegan-leather-recycled-wood armchair in Heelis' lobby. With her family history, she should have been able to take Gil in stride, like a spider living in the medicine cabinet. In theory, that was true. But all the lectures and warnings from her mother, all the Irish folk tales from her father, the family stories from her great-aunts, the warnings from her posse of Welsh witches…

Nothing had really prepared her for the shock of meeting a not-exactly-dead-or-alive man. In the flesh, as it were.

And why the hell hadn't she felt the tingling her mother said she'd feel around him?

"Ms. Gowdie?"

Fee involuntarily squeaked as she looked up. An intern was hailing her from the curvilinear bamboo reception desk. "Ms. Cookson and Mr. Bellwether will see you now."

She gathered up her courage and her Tesco bag. *Cry havoc,* she told herself, *and let slip the dogs of war.*

NINE

"Um, suggestive." Marcus Bellwether's lukewarm assessment echoed hollowly in the cellar.

"I'd say, definitive." Fee poured uncompromising belief into the words. At Heelis, the Charles First coin hadn't been sufficient inducement for Bellwether and his senior officer, Anthea Cookson, to drop everything and rush to the Olympiad. Fee hadn't expected they would. Or that they would summarily slap a work-halt order on the site to allow genuine archeology to take place. Bellwether had just looked disapproving throughout the meeting, though he'd held on to the Charles First coin for the duration. Fee suspected he would have pocketed it if she hadn't asked for it back.

Anthea Cookson had said very little in the meeting, and what she had said wasn't encouraging. "London is nearly two thousand years old, Miss Gowdie," she'd told Fee coolly, her tone a match for her immaculately tailored suit and tidy, pale blonde coiffure. "It holds literally millions of artifacts and hundreds of thousands of meaningful sites. It's frustrating but true: we'll never find them all."

In the end, Fee had pushed hard to get one of the officers to make room in what Bellwether called their "shockingly crowded" schedules to visit the Olympiad's cellar, which he only did after making her wait two more days.

Now, she wasn't going to let him leave without concessions. "My hypothesis, Mr. Bellwether, is that what I've uncovered is a theatre coin collection box from no later than the 1640s. Any later and the Charles First silver penny would have been out of circulation."

"Yes, yes, so you told us." Bellwether pointed at Fee's hand. She was holding the tiny coin up like a charm against evil, the King's head outward. "That penny. You're positive it's from..." he angled his index finger toward the hole in the cellar floor, "here?"

No, Marcus, I bought it on eBay. "Absolutely. I took the coin from the remains of a ceramic collecting box I uncovered. You can see the shards." While Bellwether crouched to inspect the hole, Fee furtively inspected the cellar. It was lit not only by the overhead bulb but by every battery lantern she'd been able to get her hands on since her meeting at Heelis. The additional light still left dark corners. She hoped Gilbert Sorley wasn't lurking in one of them.

At her knees, Bellwether sighed and clucked as he peered at the disturbed dirt. "There might be another box somewhere," Fee suggested to keep him on task.

"Elizabethan and Jacobean theatres often had more than one."

"We don't yet know it's a theatre, Miss Gowdie." Bellwether screwed his face into a critical moue. "And we certainly can't determine its age."

"The coin—"

"One coin is not sufficient to date a site, I'm afraid. That penny could simply have fallen out of someone's pocket in 1924."

Oh, yeah, sure. Because lots of Jazz Age theatergoers kept spare change from the Carolean Era in their trousers. "I understand what you're saying, Mr. Bellwether. But if what I've found is a coin box from a theatre and knowing, as we do, that the coin boxes were features of theatres in London in the sixteenth and seventeenth centuries, then that means the structure I'm uncovering may be a theatre several hundred years old. I'm sure an organized dig would uncover plenty of evidence if we can only—"

"Don't get overconfident, Miss Gowdie." Bellwether stood, his knees cracking like walnuts. "Good archeology is born of skepticism."

And throttled in its crib by unbelievers. She took a breath and let it out in a gust of bravado. "I'd like to suggest that the box and coin are enough for the National Trust to put a hold on the teardown plans. Ideally, to put the site on the Theatres at Risk Register."

Bellwether hummed noncommittally. He jutted his chin toward her hand, where the coin winked dully in the uncertain light. "Pity you cleaned it."

Yeah, yeah, I've heard that before. She closed her

fingers around the coin and dropped her fist to her side. "What's really needed is a crew from MOLA. If we can get some real archeologists in here—"

"Steady on, Miss Gowdie. MOLA is stretched very thin and so is the Trust. We'll just take it one step at a time, shall we?" Even though he hadn't touched anything, Bellwether plucked a neatly pressed linen handkerchief out of his jacket inside pocket and used it to wipe his hands. He did it carefully and slowly, one finger at a time. Fee waited, cramming a scream of frustration into the corner of her mind that was already getting crowded with other things she wasn't ready to deal with, most of them having to do with Gilbert Sorley.

The National Trust officer suddenly froze, his handkerchief jammed between two fingers. "What's that?"

Oh, God, no, not now, Shakespeare. She'd heard it, too, the tiny scratching from the ceiling timbers above their heads. A scrabble, a scritch, the noise made by little mouse feet up to no good. She didn't dare look up, for fear Bellwether's scrutiny would follow the same trajectory. "I didn't hear anything." She shoved the Charles First penny into the pocket of her UNC Lacrosse hoodie. "When can you let me know about a work-halt order?"

Bellwether gave his hands a final swipe with the handkerchief and restored it to his jacket. "Can't say," he drawled. "We've a dreadfully crowded docket, just dreadful." Where *did* he get that plummy voice, and those Bertie Wooster expressions? Hardly anyone in the U.K. spoke that way anymore. "Just carry on here, if you like." He smiled and waggled a finger at her admonishingly, like a headmaster correcting a wayward student. "But no more silver polish, please."

She could be patronizing, too. Crossing her heart, she held up two fingers like the Brownie she'd never been, since they didn't have those in 1760s Paris. "Scout's honor. I'll walk you up to the street level."

"Jolly good. Those stairs are deadly."

———

"What a scabby pustule of a man."

Fee's body jerked violently. "*Nom de dieu de merde!*" She'd barely pushed Marcus Bellwether out the stage door to the alley and shut it behind him when Gil oozed out of the gloom and to her side. "Don't creep around like that!" she hissed.

"I wasn't creeping, merely observing. The man's a pustule. I'll end him if you want. You swear most color-fully. French, is it?"

"Yes, I grew up in—could you really kill him? I mean, no, of course not!"

"The stairs are deadly, he said it himself. He might have taken drink with his lunch. A slip of the foot and he'd be done for."

"Don't be absurd, Gil."

Even in the gloom of the auditorium, she caught the flash of his grin. "You called me Gil, Aoife."

"Oh, hell, whatever."

"Now that we're on an intimate footing, would you care to see my lodging? It is close by, at the top of the house."

He advanced, just one step, but suddenly he was too near and not near enough. For the first time, Fee caught his scent. Some scent, anyway. Old theatre, wood smoke, male body. Faintly musky, faintly sweaty, whiffs of spilled ale and copper. The last...that would be the blood.

Her eyes locked on the stain fouling half his shirt-front. Like his nearness, the stain both beckoned and unnerved her. Determinedly, she slid her eyes up to his face. "There is nothing intimate about us, Gil. And no, I wouldn't care to see your lodging. Or your etchings."

"I sigh with relief about the etchings, since I am freshly out at the moment."

"Are you seriously asking me to be alone with you in your—bedchamber?"

"Aoife, Aoife...I have two full rooms, a palace for a playwright. You may take your ease anywhere you like. There are chairs—one with all four legs—a writing desk, a bed—"

"Not on your life." Fee winced. "Sorry. Poor choice of words."

"You're perfectly safe with me, you know. I haven't sixpence to my name but am finely cloaked in honor." Retracting one of his steps, he bowed. Fee had to admit, Gil's bow was a masterpiece.

He rose and extended his hand. She ignored it. He ignored her ignoring it. "No harm shall come to you in my company, mistress. 'And manly hearts to guard the fair!'"

"That's not even from your time. It's a line from a song. *Rule, Britannia*, I'm pretty sure."

"I have heard you sing. You like songs."

Honestly, the man's brain hopped around like a rabbit. "Some of them."

"I was quite the lark before my voice changed. Sang *Mirie it is while sumer ilast* with the best of them. Though, being trapped in this theatre during the 1920s cast a pall upon the muse. A panegyric to musical silliness, that decade. And the plays!"

"I hadn't thought about that. I suppose you were here for all of them."

"Yes, and woefully, I am dead but not deaf and blind. Year after year, I endured a regiment of actors tramping the stage and bellowing lines from the sublime to the scrofulous. I thought *A Shilling for Edgar* would drive me mad in 1926."

"Never heard of it."

"Alleluia, there is a God! *Edgar*'s faded into oblivion, then. Would that my memories of that turnip went there, as well. A year's run—can you imagine? And the players! Talk about chewing the curtain."

"I think you mean chewing the scenery."

"Curtain, scenery, the orchestra." He pulled away a strip of red cloth binding his hair and scrubbed his fingers roughly along his scalp. The action tumbled straight, dark locks around his umber face, turning him into a Hindu idol. Lord Shiva, without the extra arms.

He stepped closer again, and again his scent beckoned. Fee froze, knowing she should back away, but she was held fast by the smell of him. Wild things, the woods in fall, the undercoat of a cat when it was stroked. It crept through the cracks in the wall of her defenses, like incense. How long had it been since she'd been close to a man who smelled of something other than cologne or body wash? Paris, of course. Ten years ago, which was really 1774. Even there and then, men of the class her family knew doused themselves in oils and powders. Not Papa, of course, who bathed.

Papa. Her *leathling* father. A man almost certainly like the one facing her, the one who wanted her to sit on his four-legged chair. *Don't do it, Fee, don't do it.*

"No, thanks, Gil. I won't see your lodging." She turned to go, but he caught her sleeve and held it. Maybe it was her imagination—a darkened theatre, an attractive man a foot away—but Fee was sure she could feel the heat of his hand through the cloth.

Gil rubbed the sleeve between his fingers, once, twice. In the still atmosphere, Fee heard the tiny rasp of calluses against fleece.

"The mouse lodges with me," he told her in a deep, velvety voice.

God help her, she sank like the *Titanic*. "Five minutes. And then I'm out of there."

TEN

"Not quite a palace, as you see," Gil waved a hand, taking in his two rooms in the Olympiad's attic, "but it suffices. I am snug as a bug in a bottle."

"Rug," Aoife corrected. "Snug as a bug in a rug."

"Ah, just so."

Gil had given her the four-legged chair, while he leaned his hips against the scarred oak kneehole desk (discarded following the 1936 run of *French Without Tears*) in the center of the room. Crossing his arms, he watched her, trying not to display his unfettered delight. It would always be a delight to watch her, the way she sat with queenly grace, the mouse in her lap. Her hands rested on her thighs—her delicious thighs, revealed so maddeningly in those faded blue breeches—and the creature scampered back and forth across them. With its mistress beaming and crooning, the picture was one of maternal love. *Madonna and Mouse.*

"It's like cool water flowing over my hands," she said

to her pet, though Gil knew she meant the remark for him.

"You've the knack of it, now. It is not a case of touching the shade, but of letting the shade touch you." *As I'd like to touch you. And not at all like the accursed rodent.*

Aquamarine eyes lifted to his, startling him pleasurably as they'd done each time since the first. So rare, those eyes. They pierced him with pleasure.

"Are all ghosts like this?" she asked, her face guileless with wonder. "Sweet and silky and—"

"Nay, not all." The last thing he cared to discuss, now that he had her in his rooms, was the range of horror that most ghosts brought with them.

Her eyes darted around what he'd jokingly labeled "the First Room." Neither it nor the bedchamber—the Second Room—was very spacious, but the apartment was private enough, being right at the top of the theatre, under the roof.

"Are there many here like—" Aoife dropped her chin toward Shakespeare, who sat winsomely on his hindquarters and groomed his whiskers with tiny front paws.

"A few. You'll see them not, I vow to you." *And I'll hurl into Hell the first one who tries to sit on your lap like that mouse.* "I am not of their ilk." *Not a gentle river trickling over your thighs. More like a roaring cascade of desire.*

"I'm pretty sure I know what you are."

"Because of your father."

"Because of both my parents. They told me what they were. And what they were to each other." Disquiet passed fleetingly across her face. Gil sensed a secret kept, a resolution showing its sharp teeth.

He wouldn't press her for it. First trust, then secrets. "Be thine own privy counsellor," he said without thinking.

"Shakespeare? The Bard," she amended, "not the mouse."

Gil shook his head. His unbound hair fell over his eyes and he made an effort to pull it neatly back. He'd lost his hair tie again. "Benjamin Disraeli, that self-serving Tory nitwit."

"For a g—person born in the 1600s, you have a wide range of historical knowledge."

He shrugged. "Nothing else to do in the last forty-eight decades but see the world pass by, Aoife. One watches and listens, one learns."

"The way you speak…I only know it from writings, of course, but you don't always sound 17th century."

"Credit me with not wallowing in my own time for all those years, dove." He waved a hand at the stained and peeling walls. "To the extent it can be watched from this tiresome ruin, I have seen and heard a plentitude of history. And I am a poet. Words are my work. I'll converse in any style you like, should you ask. I must say the 1940s were most entertaining in that regard, even with sandbags piled on the Olympiad's doorstep and the fireball from the sky that took out the east wall. What think you of this rich bit? I learned it from Bert the stage-hand." He gave her a broad wink. "Cor, you're a jammy bit. Fancy a spin in me loan car?"

Her grin emboldened him. "Or the Prince Regent's

era. That one was fine in a flowery way. All those 'excessively kinds' and 'agreeably disposeds.'"

She giggled, a girlish sound with a squeaky little intake of breath at the end. Coming from her wide, soft mouth, the sound fluttered down to his groin and did excessively kind things to his manly parts, which were agreeably disposed to return the favor. *Tell her not to make that sound,* the angel in the region of his heart told him. *On the contrary,* the demon somewhat lower in his belly said, *tell her to make it again.* While he shifted to accommodate his tightening breeches, Aoife lectured about styles of utterance, as sober as a magister in cap and gown.

"Slang, that is, cant or common speaking—it's always more colorful and true than literary speech." She took a hand away from the mouse and pointed at the one window, overlooking the alley. "Living here, I imagine you absorbed some pretty rich language."

"Ah, but here is not where I lived." He pushed away from the desk and crossed to the window. The view, being much the same for decades at a stretch, had made him melancholy, and so for the last century he'd let the glass fog with grime and dust. In the mad hope that got its hooks into him when the woman arrived, he'd washed the mullioned panes.

The view was still uninspiring, a row of tall buildings across the lane. It had changed since last he paid attention and was now mildly diverting, if puzzling. A rope factory from George Fifth's time had become a blank wall, dotted with irregular windows and bearing no signs at all. He supposed the locals could say what manner of trade went on there, but bugger all if he could. When had buildings become as faceless as cliffs? He should have been more attentive, he supposed, but attentiveness hadn't seemed important. Until now.

He shifted to look at the woman, a view of her being infinitely better than the one out the window. "I lived in St. Giles," he said, hoping she knew less about it than he did.

St. Giles in the Fields. The name suggested grass and sheep and God knew what manner of pastoral delights. It possessed all those until the leper house and the monks who tended the surrounding fields were sent packing by Copper Nose Harry in the Dissolution. In no time at all, the place swarmed with beggars and thieves, the dissolute and dispossessed. People like him.

Aoife's brow, ivory white under raven curls, wrinkled charmingly. "It all burned in the Great Fire, didn't it?"

"It did, in 1666. I was well away, by then." He rested his weight on the window frame. "Away from all and everything."

Unnecessarily, she used great care to place her pet on the table. Despite her waggoner's foul tongue, she did everything with art and delicacy. Watching her soothed him, like music. She rose and came to stand beside him at the window, not as close as he'd like. "I'm not sure I understand. You're here, but if you died in St. Giles…" She cast a rueful look upon the mouse. "Well, Shakespeare died in Bloomsbury, and he's here."

Ah, Bloomsbury. Where the Earl of Southampton raised a great house while the less privileged parts of London burned. Gil had wondered where the creature had met its end. If her pet had been housed there, then so was she. Not that Gil would be able to make his way to her door, clothed as a grave gallant, a nosegay of violets in his hand. She might be in the New World for all the chance he'd have of that.

"The mouse is a ghost," he reminded her, "and ghosts do travel betimes. Whilst I am different, as you so graciously pointed out." For a long moment, they both looked at the mouse on the table. It looked back at its mistress with a squeak, making her face brighten like the sun. Pressing his advantage, Gil spoke again. "I lived in St. Giles, but it was here I died. Not on this spot, but in this same place, when it was still the Coronet Theatre."

To her great credit, she didn't shriek or leap away or even recoil. Nor did she ply him with questions about how and when and why he went from mortal to moribund in a wet red second. She stayed rooted, though her gaze ascended. A tiny shadow darted across her eyes like a startled minnow.

Knave that he was, he couldn't resist bending over her. He spoke low, against her temple, knowing his breath sent shivers along her skin. "It's not catching, my sort of death."

She stood her ground. Saints and martyrs, what a woman. Without a twitch or a tremor, she merely lifted her chin. The movement brought her mouth within inches of his. Sensation almost felled him like an axed tree. He could take that mouth, sink into it, into her, lips, breasts, body...

"It must be hot up here," she said levelly. Her scent, roses and mint, and the little gusts of her breath feathering his jaw would drive the Archbishop of Canterbury to rapine, but her voice was as bland as if she remarked on the latest Act of Parliament. "Under the eaves, I mean." Her eyes, turned up to his, were limpid pools, clear and undisturbed.

She was playing him, the minx. Ye *gods*, how she played him and how willingly he succumbed. In an instant, he went from a rake with his tongue nearly in her mouth to a hound at her feet, craving nothing but to whimper and obey. He whispered, trying to get the leash in his teeth again. "I like it hot."

"I'm kind of a cold weather girl, myself." She pushed away from the window and Gil actually had to grab the sill to keep from falling. With studied nonchalance, she pulled the good chair up to the desk. The mouse was still there, playing with its own tail in some mouse-ish game. Its mistress cupped her hands and the creature hopped obligingly into them.

Gil pressed against the window, panting like the dog he was. He'd felt her withdrawal as physical pain, the kind he'd not known since he'd taken a blade to the neck.

Satan's cloven hooves, he'd known the woman for barely a week and he was losing his mind to desire. How could it be? It had something to do with the crawling sensation under his skin, he'd warrant. Perhaps, it was a mark of the Old One as was left on witches. Could he have sold his soul sometime in the past few hundred years and forgotten about it? Could one forget a thing like that?

Because if the woman sitting a few feet from him wasn't Hell-spawned, he was Oliver Cromwell. It must be that. *She* must be that. He'd opened his door to a demoness, a succubus. One of those could drug a man with lust, slip into his bed, slither up his body, and suck the life out of him through his—

He cleared his throat so loudly both the woman and the mouse jumped. "The pustule."

"Marcus Bellwether? He's from the National Trust." She formed a hurdle out of her thumbs, touching them tip to tip, and the mouse jumped over, making her smile. "That's an organization, a sort of guild, that decides if a building is historically significant and should be preserved." She chucked her chin at the ratling, who jumped back over the thumb-hurdle and looked up for the smile. She gave it. Gil knew exactly how the mouse felt. He, too, would be on all fours, jumping hurdles for her, in no time at all.

He cleared his throat again, not so loudly. "What, in the estimation of this Trust, decrees that a building is significant?"

Now, she'd formed her hands into a tunnel, and the mouse was wriggling through. In and out, in and out. The diameter of her grip was just the same as...another minute watching and he'd have to pull his shirt from his breeches and use the tail to cover his groin. Aoife, thankfully, had her eyes fixed on her performing playmate.

"Different things. In the case of a residence, someone important might have lived there. If the building's a theatre...well, the Rose and the Curtain theatres here in London are both Listed, though there's hardly anything left of either one. At the Rose, there's an ongoing dig. That's a—"

"I am not ignorant of the term. People leave broadsheets lying around, you know. Jack Finley—he was the offstage prompter in the 1920s—brought the *Times* to read when he wasn't shoveling lines at piffle-headed actors. I learned about Howard Carter and the digging in Egypt from it."

The mouse had crawled into Aoife's hand tunnel and fallen asleep. From the look on its mistress' face, she might have been cradling the remains of a saint. Time to wrest her attention from mouse to man. "I knew the Rose. In Bankside it was, hard by London Bridge. The Grocer's Folly, we called it."

Success. Her eyes snapped to him. "It was built by a vegetable seller."

His mouth quirked. "Aye, so they said. Methinks he was hawking more than cabbages. 'Twas suggested, by some too stupid to keep their gobs shut, that it was counterfeit coin."

"You knew the Rose." Soft and dreamy, her utterance, as though he'd told her the Faerie Queen was a friend of his youth.

"Nor was I a stranger to the Phoenix."

"You mean the Cockpit?"

He would try hard to ignore her last utterance. "I knew it as I knew the lines of my hand. The first one burned to a cinder in—"

"1617. But it was rebuilt as the Phoenix." The mouse woke, stretched its forelegs, and shot out of her cupped hands like a pea from a reed. Without so much as a backward look, it scrabbled down her pantaloon leg and across the floor, disappearing into a hole in the boards.

Aoife's face registered such dismay that Gil swore under his breath. God *damn* that mouse. "The affairs of mice are inscrutable," he soothed. "He'll be back."

She hesitated, then nodded and rose to her feet. "The National Trust is skeptical about the Coronet. I'll need to dig, find more evidence."

Eager as the pup he'd become, he pushed hastily away from the window. "There is a second coin box. I can show you where it is."

She shook her head. Her hair had largely escaped the topknot in which it had been loosely trapped, and dark tendrils danced around her fair face. There was a tiny spray of freckles across her nose. The sight was so artlessly sweet that Gil's heart turned over in his breast.

"Not today," she told him crisply. "I need more tools, better ones. And I need to transcribe my latest research notes. I have a quarterly review coming up and I haven't examined the Bodley Head Quartos for pertinent content."

Gil tried to infuse his, "Indeed, I see," with a learned air, despite her explanation casting him adrift. He had known women of all sorts, or so he thought. Farmwives, fishwives, alewives. Virgins in white, nuns in black, drabs in brown. Milkmaids of the lane and soothsayers of the Romany camps. Women with grand titles, women entitled to nothing but the right to sell themselves against a wall. He'd never known a woman scholar before; it was passing strange.

He braced himself for another farewell, but she didn't make straight away for the door. Instead, she stared, forehead pinched, at his shirt. He couldn't help but follow her stare, and for a half minute they both frowned at the splotched linen.

Finally, she tsked and held out her hand. "That's disgusting. Give it to me and I'll wash it."

She was offering to launder his clothes. They were halfway to a house in the country with a babe and a cat. Stunned mute, he tore the shirt up and over his head, then thrust it at her. She took it gingerly, like the shift of a plague victim, without once looking at his bared torso. Bundling the garment quickly and tucking it under her arm, she turned for the door.

Alarmed, he fired a question at her back. "When will you—that is, er, when might you..." He trailed off, embarrassed. The hound would be *aah-rooing* any second.

She supplied the answer over her shoulder without his having to debase himself further. "I'll be back in a day or two."

Out the door and away she went, while he hearkened to her passage. Down the stairs, more stairs, still more stairs, her footfalls grew distant and then she was gone.

His surroundings instantly diminished in a subtle way. The desk he'd thought rather fine, the chipped mug with his quills, the stack of pilfered paper with his scratched-through verses. Even the good chair, which had a glorious tenure during a long run of *The Man of Mode*, was shabby now that Aoife's body was not curled prettily upon it. The chair, like all the rest, became what it truly was: a cast-off, a wreck.

As was he.

Nay, none of that. She'd come, she'd visited his lodging, and she'd be back. On that encouraging thought, the mouse appeared again. Like him, it stared at the empty door for a while, then moodily began cleaning its whiskers.

"You have the right of it, mouse. Work is melancholy's bane. I shall write a poem to my lady's hair."

ELEVEN

At the Bloomsbury flat, Fee opened her laptop and clicked on the folder labeled *NEH Jul-Sep*. Then, she started cursing in both English and French and didn't stop for a while. The folder's contents made it clear: she'd mostly given up already on the kind of results the grantors wanted. In the past few months, she'd done little besides paste in the URLs of digitized ancient London maps, save some articles off academia-dot-edu and JSTOR, and make notes on the now-famous video debate between Anthony Perea and Sheila Gretsch-Norbert about gender in Restoration drama.

Gender in Restoration drama? Why had she made notes on that? It wasn't anywhere near her thesis. *The Loss of Lesser Lights: Vanished Theatres, Poets, and Playwrights of the Jacobean and Carolean Ages*—that was the supposed name of the supposed book she was supposed to be writing with her NEH grant. Thus far, she had the title, six chapters, and a pathetic smattering of sources. The six chapters were strong, they'd gotten her the renewals of her grant. But after that, she'd run completely, depressingly, dry.

Failure was becoming a tangible possibility. A guilty admission sloshed in her gut: she'd been over-confident in grad school. The Provost's Award, a Graduate Teaching Award, a 4.0 GPA: she was the department's star. When she was awarded the NEH grant, she'd acted ten kinds of humble, but secretly she thought she deserved it. The scholastic dead-end road she was traveling now was her comeuppance. Retribution, hubris, pride goeth before a fall, et cetera.

If she really had the brains she thought she did, she'd dive into her book, now, today, this minute, and not come up for air until it was done.

Excellent idea, but...

Either she didn't have brains or other parts of her anatomy were outvoting them, since her thoughts wandered right back to Gil when she'd been sure he was about to kiss her. His eyes...they were pewter, blue, gunmetal, depending on the light and something else, something that ran just ahead of her memory until she caught up to it.

One day when she was eleven or twelve, she'd gone with her mother to the Île de la Cité in Paris. Under the looming shadow of the cathedral, Mom had shopped for flowers in the stalls of the Quai aux Fleurs along the Seine, where the flower sellers gathered. Bored, Fee had walked away to stare at the river, where people, goods, and watercraft were always entertaining. Beneath the barges and boats, the great waterway flowed sluggishly, a moving mirror of the sky. That day, the sky was temperamental, the river married to its moods. One minute, the water reflected a saturated blue, the next, a mournful slate, reminding her that people drowned in it.

Fascinated by the changeable stream, Fee had to be called three times before she left the balustrade and took the bunches of long-stemmed carnations and lilies Mom gave her to carry home.

Gil's eyes were like the Seine that day, shifting, ambiguous, moody.

Dangerous.

She shook herself. She was doing a D-minus job of keeping her mind off Gilbert Sorley. It was as though she was attached to him by one of those retractable dog leashes. The second she stopped pulling away, it reeled her in.

Her laptop had gone into sleep mode. Tapping a key to wake it, she logged in to her bank account. From the moderately good news there, she spent half an hour browsing London web listings for camping equipment.

The first summer after she'd come to the U.K, she'd done an archeology internship at Manchester University, and it included two weeks at an Iron Age excavation. She had a working notion of what she needed to dig up a cellar in Covent Garden.

———

Listing the essential equipment took thirty minutes. Assembling it took two and a half days. She had to criss-cross London on foot, by bus, taxi, and the Underground. That, and deal with some stores that had odd business hours and others whose staff clearly felt people who dug up the past had no sense of time. Now, she'd cleared everything off the kitchen table in the flat to lay out her makeshift archeology kit.

She was nearly finished when Abeni came home from the Slade. Instead of the books and student essays her flat mate expected to find on the table, there was a long-handled trowel with a T-square at one end, a stack of zippered clear vinyl pouches, a plastic tarp, a clutch of brushes, some neon orange marking line with U-shaped pins to hold it down, a folding ruler, a large handled magnifying glass, and a five-gallon tub for dirt or bulky artifacts. Fee had added a decent compass from the Internet and a pack of surgical gloves from Boots.

"Let me guess," Abeni said after a protracted, silent survey, "your acting dreams have come true and you've been cast in a remake of *Raiders of the Lost Ark*."

Fee clucked. "Just be thankful my budget didn't stretch to a metal detector. That would've come in really handy."

Abeni picked up the trowel, put it down, and leveled a critical look at Fee across the table. "I'm not sure I want an answer to this question, but does all this—" she waved at the mess of goods, "—have something to do with the key you lifted from Javier Almeida's keyring?"

La moitié de la vérité est un mensonge. Her Great-aunt Hélène always said it in French, her language for moral instruction. A half-truth might be a lie, but Fee wasn't ready to tell Abeni the whole truth. At least, not the half that had Gilbert Sorley in it. "It does and it doesn't. I was poking around in the theatre, like I told you I wanted to do, and I found some old bits I want to examine closer."

"Old bits?" Abeni said it like *fish guts* or *dead worms.*

"Really old bits. From something far earlier than the theatre."

"How early? Like, Roman Britain?"

"No, no, of course not!" In fact, she couldn't be sure there weren't Roman remains under the Olympiad. London was full of them. Just recently, MOLA had uncovered a large section of Roman mosaic tilework in Southwark. "Jacobean, maybe. Elizabethan at a stretch."

Abeni grunted, but Fee wasn't sure her friend was really listening. She'd picked up the compass and was turning around with it, facing different directions. "Southern exposure," she muttered to the French doors.

South, that was nice. Shakespeare's grave got the sun when it butted its way through London skies. Except, Shakespeare wasn't in the garden, not really, not essentially. He was at the Olympiad with his—and her—new dead friend.

Crap, the shirt. She'd forgotten about it, still balled up in her backpack. It was three-thirty and Abeni would leave any minute for her four o'clock class at the Slade. The second she was out the door, Fee would wash Gil's shirt. In the attic, when he'd pulled it over his head and off, she'd gotten an eyeful of his body. It might be wise to let that be the last eyeful she got. The flash of bronze, sculpted torso had sent a strong and unwelcome surge of interest into parts of her that had no business being interested in any part of Gilbert Sorley for any reason whatsoever.

If Gil was going to be hovering around her dig, as she knew he would be, she needed to get his too-interesting parts covered, fast.

Abeni put the compass back on the table. "Where'd you hide my laptop?"

Fee pointed at the lounge. "Sofa. I sorted out your books and papers, too."

"Brilliant. Now I'll never find anything." Abeni started collecting what she needed for class and stuffing it into her messenger bag. "See you later, Indiana."

"Very droll. Teach good."

"Right. Dig good." Abeni waved and left the flat.

Twelve

"I'm sorry about your shirt." Fee stood on the plastic tarp at the edge of her "dig" and held up the strip of discolored linen. It was still shedding fibers. They sloughed off even as she and Gil watched. "This is all that's left. I don't know what happened."

"It's called death, my gem." He took the cloth from her hand and flicked it to the side. The fragile scrap fluttered briefly, like a dying moth, in the light from the battery lanterns, landing pale and somehow sad on the packed earth of the cellar floor.

Ice water unexpectedly sluiced Fee's insides. She didn't take her eyes off the scrap as her question came out small and cold. "If you were to leave this place, would that happen to you?"

Whatever answer he had to her question, he side-stepped it. "Tell me of your past, Aoife." He said it offhandedly, at the same time closing the distance between them.

The icy fear in her gut vaporized under a surge of heat from his nearness. If it was risky to see his half-nakedness across a room, how much more risky was it a foot away? Not even a shirt between them, just hard male body all the way to his hips, where the waistband of his breeches clung precariously. He didn't seem to be carrying an ounce of fat anywhere, but she'd never have called Gil skinny. Lean as a greyhound, maybe, with the same deceptively languid ease over latent power. His forearms, smooth brown, were dusted with dark hair. A matching triangle nested between his pectorals, sending a narrow trail down his belly and into his breeches. Close, he was too close. If she moved her hand just a few inches, she could drag it lightly along that trail...

Abruptly, she bent and snatched up her stack of small vinyl bags. With studied concentration, she thumbed through them as she spoke. "My father—I told you about him. He was a leathling. At least, that's what my mother said. She learned the word from my Auntie Jana. She's a—"

Fee stopped herself. Knowing what she knew about the witch hunt fever of the 1600s, she might hold off awhile before bringing cauldrons and pointy hats into the conversation.

"A sort of expert on those things," she finished lamely. "Leathling is Irish. It comes from the word for 'half.' One part living, one part not."

*Oh, please move away, Gil, please. Because if you don't...*Her feet were stuck in place and she wasn't moving, but she felt herself sliding toward him, as she would down a slick riverbank. If she fell into the waters at the bottom, could she ever climb out again? Would she want to?

"You're all alone," she blurted, to her shock and probably Gil's, too.

"No more than you."

No more than me. No different *from me.* Fee could rant and rail all she wanted to about the unfairness of her souler inheritance. She could shout her bloody independence to the skies, stick her fingers in her ears, and hum denial like a turbine. But the singular loneliness of their conditions, hers and Gilbert Sorley's, bound them together as they were bound to no one else in the world.

The truth gave her a sharp yank and she did fall, almost literally. The plastic bags tumbled out of her hands. They spiraled to the floor like glistening leaves, while she leaned or slipped or *melted* over to close the few inches between her and Gil.

It was he who stopped her fall. The breath pushing his words—scented with ale and ginger, not at all what she expected—feathered her face. Grinning, he whispered, "The mouse is in your pail."

"What?" She dragged herself back from the edge of— something—and reached down for the white plastic bucket on the tarp. Carefully tilting it toward her, she looked inside. Shakespeare looked back.

"Silly mouse." Shakespeare shot up the side of the bucket and along her arm to the front of her hoodie, disappearing into the pocket.

Gil chuckled. He had a nice laugh. Fee added another dangerously attractive Gil quality to her list.

"Root around in your stony garden, as it pleases

you," he said. "Doubtless, you need more light. I'll find a rag to clean the windows."

"Windows? This cellar has *windows*?"

"It does, though I would not lay odds on opening them." He waved at the wall abutting the alley. "At the top, if you can see them through the filth, there is a row. Three or four, as I recall."

She followed his wave and there the windows were. Just below the seam of the ceiling and wall, a row of narrow horizontal panes were placed to admit daylight or what, in Victorian London, passed for daylight, an acrid, yellow, coal-smoke haze. If she went outside and inspected the ground floor of the Olympiad, she'd probably find the windows at the level of her ankles. From inside the cellar, when the panes were cleaned, she'd have an interesting view of the boots and shoes of the rare pedestrians who took the alley between Arne Street and Drury Lane.

She had no idea what the pedestrians might see if they crouched to look into the cellar.

Fee had read somewhere that on average, London's current streets and alleys were laid three meters above the 16th and early 17th century streets. At that time, the area had the thickest cluster of theatres in the history of England. She was putting two and two together to get five—a theatre under a theatre—but it wasn't impossible. And she had a primary source, right in front of her, pushing his sleeves up to his elbows.

It would've been easier to interview the primary source if he weren't so distracting. He'd found a rag in the litter of the cellar. Dragging a wooden box to the wall with the windows, he stood on it. With one hand braced on the wall, he scrubbed energetically with the other at slowly emerging glass.

Fee's thoughts about London history evaporated at the sight of Gil's muscular back, flexing and rippling as he worked. His breeches had slipped so low that she could see the dimple at the base of his spine. A voice inside her whispered that it would only take a second to pull the breeches a bit lower and expose his tensing buttocks.

Somehow, she forced a question out of dry lips. "You know a lot about the theatre here, don't you? The one right before the Olympiad, I mean."

"Know it, wrote plays for it, watched it fall." He stepped down from the box and crossed to her tarp, hefting one of the two-liter bottles of water she'd brought. Wrestling the top off, he sniffed at the contents. "Gin?" he asked. Fee shook her head, and he grunted, "Pity."

Pouring water on the rag, he capped the bottle and dropped it back on the plastic sheet. "Marvelous how that new glass doesn't break," he said as he mounted the wooden box again, talking over his shoulder.

"The Coronet Theatre, directly beneath us, rose in 1603. James had got himself down from Scotland and up to the Palace by then, and theatres were plentiful as fleas. The Red Bull, the Hope in Southwark—that one had a nice view of the Thames if you could stand the reek. The Globe, of course, both the first and second. Porter's Hall as became Blackfriars Theatre. Some burghers raised Salisbury Court Playhouse in Whitefriars. A gem, that one, between the Thames and the Fleet, and *not* for common folk."

Not for common folk. She'd been inside a theatre once that catered to uncommon folk, though she'd forgotten about it until that moment. La Comédie Française was housed, in the 1770s, in the palace of the Tuileries in Paris, and she'd been brought by her parents as a treat for her sixteenth birthday. She'd thought herself a *très coquette* in the emerald satin of her birthday dress. Quite a few dashing young bucks in the audience agreed, until they were turned hastily aside by Papa's homicidal stare.

Later, Fee couldn't have said what the play was about because she'd been hypnotized by the Parisian elites in the audience. The ladies of the *haut monde* perched in the galleries like exotic birds, draped with feathers and diamonds. She'd imagined herself a grown woman among them, gowned in gold.

As though reading her mind—perhaps he could, she wasn't prepared to say what Gilbert Sorley could and couldn't do—Gil stopped scrubbing and turned on his box to face her appraisingly. "You'd have found a seat in Salisbury Court, my dove. In the gallery, clad in a gown of shot silk. Gold, I think, with a fur-collared mantle."

Fee's brain whirled. He'd seen her as she'd dreamed of seeing herself. *Stop that*, she wanted to tell him. *Stop showing me magical things, impossible things.*

Like you.

She wrenched her thoughts back to period theatre.

"Salisbury Court. There's some debate about its date. Was it built before or after the Cockpit?"

He twisted on the box again and smiled. A smile so wicked and handsome she didn't know if it belonged on Lucifer or the Archangel Gabriel, and so magnetic it made her want to crawl to him on her hands and knees. The same part of her that had thought about pulling down Gil's breeches said what a wonderful idea the crawling was. Aoife Gabrielle Gowdie, 21st century scholar, had a different opinion. *What are you thinking, you idiot? Do you want to wake up tomorrow in the reign of Charles First? No toilets, no antibiotics, no tampons?*

Gil was still smiling. "The what?" he prompted.

"The Phoenix."

"Ah, but it wasn't the Phoenix, then, my adorable scholar. It was the...?"

"I'm not your adorable anything and you can't make me say it again."

He stepped off the box, hands raised in mock amazement. "How, now? You'll not name the Cockpit? For an actor, you are strangely reticent to say the word when it is so freely used upon the stage. 'Come, stir, stir! The second cock hath crowed!'"

He'd called her an actor. Pleasure fought with indignation. "Act 4, Scene 4, *Romeo and Juliet*. But that doesn't mean—"

"And your paragon Ophelia drags it out again, in *Hamlet*! 'Young men will do't if they come to't. By Cock, they are to blame.'"

"I'd call that social commentary, not—"

"Why, the word is in Holy Writ! 'Verily, verily, I say

unto thee. The cock shall not crow, 'til thou hath denied me thrice!'"

"The Bible has to *nothing* to do with the—"

Gil swaggered toward her. "There's Wycherly's romp, *The Country Wife*." He was right in front of her again, almost touching. "Past my time, but it's a pretty piece." Gripping himself, he bent over her and spoke low, into her hair. "The character Sparkish says, 'Let us come together, at the *Cock*.'"

She reared back. "Stop that!" Shakespeare emerged from her hoodie pocket with a squeak and jumped to Gil's shoulder. "Turncoat," she snapped and spun around for the door.

Behind her, Gil laughed, rich and low. Fee was glad the half-cleaned windows weren't admitting enough light to show the flush spreading up her neck and into her cheeks as she stormed out of the cellar.

———

Maybe she should take up vaping. There wasn't much else a person could do when they were holding up a wall in an alley, trying to look nonchalant as they fumed. She had chewing gum in her backpack, but she'd left it in the cellar with an irritating ghost.

Compounding her irritation, it was raining. Not heavily, but with that sporadic, leaky quality that English skies inflicted on the populace. "Spitting," Abeni called it. It was getting colder, too, and she was hungry. A wind with no manners at all nosed under the hem of her hoodie. Pulling the hood over her hair, she shoved her hands into the pockets.

Looking to her left, she saw Arne Street. To her right, Drury Lane. On both streets, people scurried along, umbrellas open, feet splashing on the pavement. Only a stone's throw away, they might as well be scurrying in Sri Lanka. In the bowels of the Olympiad, she and Gil were in a world of their own. Not one they'd made, one that had been made for them, by accident or ancestry—did it matter which? It had been enclosing them more tightly by the hour, ever since the LUCIES crashed the Olympiad.

No, the Coronet. The LUCIES had crashed the *Coronet*. She should get used to calling it that, since the only part of the Olympiad that interested her was the cellar, where day by day she was uncovering the Jacobean theatre that would be earthshaking and career-making when she revealed it to the world.

Trouble was, the Olympiad had a fully dead mouse and a half-alive man in it. The rare historic theatre beneath demanded the world's notice, but the Olympiad's two ghostly inhabitants couldn't be dislodged or explained. The conflation of those conditions made her head feel like it was exploding.

She sniffed and rubbed her sleeved forearm across her nose, dripping from the cold. Had she ever run across the Coronet in her 17th century studies? She didn't think so, but for every known theatre in London before the religion-driven Parliament of 1642 shut them down, there were at least ten unknown ones. Gil had ticked off the more important knowns, but he surely knew the others.

She could ask him. If she took careful notes, her book might be the first to present a comprehensive list of—

List of what, Fee? Theatres her dead collaborator named but that she, the live one, probably couldn't prove existed? Playwrights and players who'd slipped so far into a crevasse in time that there'd be no trace of them to substantiate her findings?

It was an investigative impasse, but it was the least of her worries. Top of the Worry List was that she was getting chummy with a man who'd been dead since the mid-1600s.

She pushed away from the frigid, stone-clad wall of the Olympiad. If she was going to stand outside, holding no-exit conversations with herself, she should exercise to keep her body temperature up. She walked briskly toward Arne Street, dodging puddles.

She'd made a sure and sensible life for herself after she came back from Paris. A life without hocus pocus in it. It was increasingly obvious that hocus pocus had found her, anyway. She might as well start reading Tarot cards, like Auntie Jana. Maybe she should just buy a shop and stock it with pentacles and potions like The Broom & Bottle. At the rate she wasn't writing her book, she should have a career backup plan. The closer she got to Arne Street, the wilder and more argumentative the voices in her head got.

Keep going, keep walking. Disappear into the crowds of ordinary people in Covent Garden.

Go to him, go to Gil, now. He wants you, you want him.

She stopped quick-marching with her toes right on

the line where the rough old bricks of the alley joined the rain-slick sidewalk along Arne. The order went from her brain to her feet, as though to a plough horse. *Walk on, walk on.* But her feet didn't move. Passersby gave her sidelong looks that said they were trying to determine if she was lost, panhandling, or crazy. She sighed and reversed directions.

Plod, plod, plod. Back to the Olympiad where she sat on the top of the four damp steps to the stage door. There was a stub of an overhang, but it was Swiss-cheesed with rot. She'd be soaked top and bottom, with drooping wet hair and water-soaked jeans.

The rain abruptly stopped, replaced by a gusting wind. Brown leaves blew into the alley and danced around a bit, then stuck to each other in clumps. The leaves came in from Drury Lane, where there were rooftop gardens and restaurants with potted foliage at the entrance. In Gilbert Sorley's day, there were lots of trees in the district. Even small, cultivated fields with cows and farmers to tend them.

A flock of pigeons, frightened by something, burst into flight overhead, then fluttered and soared against the leaden sky. How stupid, stupid, stupid she was. Stupid as the stupidest pigeon in that flock. She'd thought she could shrug off her souler baggage. *Just Say No to Magic,* she'd joked to herself in Savannah, in North Carolina, and in London. But now that it was happening, she knew she couldn't say *No,* couldn't even say *Maybe.*

Strangely, when she looked critically into herself, she wasn't as cut up over her tumble into an unaired episode of *Supernatural* as she probably ought to be. She'd had that one outburst of shouting when Gilbert Sorley introduced himself. After that, she'd started subsiding into resignation. Like the autumn leaves, she was being driven by an irresistible wind.

The wind being Gil, of course. He wasn't what she'd visualized, and part of her come-lately honesty was admitting that she *had* visualized her possible leathling, when and if he appeared in her life.

She'd had only her leathling father for a model, and all the boys she met in Paris seemed so much *less* than him. Would her leathling be like Papa? Big and handsome and educated and funny and forceful? What if, God forbid, the soul with her name on it belonged to a spoiled, spindly, pimpled aristo, like the son of her parents' friends, the Comte and Comtesse de Bauffremont? Or a good-looking dullard like the young fish vendor, Jacques Doudon, who stuttered *"B-bonjour, m-mademoiselle,"* in a waft of mackerel whenever he saw her in the market?

She'd never been so much of a stupid pigeon that she'd thought her leathling would be a ghostly figure moaning *"You are miiiiine"* from a rampart. But she certainly hadn't expected Gilbert Sorley. He looked like a pirate who'd walked out of a port city in Ancient Carthage and into the Olympiad Theatre.

Holding her hands out in front of her, Fee watched the chilly mist settle on them. The mist felt real. The cold felt real. Gilbert Sorley felt so real she could see herself in his arms. His bed.

Maybe Mom's souler indoctrination had worked on some deep, unconscious level. Maybe Fee was like one of those Soviet sleeper cells, conditioned to live an outwardly normal life until some codeword launched her secret identity into action.

Was Gil her codeword?

A shiver ran through her, and she tucked her damp hands into her armpits. The weather was getting colder day by day, the first howls of winter waiting just beyond the last murmurs of fall. She'd need to wear more layers when she next came to the site. Because she would come back.

Before she did, she needed to *prioritize.* Instead of obsessing about Gilbert Sorley, she really should be thinking about the precarious future of the Olympiad. Marcus Bellwether and Anthea Cookson didn't give a rat's ass about presumed Jacobean Era remains under a building slated for demolition. To change their minds, Fee needed proof. Artifacts. Bricks and mortar. That's what the two officers would want to see before they put the National Trust between the buried Coronet and a pack of suits with redevelopment plans in their cellphones. She had to believe she could make it all happen. Save the theatre, write it up, and make her mark.

She had the shards of the ceramic coin collection box and Gil said there was another. There were layouts of period theatres, showing where the boxes were usually situated. She'd make a rough architectural drawing from that. Then, she'd dig. That's what she was there for, wasn't it?

It was time to go in and face Gil and his penis jokes.

———

Even though she pushed back her hoodie and rolled up her sleeves for work, the urge to dig receded by the time she got back to the cellar. The day was getting long, anyway. Gil was sitting hunched over on the wooden box he'd used to reach the windows. The now-very-clean windows, through which fading daylight seeped, not unkindly smudged him and the shadows together like a finger running across a charcoal sketch.

Gil's elbows were on his thighs. His hands—one with his window-wiping rag still in it— dangled limply between his knees and his eyes were fixed on the floor.

He'd pulled another box next to his. When she came through the cellar door, he rose and wiped his rag across the second box with a flourish, then gestured her toward it as though he were Walter Ralegh and she Elizabeth Tudor. She resisted the impulse to nod regally and just sat on the box. He folded again onto the one next to her. He'd put the boxes very close together; that didn't surprise her.

Subdued, neither of them wanted to speak first, but Gil obviously had ready-to-go words.

"I most humbly crave your pardon, mistress. My jests were childish. I behaved like the veriest knave."

Was he being serious? She glanced sideways, looking for a hint of mockery in his eyes, but they remained downcast. His mouth wasn't curling, his shoulders weren't shaking. If he was laughing, he was tamping it down well.

She measured her words. "You were...inappropriate."

"I was rude as a bat shitting down a chimney." Ignoring the twitch of her mouth, he went on soberly.

"In the presence of a lady, a gentleman never refers to his privie parts."

"However impressive they may be." Her interjection brought his eyes up, just for a second. Long enough to see—yes, there it was, the twinkle, brightening the gunmetal blue. It faded quickly, though, and his next words were solemn.

"Be that as it may, mistress, I should remember my place and never do anything to offend you, the object of my esteem. If I may make bold to tell you, you are the cat's pajamas."

She tried to suppress it, but laughter bubbled up like seltzer and finally exploded through her mouth and nose.

Gil's face fell. "What? Is that not said anymore?"

"Not often, no," she forced through a chortle, "but I take your meaning." She counted to five and then gave him what he wanted. "Apology accepted."

"Truly, shining one, I cannot say what overcame me."

"Was it your idea of flirting?"

"Flir—nay, nay! It was just such japery to make you color. By gad, I couldn't resist saying it again and again." His smile brightened his face even in the uncertain light, making him look young.

They ran out of words for a minute or so, and then Gil piped up. "Your other friend intrigues me."

Her other friend? Oh, right, the not-the-dead-mouse-one from the LUCIES' visit, when they'd all swarmed into the Olympiad, Ben, Abeni, and her in the lead. She was pretty sure Gil wasn't interested in Ben.

"Abeni," she said, rocking back on the box and stretching her legs out. "Her name is Abeni Addo."

"Midnight and pearls, that one. Most comely."

"I'll tell her you said so. Don't count on anything, though. Abeni doesn't care for men."

"She and I should get along famously, then. Men have done me no favors."

She caught herself before she said something sarcastic. Gil thought Abeni was attractive. No surprise, many men did, for all the good it did them. Did the one at her side think Abeni was more attractive than her? "Oh, for fuck's sake," she grumbled.

"You have surpassing filthy speech for a woman, Aoife. I've known drovers with more cleanly tongues."

"You're the man who said 'cock' five times in thirty seconds."

"You were counting, I knew it!"

He grinned, and she returned it. His teeth were good for any century, extraordinary for the 1600s. But then, he hadn't been old when he...

She wouldn't think about that. Better to let the moment between them stretch, purring and sly as a cat. The moment had a cat's flexible morals, too. Fee found herself on the other side of it before she realized what had just happened.

She could almost hear the Fates guffawing. Sitting on a ratty old box in the damp cellar of a ratty old theatre, her body came to a decision without consulting her brain. The decision had nothing to do with theatres, archeology, or the soul. It simply told her that whatever else he might be, Gilbert Sorley was a man. *He puts his pants on one leg at a time.*

Not pants. Breeches, fastened below the knee. She

sneaked a sideways glance at the one nearest, a hard curve of sexual persuasion above twine ties. As a rule, the knee wasn't a passion-inspiring joint. Shoulders could be seductive. Hips. The back of the neck, the hinge of the jaw.

But Gilbert Sorley's knee, no more than two inches away, was making a strong case for sex. His. And hers, warming between her legs in a way that made her squirm on the box, only making things worse.

The persuasive knee was joined in its argument by a persuasive thigh; she sensed the iron and heat of it through the worn-thin wool of his breeches. His scent filled her nostrils and went straight to her brain like a shot of scotch. *Too soon, too much*, said her brain drunkenly, but the restless place between her legs thought it was just in time and not quite enough.

Gil was apparently losing his own argument about restraint, if he'd ever mounted any. He'd moved her box next to his, hadn't he? And then, he'd sat there, smiling the smile she didn't even have to see to be moved by. The best and worst of Gilbert Sorley's smile was that it just happened, like sunrise, a dawning day she saw even with her head turned. Damn it all, the man could smile juice out of oranges.

There was something about his mouth, the sweep of his lower lip, the faint depression that appeared on one side, looking deeper for the dark stubble in its recess. If she kissed him, she could dip her tongue into that little hollow and taste him, salt and bristle and heat.

She jerked her eyes away as her brain fired a bolt of panic. The panic raced under her skin, alongside lust, and overtook it. She needed to get her butt off the box and out of the cellar. All her muscles tensed for flight. Gathering her feet under her, she started to push upward—

"Stay."

It wasn't his command that froze her in place, nor the urgency in the single, deeply uttered word.

It was his hand on her arm.

Thirteen

Gil Sorley's hand was as warm and strong as the hand of any living man. Sepia skin against her white. A long-fingered hand, rough but finely formed, broad across the knuckles and with a muscular wrist and forearm above it. If Fee reached over and wrapped her own hand around Gil's wrist, she might not be able to encircle it. It would feel hard under her fingers, like gripping a wooden cricket bat.

For seconds that seemed to stretch infinitely, they held absolutely still, both of them staring at his hand on her bare forearm. Touching skin to skin, while sensation washed over Fee until the sheer weight of it forced her to slump back onto the box.

Gil's hand slid away, but the place where it had rested sang with memory. Fee had no idea how or if Gil was affected, but for her, his touch changed everything. A fragment of history skipped into the scene. Tomaso Garzoni in 1585, describing Venetian courtesans as "more menacing than a lightning bolt."

Fee half expected to see scorch marks where Gil's lightning had touched her.

"Your *name*, mistress." Gil said it as though he'd said it before. He probably had, while she was in shock from the virtual live wire he'd dropped on her forearm. Her head swiveled toward him, but she was unable to answer his question, if that's what it was.

"Aoife," he clarified. "'Tis your name, is it not?"

Today, class, we learn English greetings. Hello. What is your name? Is your name Aoife? She nodded blankly.

"But your comely friend addressed you as...Fee? Tell me, what manner of name is that? Or is it a title, as in, Your Feeship?"

She gawped, open-mouthed, and stammered, "It's a f-familiar name." Swallowing, she gained control and went on in a rush. "When I was a small child, I couldn't say my Irish name properly, *ee-fuh*. I turned it around, somehow, and called myself *fee-uh*, and finally it became Fee." She paused for breath. "After a while, everyone called me that."

Except Papa. Sometimes, especially when he was piqued, he used all her names. "*Aoife Gabrielle Gowdie Ó Loinsigh, behave yourself!*" Her eyes unexpectedly filled, and she coughed into her hand. "You can use it if you like. Call me Fee, I mean."

"Ah, but what I like is the Irish name. It's exotic and rare, a shining name. Will you favor me by allowing me to address you by it?"

Having used all her English words in the class on greetings, Fee nodded mutely again. Gilbert Sorley was a master of fine compliments, humble apologies, and artful bows. Her ghost knew his way around women. Maybe she could enjoy his company without being swept away. *Those pigeons in the alley?* scoffed her brain. *They compare favorably to you for intelligence.*

She steered the talk to theatre history, a safe topic. "A favor for a favor. What's your favorite passage from a play? A play from your own time, not one of the many turnips you've had to endure from later eras."

"Alas, the turnip crop was ever healthy in my own time, but since you ask for one of the better ones..." He leaned back, resting his head against the wall, and spoke simply but with feeling.

'Unweave my age, O Time, to my first thread;
Let me lose fifty years in ignorance spent,
That being made an infant once again
I may begin to know what, or where, am I
To be thus lost in wonder.'"

"I know that!" She sat up excitedly. "It's from *The Late Lancashire Witches*, about the Pendle Witch Trials."

"True, but the play was penned long after that sad affair."

"Thomas Heywood wrote it. That speech—it's from a character named Mr. Gentle—no, Mr. Generous. It was published in 1630-something."

"1634. And was, more's the pity, a great success, despite it being no more than a sop to a feckless monarch. An able poet, was Thom, but a lickspittle to Charles the First."

"Lickspittle or not, he wrote over a hundred plays."

Gil shook his head. "Published over a hundred plays. He wrote half of them and I wrote the other half."

Well, that was a shocker. She trod carefully with her next question. "Did you do a lot of that? Writing plays that were published under other playwrights' names?"

"I wrote no other kind. It was my trade."

His trade. She goggled at him for a bit, and then a new, brilliantly bright window on her thesis opened. Maybe the unknown poets and playwrights she was looking for were so hard to find because they were hiding behind known poets and playwrights. The man sitting next to her was one of the hidden ones. He was a—

No way. All the tea in England couldn't make her say he was a ghostwriter.

His smile, the one that charmed and unhinged her by turns, glimmered in the gloom. "In the version of the play *I* wanted Heywood to publish, Generous bore false witness to his own wife. She was convicted of witchcraft and hanged. The husband was afterward wracked by remorse. These are some verses I supplied, but Heywood declined to use."

He recited them in the same deep and resonant English timbre she'd first heard from the dark wings of the stage.

"Gone, thy hand, its tender reach,
Nor do I hear thy gentle speech;
Nearer, the moon, than thy pale breast,

Where ne'er again my brow shall rest.

For brutal lies, for savage death,
Have stolen fragile Beauty's breath,
And blacken'd sight where once was thy
Dear countenance, that sooth'ed mine.

Come, ye angels, or if demons, come,
And bear me to thy selfsame tomb,
Where arms now lifeless, body wronged,
Might yet enfold and bear me home."

Silence followed, Fee's heart a too-loud drumbeat in it. She was speechless for so long Gil finally asked her, "Did my humble verses disquiet you, mistress?"

"No! I—I—" She coughed to clear the emotion from her voice. "They're very fine, Gil," she finally got out. "Better than Heywood's verses by a mile. Is that why he didn't like them?"

"He did like them, most heartily. But the King did not, being at the time bent like a sapling by the strong wind of witch-hunting. He later bent in the other direction and ordered the witches exonerated."

"True, but they were all dead and gone."

His silver-blue eyes glinted. "Perhaps. Perhaps not."

There was an idea. Had some or all of the Pendle witches, betrayed and executed, ended up like Gil? Floating around in a half-life, waiting for someone to rescue them?

Not just anyone. A souler, like her. "My parents," she began tentatively, "didn't feel the same about dead and gone. My mother thought it was tragic. *Mais Papa, il a eu la conviction*...sorry." Other than curse words, it had been a long time since she lapsed into French when she was confused or distraught. *I'm a lot of both, right now.*

Carefully, she restated her sentence. "My father was convinced it was better to be dead and gone, rather than just dead."

"I don't think of myself as dead."

"That's...healthy." She fidgeted with a loose thread at the cuff of her hoodie sleeve, rolled up over her elbow. "My father said that until he met my mother, dead and gone would have been better than what he was."

"A man like me."

Yes, to that, though she couldn't make herself say it aloud. Her right hand moved of its own accord to her left forearm. She wasn't sure what it intended to do. Rub the spot where Gil had branded her flesh? Or cover it protectively, keeping it—keeping her—safe? She forced her hand back to her side, clutching the edge of the box.

A tiny chirrup alerted her to Shakespeare's arrival. The mouse came out of nowhere—literally, she supposed—and crawled up Gil's leg to his lap. Once there, it paused, alert, nose quivering, and looked over at Fee. Then, it sprang from Gil's lap to hers. Circling around itself several times, it curled into a ball with an audible sigh.

Fee let her hands play over and around the mouse without touching. She was used to it, now, the slight buzz, the not-quite brush of the white fur. "My baby," she murmured.

Gil leaned in, his mouth at her ear. The graze of his

lips sent electric shocks through her whole body, and she thought she might faint from his scent.

Softly, so softly, he murmured, "He really does love you best, you know."

And you, Gilbert Sorley, she thought, *who do you love?*

FOURTEEN

She went home to a crowd. Three people didn't constitute a crowd in most places, but in the compact lounge of the Bloomsbury flat three people overflowed the one small sofa and single armchair, their collective knees so close to the mid-century modern coffee table they almost touched it.

Sarah and Abeni were on the sofa looking, as usual, like a Diesel ad. Abeni, living up to Gil's "midnight and pearls" description, was showing off her grin and her cross-trained body in knee high boots and a black matte velvet romper unzipped from neck to breastbone. She'd coaxed out the twists of her 4C hair to make a glossy, textured cloud around her face and shoulders. Her partner, Sarah Georgina Soames, made the Top Five Botticelli Models List again—skin like porcelain, ginger hair artfully mussed, nose long and aristocratic under violet eyes, perfectly upright posture. Her ballerina legs, now beautifully crossed, went on and on past the hem of her autumnal print mini-dress. She always seemed to be listening for *"5-6-7-8!"* so she could leap into a grand *jeté.*

Then, there was the man. Some other time, the presence of a strange man in her parlor might have made Fee painfully aware of the dirt streaks on her hoodie. The smutty patches on the knees of her jeans. Her hair, which undoubtedly looked like a stick blender had gotten into it.

Now, she couldn't be bothered. She just stared at the smiling blond in the smart trousers plus white tee and bomber, and waited for someone to tell her who he was.

"Hey up, Fee." Abeni waved at the man, who smiled more broadly. "Meet Roger Bowkes."

Sarah chimed in. "Rog is a colleague. He's in Accounts." Which put him in his place relative to Sarah, who did something vague and prestigious in the auction rooms of Sotheby's.

Abeni again. "Get a wiggle on, Fee. We're going out for a meal."

They were, were they? She was too tired and hungry to argue, just stamped off to shower and change, giving everyone, as she went, a good look at her damp and dusty bottom.

Once the bathroom door was shut and the shower was pummeling her with hot water, she gave in to revelation again. Gil's hand on her arm in the cellar could have been a careless gesture on his part. Or an opportunistic touch, what a woman in his time might have called "making too free."

Fee knew it for what it was: he was claiming her. Had she really thought that her leathling—when he arrived, and if that's what Gilbert Sorley was—would be a passive dance partner? That he'd stand around politely waiting for her to favor him with the salvation waltz?

His hand on her forearm had been the farthest thing imaginable from him asking her to pencil him in on her dance card. It was him plucking the card from her hand, tearing it into pieces, and tossing it away as he whirled her into a hot tango.

A revelation, to be sure, but not the most powerful, life-changing one. That one had to do with what, all these years, she'd thought a leathling *was*. Sure, she'd memorized the catechism, could almost recite it in her mother's voice, or maybe Auntie Jana's. A soul trapped between conditions, arrested on its journey through planes of existence. Neither dead nor alive, awaiting redemption *only if the coin be whole, then will we be merry-o, soul soul soul...*

Why had no one ever mentioned the *body*?

Her weight was braced on her left hand against the shower tiles. With a start, she realized she'd soaped and rinsed her whole body except her left forearm, those few inches where Gil had touched her. Illogically angry, she ran her loofah over the spot so hard it reddened. Then, she gave the shower handle a vicious wrench to turn it off.

Out of the shower, she grabbed a towel and dried herself brusquely. She'd brought fresh jeans and a pullover into the bathroom and wriggled into them.

She'd clearly been deceiving herself for years. Thinking of leathlings as ghosts had been so much easier.

Ghosts stayed ghosts, unless, she guessed, they were exorcised or banished in some way.

Ghosts also didn't have bodies. They were mist, fog, gossamer visions in graveyards. They might even be diaphanous balls, like Shakespeare.

Loss skewered her heart. *Oh, Shakespeare, my poor little ghost mouse.* With a ragged sigh, Fee reminded herself that she'd held him—sort of—in her lap an hour ago. His ghost was comforting, but not Shakespeare, not really, and nothing at all like Gilbert Sorley.

Who had muscular thighs in worn breeches. Who smelled of ginger, sweat, and ale. Who curled strong, warm, possessive fingers around her forearm, making her want to know what those fingers felt curling around her breast, her ass.

Oh, goddamn it to hell. If the revelation that leathlings had actual bodies was making her uncomfortable, she couldn't pin it on her parents and Auntie Jana, even if they hadn't highlighted it in the syllabus. They probably thought she was smart enough to have figured it out by herself. She certainly should have. If her father hadn't had a body before Mom rescued his leathling soul, he and she wouldn't have been able to...

Fee dragged a brush brutally through her tangled hair. She'd never been able to and couldn't now wrap her head around her parents doing the very *bodily* things they'd done to conceive her. Not on an empty stomach, anyway.

The four of them walked to a gastropub in Neal's Yard, the New Young, whose name was a pun on "Foo Yung." Sarah was vegan and could get something to eat there, Abeni liked Asian food generally, Roger knew the owners, and Fee didn't care. Even with a reservation, they were told *it'll be a forty-minute wait for a table, so sorry, have a round of drinks on the house.*

They went to the bar. Sarah and Abeni almost immediately sloped off, leaving Roger, Fee, and two glasses of Glenmorangie alone at a two-top. Fee made noncommittal noises to Rog's date chat until he stopped talking. In the blessed lull, she scanned her cellphone screen. After a few minutes, she found a website for a London company called *Gauntlet and Gown, Garb for Reenactors: Tailors to His Majesty King Charles I.* Oh, ha ha, very funny. She scrolled through a few pages of the site.

Finally, she raised her eyes and stared at her date. The length of her stare would have been antisocial even in countries where staring was normal. Roger averted his eyes.

"How big are you?" she asked in a voice roughened by her day in a damp, cold cellar, chatting with a ghost about witches, drama, and the cat's pajamas.

Roger startled but recovered quickly and summoned a smug grin. "Well, I haven't had any complaints."

"No. What *shirt* size are you?"

The grin slid off his face. "Uh, large, I suppose."

Fee conjured Gil's tall, lean body and the span of his shoulders in her mind. XL, maybe. She checked the size chart on the webpage. "Yeah, that's about right."

"Are you buying me something?"

"No." A waiter was heading their way, menus clutched in his fist. Fee put away her cell. "Let's order. I'm starving."

Fifteen

Abeni looked up from the kitchen table. From the way her eyes snapped, she was a lot more awake than Fee. No *hey up, pet, how'd ye sleep?* Just, "What the fuck, Fee? You were an ice maiden last night with Roger, but he still sent you a nice thank you text when he got home."

"How do you know that?"

"Sarah. Rog told her. He said you ghosted him."

Factually speaking, Rog couldn't be more right. "I don't want to see him again, that's all."

"Because you're in a meaningful relationship with your laptop."

"I didn't ask you to pimp out Sarah's workmate, Abeni."

The kitchen filled with sixty cool seconds of nothing. They'd both slept late. It was Saturday and the workday din of London traffic had stilled. In the quiet, Fee heard the crunch of Abeni's teeth on her Weetabix and the dull hiss of the teakettle heating up. She switched it off since she'd awakened jittery enough.

She slid into the other chair at the kitchen table. "I'm sorry, Abeni. I'm stressed about my grant, I guess. No reason to take it out on you."

"Or poor old Rog." At that, they both looked up and smiled. "He's a bit of a *dimlo*," Abeni admitted.

"He's all right. I'm just not in a socializing place in my life, that's all." Picking up the Weetabix box, she shook it, then tipped one onto her plate, even though she hated shredded wheat. "And I really do need to focus on my book."

She jabbed her spoon into the Weetabix to break it up. When it didn't look quite so much like a hairy Milk-Bone, she ladled blueberry yogurt on top. Maybe if she ate more fiber, her brain would clear.

"Not for me to say, pet," Abeni began, "but ever since you got the key to that chaffy old theatre, you haven't been yourself."

If you knew I was a souler, Abeni, you'd say I was being exactly myself. "It's not that. I just need to get my nose out of my research, like you said. We'll go out again Friday night, okay? That salsa club you and Sarah like. But no setting me up with anybody."

"If you don't come with a partner, you'll end up dancing with every wannabe *salsero* in the place, you know that."

"They should be so lucky."

"Well, then, *señorita*," Abeni picked up her empty bowl and headed to the sink with it, "eat your cereal. You'll need your strength."

Sixteen

The pustule had returned with Aoife. Gil spotted them from his First Room, the one with the window overlooking the alley. The day had been uncommonly long, spent waiting for his radiant woman, and he'd nearly surrendered any hope of her arriving. Catching sight of her at last, his heart had leapt like a hare, then plummeted when he saw she wasn't alone. She and the pustule entered the Olympiad by the stage door, and he knew they were bound for the cellar. With choler rising, he'd followed them.

Aoife was vexed to see him. Even knowing, as she must, that the pustule could not so much as sense the quiver in the air of a ghost, she scowled and grimaced and made waving away gestures whenever the pustule's back was turned. Finally, since he was discommoding her, Gil took himself off, but not before he mouthed a few silent but juicy opinions of the living man's bollocks.

An hour later, with barely dampened fury, he watched Aoife usher the man out of the theatre and into the alley. In the fading light of the day, the lane was a narrow strip of darkness with brighter mouths at each end, emptying into Drury Lane and the street now called Arne, a muddy path in his day. On her way out the stage door, Aoife touched the switch that ignited the flickering bulb above it. In the sudden pool of light, Gil saw how pale and pinched her face was. The pustule was giving her grief again.

God's bodkins, he didn't know which rattled him more, the fact that he was so angry or the speed with which he'd arrived at the junction of Venus and Mars. In barely a fortnight, he'd gone from wanting the woman—ferociously, carnally—to caring for her enough to want to murder some inoffensive toady who gave her a bad day.

Shakespeare the Mouse, being more prudent, had not accompanied him to the cellar. Now, it skittered across the windowsill and up Gil's arm. Since his arm was bare, his shirt having gone to the washing tub with Aoife and come back a memory, the mouse's claws were like a hearth broom of tiny twigs. When it reached his shoulder, the mouse sat quietly enough, looking alternately out the window and at Gil. It squeaked.

"Don't distract me," Gil grumbled. "I am having a philosophical discussion with my spleen."

A buzzing noise intruded on his thoughts. A blue-bottle fly batted against the windowpane, seeing the world outside but unable to reach it. Gil knew the way it felt. He banged at the sash with the heels of his hands until it opened, and the fly swooped through the gap. The mouse twitched its nose at the rush of air and Gil moved hastily to lower the sash, until he remembered a drop to the stones sixty feet below would do nothing to the creature. Or to him. In a fit of melancholia some years before, he'd tried it.

In any case, the mouse lost interest. "That's right, keep ye home," he told it. "You never know when a dead mouse of the female sort might turn up."

The diversions of the fly and the mouse were not enough to put Gil off his ruminating. Jealousy. He'd thought it had died with him. He was wrong. Perhaps, what burned in his gut wasn't jealousy at all, but pique. Aoife would never be troubled by his former lovers; they were in their graves ten lifetimes past. But any man for whom she'd had a fancy would still be walking in the world, on two sound feet.

No, by the Furies, what he felt wasn't pique, either. Watching the man from the Trust—a misnomer if ever there was one, because the imbecile looked as though he couldn't be trusted to piss outside his breeches—lecture Aoife in the alley, smooth hands waving and lips flapping, while she nodded glumly and her face fell further...

Protectiveness awoke and rolled through Gil in a hot, red tide. How dare the ewe-swiving popinjay put that look of dismay on his woman?

His woman. 'Swounds, he liked the sound of that. He turned the words over a few times in his mind. They floated bravely on the red tide, possession and protection being two oars of the same boat.

He'd felt things for women before, in his living years. Lust, mainly. Boredom. Betrayal. For his mother, he'd felt yearning. That had clung to him long after she had left him, a child, on the kitchen steps of the man who sired him. He'd had comradely affection for poor Polly Makepence, when she wasn't driving him up a wall with her airs and notions.

What he felt for Aoife Gowdie, she of the Gaelic names and jade eyes, the dove-soft skin where he'd laid his hand upon it—that was as strange and new as if he'd touched some traveler and taken away an exotic sickness. Feverish under his skin, restless and benumbed all at once, he could think of no remedy save another touch, and another.

Polly would have said he dared too much, thinking of her that way. She might have argued that he was driven into a fever of desire only by the need of a woman, any woman, and Aoife Gowdie just happened along at the same time his solitude sidled toward the halfway point of the Roman Empire's duration.

Polly would not be entirely wrong. She would also say he should divert his eyes from the top of the pustule's head until he stopped seeing himself caving it in with a piece of cordwood. He turned away from the window.

He'd answer Polly's argument about what he felt for Aoife in the simplest, truest manner. Lust was one thing. Tenderness was another. Tenderness had been naught but an encumbrance in his living years, and so he had locked it away like an old suit of clothes. Now, it was back, draped awkwardly and with no small amount of pain upon his limbs. He couldn't imagine it would fit him again. Whatever love he'd once felt in life, it could only, in death, bring unimaginable pain to him, and to others.

She was not for him. *Why, then, does she see you?* a persistent voice asked. *Why does she desire you?*

Because she did desire him. He wasn't such a fool he had not sensed it. But if not a fool, was he such a villain that he would ignore what consequence attended the reach of her desire into his world?

He left the window, too restless to stand there counting minutes until the woman cast off her pustular companion and came to him. Without the slightest plan or intent, he paced his paltry pair of rooms, picking this up, putting that down, his thoughts still flapping like sails in the wind. He was always like that out of her company, now, every part of him at war with every other part. One minute, he wanted to glide about in some well-mannered English reel. The next, he wanted to stamp the floor, snapping his fingers in one of the dances of his mother's people.

His mother's people and his. Never his father's. Perhaps, that was why Polly Makepence had been his particular friend. Apart from being despised for their other sins—he a forger, she a whore, both of them what the Privy Council called "vagrant and lewd persons," to whit, actors—they had the bond of bastardy. Polly, born Pauline Stubb, had a dairymaid for a mother, a minor viscount for her sire. At least the viscount had saved Polly from the foundling home or the streets, in the same way that Gil's father, a Kentish baron, had given a roof and some grudging tutelage to his ill-got spawn. Charity in neither case was for the mother's sake, and barely for the child's.

Even so, Polly had it a bit better than Gil. She was

aware of the trifling eminence her father's title gave his baseborn daughter and, for the most part, did not lord it over Gil. When she did, well, it was no fault of hers that the world esteemed the lowest of her kind to be more worthy than the highest of his.

But Aoife, diadem of brilliants that she was...Not a single fleck of disdain showed when she looked upon him. In that alone, she was unlike any woman he'd known. Some had tumbled him, to be sure, for coin or favor. Some had even been fond of him, briefly, the way one was fond of an exotic pet. A falcon, perhaps, or a civet.

With Aoife, it was profoundly different. Everything between them seemed so fitting and right, as though their stars aligned in sweet concordance. Could such an attraction possibly be an illusion? A pantomime on a spangled stage, glittering in the candles' glow but, in morning's light, a shabby spill of puppets on a board? Surely the universe could not be so mortally cruel.

Ah, but it can, fool. He'd dealt in pretty lies; they had been his life. It would be only fitting if they were his death—again. For the flash of pain that had brought the death of his body would be as nothing to the long death of loss, should she leave.

Despair, his old companion, joined anger in his belly and sickened him. He slid down the wall to the floor, where he sat like the heap of uselessness he was. Surely, notwithstanding the augury of his instincts, he deluded himself if he thought he and Aoife had a future.

Perhaps, he was wrong about her, about everything. He was no John Dee to read stars and symbols. A tree to him was just a tree, a stone no more than a thing to stumble over. What she felt when she looked upon him, what he'd felt when he touched her delicate skin...

How could he, with any certainty, say those were love ordained? And who was he to say whether it brought Heaven or Hell to her, to him, to them both?

But you do know. Rot his worthless soul, he did. Three hundred years of his damnable fate had taught him things. Wisdom floated in the very air he did not need but took into his dead lungs, anyway. Awareness came with the rain he let pour upon his head when he stood on the roof, under the sky, and shouted his loneliness to the moon.

He could give her so little. One thing only, perhaps, and that he would do. She had a dream, small but stubborn, that pricked at her heart every time she walked upon a stage. Why she yearned for the life of a player when it was so fraught with penury and mischance, he could scarcely imagine. But if anyone could shape an actor from Aoife Gowdie, it was he. To please her, he would do it.

After that, and with no regard for how it pained him, he would let her go. He had been unwise throughout his life, a simpleton in many things, an outright rogue in a few. In this, though, with her, he must be wise as the wisest of men. He must let her go, before they were torn by the severance into pieces so small they blew away on the wind like cinders.

The mouse chirped again in his ear, so he levered himself up the wall to stand, peering through the window into the alley. The pustule was taking his leave, *gratias Deo.* Aoife stayed in place for a moment, watching the man pick his way, careful of his fine shoes, toward Arne Street. As the man departed, Aoife turned and reentered the theatre, pulling the stage door hard behind her.

Gil stood a minute longer at the window, held fast by memory. Night was coming on, the smells and sounds of Covent Garden receding. In his time, the market at all hours had issued a homey reek of withered cabbages and the farm dirt clinging to them, of wet forest from the vast stand of trees beyond the stalls, and whiffs of the Thames when the wind was right. From long before dawn to past noon, the din of costermongers and squeaking carts entertained the ear. Smoke rose from fires built on cobbles, where there were any, on bare earth where there were none, while flying embers sparkled in the air.

These days, from dawn to dusk, the Garden was all hard stone and the clamor and stink of machines. Like the past, everything was transmuted into a present he did not recognize.

Hark, she comes. Her footsteps climbing the stairs to the attic were sweet as the notes of a song, as reassuring as the wave of needle pricks under his skin that announced her nearness. The mouse flew from Gil's shoulder to the floor and streaked across it, a blur of white, to greet her.

She arrived and stood in the doorway. Golden light from the remains of the day fell upon her, making a gilded corona around her hair and a Verocchio angel of her face. She smiled. In all the days of all the years of the world, there had never been a smile like that. It was all welcome, all warmth. All, he dared to hope, for him.

His resolution to part from her burst upward and flew away like a skylark. Wheeling and soaring in an aerial ballet to the Thames, it plummeted into the water and disappeared.

"You were inappropriate again," she chided, but gently.

"No one saw it."

"*I* saw it."

"If you'd let me kill the pustule when I first wanted to, you'd not have seen it."

She waggled her fingers and Shakespeare Not the Bard ran up her body and down her arm, jabbering mouse words. Cupping the creature against one breast, she shrugged her bag off her other shoulder, dropping it on the table with a sigh. "I had a few murderous impulses toward Marcus Bellwether myself today." She coddled the mouse in both hands, spilling him lightly from one to the other. "I know he's just doing his job, but he barely looked at the second coin box. Mostly, he droned on about trade-offs for development in Covent Garden. The price of progress. The generosity of the investors toward the Trust."

Investors, denoting many. Gil held his tongue. If she didn't like the notion of him killing one pestilent modern, she probably wouldn't care for his killing a job lot of them.

She looked up from the mouse, her eyes crinkling with jest. "Anyway, even though you're rude, I brought you something." She lifted her chin toward the bag on the table. Gil took it up, wrestling with the closure until he got it open. The folded length of linen, when he extracted and shook it out, was a shirt.

He held it up, amazed. The cloth was as white and tightly woven, and the fashioning as fine, as anything a King's courtier might put on his back.

"Try it on," Aoife said. "I hope it fits."

He hastened to obey. The slide of the cloth against his skin was excelled by nothing in the Known World except, Gil suspected, the slide of her hands along his flanks, should the lucky moment arrive when he felt it.

Shirt on, he settled his shoulders and tugged lightly at the tails. His voice came out gruff and halting with emotion. "I-I am moved beyond measure." He stretched out his arms, turning them this way and that in the sleeves. The linen was the flesh of lilies, new snow, summer clouds, and all things fine and flawless. "I've not received a gift of clothing since I was a child." He examined one cuff, then the other, as he closed the ivory buttons. "The stitchery is surpassing neat. Is it yours?"

Her laugh echoed in the building, gone quiet after she and the pustule had ceased scuffling and thumping in the cellar.

"If you saw my stitchery," she told him, "you'd say it was surpassing only for how crude it is. I think the last thing I sewed was a doll dress when I was twelve. The shirt's from Gauntlet and Gown, Tailors to His Majesty."

"They hold a Royal Warrant?"

"Not really, it's just something they say. Or, I don't know, they might actually have one. For all I know, the King loves living history, and does it every weekend. English Civil War reenactment."

"Why in God's name would anyone wish to reenact—"

"He doesn't, they don't! I mean, some people do, but —never mind. I ruined your only shirt, so I had to replace it. You can't just walk around naked."

The word triggered a vivid image, and for a few seconds it floated between them. Floated in his brain, anyway. Their bodies, the light and the dark, with not a snip or stitch between them. Entwined, their limbs entangled. His gaze and Aoife's clasped, and Gil knew she saw it, too. For the space of a half-dozen breaths, their eyes conversed quite blatantly about the unspeakable.

She tore away first. Crossing to his desk, she carefully placed the mouse upon it and began fidgeting with the things thereon. A pile of his verses lay there, the first scenes of a new play, and she shuffled through the pages.

"What's this?" She pulled a sheet from the middle and held it aloft.

"'Tis my poor attempt to render the Coronet in its day, since you show interest in the old dame."

Aoife scrutinized the sketch. "It's very good, Gil." She pointed to the roof, as sketched. "Is that a flag on top?"

"It is. The theatre could not boast of any great person's patronage, but it was politic to fly the standard of the Lord Mayor."

She returned the sheet to the stack. "Would you like more ink? And paper? I can bring you some." Picking up his quill, she ran her fingertips over the plume, cut short and angled, the way he liked it. "Is this a pigeon feather?"

"To the brim with questions, is my lady today. That

is a crow feather. Pigeon quills are too soft to be of much use. Goose would be best, but I've yet to see one waddle in and die here."

"I can bring you a dip pen, if you like, a metal one."

"You spoil me with gifts, beauty. First, a garment fit for royals, and now the tools of my poor occupation. I've never been a kept man, but I may gain a taste for it."

He tucked his very new shirt into his very old breeches. "Come, now. Let us visit the roof."

SEVENTEEN

They passed through Gil's Second Room, where Fee steadfastly refused to look at the bed, and climbed stairs no wider than a ladder and just as steep. At the top, they went through a dormer window to the roof. With Gil's rough hand anchoring hers, Fee stepped out onto a fiery sea.

The fire came from the setting sun. She supposed if one had a penthouse apartment or an executive office in a high-rise, they actually got to see the London sunset every day. For everyone else, the city went from bright to dark by colorless degrees, the sun blocked by tall buildings long before it reached its azimuth.

Atop the Olympiad, solar fire poured onto the roof like lava, broad orange and gold ribbons striping the dull zinc shingles. She shielded her eyes as Gil led her to the protected angle of a chimney, its crowned pot making the stout brick rectangle into a huge chess piece. Five or six such monarchs rose from the roof. She'd noticed them when she came to the Olympiad the first time, with the LUCIES. Then and now, they surprised her.

"I didn't see any fireplaces in the theatre."

"Nay, long gone. Bricked up to lessen the threat the place might burn with actors and patrons within, like blackbirds in a pie." He turned to grin at her. "You know what ruffians actors are, sneaking teakettles onto the hob, toasting bread." He shook out a blanket tightly rolled against the chimney base. "Stopping the chimneys brought a different danger, that everyone might freeze to death in winter. Here—" he spread the blanket, "sit ye down."

Gil had wisely chosen the spot to face east, not west, so they weren't blinded by the sunset. When he lowered himself beside her, they sat in relative comfort, knees drawn up and nearly shoulder to shoulder, as they had on the boxes in the cellar. Had that been only a week before? It seemed they'd known each other for years.

For the longest time they didn't speak, as though they were two people without a common language. Surprisingly, the shared silence wasn't uncomfortable, though it was filled with unanswered, maybe unanswerable, questions. She would always be curious about Gil as a child, a feral adolescent before his voice changed and his beard came in, then Gil as a young man, adrift in the worst environs London offered up in the 1600s. The things he'd done, the things that had been done to him. Had he known anything in those years, *intuited* anything, of the violent death and bizarre after-death that awaited him?

She'd dropped into his life without backstory, too.

The mouthy kid she'd been, the rebellious teenager who'd escaped her tutor—tutors, since she'd driven away several—to drag a maid with her while she wandered Parisian markets and spent her loose change on ribbons and buns. The eyes-wide-shut university student in North Carolina, with her shoulder to the academic wheel, never so much as reading a novel or watching a movie about the paranormal in case it slammed her into the uncomfortable reality of her heritage.

Maybe the blank slates of their pasts accounted for the way their silences fit like joined hands. With nothing to look back on, it was all now for them, all the moment, the hour.

Acutely aware of Gil's body inches away, Fee still appreciated the city view from where they sat. In her three years in London, she'd gawked at all the usual sights. The Palace, the Tower, the Houses of Parliament, Westminster Abbey, the London Eye, Hyde Park. She'd taken the Jack the Ripper Tour, the Catacombs Tour, the Harry Potter tour. Day trips to Stonehenge and Windsor Castle.

Compared to all that, the Olympiad's roof offered not much more than surrounding buildings, most of them taller than the theatre, and glimpses of streets between the buildings. Treetops here and there. A narrow gap east, through which she supposed Gil watched sunrises. A distant sparkle that might be the Thames. But the feeling of being above it all, above and apart from the pulsing, clamoring metropolis—it was intoxicating.

She leaned back against the chimney, still warm from

the day's sun, and took a deep, grateful breath. After the hour she'd spent with Marcus 'Bad News' Bellwether, his cologne battling the smell of mold rising from the cellar floor, it was bliss to have fresh air and a view of sky.

And to have Gilbert Sorley by her side.

The happy silence persisted for minutes, but not absolutely. London was never without its voice. When it wasn't scratchy and sharp with human cries and ululating sirens, it was rumbly and visceral with underground railways, buses, and tires on pavement. The distant horns of watercraft sounded eerily from the Thames.

Gradually, though, Fee became aware of another, different voice below the city's. The subtle voice of what she and Gil were creating, a world below the world. A buzz at the bottom of all they said and did, a sound like bees who whispered among themselves of secret things.

Had she ever before had thoughts like those? Of active silence, gossiping bees? She was sure she hadn't. Like Gil, the thoughts came from the shadows. Fantastic creatures and encoded signals came with them.

Or maybe they were the signs and portents Jana had warned her about. What Mom called "magick with a *k*."

The sun finally dropped into the sea, and the daylight with it. Still, the silence lengthened, as did the shadows spawning it. Unable to stop herself, Fee turned her head to watch them slowly capture Gil, painting him in shades of gray and brown and black. Deeper in some places; the underside of his jaw, the seal-brown slashes of his hair, the hollow of his throat. In martial opposition were the bright white of his new shirt, the highlighted angles of his hands resting on his knees, and his emphatic nose and smooth brow.

The rising moon slid away from a screen of clouds, and all Gil's black and rust turned to silver, pewter, and smoke. She pushed up one sleeve of her hoodie, holding her bare forearm to the moonlight. If he was so transfigured by it, what had it done to her?

Gil's soft baritone didn't so much break the quiet as slide into it, words boarding the drifting craft of her thought. "Pale as a moonbeam fine, her form, that sails upon the liquid night. Shaming the orb of Venus, she, and ever lovely in my sight."

He reached for her hand, brought it to his lips, and kissed her knuckles, then rested their joined hands on his knee. Touch, touch, he was touching her again. The warmth of his mouth and the hardness of his body made heat rise everywhere inside her.

She had to try twice before she managed, "That— that's exquisite, Gil. Is it from a play?"

"It is from my heart, radiant one, that in this moment can but spill words, however humble, for you."

He had written her poetry, a first. For her, anyway. For all she knew, he'd spouted verse for a string of women in the 1600s. He might have had a fan following. Women dogging his steps in the lanes of Covent Garden, wrapping their stockings around *billets d'oux* and hurling them into his window. Before she could follow that thought to a disappointing conclusion, Gil moved her hand to his chest and held it there, so she felt the vibration of his voice through her fingers.

"I pray you, mistress, despise me not for being just

the latest in a string of besotted fools to write verses to a woman under the moon. This other, you may know. 'Stars around the brilliant moon now hide away their shining forms, when She fully floods the earth with silver light.'"

"Not as nice as yours, but still pretty. Sappho, isn't it?"

"It is, and predictably fervent from a pagan priestess of Aphrodite. Though, even the very Reverend John Donne spoke warmly of the moon and stars. I imagine he saw a lot of them, up at night as he was, siring his twelve offspring."

She pulled back her hand with a mock-indignant cluck. "You show no respect at all for the greats of English literature."

"Oh, aye, *now* they're great. Do you remember, please, that they were, in another time, simple mortals, walking the earth. *Dimlos*, even. Eating, belching, rutting. Cursing."

"Not John Donne."

"Aye, I'll warrant he swore like a swineherd when he cracked his shin against the bedpost of a midnight. Or reached a peak of pleasure with his poor wife, which he had to have reached at least a round dozen times. 'Nails of the Cross, Anne! Thou hast most fuckingly fucked me!'"

"Gilbert Sorley!" She laughed and swatted him at the same time. "He was the Dean of St. Paul's!"

"Oh, Johnnie!" Gil warbled in an excited falsetto. "Thy vigor compels me to beg for it again! Doff thy cassock and cap this time, that I may view the stallion of the Church of England in unclothed glory!"

"You're awful, stop it!" But she was laughing so hard she could barely breathe.

Gil slid down to his elbows, bucking his hips and shrieking. "Oh, oh! The rapture takes me, Johnnie! Alleluia! Alleluia!"

They both laughed like hyenas, clinging together helplessly, falling against and atop each other.

And then, somehow, they were kissing.

His arms enclosed her and hers went around his neck as though they'd known all along where to go, what to do. Her fingers thrust up through the satiny waves of his hair and cupped his skull, holding him to her. Mouths joined, their bodies fit together like the pages of a book.

His mouth was hot and demanding, bent on taking hers. Sliding his hands down her back to her buttocks, he clutched them as though they were the only things anchoring him to earth. He dragged her up against his groin, once, twice. Pleasure shot through Fee's veins like a drug and she couldn't stop her whimper of need.

She felt more than saw the moon go behind a cloud, submerging the roof under a wave of shadow like the tide washing over a half-sunken ship. No West End evening was ever truly lightless. Illumination spilled and sparked from hundreds of sources, from neon signs to windows lit blue from within by television and computer screens. But with the moon in hiding, the space behind the chimneystack plunged fathoms deep into night. She and Gil swam, twining, like eyeless fish in a dark abyss.

Fee was suddenly one with all dark things. Black pearls, black cats, black diamonds. Black volcanic sand under her feet on the beach in Iceland, where she'd spent a three-day elective layover on her way to London from the States. Black velvet on her body, the dress Great-aunt Sophie had made her to go under her UNC commencement gown. Black magic, transforming all the glaring impossibilities of life.

"Gil." She whispered his name, a plea and a spell, and his whole body trembled in her arms. The ferocity of his hunger and the force he was using to control it—they were the razor edges of risk and ecstasy. In seconds, he might be beyond control. She was as sure she wouldn't be able to stop him as she was that she didn't want to. Her own need was raging, breasts taut, nipples pebbled, buttocks clenching under Gil's hands. They lay on their sides, joined mouth to mouth, but the flooded, aching core of her screamed to pull him atop her.

The night swallowed every sound except the ones they made, the low and breathy sounds of lust. Hers, his, theirs. Rapid and hoarse, laced with moans and sighs.

The heat of him washed over her, bringing taste and smell. The ale she'd scented on his breath, and that other flavor, ginger or pepper. No blood—that had gone with the old shirt—but a tang of randy male. If she'd been inhaling nitrous oxide, it couldn't have made her any dizzier.

"Aoife, Aoife..." He crooned it between kisses, teaching her how sweet her name could be. She'd never really liked it, though she'd never said that to Papa, for whose mother she'd been named. Or to Mom, who'd given the name to her at birth, when she thought she might never see Papa again. Parisians had struggled with it. There was no equivalent in French and it often came out as "*Oui*-fay" or something equally garbled. American English was even worse. In North Carolina, Aoife became "Oy-fee" and Gowdie rhymed with "howdy" instead of the Scottish "*Goh*-dee."

But when Gil spoke her name, it was poetry, passion, a sibilant rush of vowels, a distinct and suggestive *f* between them. "Aoife, Aoife," he growled, and with every syllable Fee fell deeper into the spell he cast with his voice and body.

There wasn't much art in their first kisses, but they weren't clumsy, either. Arrow straight and intent, they were the kisses of two people who were sweeping every-thing out of the way to get to each other. Pulling her mouth from his, she dragged it across his jaw, and the scrape of his beard blazed a trail of heat down her legs.

She ground against him, hungrier than she'd ever been for a man inside her. Gil's body whispered approval. Under the age-thinned cloth of his breeches, she felt the outline of his erection as perfectly as if she had it in her hand. *Cock, cock, cock...*She was pretty sure she could say it aloud, now. More than say it. Grip it. Stroke it. Take it into her body, her mouth. Tugging up the long tail of his shirt, she worked her hand beneath, wriggling it into the waistband of his breeches.

Gil's movements stilled. His handful of words emerged on a ragged exhale. "If your hand strays there, Aoife, there is no turning back." The words cost him; she heard it in the gravel of his voice and felt it in the thudding of his heart against her breasts. He said them none-theless, dashing ice water on her arousal.

Mom had used those very words, *no turning back*, to describe Papa's warning about making love to a leathling, to him. It was sobering enough to envision her parents in a clinch like the one she was in with Gil. Remembering how her parents' defiance had led to her mother almost disappearing from the physical plane, her parents separating before Mom even knew she'd conceived, then staying apart for five years...

That was a whole new level of sobriety.

Breaking off the embrace cost her, too, but some beleaguered voice of sanity agreed with Gil. She rolled onto her back, panting, and tucked her hands behind her head, where they couldn't get her into trouble. More trouble. Worse trouble.

They lay side by side, barely touching but breathing like racehorses. Fee counted backwards from fifty as her mind staggered drunkenly back into her body.

Talk about something else, something else, something else. She harshly cleared her throat. "That word, *dimlo*."

"What?" Gil was still visibly fighting his own battle with arousal, trying to get his own mind back where it belonged.

"*Dimlo*. You said historical figures in their time had been, among other things, *dimlos*. Abeni used the same word the other day."

Gil had pulled the rest of his shirt from his breeches and was tugging down the tails. They did little to conceal the formidable jut of his arousal but, like her, Gil was making a stab at ignoring it. "Not used in reference to me, I hope."

"She doesn't know about you." *And it's probably better if it stays that way.* "She was referring to a man I went out with."

"Went out with. Out of the house, you mean?"

"It's an expression. It means we had a meal together."

"Alone?"

"No. In...a tavern."

"I see." After a pause, he added, "This man. Does he aspire to your affections?"

"If he does, he can put his aspirations where the sun don't shine. I'm not interested."

"Because he is a *dimlo*?"

"I'm still not sure what that means, but I'll say no, that's not why."

"Why, then?"

Should she say, '*Because I'm only interested in you*'? Definitely not. She turned the question aside with another. "Are you jealous?"

"I am possessed of not a single right to jealousy. Nonetheless, I shall ask you this man's name and dwelling place. It will shorten the time between my learning of him and his death."

He was joking. Wasn't he? She rolled toward him, on her side again. "Gil, you must stop offering to kill men who displease me."

"Why? Have you another protector?"

A protector. Could he be a mortal danger and a protector, too? Just her luck that he was the first of either one she'd known. "At the risk of sounding like a line from a turnip, the *dimlo* means nothing to me and I'll never see him again."

"You please me, *chavi*."

"I'm overjoyed. So, what's a *dimlo*, anyway? And a... what's that other thing?"

"The first means an oaf, a lackwit. A boffle-head, a clod-pate, a—"

"Got it. And the second word?"

"*Chavi*." He pronounced it *djav-ee*. "Girl child."

She huffed dismissively. "I'm almost twenty-seven."

He reached across to run a finger down her cheek. "We are like in age. If you give no heed to the few hundred years between."

She'd do that. At no point did she want to be reminded she was cuddling a senior citizen. A sharp squeak made her look up and there he was, Shakespeare, perched atop the chimneystack.

She sat up and stretched her arm along the stack. The mouse ran down it, chittering, and into the neck of her hoodie.

"Ack! Shakespeare! No, stop! That tickles!" Fee squirmed, holding the front of her hoodie away from her chest, while Gil howled with laughter.

"The wee beast is a rake, God's hat! Go on, then, mouse, make yourself snug between those warm hills, and tell me all later when your mistress is gone and I have only my right hand for comfort."

Scowling at him, Fee shook out the hem of her hoodie and Shakespeare dropped into her lap. With what sounded suspiciously like a mouse giggle, he scurried across her thighs to Gil.

"There are times when your presence is welcome, ratling," Gil sat up and cupped Shakespeare in one hand, "and times when it is not. A mouse of discernment knows the distinction." Getting his legs under him and rising, he crossed the roof to the dormer window, still open to the attic, and carefully deposited the mouse inside. "Attend to mouse affairs," he said, closing the window, "and await the return of your betters."

Gil smiled down at her as he returned, folding his long frame and pulling her down to lie alongside him again. Flank to flank, shoulder to shoulder, they felt as right as the sky, as right as any couple who'd lain together since the dawn of time. She reached for his hand and held it up, interlacing their fingers. The contrast in their coloring was striking. "You're not English, are you?" she asked.

"I daresay I'm more English than anyone now in London. Old English, you might say."

"That wasn't what I meant, and you know it. You look—are you Indian? From India, that is, a country—"

"I know of India, shining one. Knew it in the time when James and then Charles propped their royal hindquarters upon England's throne. India is a land from which come rare and wonderful things."

Hot yoga. Tikki masala in a ready-heat bag. Bollywood. None of which Gil would know about. She rubbed her thumb against his. "I only asked because those words, *dimlo* and *chavi,* they sound Indian to me."

She felt his shrug, a barely perceptible twitch in the shoulder that pressed hers. "Perhaps they are. My mother and her people spoke the tongue from which those words come. I remember only fragments."

She brought their clasped hands to her heart. "That's a shame. You might have kept your heritage."

"I might have swung from the gibbet." He extracted his hand from her grasp and rolled atop her, taking his weight in his arms. His broad shoulders blocked the moon's milky light and there were only a few inches between his body and hers. In the sudden shadow, his eyes seemed darker, his skin darker still.

She forced herself not to seize his shoulders and pull him against her. "Swung from the—because you were an actor?"

"Because I am a 'Gyptian."

Eighteen

Fee struggled to sit up and finally did, forcing Gil to lie back. He crossed his hands under his head as she had done before.

I'm a pluperfect idiot. Why hadn't she figured it out earlier? The singular color of his skin and hair, his self-deprecating references. They joined every pejorative from the past, a tumble of words and images and sudden comprehension.

'Gyptians. From "Egyptians," what the Rom called themselves—or were called, the etymology was still unclear—at the start of the 1500s, when they first arrived in England. The label was later diminished to "Gypsies" and the people diminished and despised by English society. *'Gyptians.* Synonymous with thieves, idlers, liars, tricksters, heathens, and child-stealers, they were hunted, cast out, and reviled.

She was late off the mark, but she could show him she wasn't a complete *dimlo.* "Henry the Eighth ordered your people out of England."

Even though she leaned over him, he looked past her into the night as he replied. "Ah, far better to call them my mother's people. How much they were mine depended on whom you asked and whether I felt, on a particular day, that I had any claim upon them or they on me." He took a handful of her hair, twining it around his fingers. "Old Henry exiled the 'Gyptians in 1530, on pain of death. A hundred years on, each setting sun still might have been my last."

He didn't say more, so she lay back again and edged closer, nestling into the curve of his shoulder. Everywhere they touched, flames of sensation leaped up, while everywhere else chilled with fresh understanding. As with everything he said, Gil was schooling her, and she needed a few minutes to catch up with the current lesson. "How long were you with them, the—your mother's people?"

"Not long. Four winters, I think, maybe five. I remember the camps, moving with the harvest. Hops and berries in summer. Apples and pears before the first frost. Then, potatoes."

He lapsed into silence again, so Fee nudged him with her elbow. "Go on. You can't leave me with a little boy and a basket of potatoes."

Gil reached his other arm over and raked his fingers gently up her thigh. The sensuous scrape of his nails on the taut cloth of her jeans said the story didn't matter and taking off her clothes did, but she forced herself to listen.

"At whatever age I was, I became part of the household of Samuel Roderic Sorley, a baron of no particular note but some particular wealth. When my mother, his occasional whore, left me upon his doorstep, my sire's reluctant sense of duty compelled him to take me under his roof. It did not compel him to preserve any aspect of my former life. If I had a name among the 'Gyptians, it was torn from me," he fingered a healed-over scar bisecting his left earlobe, "along with the gold ring in my ear. The baron did not bother to open the hoop before he gave it a good tug."

Fee flinched. She'd try to bin that image, but somehow, she knew it would regularly return to sicken her.

"I was with Sorley until I reached what I believed to be my fourteenth year. Then, I was not."

"Do you mean you ran away? Or that he kicked you out?"

"Let us say the lure of adventure was strongly enhanced by my few possessions being bundled and placed outside the gate of the kailyard. I was given six shillings and an instructive boot to the backside to ensure I knew where the road to London lay."

A minute passed while Fee considered the enormity of that ejection. He was a boy of fourteen with no trade and no family or friends, alone with only six shillings to ward off utter destitution. A shield the thickness of a leaf.

"Obviously, you made it to London. How on earth did you live once you were here?"

"I stole."

"You mean…"

His smile contained equal parts mirth and chagrin. "Is there more than one meaning? Thievery, robbery, nimming, lifting, footpadding, cutpursing."

"You could have been—I don't know, exactly. What was the penalty if you'd been caught? Would you have been hanged?"

"Nay, gillyflower. Branded, certainly, with a *T*," he traced the letter on her cheek with his forefinger, sending a cold tremor through her, "just there." He bent to kiss the spot, banishing the chill. "I was too fine a practitioner of the trade to be taken, and quick as a flea, besides."

"Did someone teach you? How to steal, I mean?"

"They did not. Neither did I know how to starve, but at the time I seemed to be taking to it with astounding speed. Methought I must learn to steal, and faster."

Fee let that sink in for a bit. It conjured a disturbing image. Gil as a young teenager, his natural leanness whittled by hunger to that of a famished cat, pale eyes large in a gaunt face. She jerked away from the picture. "What did you steal? Nothing very large, I imagine."

"Bits of this, bits of that. My first cop was a fine-stitched cap of velvet, right off a tyke's head." He smirked. "Terrified, I was. Made off with it like the hounds of Hell were at my heels, and his nurse screaming the while. Traded it for a good knife." Gil's smirk widened into a grin. "Having tools, then, I became a cutpurse, and a very fine cutpurse was I."

At fourteen, he'd been an orphan, a starveling, and a thief. What had she been at that age? A carefree girl in a Parisian family of means, she was well-dressed, well-tended, and well-fed. Not to mention more than a little spoiled by doting parents.

"Your father sounds like a complete prick," she said

acidly. "When he kicked you out, did the prick tell you why?"

"The filthy things you say, sweetling, they inflame me." Gil chuckled, then shook his head. His hair caught glints of moonlight, as though lightly brushed with silver paint. "The baron was not one to waste breath on explanations. I was never entirely sure why he kept me for the nine years he did. The heir of last resort, I surmised whilst footing the long road to London, an heir he could claim if all else failed. Old Sorley had neither son nor daughter in wedlock, you see, his wife being barren. When she died, he wed anew, quick as quick. The new wife doubled his prospects and ensured my doom in the first year, giving him twin boys."

Fee scraped her memory for what little she knew of English heirs and titles. "If your father had married your mother, you'd have been the Honorable Gilbert Sorley. People would have said 'yes, sir' and 'no, sir' to you."

"Aye, I suppose they would have done. Had it come to pass, which it did not." A low chuckle vibrated in the body pressed against her side. "For spite, I took and kept his name, though he had given me no right to it."

"Even if he didn't acknowledge you, Gil, you were still his first-born son. You should have been his heir."

"Huh." His grunt was darkly amused. "As Polly would say, a nod's as good as a wink to a blind horse."

"Polly?"

"Polly Makepence, my friend."

Fee took a minute to think about that. "Was she your...girlfriend?"

Bemused, he looked down at her, one eyebrow arching. "She was but a girl and I a boy when first we met, if I take your meaning. We thieved together, for a time." He entwined his fingers in her hair again, sifting through the curls and gently rubbing her scalp.

Driven by an impulse she didn't fully understand, Fee rolled to the side and flung her arms around him. Holding him tight, she buried her face and the grief that overtook her in the warm linen of his shirt. "I'm sorry," she mumbled into his chest. "I'm so sorry."

"Sorry?" he asked the top of her head. "For Polly and me? God wot, we were quite excellent thieves, for ones so young."

"No! For your life, what you went through, your mother, your—"

"Sweet mistress, if your gentle spirit is so pained by my childhood, what will you do when you learn of the years I then passed among pestilence, penury, coney-baiters, and bawds? And incomprehensibly worse than those," he gave a violent shudder, "*actors*."

"It's not funny, Gil. You were a child. It wasn't your fault. You shouldn't have had to—"

He dragged her over him, into a kiss. Not a desperate one, as before, but achingly tender. Also as before, the line between the night and Gil disappeared. Fee opened her mouth, and both came in, night and Gil together, spilling over borders, erasing them.

The kiss subsided, but she still lay half atop him, feeling the thud of his heart. *We're in a new place*, she thought. *A new land.* A strange land, not on any map, unless it was printed on her souler heart.

Gil pressed his face into her hair, inhaling her scent.

"Our embraces are pleasure, they go to my head like wine. Thank you."

He was thanking her for hugs. When had a man ever done that? "I want them, too."

He took her hand and put a kiss in the palm. "What I mean to say is, you hold me to your body when mine is filthy. It must be like embracing a beast of the fields, though I hasten to assure you I have no experience of that."

"You're not so bad. And I spend most of my days here digging up the cellar. I'm not fresh as a daisy."

"You are a garden of ineffable sweetness."

"Not so. We're a pair of sheep."

"There's a pastoral charm to that, *chavi*. Innocence, wool, clover, all under the English sky."

"Have you ever had a bath?"

He threw his head back with a groan, toppling her off him. "Oh, mistress, how you wound me! Am I that odorous that you would soak me in a vat of hot water, like a pudding in a sack?"

"No! I didn't mean you *need* a bath. I was thinking of...something else." Not a bath but a bathtub, a large one, claw-footed porcelain with gauze curtains all around. The two of them in the warm water, soaping, rubbing...

"Sorley's house had coopered oak tubs and servants to fill them with buckets of hot water brought up from the kitchens. I was forbidden, alas, to bother the servants for water even if my scrawny hide were to take fire. There was a lake, though, on the grounds. When I wasn't fishing in it, I was splashing about, naked as an eel."

"Not in winter, I hope."

"Nay, nay. Sorley's cook was not unkind. In winter, she gave me a bucket of water heated on the hearth, and a rag. I washed myself in the kitchens."

"The female servants must have found that entertaining."

"They paid me less note than the cat on the hearth. Paid the cat more, forsooth, since it was a ratter of great worth, whilst I did little beyond eating and reading and growing."

"Gil." She'd asked him once and he hadn't answered. She'd ask again. "What happens if you leave the Olympiad? Just walk out the door into the alley or the street?"

"Not a thing. Before so much as drawing a breath, I find myself back where I started."

"Have you tried it?"

"Tried it, failed at it, cursed my fate. At the start of my long stay in this place, I was like a wild ram mewed up in a barn. I drove my head against the stall day in and out, but to no avail, other than a sore head and deep despair. After a time, escape lost its appeal. Even a 'Gyptian becomes resigned to the loss of liberty.

"Besides, doth not the Bible say, 'Good things come to those who wait'?" He pulled her tight against him. "Sore long have I waited, and hath come now the best of things."

They kissed, Gil smiling and Fee trying to, into each other's mouths. The kiss turned questing and hungry, then became lost and cast away. They had no hope of returning to the people they'd been before the night, the moon, and each other.

Fee felt the very instant the knotted cord holding her to her old life unraveled and fell. It was lightness and pain at once, the letting go of a great weight followed by the rushing in of fear. *Aide-moi*, the confused girl she'd been in Paris begged, *help me*. But who could help? Her mother and father? They'd taken her to the Dordogne and put her feet on the crossroads of time. Her witch-aunts in Wales? They'd ladled warnings into a cauldron of predictions and brewed them into useless spells. Her great-aunts in Savannah? Despite the harm they'd done by keeping secrets from Fee's mother, they kept right on trying to pretend they didn't exist.

Aide-moi, aide-moi. There was only one being in all the world, in all of time, who truly understood. Only one who could help.

But he was the one pulling her with him into the endless night of his soul.

Nineteen

"Where the bloody blazing hell *were* you?" Abeni wasn't usually a shouter, but she was shouting before Fee's feet even crossed the flat's doorsill.

"Out," Fee answered curtly.

"For *two days*?"

"A day and a night. Part of another day, but that's only because on the way home I remembered we were out of coffee." Fee raised the sixteen-ounce Costa cup. "There was a queue."

She came all the way into the flat and shut the door behind her, shrugging her backpack onto the coffee table. The seconds it took to do both enabled her to tamp down her irritation before she added, "I'm almost twenty-seven, Abeni, not seventeen. Which was the last time I had to report my whereabouts to a parent."

Because, not long after her seventeenth birthday, she'd zipped through time and space to her great-aunts' house in Savannah. If she'd stayed with her parents in

1770s Paris, she was pretty sure she'd still have a curfew.

Abeni, at the kitchen table, wasn't buying the *I'm an adult* argument. "I rang you six times. Didn't you check your mobile?"

"It was turned off. I didn't expect my parole officer to be calling."

"Funny as fuck, Ms. Gowdie."

Fee schooled calm into her voice. "Abeni, I'm sorry I worried you. I don't worry when you're out all night."

"That's because you know where I am, Sarah's house. You *never* stay out all night, Fee."

"I'm turning over a new leaf. You're the one who said I needed to get out more."

There was a short, prickly pause from Abeni, then, "So, where were you?"

"At the dig."

"The dig."

"The dig in the Olympiad."

"The *theatre?*"

"Christ, Abeni, you make it sound like the Roman Coliseum on All You Can Eat Christians Day."

"Let me sort this," Abeni said through clenched teeth. "You spent the night alone in a derelict theatre in Covent Garden."

Not alone, no. "We've talked about how important the dig is. For my book, for the site. I only have so many hours I can devote to archeology, and I—well, I lost track of time."

From the presence of a milk carton and cereal box on the table, breakfast had been underway before Abeni started kvetching. She pushed back her chair and stood, snatched up her bowl and mug, and took them to the sink. "You've been in London for three years, Fee. You know there's no such thing as a totally safe part of the city, especially at night. You remember in April, that nurse who was walking fifty feet to the bus stop and—"

"I said I'm sorry! I won't do it again." Now, there was a fat, festering lie. She'd probably do it every night if Gil asked her to.

Abeni blew out an exasperated breath but didn't pursue the rant. She hefted her messenger bag and a thick folder of student work from the table and headed for the flat door. Just before she went through, she said, "There's some post for you. I put it in the fruit basket. And your Aunt Jana texted me. She's looking for you, too."

"Brilliant, fabulous, life can't get better."

Abeni left the flat. Just as she wasn't usually a shouter, she wasn't a slammer, but the heavy *thud* of the door was eloquent in its own way. The quiet afterward was a relief, even though the air still quivered with unspoken things.

Fee lifted a yellow plastic folder off the fruit basket on the table. Under it, tucked between two aging apples, was an envelope. Even from two feet away Fee could make out the *Savannah, GA, USA* postmark. Well, well. Just because she'd sarcastically said life couldn't get better didn't mean it wouldn't get worse. She'd open the letter later. She wasn't sure she was up to tackling its contents first thing in the morning. Or ever.

At least with Abeni gone, she didn't feel cornered, like she had to defend herself. She admitted it, she'd been inconsiderate. She'd stayed out all night without telling Abeni where she was and scared her roomie half to death. That was a mistake. But the bigger mistake had been made while she was making the smaller one. Almost without seeing it and definitely without willing it, she'd crossed a line between her and a not-alive man on a roof.

Gil would be with her all the time now. The faint rustle in the back of her mind—that was the brush of his clothing as he took her in his arms. The bee hum of awareness in her body—that was her readiness to take him into her. Any time she remembered his voice, she'd crave the low moan he made when she opened her mouth to him. Thinking of his hands would conjure those hands cradling her buttocks as he moved her against him.

There'd be no peace anymore in a world that had Gilbert Sorley in it.

Fee let all that sift and settle while she made a toaster waffle. She couldn't remember the last time she'd eaten.

Her practical clone, who pretended nothing had changed, banged around in the kitchen cupboards, looking for syrup. The original of her was still on top of the Olympiad with Gil. If they hadn't torn off their clothes and coupled under London skies, it wasn't because she hadn't wanted it.

Oh, how she'd wanted it.

As he'd wanted it. Wanting was in his wound-tight caress, his musky taste. The hard proof of it rubbing against her had brought them both close to explosive release, even as his body quaked with restraint. And yet... and yet...

He'd handled her as though they were lovers outside

of time. Not hurrying, not spreading and mounting and plunging. Instead, he'd given her a slow-moving stream of moments, each one long as eternity. She'd never been touched the way Gil touched her. He took the elemental fire that burned in both their bodies and turned it into gold. *Alchemy*, a thing of his time. The transmutation of base metal, the flare of dragon fire.

The Philosopher's Stone, that brought life everlasting.

Reality came back with a thump. There was no syrup. After more banging around in both the cupboards and the fridge, she determined there was no jam, either. Nothing as grounding as a waffle without syrup or jam. Settling for butter, she ate standing up at the kitchen counter.

She absolutely had to stop thinking about Gil, the roof, his body, their embraces. She'd be a lot better off thinking about what had happened to Mom, who ended up in the 1700s with her restored leathling.

If Fee couldn't renegotiate her relationship to her souler heritage, her ultimate destination might be the 1600s. Last stop on the Plague, Pox, and Puritans Tour.

And what about Gil? Where will he end up? She locked the door on whatever crazy room those questions gibbered out of.

Her plate was empty, and she looked at it stupidly. She'd finished the waffle without tasting it. She washed up and then roamed the flat for a while. Showered and shampooed. Made and drank a mug of Keemun Daybreak tea, since even the large latte hadn't put enough caffeine in her bloodstream to clear her head. Ran her cellar-filthy clothes through the wash and hung them to dry on the carousel drying rack in the garden. While she was out there, she stood vigil at Shakespeare's grave for a few minutes.

Fee had never figured out why the garden thrived when no one paid any attention to it. If she were a garden, she'd find that discouraging. Maybe the plants were ecstatic to find any un-concreted earth at all in London. A few roses were still blooming, so she pulled off their petals and scattered them on Shakespeare's small mound of dirt. It seemed odd, leaving flowers on the grave of a mouse she'd chased out of her bra a few hours before.

She went back inside and cleaned the kitchen and the bathroom. Vacuumed the carpet in her bedroom and reorganized her closet. She would've cleaned the neighbors' apartments if it helped her fight the almost over-powering urge to return to the Olympiad. To Gil.

Finally, she ran out of distractions involving household furnishings. That only left research, so she changed into clothing decent enough to wear to the British Library. Rooting around in the stacks always had a soothing effect. Her laptop bag was weighing down her shoulder and she was standing half in, half out of the flat door when her cellphone sounded. *The Sorcerer's Apprentice.*

Ignoring it wouldn't work; her witch-aunt would keep calling. And if she didn't reach Fee pretty soon, Jana would contact the great-aunts in Savannah and then, they'd *all* be on her case. She snatched the phone from the outer pocket of her bag. True to custom, Jana plunged right in.

"Aoife, let's have that conversation again." Her witch-aunt didn't sound angry, but her voice had a *don't-shit-me-girl* quality. "The one where you told me nothing was happening, and I didn't need to worry."

"Hello, Jana. How are you? I'm fine, thanks for asking. I didn't say nothing was happening. I said I'd met a man, but there was nothing to it."

"And I said if that was true, I wouldn't see him in the cards again."

Clack clack clack. The sound distracted Fee. One of the neighbors was passing by in the hall, her high-heeled boots noisy on the tiled floor. On her way somewhere nice, judging from the boots, the belted Burberry trench coat, and a scarlet beret. Normal-nice clothes on a woman doing normal-nice things, things without witches and trapped souls in them. *Clack clack clack.* The woman nodded at Fee as she passed. Fee gave her a stock "Hi, neighbor" smile.

She moved inside the flat and dropped her bag, pushing the door closed with her foot. "I guess this call means you saw him in the Tarot again."

"Him. You. A couple other things I didn't like the look of. The Three of Swords, Aoife, and the Two of Cups."

"Uh huh. And those mean..."

"You're the research wizard, figure it out."

Fee swore under her breath, then to Jana, louder, "Gosh and golly, I left my decoder ring back in North

Carolina. Give me the abridged version, if you don't mind."

Jana's irritated sigh rode the electromagnetic waves from Wales to London like a fuel-injected surfboard. "It's a gross oversimplification, but the Two of Cups signifies deep love, often at first sight. The Three of Swords foretells the catastrophic rupture of a bond."

Fee sank down on the sofa. "All right." She took a few seconds to gather her wits. And her courage. "I'm going to need more information, Auntie."

"Oh, *now* she wants information!"

"Don't be sarcastic, Jana. I just—"

"You've turned a blind eye to what you are for years, Aoife."

She couldn't argue with that. Most of her life had been a pitched battle with her parents on the subject. Once she "transited" from France to Wales and the ring-ing/buzzing/tingling in her body stopped, she was fine and dandy with forgetting the entire souler-leathling business. With every passing year and no return of symp-toms, it had become easier to think they'd never come back.

Then, Gilbert Sorley appeared, sans symptoms but with a ghost mouse in tow. Her own fault for pretending it could never happen, but she'd been totally blindsided.

"Aoife. Are. You. *Listening?*" Jana bit out the words impatiently.

"I am, and I know, I haven't always paid attention." Another lapse in conversation ate up a minute. Fee used it to visualize Jana in her shop. Her substantial form was probably parked in a chair at the small table where she practiced divination, cards fanned out in front of her. She'd be crowded on three sides by books and herbs and racks of potion bottles. What color was her hair this month? Jana had a penchant for blue dye, leaving broad streaks of white at the temples. She used to bleach the streaks, but they'd turned stark white of their own accord in recent years.

Fee didn't have to force humility and a dash of unease into her question. "Do you mind if I—can I ask about a few things?"

"Better late than never," Jana harrumphed. "Fire away."

———

Ten minutes after Jana rang off, Fee was still sitting on the sofa, turning the call over and over in her head. She'd asked her witch-aunt some tough questions, so she shouldn't be chagrined at the uncomfortable answers. Sometimes, she got carried away with confidence in Jana, assuming she could supply solutions to every problem. Fee supposed she'd taken it for granted, having a powerful witch in the family. Especially the most powerful of the witches she knew in Wales now that Selene was gone.

Selene had scared her silly. The elder witch had such an astonishing gift of sight it made Fee feel like a fishbowl, every secret of her soul floating around for the world to see. She couldn't even imagine what Selene would say about her now, about her grant going off the rails while she dug like a manic gopher in a cellar. About the theatre and Gil and a silver Charles the First penny that, according to Jana's latest Magic Advisory, wasn't a penny at all.

"It's right there in the song," Jana insisted, and she recited the last verse.

"'Soul, soul, ransom a soul,
Only if the coin be whole.'"

The song came uncomfortably back to Fee, like an embarrassing memory she'd deliberately forgotten. She wasn't sure she'd even known it in the first place. Unlike her mother, she hadn't sung it as a child, when she was making those drawings that got everyone around her so riled up.

At least, she didn't *think* she'd sung it. Surely, someone would've told her if she had. Mom had taught it to her later, wedging it into her years-long curriculum, *How to Be a Souler, Parts I-XXV*.

Now, Jana was reminding—or warning—Fee that *she* was the coin. The one she'd found in the cellar, Jana said, was just an avatar, an ensign. A serpent on a map with a tiny motto underneath. *Hic Sunt Dracones*. Here there be monsters.

"Okay, Jana," Fee had persisted doggedly, "here's something I don't understand at all. My mother always said that you and the other witches warned her not to get —" Holy flaming shit, were they really going to chat about her parents' sexual history? "—um, physically close to my father."

"Because the coin of the song," Jana interjected, "is

the souler, and the souler must be whole to ransom the leathling."

"Okay. You're telling me the intimacy caused Mom to start fading, losing her...wholeness."

"By bits and pieces, yes, which forced your parents to separate so the fading would stop and, eventually, reverse itself. Fee, surely you know all this. I wasn't with you in Paris, but Celeste was very conscientious. She must have told you."

Fee nodded, even though her witch-aunt couldn't see it. Maybe they should've had a Zoom conference. Oh, no, delete that. She was *not* going to look Jana in the eye for this conversation. "She was, she did. I mean, I understand that much. But Jana, I wouldn't be here if my parents hadn't had, you know, s-e-x."

"Hecate's hounds, Aoife, you're a grown woman! Considering the profanity I've heard from you at other times, I think spelling out sex is unnecessary."

"Just answer the question, please, Aunt Jana. Was it or wasn't it wrong?"

"Aoife, nothing that brought you into the world could ever be wrong. My concern, and the concern we all had at the time, was that the damage done to the souler transaction would take a very long time to repair. As it did. Over four years."

Four years and nine months, give or take a couple weeks. The time from when her mother conceived and then, four years after Fee was born, had an astounding dream that told her she could rejoin the father of her child if she went to a crossroads at the heart of a stone circle on All Hallows' Eve.

Fee's next question followed, at least in her own mind, the one before. "Are you saying that my father would have been rescued from where he was sooner if my parents hadn't gotten physical?"

"I wish I could say that with certainty, Aoife. I can't, and I don't know any witch who can. There's no instruction manual for this. I can't just click on soulers-and-leathlings-dot-com. There are references in old grimoires, but they're fairly nebulous, as you can imagine. Back in the Burning Time, the consequences of writing anything down, even talking about it openly..."

Jana let the sentence dangle while Fee thought about consequences. Denunciation, trials, torture, hanging. *The Late Lancashire Witches.*

"There are other consequences, too," Jana resumed. "What your mother and father did was daring and probably foolhardy. Though, it came out well in the end."

Did it?

"The thing you must remember, Aoife, more than any other, is this: What happened to your parents was an exception to the rule of souling, at least as we know it from grimoires and tradition and hearsay. Release the soul, that's always been the rule. As a souler, your calling is to set the soul free, not to set up housekeeping with him, if that's the idea you're getting into your head."

Was it? "Believe me," Fee told her witch-aunt truthfully, "I'm not at Harrods looking for china patterns."

Jana harrumphed again. "I won't tell you not to bed him," she summarized grumpily, "since I have a feeling that horse is out of the paddock. But you're on a dangerous path, Aoife. Mind how you go."

Beware the Ides of March. Stay on the Yellow Brick Road. Harry must not go back to Hogwarts.

And just how did Auntie Jana know "bed the leathling" was already on Fee's Google calendar? It gave Fee what her Savannah aunts called the collywobbles to think her sex life could be viewed by anybody with a Tarot deck, like on closed circuit TV.

Before she ended the call with her usual abruptness, Jana dispensed witch-guru wisdom, as vague as that stuff usually was. "Be wise," she said. "Never forget what you are, what you owe, and to whom."

And then, Jana was gone. Fee was on her own again.

She went to the kitchen and took the water pitcher out of the fridge. Pouring herself a tall, ice-cold glass, she drank it while she stood at the kitchen table. The water just added to the chill in her belly. Hot tea would've been a better choice, but she was rattled enough that she didn't think she could manage the kettle. The envelope with the Savannah postmark thrust up from the fruit basket like a white flag of surrender. *Later*, she told it. *I'll read you later.*

The takeaway from Jana's call was that Fee could and couldn't take her witch-aunt's advice. The rebel in her didn't want to take any of it, especially, *"Never forget what you are, what you owe, and to whom."* Not *who* you are, but *what*. Did Jana really expect her not to resent being reduced to an object, a thing? A thing with regalia, drawings, songs, symbolic coins, and grimoires. A thing with obligations, secret vows, instructions written in disappearing ink and stored somewhere in the Ministry of Phantoms.

The deeper into souling she got, the more she felt like a walking magic shop, like Jana's Broom & Bottle.

The idea that each soul had just one souler assigned to it? That part seemed too neat and orderly to be real. Maybe Jana made that up? Jana's insistence that she had to follow the rules of souling—just who the hell wrote those down? Maybe there really *was* a Ministry of Phantoms and she just hadn't found the secret entrance to it.

Now, her witch-aunt was waving the Three of Swords and the Two of Cups at her. Fee could barely play poker, but Jana expected her to seek enlightenment from Tarot cards?

And then, there was the legacy angle. For fuck's sake, was she really expected to accept that souling was a family business? Gowdie & Daughters, Inc. It defied science that souling was in her DNA. Nor was it a calling, like being a nun, something she, like most good Catholic girls, had wanted at age eleven.

She wasn't a preteen anymore. Or a good Catholic girl. Speaking of which—she rinsed out her glass and put it in the dish drainer—it was time to visit the nearest NHS clinic and get a prescription for birth control pills. If there was any chance she might end up in bed with Gilbert Sorley, she ought to at least *"Be wise."*

On her way from the kitchen back to the lounge, she glanced through the French doors into the garden. The shadows were lengthening. If she was going to get any work done at the Libe, she'd better get moving.

There was one thing she was sure of. Jana would really get her knickers in a twist if she learned of the conviction that had taken root deep inside Fee. Hopefully, Jana's clairvoyance couldn't reach that far. Because Fee's new and disturbing conviction was that her night on the Olympiad's roof with Gil was the fateful first taste of a dangerous drug.

She wanted him, now. Fiercely, constantly. How long before she had to have him, and couldn't let him go?

At that question, her hands began trembling. They trembled while she snatched up the letter in the fruit basket, shoved it into her laptop bag, slammed the flat door even harder than Abeni, and pointed herself toward the British Library.

It's fine, she told herself over and over as she went. *Gil and I didn't really do anything on the roof. I can stay on top of this.*

Could she? On the rooftop, she'd seen a straining but controlled Gilbert Sorley. What would he be like unleashed, uncaged by convention? He was a man from a coarse and violent era. Educated, yes, and mannerly, when it suited him. But he probably wouldn't be held in check by the constraints of the modern world.

And her, what about her? How long before she stripped away caution for his pleasure and her own?

I don't love him. I don't love him.

Who was she kidding? If she needed to tell herself that now, it was already too late.

TWENTY

September 28
882 Bull St.
Savannah, GA

Ma chère Fee,
Now, don't get mad, honey, but Jana Smithbury-Tewkes
messaged me on Facebook. I would've liked to talk to her,
and I would have, if we both didn't have those phone plans
where they charge you an arm and a leg for overseas calls.
But years ago, I Friended her on Facebook, so she knew how
to reach me.
I'd like it even better if you and I could talk. You know, like
we used to, on the back porch when you were just a bitty
thing. Your mom and I used to do that (and I still miss our
sweet CeCe so terribly), but maybe I can express myself
better if I write things down. My memory's not what it
used to be.
Jana's message said, "Nicole, do you have any of the draw-
ings Aoife did when she was small?" I told her, yes, I did

save a few. Hélène wanted them all to go in the recycle bin, but I made sure she didn't know where I stashed them, behind the endpaper of Diane's old book on Savannah history. My big sister still gets her panties in a twist over the souler business. It's that doctor training of hers. She just can't make herself believe it, even though she saw our sister Gabi disappear with her own eyes. Not to mention she was there that night in Wales when CeCe took you "to Paris." That's how she still thinks of it. Just the other day somebody asked her about your mom and Hélène said she'd married a Frenchman and was living over there.

I can't really blame her for telling a story like that to strangers, but inside the family? By family, I don't mean the cousins in Moniac. They have trouble wrapping their Cracker heads around anything but hunting and fishing. But her own sisters?

Even Sophie and Diane, who know what really happened, don't talk about it. Of course, they're busy. Diane's still making money selling houses and Sophie's design business is bigger than ever. She redid the interior of two rooms in the Harper-Fowlkes House, did I tell you? Sophie felt the job cramped her style. You know, all that Victorian clutter. If she'd had her druthers, she'd have ripped everything out and replaced it with Scandinavian. Guess that's not done in a historic house museum, ha ha.

Before I forget, Leonora's just fine. She's getting a little tired of the store. We both are. Business is up and down. It was up when everybody was doing Mindfulness, but now it's back to soaps and essential oils. It's been years since I heard anybody even say the words "New Age." Nora and I are both close to retirement, so maybe it's time to give up New Age before we get to Old Age.

That's all the news from Savannah, sweetie pie. I hope you are taking care of yourself. I know you get all wrapped up in your studies, but balance and harmony are everything. You don't need to change the world, just change yourself. Be positive!

Love always,

Great-aunt Nikki

P.S. I enclosed what I think is the best of the drawings you did when you were little. Second best, maybe. You took the best one with you when you went "to Paris."

Fee folded her aunt's letter and put it aside. Libraries were quiet, as a rule, but she didn't think the British Library had ever been as quiet as it seemed that afternoon. Even the usual background noises—the faint *shush* of turning pages, the muffled sneezes or coughs—were absent. The rustle of her aunt's letter as she handled it sounded, to her ears, like gunshots.

With the care she'd use to pick up a grenade, she reached two fingers into the envelope and pulled out the second sheet of paper, stiffer and thicker than the other. She unfolded it. Her hands were icy, and her heart was racing. She hadn't had any caffeine since the Daybreak tea hours ago, so the jitters weren't from that.

Even guessing what she'd see on the paper, it was still a shock. The Coronet Theatre, built 1603 and standing, more or less, until 1881. The Coronet as a precocious four-year-old would draw it, with a good set of colored pencils from her Great-aunt Nikki and a quality sketch pad from her mom. The Coronet with a squiggle on top that Fee now knew was the Lord Mayor's standard.

Gil's Coronet was in pen and ink. Hers was one up on his, thanks to those colored pencils. How accurate were her colors? She could ask him, and wouldn't that be one hell of a conversation? His memory of a theatre that disappeared in the 1880s and her memory of it from twenty-three years ago.

Employing bomb disposal delicacy again, she folded the drawing around Aunt Nikki's letter and worked them both back into the envelope. Then, she slid her laptop into her backpack, along with all her study materials, and pushed away the small stack of books she'd pulled from the stacks.

The titles should have been about 17th century theatre, considering how far behind she was on her book. Instead, the worn paper under the clear vinyl cover of the top one read *Hallowtide Customs in Old England: A Study of Souling.* She'd thought of checking it out, but it wasn't necessary. By the time she'd read page 146 seven times, she'd memorized it, especially the strangely familiar yet totally strange song the author had extracted from a 17th century Scottish document:

Soul, soul, tak ye the coin,
Let thy Death and Life unjoin;
Up the Kettle and down the Pan,
Leave as a soul, return as a Man.

Gil. She wanted Gil.

Twenty-One

There were six of them. Five men and a woman, all in suits the color of a drear day. The linen on the men was white, yellow, and a grayish tan that in Gil's day was called Dead Spaniard. One wore black from head to toe, like a Puritan witchfinder. All of them, even the woman, had hair so neatly and closely shorn that Gil wondered if they'd had lice.

They entered the alley from Drury Lane and moved in a tight group, purposefully, toward the stage door of the Olympiad. There, they paused and milled around, talking. The woman, trousered like the men, held a flat tray of some sort, cradled on her forearm. She pointed at it, said something to the others, and they all walked away, following one man. He talked and waved his arms as he led the group along the perimeter of the building. None of them struck off on their own. They moved as a swarm, a herd—no. A pack.

Memory delivered something sharp from long, long ago. It was winter, bitter cold. All the winters in London had been cruel, then, and the Thames froze to greater or lesser degree in many of them. That winter—1639, if he recalled aright—the ice was deemed insufficiently thick to support a fair, as had been held on the frozen river in an earlier year. The holders of stalls and purveyors of sled rides were keenly disappointed, but none so much as the actors, himself included, who had hoped to stage drolls and penny pantos, tiding themselves over until the spring when the theatres could open again. A clutch of them argued with the King's men in front of the Boar Inn at Thameside. There were raised voices and much pointing at the river, which looked solid enough from where Gil, at the side of the fray with Polly Makepence and some others of his raggle-taggle friends, took bets on the outcome.

Because they weren't inside by the fire, but outside, they spotted the wolves. Polly saw them first and shrieked. They all looked toward the Thames, staring open-mouthed, breath frosting, as the six gray shapes advanced westward, fast, along the white divide between the Tower and Southwark.

Everyone screamed for the Watch except Polly, who just screamed until Gil shook her brusquely. In any case, the wolves had been sighted earlier. It was only moments before a company of archers poured onto the ice and brought the beasts down, all but two who streaked back the way they'd come and were soon out of range.

Gil did not join the fools who tramped onto the river to see the carcasses. Those left behind speculated wildly that the wolves had come from Hampstead Heath, or even as far away as Epping Forest. Cooler heads suggested they'd spilled from the Moor Fields, where they'd tired of dining on beggars and laundresses. Perhaps, they'd even crossed like good citizens through Moor Gate, on their way to better-fed prey in the Town. The sanest suppositions came from those who said they must have escaped the Menagerie at the Tower.

Within the hour, when the carcasses were dragged back—the Boar's owner having paid for their pelts to tack upon his wall—the onlookers learned the pack were not wolves at all, but some mongrel mix bred in the Fields. Perhaps, the new King would hunt them for sport, as old King Hal had hunted real wolves until there was not one to be seen in all England.

Polly came in for no end of jibes when the gawkers tramped back to the Boar and resumed their drinking. Howls made the rafters ring for an hour and Polly flushed the color of beetroot. Gil gave her his last tuppence for ale in which to drown her shame.

Now, watching a latter-day pack sniffing around the perimeter of the Olympiad, Gil had a mind to bring back wolf hunts.

Or he might try prayer. He was certain that invoking a saint to entice persons to bodily harm was ungodly in the extreme. Despite that, he ran through the list of saints he knew, wondering if St. Dismas of thieves or St. Michael of warriors would be his surest bet. There was nothing he could do to defend the Olympiad from the gray-suited predators if he couldn't get them inside its walls. Even within, and despite his offers to murder Aoife's enemies, he doubted he could accomplish more than a stumble over a doorsill or a misstep on the stairs. Still, the stairs in the Olympiad were fairly steep.

The group of six made a circuit of the theatre but did not attempt entry. Their straggling numbers collected again at the stage door. As one, they tipped back their heads and looked toward the roof.

If only he could be seen. Invisibility took the joy out of turning his backside to them, dropping his breeches, and bending over. Even the talent he'd mastered in his youth, deliberately breaking wind, was wasted since he couldn't be heard.

The gray-suits gabbled for a while, some pointing at the roof, some at the tray in the woman's hands. They finally seemed to reach accord and went out as they'd come in, by the alley, toward Drury Lane. They were smiling, each and every one. That, more than anything, enraged and depressed him. He disconsolately trudged back to his lodging.

Once inside, he flattened his palms on the wall and thudded his head against it, twice, thrice. *You are a damned, doomed, wreck of man, an eternity of woe is less than you deserve.* That was the thought ringing in his brain. 'Sdeath, no part of him deserved the sweet glory that was Aoife, her radiance, her joy.

And yet, he'd give all his tomorrows for one more night with her in his arms.

The mouse, who always seemed to know when he was melancholic, appeared at his foot. It could easily have scurried up his leg, but it chirped and chittered instead, like a tiny monkey. It had developed the trick of distracting him from sorrow by demanding attention. A kind trick, so Gil honored it by reaching down a hand for the mouse to crawl into.

"As you remind me, little friend," he answered as he moved to his desk and sat, tipping the mouse to one side where it also sat, cleaning its whiskers. "It was a short enough play and had a long enough run that I remember the lines. Let you observe, now, as I put them to foolscap." Gil moved some sheets to the center of the desk and picked up the metal quill Aoife had brought him. He began writing. "*The Alchemist. Act I, Scene I.I. A room in Lovewit's house...*"

Twenty-Two

"I thought you hated Ben Jonson." Fee's voice echoed in the high-ceilinged vault of the Olympiad's auditorium.

"Hated him, loved him." At stage center, Gil fanned a stack of paper, what he called foolscap when he forgot the modern word. "Everyone did. Ben was a singular nuisance. A brazen-faced, breedbating, firefanged, tent-bellied—"

"I have no idea what—"

"—fart of a man."

"Okay. I get that."

"But he could," Gil added, "pen a play, and that is why we are here."

'Here' was the stage, only slightly brighter at noon than at midnight, even with the old electric footlights—half of them, amazingly, operational, though they flickered—along the lip of the proscenium.

Fee squirmed in the tight-bodiced gown Gil had dragged out of a chest in the attic and declared perfect for her. Apart from it being so old the sea-glass silk was shattering along the seams, it had an odor like soured wine and mothballs. She couldn't begin to place the style, historically. The Crimean War, maybe?

Gil stood in front of her, wide-legged and stolid as a captain on a ship's deck. He held aloft the sheaf of papers. "You said, if memory serves, that you wished to be an actor."

Had she said it? Dreamed it was more accurate. And futilely at that.

"You put great feeling into Ophelia's lines," he prompted.

When had she—oh, right. He'd heard her orating to the dark the night the LUCIES arrived to pillage the Olympiad. She hadn't been embarrassed, squawking those lines like an audition for a high school talent show, because she hadn't known a real actor was in the wings, listening. Now, knowing what she did about Gil, she cringed to remember she'd called him a wanker.

"Great feeling," he pressed her, "though very little skill."

Agreed, but she could do without an actor who'd been to William Shakespeare's funeral telling her so. Maybe she could steer him somewhere else. "This costume doesn't seem like something Ophelia would wear."

"We're not here to do *Hamlet*." Gil shuffled the papers and didn't look up from them as he spoke. "Nor will you be playing Ophelia."

They weren't? She wouldn't?

"I will not say Shakespeare's women are unimpressive, as a lot," Gil lectured, "but the mad maiden is not outstanding."

"She's the essence of tragedy!"

"She is an insult to your talent."

He thought she had talent? Maybe she could live with the dress. She rubbed a fold of the thin skirt between her thumb and forefinger and wriggled in the breath-robbing bodice again. The costume was elderly, true, but the color matched her eyes. Maybe someone famous had worn it, in that very theatre. A young Billie Burke, maybe, in her stage acting days before she became Glinda the Good Witch.

The short, happy flight of her heart crashed with Gil's next words. "You will learn the part of Dol Common."

"Dol Common?" she blurted. "From *The Alchemist*? But she's a—" Gertrude the Whore leered from her past, "—prostitute."

"She thrives in a world of commerce with the goods she has to sell, and what of it?" He strode to her and, as always, his approach turned her wits to scrambled eggs. "It's not what lies between her legs that makes the play." Bending slightly, he kissed one of her ears, then the other, and the last scrap of her resistance dissolved under his lips. He tapped her forehead gently with his forefinger. "It's what lies between her ears." Walking away, he left her wanting more.

"Take your mark, Mistress Gowdie." He was suddenly all director from his sleek, sable hair to the soles of his feet. "Repeat after me."

They started with Act One, Scene I, when Dol—

sneak thief, confidence trickster, wanton—broke into a house with her two accomplices. Gil fed Fee her lines and told her where to stand and move.

At first, she balked the way she usually did, grumbling and deliberately misinterpreting his stage directions. Whether it was a reaction to the weird truth of her family or just her nature, she'd always turned into a doorstop when anyone told her what to do. She'd done it with her *tuteurs* in Paris ("I am sorry, Madame and Monsieur, but I cannot teach her the pianoforte with her arms crossed."). And her mother ("Listen, Mademoiselle Stubborn-to-a-fault, you *will* wear stays like all the other girls your age."). And her theatre profs at UNC ("Do you think you could deliver Edward Albee's dialogue as written just once, Miss Gowdie?").

She preferred to call it independence of spirit, but she knew in her heart it was sheer cussedness, and self-defeating, too. Gil wasn't having it.

His way of getting her to do what he wanted was subtle. Implacable. Irresistible as the tide.

Lightly, by the very ends of her fingers, he pulled her to him, then dropped her hands, walked away, and came back. Circled casually but with intent, a lazy wolf deciding whether something was worth the effort of attack. Made her follow him by the simple tactic of drifting away and lowering his voice in the middle of a sentence, so she couldn't resist getting closer. Touched her, but barely, the lightest of touches, like gentling a colt. Turned her this way, his hand on her waist. Nudged her that way, shaping her into a static pose so the audience had a chance to read the disdain of her back, the coquetry of her jutting hip.

Gradually, as she understood the artistry of his direction, her resistance dissolved. She relaxed. She *trusted*. In the end, he moved her around the stage as though she *were* a doll.

Without missing a beat in his role as director, he deftly acted whatever role was needed to partner her in each scene. As Face, the greedy housekeeper who invited the conmen to his master's house, he assumed a squint and a shambling, sneaky way of walking, one shoulder lowered as though habitually looking over it for his employer. He turned into Subtle, Dol's criminal associate, a huckster who could talk the Crown Jewels out of the Tower. All smiles and winks and an oily, insinuating voice, he made even Fee believe he was an alchemist who could pull the Philosopher's Stone from his pocket—for a price.

In the next instant, he was Dapper, a timid law clerk, so naive that he confused Dol with the Fairie Queen and was ready to give her anything for her magical gifts. Gil as Dapper disheveled his hair to hang over his eyes. He spoke with a lisp and a stutter. His hands twisted together nervously and he took small steps, as though afraid his body might do something impulsive if not kept under strict control.

The play grew as they acted it, grew and bloomed like the witty, thorny rose of Jacobean satire it was. The synergy between Fee and Gil grew along with it—dance, theatre, sexual attraction, all enmeshed and simultaneous, with no way to tell where one left off and another started. Line by line, Fee opened. Scene by scene, Gil entered—voice, hands, breath, body—along with the play.

She'd never seen him like that, making her wonder if she'd ever really seen him at all. He'd been a jester in the cellar, making adolescent jokes, cock this and cock that. A poet on the roof, quoting Sappho, John Donne, and his own lyrical verse. A tattered gallant, ashamed of his spoiled shirt and absurdly proud of his new one.

But this Gil, *this*, was the essential and unvarnished Gil, the one in his native element. He ranged the stage, roaring, like the jungle cat he was in his day. Power spoke from the wide sweep of his shoulders. The lean muscle of his back flexed beneath the loose folds of his shirt. Taut hips, long thighs, bunched calves: this was a man who'd walked the forty miles from Kent to London and thought nothing of it.

Mastery, ferocity, sexual potency...they rolled off him in waves. Watching him, Fee's mouth went so dry she could barely deliver her lines. Talk about bringing a knife to a gunfight; she'd been a fool to think she could control anything about Gilbert Sorley.

"Dol brims with the juice of harlotry. Give it to me." His base order nearly dropped her to his knees. "Ensnare and beguile," he demanded, his voice roughened by desire. "Seduce me, Dol," and God help her, she did, giving him heat for heat, feeding his arousal and her own.

She couldn't say she'd never been aroused on the stage, she had. Once, when her UNC prof inflicted a scene from *Bus Stop* on the class, he'd paired her—in the Marilyn Monroe role—with a student cast as Beau

Decker. A strapping Carolina farm boy, her co-actor wasn't so different from the rodeo rider of the play. Tall, brawny, strong chinned, he wasn't averse to touching Fee more than the scene required, and letting his big, callused hand rest wherever it landed. Fee forgot or muddled her lines throughout the scene, which got her hollered at and humiliated in front of the class.

That young farmer was a Cub Scout compared to Gilbert Sorley. And what she'd felt in the class, the sweating palms, the clenched thighs...they were a campfire compared to the Bikini Atoll blast of Gil as he coaxed sex out of her and into Dol Common.

"Harden me, Dolkin," he growled, cupping his hand at the front of his breeches. "Make me rise."

Fee was lost. Lost to him and desire, lost to the knowledge she had—and that he knew she had—of what swelled and lengthened under his hand.

She did as he commanded, purring and arching, slathering her words with invitation. "Troth, I am taken whole, sir," she cooed as she ran her hands up her body and paused to cup her breasts, "with these studies that contemplate—" She ran her tongue along her upper lip, "—*nature*."

Gil gave her a wolfish grin of approval. "I have cast mine eye upon thy form," his smoky gaze stripped the gown from Fee's body, "and I will rear *this Beauty*—" he whirled around, grabbing his crotch and shouting at the rows of empty seats, "above all Styles!"

Fee totally blanked on her next line. The vacant auditorium shimmered and dissolved, then filled with row upon row of groundlings standing, shouting, eating, and drinking. Some stared, gape-mouthed, at the play before them, some hailed friends or shoved their neighbors to gain more room. A sea of hats undulated, feathers and fur tippets wagging. A stench of unwashed bodies and ill-washed clothes rolled toward the proscenium like fog. Behind and to each side of the mob, wooden galleries rose three stories high, with boxes on the ends. Much closer than in a modern theatre, the seated patrons were as loud and coarse as the raff on the floor. They looked more than ready to hurl fruit, vegetables, and insults into the actors' faces. The most moneyed patrons crowded together in the wings, their stools occupying so much of the stage that actors had to dodge around them on entrances and exits.

Noise and stink and fury and exaltation: it was Gil's theatre, the privileged province of great talent and greater hardship. The world he knew. The world he gave her, freely, completely, for no other reason than that she wanted it. Swaying with vertigo, Fee shut her eyes, then snapped them open, unwilling to miss a single second of the mad spectacle, whether it was real or a hallucination.

She shouted her lines until she was hoarse, spun and paced and posed until every muscle shook with strain. The more she threw herself headlong into risk, the more tenderly he cradled her. The stage was no longer a stage, and she was no longer a player. She was a planchet in a green silk gown, moved by Gil's hand across a Ouija board to spell out magic-bearing words.

Grateful. Hungry. Desperate. Soaring.

By the end of the play, she was utterly wrung out, wanting more but not having it in her to *do* more. In a dusty backstage dressing room, she hung the silk gown on a hook and put on her street clothes. Back in the auditorium, she fell into Gil's arms for a goodbye kiss, but barely heard the words he said or her own responses. As she stumbled through the stage door into the waning daylight of Covent Garden, the final, life-altering spell word rang in her ears, deafening all else.

His.

Twenty-Three

He was lost. He knew it with the certainty of a man swept into the sea. For the whole glorious, torturous day, everything in his body had urged him, his privies gone tense and heavy. He'd been but ten lines into that pestilent play before his prick was straining at his breeches. No lines of Scripture, no thoughts of dead dogs in the Fleet nor of vomit outside tavern doors worked to lower the impudent spike of flesh demanding to bury itself in the silk-clad vixen capering before him.

Still hard as a mallet an hour after her departure, Gil sat disconsolately on the vacant stage, pining. So black was his mood that even the mouse could not bear his company. Perhaps, the red spark of anger in his longing repelled it. The creature, like all small prey, sought safety when an ill-humored beast was near. In whatever mousely diversion it engaged, may God grant the mouse joy.

For Gil, there was none.

He and Aoife had made their farewells, both of them subdued by the pleasure of what they had done and the agony of what they had not. He'd kissed her lightly, almost formally, like a courting youth within eyeshot of the maiden's father. Not a flicker showed of their wild ardor on the roof. He'd not dared get anywhere near that lustful temper, had skirted it like a plague-ridden town. The play had driven him to such a pitch of lust that if he'd delved her mouth as he'd done two nights before, and had she responded in kind and pressed her devilishly fine body against him, he'd have had her there on the bare boards of the stage, instead of the bed where he was determined it would happen. *Ye gods, let it happen!*

That thrice-damned play. He'd never despised and admired it so much. Despised it, still and always, for Ben's self-praising thicket of Classical allusions and political tripe. Despised its success and the success of its maker, who somehow managed to remain a prince of the theatre despite doing everything he could, including murder, to damage his own reputation.

But Gil admired it for the best female role Ben ever wrote. Dol Common. Dorothy. Dolly. Dolkin. Deceitful trickster. Honest whore. A role completely unlike Gil's learned beauty of the modern age, and yet, at heart, the same burning brand of frank carnality that set him afire from head to foot. It all but unhinged his reason to watch Aoife strut and posture, pouting and scolding by turns, her arms cutting graceful arcs in the golden lights of the proscenium's edge, her body a twisting helix of perfection.

Did she know how often he had unclothed her in his

mind? He'd done it every day from the first hour he'd seen her and that was torment enough. Those breeches of hers plucked sanity from his brain and replaced it with ravening want. Seeing her move and stand and sit, day upon day, every curve of her nether parts tempting him to toss her onto the nearest table or bend her over the nearest chair—

But the gown he'd put her in! What perverse elf had guided his hands to that relic at the bottom of a trunk, and then offer it to Aoife? A rag of blue-green silk, barely whole after decades of use and a century of neglect, it clung like a lover's hands to her bosom, her waist, her shoulders, one of which it bared every time she spun and the sagging sleeve slid downward.

He'd warned himself, when he neared her, not to leer down the front of her garment like an alehouse sot lusting after the drawing wench, but his eyes had their own orders, given by the region south of his top breeches button. The bodice of the gown was tight and low, skimming the tops of her nipples. God's bones, he'd had to find a dozen other uses for his hands to keep them from dragging down the silk to free the breasts he ached to hold.

And then, her limbs! 'Struth, he didn't think he'd directed her to twirl so often in the role, but he wouldn't put it past that same southern region of his body to have added more turns than were strictly necessary for the play. And every time she whipped about like a wind-blown leaf, the flimsy silk petticoat lifted, showing long, pale legs, perfectly formed by some demon sculptor to drive Gil mad. At times, her hem had risen so far as to give him a glimpse of thighs, torturing him with visions of what waited between them for him, for them both.

Except, he was reminded by the parts of him north of his breeches, *she is not for thee.*

His groan was hollow and loud in the empty auditorium. Lying back, he stretched and gazed into the rigging above the stage. There'd been talk of replacing it before the Olympiad closed. Half the beams were riddled by worm and one stagehand had crashed through broken planks to the stage while securing a flat. A broken leg only, but it could easily have been his neck.

Gil would climb up there and have a look, later. Not that he worried about his own limbs, should he or the beams fall. But as he lay beneath, a fine rain of sawdust trickled down to the stage each time the adjacent roadway shook from heavy conveyances. It would not do for the fly loft to come crashing down whilst his woman was beneath.

"My woman." Aye, it was pure delight to think and say it. But nay, she was too much, too good, for the likes of him. Hour after hour as they trod the stage, he told himself that his work was to give her something she craved, the actor's art, and ask nothing in return.

Because, if experience was an apt teacher, nothing was his due. The injustice of it ate at his gut as though he'd swallowed lye from a cup. All his life, everything he'd wanted, everything that should have been his, had been torn away. Family, name, home, respect, work, life itself: all taken for no reason beyond what he was. A bastard, a foundling, a 'Gyptian, a player on the stage. And now, not even a man.

Was there no end to the taking away?

She had a future, and he had none. She lived and breathed, while the breath he drew in and let out was a mockery, as he would be no less dead if he held his breath forever. She was not now and could never be his. He should never touch her again. Never, never.

But, by Heaven, the thing between them had gone beyond their power to stop it. Even when he lived, he would not have had that much power. Now, he could summon barely the strength to think of it, much less turn away from Aoife Gowdie, back to the void, to the aching prospect of a future without end. Without her.

Perhaps, if he couldn't sense the same craving seethe in her blood...

But he could. It rose, sparking and jumping, when he so little as brushed her skin.

This. Them. It made up for the thousand thousand nights he'd spent alone in two rotting theatres. For the endless suns he'd watched rise and fall, shadows crawling across the cobbles of Wych Street, then the tarmac of Drury Lane. It was the restoration of everything he'd lost, a flood of sweetness that washed away the bitter taste of his short life and long death.

Love, at the end of days. As though he'd handed a farthing to God and been given the keys to Heaven in return.

Damn him, damn all, he and the woman would have each other. They might burn in Hell when all was done, but first, they would burn together in his bed.

TWENTY-FOUR

Gil was between her legs. The hot, hard length of him rocked into her, and her hips arched to meet him. *There*, she told him, *oh, yes, there,* and he shifted so the angle was right. She lifted her knees to give him deeper entry and—

"Fee! Fee!"

Why was he hissing that into her ear? He loved her Irish name. *My Aoife*, he called her, *my gem, my downy duckling*—

The bed shook. How was Gil doing that?

"Fee! Wake up!"

It wasn't Gil. It was Abeni.

"Gargh." Fee rolled to the edge of the bed and sat up. Abeni had hold of her shoulder and had gone from shaking the bed to shaking her.

"On your feet, girl. Some sticky beak from the AHRC is here."

"The—what?" Fee rubbed her eyes. Morning. Early.

No Gil. One too many flat mates. She swatted at Abeni's hand. "Stop that! I'm awake."

"Good, 'cause a Dr. Gretchen Hyde is on the sofa, and she's asking for you. She said she's from the AHRC."

Fee stumbled to her feet. "I heard you the first time, Abeni, but I don't know the AHRC from the ASPCA." Where the hell were her yoga pants and sweatshirt?

"Get dressed," Abeni said. "I'll put the kettle on."

Right. Let's have a cuppa. That'll solve everything.

AHRC, the Arts and Humanities Research Council. Fee remembered what it was as she pulled on her clothes and tugged a brush through her unruly black curls. AHRC was a major UK support pool for projects in philosophy, design, art conservation, and more. While all her grant paperwork had come from the NEH, she knew the American and British organizations sometimes shared funding and administration. Had she missed that in her contract? Papa, ever the canny businessman, had warned her about reading the fine print, but she'd mostly ignored him.

———

"I'm so sorry to have awakened you, Ms. Gowdie." Gretchen Hyde smiled.

Facing her from the armchair in the lounge, Fee thought her visitor didn't look the least bit sorry about her wakey-wakey visit. She looked alert and administrative. Neat rose-colored suit, cream blouse, stockings, heels. Stylish eyeglasses. Business card handed over, now in Fee's hands. *Gretchen L. Hyde, DPhil., Arts and Humanities Research Council.*

Fee cleared her throat, dislodging the sleepy raspiness. "Not at all, Dr. Hyde. I was working late last night on... an archeology project, and I overslept."

"Archeology, how exciting! Is it to do with your book?"

Ah, her book. The book that hadn't taken Fee's repeated hints and gone away. "Yes. Indirectly."

She put Dr. Hyde's business card on the coffee table with great care, as though it were a priceless artifact. Or a tarantula. Then, she lifted her mug and took a hefty swallow of tea. As usual, Abeni had made it strong enough to strip paint, and it was so hot it burned her tongue.

Fee forced herself to look composed, or as composed as someone could look who'd been alternately rehearsing a Jacobean play and lusting for a dead man all the previous day.

Abeni, in a kitchen chair she'd dragged into the lounge, had her own cup of tea. Knowing the liquid was the temperature of lava and being more awake than Fee, she was holding it, rather than trying to drink it. Dr. Hyde apparently had lips of steel; she was sipping away, unfazed.

Fee cleared her throat again. "Dr. Hyde, have you met my flat mate, Ms. Addo?"

"I have, yes. She was kind enough to let me in and, again, I apologize to you both for such an early morning visit." Dr. Hyde smiled again. Her smiles went with her suit. Rosy. Professional.

Fee nodded. Dr. Hyde sipped. Abeni lifted a shoulder and one eyebrow at Fee, as if to say, *Who is this person and why is she on our sofa?* Fee returned the lifted shoulder and eyebrow. *How should I know?*

"Dr. Hyde," Fee began, "the AHRC is in Swindon, isn't it?"

"It is!" Dr. Hyde chirped happily, as though Fee had correctly guessed the length of the Nile on an exam. "I'm in London for a two-day conference, however, and thought I'd pop in and see how you're doing."

"You mean, with my grant?"

"With every little thing." Dr. Hyde bent forward, still smiling, and neatly placed her mug on a coaster on the coffee table. "Your NEH advisor let me know your last two quarterly progress reports have wandered off. He was concerned. Grantees do take ill, now and then, or have some other problem."

Gilbert Sorley fell squarely into the Other Problem category. "I'm very well, Dr. Hyde. Just distracted by the archeology project. As I mentioned, it ties into my book."

"How wonderful!"

Wonderful, exciting, all part of the act, folks. "Yes, I think—"

"Can you tell me about it?"

Why not? MOLA and the National Trust knew. What was one more disclosure among the Suits Who Ruled. "My evidence suggests I've uncovered the remains of a hitherto unknown Jacobean Era theatre, the—" Just in time, Fee stopped herself from naming it. *The Coronet, according to the ghost who told me about it.* She took another sip of tea, cooler now, and scrambled for a sentence that wouldn't compromise her, Gil, or the common definition of sanity. "The early evidence is promising enough that I've brought in the pertinent organizations."

"Yes, Anthea Cookson's an old school chum. I do hope the National Trust can help you. There's no chance, I'm afraid, that the AHRC can do much in aid of the project. Anthea and I chatted briefly about it."

Of course, they did. Fee covered a flurry of chaotic thoughts with another swallow of tea. She didn't know which provoked her more, her Welsh witch-aunt spying on her through the Tarot or the coven of pen pushers examining her life from close at hand.

Another silent minute passed while Dr. Hyde waited expectantly on the sofa, but Fee didn't feel like chatting anymore. She didn't have anything else she could share, anyway, since the bulk of what she knew came from a source she could never disclose. She supposed if the AHRC had been able to aid her research, they would have had a right to demand the details of what she was working on. But circumstances—*what a nice, vague way to describe my growing attachment to a dead playwright*—had altered since Fee started her project. Now, any and all organizations could wait until Hell froze over for her to fill in their covert intelligence briefs.

On the other hand, she reminded herself uneasily, she was in the U.K. on someone else's nickel. Jumping through administrative hoops was the price she paid for that. If she defaulted on her arrangement with the NEH, she barely had enough in savings to cover another month in London. Another month at the dig. Another month with Gil.

And even that month was dependent on her getting a stop-work order for the Olympiad.

Fee slapped on her most ingratiating grin. Her change of expression was so abrupt the eyes of the woman across from her widened a little in alarm.

"Dr. Hyde," Fee told her, "I know I've been remiss in getting my quarterly reports to the NEH." She made a fist and struck her chest lightly. "Mea culpa, mea culpa. I'll catch up shortly, I promise." *See, Teacher, I'm a good little scholar. Don't smack my hand with the ruler.*

Dr. Hyde's whole body seemed to relax. She beamed at Fee, at Abeni, at the coffee table. "Oh, no bother, really!" She tucked her handbag—gray leather, matching her heels—under her arm and stood. "I'm just doing a favor for a colleague in my sister organization, checking up on the well-being of a grant recipient."

Fee and Abeni stood, too. For an awkward moment, the three of them grinned at each other like they'd won the Irish Sweepstakes and were splitting it three ways.

Fee forced a sentence through her bared teeth. "I'll be wrapping up the project soon, Dr. Hyde, and everyone will get my report." *Yes, everyone from the Prime Minister to the bin emptiers outside MOLA's new headquarters, since otherwise I can kiss my chances of ever getting another research grant goodbye.*

Abeni dove for the door and Fee ushered Dr. Hyde out of it. A grateful hush followed the sound of the AHRC woman's heels clicking up the hall.

At first, Abeni didn't say anything, just picked up the

tea mugs, except for Fee's, still mostly full, and carried them to the sink. After the clatter of china on stainless steel, Abeni spoke.

"Tell you what, Fee. I did the shopping yesterday and bought syrup. Let's make waffles. We can have a bit of a natter over them."

Twenty-Five

"I had to tell Abeni *something*. She has this way of keeping at you until she gets what she wants." Aoife tugged restlessly at the blanket across her shoulders, and Gil tucked it more snugly around her.

His spirited woman was at last calming, her anger quelling. She'd been in no state to put on her ragged silk gown and be Dol Common, since she'd arrived at the Olympiad in the highest state of dudgeon. Gil had been expecting the dudgeon for some time and knew its source. He'd needed no augury, only common sense. Secrets had a damnable gift for emerging, no matter how their keepers strove to cloak them. Emergent, they caused limitless mischief, a flock of gremlins unleashed and capering. Aoife was enshrouded in secrets when first she entered the Olympiad. Meeting him had given her one more, and that one was too large to conceal for long.

He'd brought her straight away to the roof, in the hope the view might calm her. Pacing and waving her arms, she fizzed and spat for a while, like broth on the boil. He listened, not interrupting, as the worst of the anger steamed away. After a time, she stopped pacing and curled between his knees, leaning back against him while he leaned against the broad chimney base. He'd enveloped her in a spare blanket he'd brought from his lodging and, over the blanket, his arms. The morning had been mild, but after the noon hour, the weather turned. Now, the sky above was heavy and gray with clouds, and wind ran cold fingers through his hair and hers. No rain, yet, but it was coming.

"Has your friend found you out, then?" He nuzzled her ear and she sighed, still vexed but less than before.

"Not entirely. I didn't tell her about you. She'd think I was crazy."

"Addle-pated. Dicked in the nob. Bats in the belfry."

"Listen to you! Elizabethan, Regency, and World War One American, I think. You're a walking encyclopedia of period slang, Gilbert Sorley."

Twitching a shoulder, he belted his arms more tightly around her. "I'd nothing but time and needed an inter-est." He kissed the top of her head. "Now, I have you."

She turned up her face, giving him the particular smile that showed he'd pleased her. His chest expanded and he fought the urge to crow like a gamecock after treading his favorite hen. He put a second kiss on her fragrant hair.

"I told Abeni as much as I could about the Coronet," she sighed out again. "Though I just called it 'the earlier theatre.' She asked why no one had found it before, and how I knew where to dig. I told her the reason for the first was the point of my book, that some theatres, plays, and playwrights have disappeared altogether in the historical record. As to knowing where to dig," she let her head fall back again and turned it, her luminous eyes seeking his, "I told her I heard a voice telling me the theatre was under the cellar."

"Oh, a voice, forsooth. And so now your friend thinks you demented."

"Maybe not. Abeni's not like most people, Gil. She's..." Aoife halted, appearing to ponder her next utterance. "It's a little hard to explain," she began again slowly, "but Abeni was raised—well, the expression might be 'between two fires.' If you asked her, she would swear the presence of otherworldly beings is fantasy. But when we moved into Bloomsbury, she did some sort of ritual involving bowls of water in the corners of the flat. When I asked her, she said it was to draw out the evil spirits."

"A singular belief for your time, perhaps, but not mine." He put a third kiss on her hair, simply because he could. "In my time, every fishwife spied portents in the guts of a herring, and every householder knew thumps in the attic were gamboling imps that needed abjuring."

Aoife hugged her knees, tucking into him like a kitten. "Abeni's not *that* credulous, but she won't stop with what I told her. She's got her own little shovel and she'll dig until she gets it all."

For that, he had no rejoinder, nor she another remark, and so they silently sat, wrapped in each other, while the sun lowered. To be sure, the lowering was a surmise on Gil's part, from the little he could see of it through the buildings that crowded Covent Garden. Above the city, clouds filled the middle distance and darkened even as he watched. A silver thread of lightning slashed them, then another.

The delight within his arms notwithstanding, his heart darkened with the sky. They had barely begun, he and Aoife, but he could see their ending. It was as unstoppable as the coming storm. The approach of it drummed in his breast, closer and closer, like an advancing army. He and his woman were but wildflowers in its path.

The irony did not escape him. Possessor of nothing for centuries, he'd had nothing to lose. Now, he'd been gifted a fragile universe of joy and naught to protect it but the circle of his arms.

Aoife also seemed to note the gathering tempest. The one in the clouds, at least. "I know we should go inside, but the lightning's a long way off. Let's stay here until the rain starts."

"Nay, by then you'll have taken an ague. Let us repair to my lodging now, before it grows colder."

"The roof's not that cold."

"Perhaps not. But my bed is warmer."

Twenty-Six

Once they crawled through the dormer window and down the steep stairs to Gil's lodging, it surprised Fee that Gil, that *everything*, went so slowly. If it had been up to her, she might have embarrassed them both by pushing him onto the bed and herself onto his thighs, making it all about sex, at least for a few hours. But it wasn't up to her, not at the start.

They stood next to his bed, both of them pretending not to notice it. *Oh, look, a bed! How did that get in here?* It was certainly visible enough in the light of the one candle Gil had left burning in a small dish on the floor. He hadn't relinquished her hand after helping her down from the roof. Apart from his light caress of her fingers, neither of them moved, while night stole into the room. A kind night, softening the dangerous reality of what they were about to do.

Finally, he brought her hand to his lips and placed a long, tender kiss on her knuckles. Everything was in that kiss. Fear and longing and promise. A shyness that moved her with its youthfulness.

Fee was suddenly oppressed by the weight and texture of her clothes. Every seam and thread confined her and her worn, old jeans and hoodie felt like an Iron Maiden. Underneath, her skin was restless, her flesh, her bones.

She didn't know where to look. If not the bed, then where? Her vision skittered nervously. First to her hand, pressed against his lips. Then, to his shirt, inches away, the open neck inviting her to the shadowed valley between his pectorals. Her gaze caught on his face. His eyelids were lowered. She savored the inkiness of his lashes, and their almost girlish length.

He opened his eyes at the same moment the storm outside broke. A loud crack from the skies made Fee twitch sharply, and the drum roll of thunder trembled through the whole attic.

"You're safe with me, *chavi*." Gil's words were the same ones he'd used a month before. Safe or unsafe, Fee needed to let go. She simply couldn't carry all her fears and doubts and memories by herself, anymore. And she didn't have to, because now she had Gil.

Whatever was too heavy for her, he would carry. Whatever hurt her too much, he could bear. He was formed by endurance, hardship, and survival. She leaned into him. He enclosed her with his strong arms. Exhaling against the safe harbor of his chest, she released everything she'd been clenching tight inside.

They sank down to the bed, lying side by side across it. Faces almost touching, they breathed into each other.

It was a dizzying moment, as though they'd rolled onto a ship that listed and swayed. Outside, the storm raged, all fury and wind. Gil's rickety wooden bed was the pea-green boat, with the Owl and the Pussycat rowing to sea with a song.

A different story, she reminded herself, *a different boat*. If Gil was in this boat, it was crossing the River Styx. And if Fee was everything she'd been told she was, she was snatching away boatman Charon's fare. There'd be a price to pay; she'd been told about that, too.

Now, though, she reached a hand to Gil's neck, playing her fingertips over the jagged scar of his death wound. Apart from the wound, the skin of his throat was smooth, lightly prickled by beard. Beneath it, hard tendons betrayed the effort he was putting into self-control.

"Please," she whispered, palming the back of his neck and pulling him to her. "Please, please, let me love you."

He would and he did. His warm, tender mouth was all permission, his hands said *yes* and *yes* and *yes*. He slid both arms under her, enveloping her. They lay that way, cocooned like drowsy moths, opening to each other.

When his mouth took hers, it was hot but gentle. A brush of lips, a scrape of beard. He could have gone hard and fast, taken her like a wildfire took dry grass. God knew she was ready enough. But he let time and the kiss drip desire into her mouth, drop by drop.

It wasn't only for her, the slow dominion of her mouth and body. She measured his need the way he was measuring it, in decades, centuries. He didn't want to overwhelm either of them, and he wanted it to last. Lying in his arms, Fee knew all that, knew it as she knew the moon would rise and the Thames would disappear under fog by morning.

Her ghost needed patience. She became patience itself, schooling herself to move at his pace.

Touch him. Her hands had slid from his neck and were curled between them. She dragged her fingertips across the linen of his shirt. Some powerful and wonderful drug let her feel every thread of the cloth.

Hear him. The hair of his chest made the faintest shush as she rubbed across the valley between his pectorals. Shifting in his embrace, she tilted her pelvis so they were groin to groin. He was hard as iron. When she moved against him, he moaned faintly, like a man on the edge of pain.

Taste him. She sought the flavors of him with her mouth, with little sucks and bites, and the flick of her tongue. He responded, oh so languidly, giving her the salt and sweat and sex of him.

When she thought she would die from not getting more, he threaded his hands into her hair, his fingers tightening to hold her fast. She knew only a second of razor-sharp desire before he captured her mouth entirely.

In the space of a breath, Fee knew that, before Gil, she'd never really kissed a man. *Been* kissed, too many times. Waited passively while some eager partner smacked his lips against hers, bit at her, slurped at her, poked his fat tongue into her. And even the men she'd liked...well, it hadn't been a case of wanting them as much as wanting sensation and eyes-shut release.

She would never shut her eyes with Gil. There was

too much to see and she needed to see it all. In daylight, candlelight, moonlight, sun, and shade. In the dark corners of the cellar, on the stage illumined by the off-and-on footlights, on the roof, washed silver by the moon. In the two attic rooms of which he was so proud. In his bed.

She wriggled her hands upward, between his arms, and stroked his hair. The strands were smooth ribbons, warm from his scalp. Her fingers wandered, tracing the proud arch of his nose, his forehead, his brows. His brows were fine, the hairs slick and short and richly sable like the hair of his head. Like the hair of his body that she'd seen when he was shirtless, a dark path disappearing into the waistband of his breeches.

So much of him to see, and no idea how much time they might have. *Not enough, not nearly enough.*

Time wasn't the only thing they wouldn't have. They'd never kiss in the ocean, standing upright in chest-high water while waves encouraged them against each other, again and again. Nor in the country, sheltering under a spreading tree while rain crashed down and cold drops made their way through the leaves. Nor at the breakfast table, when his mouth was sticky sweet with pancake syrup and she stood, laptop bag over her shoulder, giving him a *later, darling* smooch before she left for the Libe. All those things and more they'd never have.

But they had this.

"Gil," she whispered into his mouth. "*Gil.*"

Still kissing her, he shifted the two of them effortlessly to lie longways in the bed. He covered her, and Fee nearly sobbed at the perfect symmetry of their bodies.

Gil's tall, whipcord lean form suited her. It *fit*. The height she'd inherited from her father had always made her feel rangy and coltish. Her long limbs, the curves she'd inherited from her mother...until she and Gil lay pressed together on his bed, she'd never understood what they were for. Now, she knew; they were for *this*. She and Gil joined as though they'd been poured from the same mold, just tweaked in the right places to be male and female versions. His dark to her light, his steel to her velvet, but, in some ineffable way, the same. Impossible that they'd ever been apart. Impossible that they could ever be anything but together.

"Aoife, my soul, my heart." His deep murmur was full of want. She answered by pressing upward, letting her thighs part to take the length of him against her cleft, making him gasp. She pressed upward again, and a tremor ran through his whole body. Her sex clenched and throbbed.

She loved him. It came in an instant, as pure as water and as certain as the dawn. It might have been his words. It might have been his mouth, which shaped them so tenderly. It might have been her time to fall, and his time to catch her. Surrender arrived on a hot tide, rolling from her body into his and then ebbing, washing away fear.

"Gil, my Gil."

The time for patient exploration was over. Now, it was time for urgency and release, for opening and filling, for sweet, thoughtless rhythm. There was nothing between them but the weak argument of their clothes. Mouths still seeking and laving, they began the silent, inevitable baring of their bodies.

She helped with his shirt. He dragged her hoodie over her head, taking her pullover with it. He wrestled with her jeans until she pushed his hands away and did it herself, a fast and efficient unzipping and pushing downward, tugging off her shoes at the same time. Her underwear slid off her body as though it couldn't wait to get away.

He pushed up to his knees and began to unbutton his breeches. They snagged momentarily on the jut of his erection and they both smiled. Then, he shoved them down and he was bare before her. He was rampant as a stallion, his cock thick and ruddy. Her sharp little intake of breath clearly told him what she hungered for and he gave it, wrapping his hand around his length. His eyes never left hers as one downward drag from his fist pulled back his ample foreskin to expose him from glistening crown to root, his other hand cupping his balls. The gesture was clear. Everything he was, everything he had, was hers.

The next minutes were brusque and efficient. Pushing between her legs, he was inside her in one violent drive, making her cry out in shock and elation. Fee reached behind her and gripped the top of the mattress, then pressed her palms against the wooden headboard to brace against Gil's relentless pounding.

It wasn't art, it was fucking. Necessary, driven, and pure. He released a string of oaths—some she recognized, and some that owed their coarse syllables to ninth-century Saxon mouths. There was nothing else, just the hammering blows of his hips and the obscene thumping of the headboard against the wall.

She shouldn't have been ready, but heat pooled at her core. She planted her feet against the bed and lifted her pelvis, meeting Gil drive for drive. There was something so ferociously crude about their union, something she *needed.* Sparks of sensation jolted through her loins every time he slammed against her. Her response rose higher, higher—

He heaved off her as violently as he'd thrown himself on and rolled to her side. Stunned, Fee gulped air, trying to get up to speed. Was that it? Was he finished? Were they done?

"There's that," he said gruffly. "Onward."

Her bark of laughter didn't seem to affect Gil's plan of attack. He shoved his rumpled breeches off and onto the floor. "Oh, plums of my desire," he crooned, rolling back to his knees and pushing again between her legs. He was referring to her breasts, she quickly learned, when he crouched to cup them both. Fee's laughter turned to hitching breaths as his warm, roughened fingers squeezed and plucked at her. He brought his mouth down to one pebbled nipple and suckled it. Hard, then lighter, then hard again, alternating his mouth with fingers that circled and plucked at the rising bud.

Her strangled bleating seemed to inspire him, so he gave the same attention to her other breast while his free hand roamed lower. Unerringly finding her drenched opening, he plumbed it, palm up, to one finger's last knuckle, while she squirmed and gasped below him. A second finger slid alongside the first. Her hips rose, rocking helplessly against his hand. When his thumb went to work on the engorged trigger at her center, she abandoned all control. Mindlessly responsive, she clutched his shoulders and rode his hand for all she was worth. A keening moan rose from somewhere deep and primal inside her, the music of her pleasure, and he played it expertly.

She screamed.

Even as the brain-emptying spasms took her, Fee knew she'd never climaxed like that. Her body exploded with sensation, waves rippling outward from her core to shatter every cell. She defied gravity. If she was still on the bed, she couldn't feel it under her. Convulsing several feet above it—it made perfect sense.

It went on and on, hotter, sharper, until, whimpering, she grasped Gil's hand and pulled it away. She'd promised herself to keep her eyes open, but at some point during detonation, she'd squeezed them shut. *Look at him*, her recovering cognition told her. *Say something.*

Bless Gil's gifted fingers and mouth, he gave her no time for compliments. Fee forced open her eyes to see him on his knees, staring hotly between her thighs. His hand had left her still-quivering sex to wrap around his cock again. As she watched, he pumped it slowly.

Lifting his fierce gaze, he warned her, gruffly. "*Finis*, the prologue. Let the play commence."

He fell forward and into her.

———

No woman he'd known in his living years was like her, and no coupling had been like this. It wasn't only that in the past, fearful of making bastards like himself, he'd settled for rubbing the women to their release and rubbing himself to his own against their bodies, more often clothed than bared.

Through the red haze of his second mounting, a shred of alarm found its way. Was he harming her? Crushing her? Aoife was a strong woman. She might not, forsooth, be so strong as to throw him off her, but she could surely work a hand beneath her raised thigh, take hold of his bollocks, and wrench them hard enough to near geld him. That would get his attention.

Or she could shriek in his ear, next to which she panted. She had a good, loud scream; he'd brought it out of her minutes before. But he discerned no clamor of distress from her lips, despite the fact he was swiving her hard enough to drive nails. Her hands slid down his flanks and took hold of his buttocks. She pulled him against her, her utterances sounding favorable.

His name, in her voice, said over and over. Then, there were words, whorish and filthy words, from her pretty mouth. Every sound pleasured him as though she had him in her hand and was milking him to completion.

Oh, God, the sweetness of her! The hot, slick glove of her body gripped him until his control shredded and he was mad with the urge to finish. Drunk on the rose scent of her hair, he strove to hold back the inevitable even as it thundered toward him. The slide and slap of their flesh, the soft mounds of her breasts under him, the silky prison of her thighs enwrapping him. She arched and bucked, swore and begged, while the fire-tide of his peak roared in his ears.

"I must...I must..." He gasped against her shoulder

and was swept away. With a bone-deep shudder and a cry, he spent, spilling centuries of want into the narrow channel of her sex, the wracking of his loins so intense it was painful. No him, no her, just a union so complete it merged into oblivion.

———

He went…somewhere. Somewhere dark as night, sweet as Madeira wine. That he could connect Portugal to wine meant his reason was still intact. That he could feel the accursed mouse chewing the heel of his sock meant his body still lived.

Aoife. Had he killed her? Was she lying beneath him, a pile of ashes? And he, atop her, a burned-out branch still alight at both ends but hollowed by flame within?

Nay, she lived, he felt the jump of her heart under his. Slowly, the conjoined planes of their bodies also spoke of life. Sweat-slick bellies, the motion of their ribs, hair damp and tangled all together on their cheeks and foreheads.

He didn't roll so much as pour off her. Half on, half off, he wheezed like an ox, wanting but unable to speak Aoife's name. While he was scrabbling together his wits in order to say something poetic and fine, she pressed her face into his chest and gave a little cat-like sneeze.

"Why do you taste of ginger?" She sniffed his chest again, cautiously, like a housewife testing the freshness of a trout. "And smell of it, too."

"Ah, the way of a wench." 'Sdeath, his voice sounded like a man of eighty. With catarrh. He cleared his throat.

"Having had your way with me, you begin to catalogue my vices. I admit the most minor, straight away. I was, for years, overfond of ginger comfits."

He reached across her to Shakespeare, now sitting on the bed by Aoife's shoulder. The mouse had given up on the sock and was industriously ruining the shaved point of a quill. Plucking the quill out of its paws, he thrust it into Aoife's hair, declaiming.

"For Dido's sake, I take thee in my armes,
And sticke these spangled feathers in thy hat,
Eate Comfites in mine armes, and I will sing."

Giggling, Aoife extracted the quill and gave it back to Shakespeare, who scampered off with it in his jaws. Bugger, another pen gone.

"And who wrote that piece of fashion doggerel?" his beloved asked, nuzzling his chest and making him feel very manly. "It sounds vaguely familiar."

"Yes, well, *vague* is my favorite word for Christopher Marlowe. He wrote that in one of his more lucid moments. If you like that sort of thing, I can give you Nick Breton on the same subject."

Gil threw himself back in the bed and roared, "'A ginger comfit, whose taste did set my mouth all of a *heate!*'" Hauling Aoife atop him, he kept up the roaring as he bucked his hips and she howled with laughter. "Come here, my dainty Dolkin! Let me put my heated mouth upon your—"

At which very fine bit of dialogue, the bed collapsed.

Screaming understandably followed the event, as did

an impressive dust cloud. When she could speak, Aoife seized his arm and gasped, "Are you all right? Gil, talk to me!"

"I am unhurt, unmarked, and undamaged, apart from being most explosively unmanned by you before the bed let us down." He reached over her to pound the tilting headboard back in place, raising more dust. "And you, beauty, are you well?"

Aoife coughed, waving a hand in front of her face. "Reasonably. The bed must be an actor. It has impeccable timing."

"The floors are worthy of praise as well. Had they fallen along with the bed, we might have found ourselves pronging on the stage."

"Pronging?"

"A word the groundlings used in the thirties."

"Nineteen?"

"Seventeen."

"Here now, it's not a bad bed." She patted the side rail.

"'Tis only the slats were shocked into collapse by our use of them. A fine bed, otherwise."

"Did it come with the Olympiad?"

"Nay," he shook his head, then brushed damp strands off his forehead. "'Twas left behind after the mercifully brief run of *Sick-a-bed*. Three weeks and closed not a moment too soon."

"Never heard of it."

"You missed nothing."

"A production company left a whole *bed* behind?"

"Not the first to do so." He waved toward the First

Room. "Bed, chairs, desk, clothing, wigs, books. I've quite the collection. When we've nothing better to do, I'll show you."

"I think," she said as she kissed and then licked his shoulder, sending a quaver through his whole body and making his cock stir, "we'll always have something better to do."

Twenty-Seven

Six days, five nights. It was both disturbing and delicious that her first thoughts every morning were of her last hours with Gil. If she was honest with herself, and it was too late for fiction, her thoughts for the rest of the day belonged to him, too.

Mostly him. Now and then, she squeezed in a few hours of digging up more proof of the Coronet's existence. But she hadn't written a word on *Lesser Lights* in so long she couldn't remember what she'd written or when. *I'll get around to it*, she told herself.

Six days, five nights with Gil. It was like a package tour. *See London, Paris, Dijon, Amsterdam, Interlaken, Bruges!* Gilbert Sorley, the unscheduled stop, where every night she stepped off the train and stayed a week, an eternity.

With a yawn and a stretch, she registered pleasurable soreness in all the right places. Places that had been exercised thoroughly by a man whose skill in bed hadn't suffered at all from three-hundred-plus years of disuse. Last night, as always, her post-exercise sleeping was deep and dreamless. Aggravatingly, she always woke at seven, even if she'd returned to the flat in the pre-dawn hours.

She didn't think she'd overslept today, but she was too comfortable to reach over to the nightstand and check her cellphone. It was impossible to guess the time from the ambient light in her bedroom, as there was no window. Even if there had been one, the sun wasn't making too many appearances over London lately. Winter was coming, days shortening, nights lengthening.

Another luxuriant stretch and she let herself sink into the bed, burrowing under the duvet and pulling a pillow tight against her body.

Comfort wise, the lumpy mattress in the Olympiad's attic was as far from the flat's hybrid foam-plus-springs as Hyderabad was from Covent Garden, but it had the incomparable advantage of Gil's body in it. Apart from the mating at intervals—three, four—throughout the night, they talked. There'd been one challenging conversation in which she explained oral contraceptives, his summation being that she oughtn't to buy cures from strange apothecaries unless she knew they'd not killed anyone. Apart from that, they used their talk to learn about each other. Last night, she'd asked about his mother.

"Do you know her name?"

Gil was lying on his back, staring at the rafters. "I know less of her than a flea knows of its dam." He lifted a relaxed hand to his forehead, pushing back the dark locks that fell, as they frequently did, over his forehead. "I have her hair, that much I know, as my sire was yellow-haired as a Saxon ploughboy. But of her name, her family? Nothing."

"Did the Rom even have surnames at that time?" She period-corrected herself. "Family names?"

He'd been lying snug against her, one arm under her head. Rolling on his side to face her, he brought his other hand to her cheek and stroked it. "Some did. Some did and claimed not to. Many did but declined to share them with *gadje*, as a name leaves a trail and one might wish, for many reasons, not to be followed." He substituted a thumbnail for the pads of his fingers on her cheek. The gentle scrape sent liquid fire between her legs, and she struggled to stay on the subject.

"'What's in a name?'" she whispered. "'That which we call a rose—'"

"Pray don't bring Old Will into bed with us, or my pole will sag."

She reached down to grasp it, found it in no danger of sagging, and gave it an affectionate squeeze, making him growl. Before they both utterly lost track of the conversation, she said, "I'm going to try another tack to stop the investors from taking the Olympiad. The Trust isn't the only organization I can harass. I'll try the people at MOLA again."

Gil's brow furrowed. "A society of moles?"

"For all the good they've done us so far, they might as well be." She took his hand from her cheek and put it on her breast. "I can't guarantee they'll be any more helpful than the Trust, but first thing tomorrow I'll visit them."

He kissed the tip of her nose. "You are the most enterprising of women. Don't give up the canoe."

"Ship. Don't give up the ship."

"Ah. I have here an oar you may need." He nudged his tool against her thigh.

"That's not an oar," she giggled into his mouth. "That's the mainmast."

And then, there'd been sighing and clutching and arching and ecstasy. MOLA and the Coronet and greedy investors slid away as the night became another of the five in a row she and Gil had given each other in his bed. Would have been six, but she'd let Abeni and Sarah drag her to the salsa club on Friday last, as she'd promised. That night was every bit as bad as she'd feared. Men serially attached themselves to her and she spent as much time dodging propositions as she spent dancing. Abeni noticed.

"Something's different about you, Fee." Abeni leveled surprisingly sober eyes at Fee as they stood at the bar, shouting into each other's ears over the music and ordering their fourth round of RumChata and Fireball shots. It was lucky they'd been dancing the liquor off all night. Otherwise, they'd have been facedown on the floor.

"New shampoo," Fee cheerfully shouted back.

Abeni's eyebrows lifted the way they did when she smelled a rat. Their drinks arrived and they separated with them, Abeni back to Sarah and Fee to her partner of the hour. Armando? Cristofero? Whomever he was, she never let him or any man buy her drinks. It was partly a safety thing and partly that she hated dealing with the sneaking sense of obligation some men attached to the act of paying for a beverage.

Even without the dubious drink transactions, she'd had to lay down the law with her dance partners that night. *No es no*, she'd told one of them. Twice. Maybe Abeni was right. Maybe, without knowing it, she was giving off sexual signals of some sort.

She clambered out of bed and into the bathroom. The mirror reflected her usual early morning self. Tousled. Heavy-eyed. A red splotch on one cheek from sleeping squashed against the pillow. No visible signs of licentiousness.

Pheromones, maybe. They might be jacked up. Figuring it out demanded too much chemistry before breakfast, so she washed her face and shuffled into the kitchen.

"You've got post." Abeni, munching away at her Weetabix, jutted her chin at the fruit bowl on the table. Fee sagged into a chair and examined the bowl. Jammed between two bananas was a gray envelope. She hadn't enjoyed the last mail she'd pulled from the bowl, and from the Wales postmark on this one, she was pretty sure she wouldn't enjoy it, either.

If she'd had her tea, if she'd been more awake, if she hadn't still been slightly drunk on thoughts of Gil, she would've waited until Abeni left for her morning classes. Instead, she plucked out the envelope, ripped open one end, and shook out the letter inside. The single sheet of gray notepaper matched the envelope. Unfolded, the sheet displayed a familiar three-line letterhead in royal blue.

The Broom & Bottle
Divination, Botanicals, Esoterica
Jana Smithbury-Tewkes, Proprietor

The letter began like Jana's phone calls, no salutation and right to the point.

Morgana inherited Selene's collection of antique grimoires. She's been going through them, but it's slow work. Most are extremely faded with age, and some weren't highly legible when they were new. Potion spills, bad penmanship, grammar mistakes, spelling—the spelling is atrocious.

Fee knew all about the atrocious, or at least capricious, period spelling. She'd spent the past few years buried up to her eyebrows in original documents from Tudor England to the Restoration.

I asked Morgana to keep an eye out for anything Selene might have missed when she went through the grimoires earlier, before your mum and you rejoined your father. Morgana wasn't hopeful, since right up to the end of her life, Selene didn't miss much.

As though Selene had entered the room and taken a seat at the kitchen table, Fee had a strong sense of the elder witch. When, at age four, Fee first met her, Selene seemed a small woman. By the time Fee, grown tall at seventeen, came back from Paris, Selene barely reached Fee's breastbone. She remembered the old witch's hair. Unbound as always, it fell in a curtain to her ankles, as white-silver as the moon for which she was named. And she had a voice as soft as moth wings, potent for all it was so delicate. *Read on, granddaughter*, the voice fluttered from across the kitchen table. *Read on.*

It wasn't surprising Selene overlooked this bit in a 1616 Gloucestershire spell book. Just three lines, barely decipherable, and Selene's glaucoma got pretty bad in her last years. Morgana took a picture of the page on her mobile and sent it to me so I could save it. Wren helped me clean up the image and convert it to a file. This is just as it appears in the grimoire, only easier to read.

A photo was embedded in the letter. As Jana said, the writing wasn't clear—just clear enough to scare Fee.

Most grievus is the Pain suffr'd by Hester upon her Soul's conveyance. She doth weep all the daye and will take no Consolation. She wast forewarnt some-such thing was like to come, but Love brookes no Reeson.

Fee stopped reading and looked over the top of the letter. Abeni was still crunching away on her shredded wheat. She'd propped an open book against the oat milk carton and was absorbed in it. Fee went back to the letter.

There wasn't much after "brookes no Reeson." What the hell else would Jana need to add? Fee already knew she and Gil were way past reason and deep into madness. She scanned the letter's closing lines.

I've said it before, Aoife, and all I can do is repeat it. Mind how you go. Jana

Fee heard a sound and jerked her eyes up. Abeni wasn't reading her book anymore. She appeared to be reading Fee's face. *Enigmatic* was the word for her flat mate's expression. Her question was cryptic, too.

"Did I ever tell you about my *maame*?"

"Your mother?"

"Uh huh. She's an *okomfo*. An ancestor priestess."

"An ancestor priestess." Fee didn't remember every little part of Abeni's family story from when they'd first met in London, but surely she would've remembered *that*. "No, I don't recall that you—"

"I thought maybe when we came to England, she'd give it up, but she's as popular here as she was in Ghana. More, maybe, since ancestor priestesses are pretty thin on the ground in Yorkshire. Her given name is Kuukuwa, but the neighbors call her Okomfo Kate."

To have something for her hands to do, Fee folded Jana's letter and put it back in the envelope. Her fingers trembled slightly as she lay the envelope on the table, address side down.

She reached across for the Weetabix box. Why was it every time she and Abeni had these awkward chats, she ended up eating forage-in-a-bowl? "Are you telling me about your mother for a reason, Abeni?" Fee started to shake out a shredded wheat biscuit, then realized she didn't have a plate. Or a bowl. Or a spoon.

"I heard you last night."

Fee didn't reply, just left the table in search of eating

implements. She also switched on the kettle, since it had cooled. She was going to need a lot of tea for this chat. "Heard me what?"

"Talking in your sleep."

"I don't sleep talk, or whatever it's called. Nothing in my sleep but sleeping. No walking, snoring, dancing, chatting—"

"Maybe not before. But you're doing it now." As Fee returned to the table with a bowl and spoon, Abeni closed her book and put it aside, front cover up. *The Atlas of Street Art.* Very Slade.

"So, I'm sleep talking." Fee mentally sent herself a thumbs up emoji for calm control. "What about?"

"I'm gonna say a man. You were calling his name. I couldn't make it out, exactly, but it sounded...mannish."

The teakettle switched off with a click that on an ordinary day would barely have caught Fee's attention. This morning, she almost levitated off her chair. Abeni waited as though she expected more from her, but she'd have to wait all year before she got Gil's name.

Fee took a linen napkin off the stack on the table. There were only two left: her fault, since she hadn't been laundering and pressing them lately. She'd been busy. Needlessly opening and then refolding the napkin, she put it next to her bowl and spoon. "Yeah, I was dreaming. I sort of remember. Tall, dark, handsome. You know, the usual dream lover."

She thought Abeni would make one of her ribald comments. *How dark? Send him to me if his tongue still works when you're through with him. Does he have a sister?* What she did was take the talk back to her mother.

"*Maame* embarrassed me when I was young. Single mum, fine, that wasn't so rare. But an ancestor priestess? Someone who will tell you how to keep bad ghosts away from your door?" She shook her head. "The strangest parents on my street before we moved in were Mr. and Mrs. Ainsley. They taught ballroom dancing."

The reference to being embarrassed by a parent jogged Fee's memory. There'd been a woman on her lacrosse team at UNC whose parents ran a traveling oddities show. Sooz McGarvey told some hair-raising stories about what her family did from time to time, but neither Sooz nor Abeni could compete with the degree of weirdness Fee's family passed around the dinner table.

"Just because I'm kissing and telling in my sleep," she said pointedly, "doesn't mean I'm a victim of demonic possession, Abeni."

Abeni pushed out of her chair and went to the kitchen counter. She rooted out Fee's V&A Museum mug, popped a bag of Daybreak in it, and added steaming water from the kettle.

"Not all spirits are demons, Fee. Though Mum's the expert, not me." She brought the mug to the table and put it in front of Fee. "I don't know who's disturbing your nights or if he's disturbing your days, too. I just know something's not right with you." Abeni stayed standing next to Fee's chair. The hand she dropped on Fee's shoulder was warm and strong. Impulsively, Fee reached up and placed her own hand atop it.

"Just to say," Abeni went on, "when I got over being a snotty little twit embarrassed by her parent, I realized *Maame* did a lot of good for a lot of people. I'm not saintin' her, Fee, she knows things. She *sees* things." Abeni gave Fee's shoulder a rough squeeze and then headed for the shower. She turned her head and flung back a last remark. "Let me know if you want me to text her."

TWENTY-EIGHT

No texting your mum, Abeni. Not yet.

She hadn't said it aloud to her flat mate, but Fee repeated it to herself like a charm all morning as she prepped for her second visit to the Museum of London Archeology. At eleven, so preoccupied with what she planned to say in the meeting that she hardly remembered how she got there, she faced off with three staffers in the organization's offices at 150 London Wall. It was a tight squeeze in the conference room. At one end, dangerously crooked towers of taped boxes left barely enough space for a table, four chairs, three MOLA staffers, and her.

More than packing boxes contributed to an air of impermanence in the building. In one sense, the impermanence was odd, considering MOLA was jammed up to ruins so old they seemed eternal—the AD 200 wall of Londinium, the Roman settlement from which modern London eventually evolved. In another sense, it was understandable. MOLA was in the throes of relocation to new headquarters in Smithfield. Maybe, Fee rationalized, the impending move was responsible for her feeling that the staffers were trying to get rid of her as quickly as possible. They probably had more packing to do.

Or maybe MOLA had already made up its collective mind not to investigate a cellar in Covent Garden and the staffers had been hoping they wouldn't have to say so to Fee's face.

The staffer at the far end of the table was Nazir Desai, who'd given her critical looks weeks ago about cleaning her silver penny. He had his surgical gloves on again. All three MOLA people did. None of them had name badges, but Fee had one. It was a stick-on label she'd been given at the front desk that read *Aoife Gowdie Ó Loinsigh, A.B.D.* in black marker. She'd insisted on the letters following her name; she needed every edge she could get.

She didn't really know the other MOLA staffers at the table. There'd been a brisk round of introductions when she first entered the room, but she was so nervous she immediately forgot two names. She thought the women might be Maureen and Margaret. Or Marin and—

"Is this all you have?" Nazir was holding up the two clear vinyl pouches she'd brought. One held the silver penny. The other contained a few ceramic shards from one of the coin boxes. Each shard had a tiny, numbered label on the back, keyed to a sketch Fee had made of the shards in situ. Nazir didn't seem impressed with her dig technique.

Go on, Nazir. Just nut up and tell me I'm wasting your time. Fee pulled a third pouch from her bag and held it up. "I also found quite a lot of clinker." Clinker was the gray, pebbly waste used as filler in many old structures. The pouch was half full of it.

Nazir barely glanced at her or the pouch. "Clinker's everywhere."

Maybe Margaret, a plump, kindly-smiling brunette in her thirties, smoothed over her colleague's brusque comment. "I'm afraid Nazir's right. Clinker was used and re-used for centuries. Even if a particular sample can be dated as 17th century, that doesn't mean it wasn't dumped into the foundation of a later building."

Fee had known the clinker was marginal as proof went, but she still had hopes for her photos. She handed over her cellphone. "The second coin box is a little more intact than the one I took those shards from. Obviously, I didn't want to disturb it, but you can see the style of it in the photos. It's almost identical to the glazed pottery examples found at the Rose Theatre." The MOLA people huddled to peer at the phone while Nazir swiped through the images.

Fee gave them a minute and then handed over a file folder. "Here are some drawings I made of my dig, with the finds marked. And a projected floor plan of the 1600s theatre." Her floor plan was actual, not projected, but she couldn't very well say she'd copied Gil's.

Nazir frowned. "A floor plan for a 1600s theatre you uncovered by rooting around in the cellar of a condemned building."

And from pillow talk with a ghost, but let's not split hairs. Despite the unease shrilling in her chest, Fee forced out a courteous reply. "The Olympiad Theatre is, in fact, quite sound. Up until now, no one's suggested it should be condemned."

Marin/Maureen spoke. "It was bombed during the Blitz, wasn't it?"

Fee shook her head. It felt strange not to feel her thick curls brushing her face, but along with wearing office attire—plaid skirt, white blouse, navy jacket—she'd scraped her hair into a tight bun to look more professional. Less demented. "Not actually hit, not directly. A building across Drury Lane got a seventy-kilogram bomb and several structures in the area suffered cracks from the concussion. But repairs were done on the Olympiad and it's sound to this day."

"That's not necessarily a good thing, Miss *Gow-dee*." Nazir pronounced her name wrong, as people usually did. "It's harder to mount a formal excavation under an intact building than on a site where a redundant one's been pulled down."

Fee mentally kicked herself for bringing up the Rose. Now, Nazir was thinking of that site, where archeologists were still struggling to maintain a dig in the basement of a towering office building erected, despite loud objections, over the footprint of an Elizabethan theatre. "True, but it's possible to accomplish both the dig and the pulling down if everyone knows ahead of time what they're dealing with. It's all a matter of doing things in the right order. Right now, the plan is to simply raze the Olympiad and—"

"We know about that," Maybe Margaret, sounding not as benign as her smile, broke in. "Morsani-Loeb Futura, a consortium of investors, has a mixed-use project slated for next year. The site is just outside the height-restricted area, making it very attractive to developers. The plan is for ground floor shops, six floors of offices, and eight luxury flats at the top."

Luxury flats at the top. Silk purses made from Gil's sow's ear lodging. Velux skylights over Thuma beds. Smeg fridges and Aga ranges in the kitchens. Stunning décor! Breathtaking views!

Gone the scarred oak desk and four-legged chair, of which Gil was so fond. Gone the man who composed poetry and plays while sitting there.

Her knee was bouncing with nervous tension. Fee willed it to stop and spoke firmly. "I'm hoping that a serious inspection of the cellar will reveal important historical remains." *Go long or go home, Fee.* "My research indicates a circa 1603 theatre called the Coronet stood on the spot before the Olympiad was built."

The muteness from the MOLA staffers was somehow louder than any verbiage could have been. Nazir, who'd taken the Charles First coin from its pouch, froze with it held between his thumb and forefinger, like he was poised to drop it into a slot in a vending machine.

Maybe Margaret found her voice first. "Quite a detailed conclusion. What's your evidence?"

Ah, well, that. She'd known the question was coming, and she hoped her answer sounded more confident than it did when she was rehearsing it in her head on the way to 150 London Wall. "I'm compiling all my proof in a dossier." She'd chosen the word carefully. The faint whiff of espionage and state secrets might lend the project cachet. "I'll have it on your desks very soon."

Nazir dropped the coin into its pouch, then handed both pouches and the file folder back to her. "By then, our desks may be in the Mortimer Wheeler House on Eagle Wharf Road." Fee knew the address. Spacious, impressive, joining MOLA's other buildings in Hampshire, Northamptonshire, and the West Midlands.

Marin/Maureen smiled. It was a nice smile, but she stood as she made it, signaling the end of their little talk. "Miss Gowdie, you've been very industrious, but it may be necessary for you to confront the hard reality we here at MOLA confront every day. There are more historic properties in London than we'll ever be able to document, much less rescue."

Maybe Margaret, still in her seat, added, "They're like stray cats. You want to save all of them. But you can't."

Rising, Nazir chimed in. "And we still serve at the pleasure of the National Trust, as you know."

Fee jumped to her feet. To be the last one sitting would look unbearably needy. "Of course." Everyone was standing, then. With the people, the table, the boxes, and the fug of disappointment, the room felt claustrophobic. She gathered her artifacts and folder and slipped them into her laptop bag. "Thank you for your time."

Nazir squeezed around the table to open the door for her. "I want you to know we're in regular contact with Marcus Bellwether and Anthea Cookson on this." No surprise there. Along with Dr. Gretchen Hyde, they probably wore the same school tie. "We look forward to seeing your notes on the site, Miss Oh Loynsee, though we're at sixes and sevens until the move. I'm sure you appreciate that."

They exited in single file through the door, a pleasant expression on every face. The norm, in other words, for people who meant exactly the opposite of what they'd just said. In the hallway, polite goodbyes went around. Splitting up, Fee headed toward the exit and the MOLA staffers returned to desks that, for the time being, still overlooked the traces of Londinium.

None of them said *get lost, good riddance, don't waste our time*, but the words hung in the air, anyway, like a bad smell.

Gil. She had to get back to Gil.

TWENTY-NINE

"They don't believe me."

Gil gathered her to him in the bed. It had gone stone cold outside all at once, the way England did in the fall. While weather meant nothing to him, his Aoife suffered from it. He pulled his meager blankets up to cover her, bundling her shivering form.

Haltingly, she gave him the gist of her meeting at the Mole Guild, the words coming out angry, then desperate, finally not coming at all as she wept into his shoulder.

She'd been hurt, and Gil murmured comfort at the same time he fumed and boiled with rage. What sort of man was he, that he could do aught but hold her after she'd been buffeted so cruelly by the world?

When the sobbing stopped, she wiped her face on the hem of the sheet she'd brought to his lodging the week before. She'd said she couldn't stand a bed without linens. "I'm not giving up. Who the hell are those pen-pushers at MOLA, anyway? They can't lift a finger without the National Trust. I'll keep working on the Trust."

"That's my fearsome queen. Don't throw in the sponge."

"Towel. Don't throw in the towel." She smiled, and his heart wrapped around the sight, locking it away like treasure.

The moment's joy cowered under the persistent charge of his guilt. A platitude was all he could give her. A foolish aphorism about towels or sponges or standing firm. What help was that in securing her heart's desire? A man should fight his woman's battles, not leave her to strap on the bag she slung across her shoulders like a shield and stride forth, alone, to confront her foes.

He stroked her cheek, never tiring of the silken feel of it. "This old ruin. Does it matter to you so much, *chavi*?"

"Tomorrow matters."

"Ah, but no, tomorrow matters not at all. Only today, this hour. Be here with me. Let me love you."

Each time they coupled was different, as though they changed in themselves from day to day and from one joining to the next. Strangers afresh at every meeting, they found infinite joy and diversion in each other's bodies. He'd gathered from the lewd prattle he'd overheard backstage across the decades that women in the modern age were more forthright in amorous adventure than their foremothers. He did not think that true, or perhaps he'd known more than his fair share of rambunctious females in his day. But if it were true that the sisterhood of his beloved were a frisky lot, then Aoife was, to his unending delight, one of the friskiest.

She gave as good as she got, never failed to command him to touch her one way, swive her another, and rode him as hard as any Amazon with a warhorse between her thighs.

Not this day. This day, she welcomed him with poignant tenderness. Submissive as a doe, she lay quietly and let him mount her, enter her, while she did aught but enfold him like the sea. The sweet paradox was that her docility drove his lust to an almost bestial intensity.

'Twas fear laying the whip on him; he knew it. A consuming fear that lashed him, body and soul. Fear that he was losing her, that they were losing each other, that all they had was melting like April snow under the merciless sun of their diverging fates. Her yielding softness called forth the stiffest prick that had ever sprung from his loins, one that lasted uncannily. Still hard after his first too-quick spending, he kept inside her body. Before his violent spasms had even subsided, he took her again. Mad in the moment, he thought he could fuck them to safety. Delve into her, fill her...he would leave no space for that other grim lover, Time.

With their second coupling, she seemed to come alive and join his desperate drive to immortality. With a cry as much of sorrow as lust, she struggled from under him and rose to her hands and knees, facing away. Head and shoulders pressed to the bed, sweet arse upraised, she reached behind and pulled her thighs apart to open herself entirely. Fierce as a buck deer, he grasped her hips and drove into her. Every foul oath he'd learned in his hardscrabble life rose up and out of his throat. Each thrust sent flames of pleasure through his cock and balls to ignite the base of his spine. The slick, wet sheath enclosing him tightened; her body burned with his.

Sweating and swearing like a drover, he crouched over her, his body shuddering on the edge of release. "Never leave me," he forced out through clenched teeth, reaching a hand under her to stroke her slit. "Never—"

Then, they were crying out together, spending together, their breath and bodies quaking. Falling together, into the ermine-soft bed of completion.

———

For as long as it would take to say the Pater Noster a dozen times—Gil was tempted, for surely a miracle deserved thanks even from damned souls like himself— he and Aoife lay silent and full, letting their hearts calm until they found a matching rhythm. He prized that part of their union more than the rest. Well, perhaps not *all* the rest, but the hour just after they joined was always a prize. An hour untroubled and pure. Domestic. The tranquil union of two old dray horses in a barn, yoked together for seasons uncounted, so practiced in each other's ways that even their resting breaths moved in and out together.

Not that they'd have a chance to become old together, to become anything together other than the uncertain and haphazard collection of days and nights they would have before the ruined theatre came down. As sublime as was the most recent, Gil felt the weight of centuries pressing upon him. They bore him under a sea of despair like stones in the pockets of a suicide.

As in all other moments, their thoughts twinned. She breathed a question against his chest. "If the Olympiad is demolished, Gil, what happens to you?"

He kissed her forehead, brushing sweat-salty hair away with his lips. "Do not vex yourself with such questions, sweetling."

"I can vex myself with them here or somewhere else. What happens?"

"Do you imagine I know? Your faith in my prescience flatters me, but in truth I cannot say." Or could he? He began hesitantly. "There was a leech."

"A doctor?"

"Phineas Gravely, an inauspicious name for that trade. He dispensed cures from his house on Wych Street at the Strand, and there he died in the reign of Edward the Seventh."

"Early 1900s?"

"Just so. The house stood until late in the reign of George Fourth—"

"1940s?"

"In the region of. The Olympiad was dark by then, so I had not the chatter of theatre folk to keep me apprised of changes in the Garden and the passage of years. The great explosions and balloons in the sky had gone, so it was after the War, I think." He bent his head to kiss her shoulder, petal-soft like her cheek. "Displaced from his house by the new roadways, the ghost of the leech came here for a time. I found him pleasant enough company, if a little dull. After a few months, he...dispersed."

The island of warmth made by their bodies was no

match for whatever made Aoife shiver in his arms. "What do you mean, *dispersed*?"

For an uneasy interval, Gil didn't answer. When he finally did, he knew he sounded as perplexed by the incident as when it transpired. "I saw it happen, and yet I cannot say how or why. As you know from the mouse," he waved a hand at Shakespeare, who'd come into the bed after the jouncing of the mattress ended and was curled into a ball of pale mist at the foot, "ghosts have not much substance to begin with. Old Phineas had been growing less substantial for weeks, and more disjointed in his speech. One day, we sat together before the stage—there were many seats, then—and he rambled on about mercury and calomel. Then, he simply came apart before my eyes.

"It was like watching a handful of dust, blown away by a breath."

They both looked again at Shakespeare, his faint luminosity expanding and contracting with mouse breaths. Aoife's question plucked at Gil's heart. "That will happen to Shakespeare, won't it?"

Gil enfolded her. He could not change fate, that was certain sure. But he must be proof against her fear of it. "Perhaps, it will," he said into her hair. "But, if so, it will be when he has somewhere else to be. Like Phineas."

Like Gil himself, but he hoped she wouldn't force a discussion of that. His hope was futile, since she wriggled out of his arms and sat bolt upright. "You're different. You're not a ghost, you're a *leathling*."

He pulled her back to lie alongside him. "Am I? You are the learned one in these matters, Aoife. I would have called myself a leg of mutton and 'twere all the same to me."

She popped up again, like a jack-in-the-box. "Leathlings aren't ghosts."

The words had the unarguable tone of Holy Writ. *Sayeth this, the Lord Almighty.* He sighed and sat up as well. "Both are dead," he reminded her.

Her headshake was vigorous, jiggling her breasts. Like cream puddings, they were, with cherries on top. Gil's unruly prick said very approving things about them, and hoped her sermon would be a short one.

"You're only part dead," she told him firmly. "The rest of you is alive."

"If you said that in the street," he remonstrated gently, "you'd be popped straight away into a madhouse."

She didn't pursue the notion, just reached to the floor next the bed and brought up the palm-sized black implement she carried with her everywhere. Her "mobile foan," she called it. Whene'er she tapped it into life, Gil stifled the urge to snatch the thing out of her hands and fling it from the window. Surely no good could come from an infernal device like that.

"Leave me a message," she told him, looking into his eyes with as serious an expression as he'd ever seen on her features. "Like, a letter. As though I'm in France, or America. Just a few lines." She brought her attention back to the device and tapped it lightly several times, then held it up to face him. "Speak to it. It will transcribe your words."

Aoife reached her thumb around to tap the thing

again. Gil felt moon mad for talking to a tool, as though she'd held up a mallet and asked him to recite to it. But she was his queen, and whatever she commanded...he held her eyes as he spoke.

"The heart that in my breast beats, thine. Eternally, beyond the death of time."

Aoife touched the face of the device once more and then held it in cupped hands, her eyes bright with tears unshed. "Listen," she told him, and tapped the thing yet again, then raised it between them.

Gil swore as sound came forth. That it was him, his words, his voice—of that, he had no doubt. He'd seen many marvels over the decades, even trapped as he was in the moldering wreck of the Olympiad, but rarely at such close range. It dislodged his composure mightily.

"Did a necromancer sell that thing to you? Is it safe?"

Aoife laughed, wiping the wet from her eyes with one hand and poking at the "foan" with the other. "Let's hear you again."

Again and again and again they heard it, until the newness went off and Gil told himself it was naught but a conjurer's trick. He'd seen a fellow at a street fair once who pulled a live dove from a blazing pan, no harm to the bird and the fire extinguished with a shouted command.

Whatever Aoife's "foan" was, it was passing strange, but he would think no more about it. Real magic was in his arms. He kissed and petted her until she put the device aside.

They conjured pleasure, then.

THIRTY

It was late afternoon the next day before she tore herself away from the Olympiad. Earlier in the month, she'd left Gil a paperback copy of Racine's *Phaedre*, written after Gil's death. He knew the Seneca original, as most literate 17th century people did, but he was ecstatic at the spin Racine gave the tragedy of forbidden desire and betrayal. His delight was nothing to what Aoife felt when he said he'd like to act a few scenes with her. Before Gil, she'd have had no hope of a role like that.

They rehearsed the whole morning and half the afternoon. Drained but blissful, she got on the bus taking her to Bloomsbury from Drury Lane. As she walked the two blocks from the stop to the flat, her mood balloon began deflating, thoughts about the Olympiad's future poking holes in it.

Even though her emotions fought back, logic and experience told her to accept the truth of Maybe Margaret's remark about stray cats. In a way, historic sites *were* like rescue animals. It was terrible, but no one could save them all. The sad addendum to the work of everyone in preservation was that they found historic remains, exulted over them, documented them, fought for their survival...

And lost them, more often than not, to public disinterest or economic priorities. If Gilbert Sorley weren't in the Olympiad, she'd have abandoned it to its fate long ago. But Gil *was* in the Olympiad. His fate was hers. Abandoning him wasn't something she could even think about, much less do.

Christ, she was tired. And hungry, which was probably the cause of the headache she was nursing. Eating was a low priority when she was with Gil, and she routinely forgot to bring food to the theatre. Maybe she should go for a quick swim in the King's College pool. A dozen laps would clear her brain fog. Abeni might even meet her there and afterward they could go for a meal and a drink or three, anything to lift her spirits and her blood sugar. She dug for her phone, but before she could tap Abeni's name in her contacts, her flat mate's ringtone sounded. Fall Out Boy, *Light Em Up*.

"Abeni, hey! I was just about to call you. Would you—"

"Are you on your way back to the flat?"

"Uh, yeah, I'm almost there. Why? Are we out of oat milk again?"

"No, just—it's something else."

"What else? Tea? Weetabix?"

"We'll talk when you're here."

Abeni rang off and Fee stared at the screen so long

she almost missed her turn to the flat. Now, she was headachy, hungry, and confused. It must have been her week for inconclusive conversations, in which case Sunday couldn't come soon enough.

Five minutes later, she unlocked the flat door and slouched inside. The pain in her head got much worse when she saw who was on the sofa, waiting for her.

Abeni sat with a woman who looked so much like an older version of her, she had to be her mother.

Abeni lobbed confirmation over the net. "You remember my mum, Fee."

Oh, she remembered. Not from an in-person meeting, but from the conversation she and Abeni had just a week ago, at the kitchen table over breakfast. Abeni's mum, the ancestor priestess.

Fee started to put her laptop bag on the coffee table as she always did, but halted when she saw the table was covered with tea things. The good floral china teacups and saucers. Sugar bowl, creamer. Abeni's loud paper napkins. A plate of Rich Tea biscuits.

She turned away long enough to find another place for her bag and to hang her mac and scarf on the pegs behind the door. And to control her face. First Dr. Gretchen Hyde, then Abeni's mother. For the second time in two weeks, she'd been dropped into what looked a lot like an intervention. A disturbing trend.

Tacking on a smile, she turned to extend a hand to Abeni's mother. "Hello, Mrs. Addo," she said with restrained warmth. "It's a pleasure to meet you."

Mrs. Addo squeezed her fingers and released them. "Oh, my dear, please call me Kate." Her voice didn't have the broad Yorkshire vowels of Abeni's, unsurprising since Mrs. Addo had been a grown woman when she left Ghana for the U.K. Formally schooled English blended with a lyrical African accent, a nice match to the modish skirt and heels she wore with a brilliantly colored *kente* cloth blouse and head wrap. "I feel I already know you, since I have heard so much about you from my daughter."

Fee took her eyes off Mrs. Addo and planted them firmly on Abeni, but Abeni's were downcast. Her flat mate was scrutinizing the cookies as though the Holy Grail was hidden among them and she could stare it out.

"Have some tea," Abeni suddenly said without raising her eyes.

"Tea's good," Fee told the pair of *ambuscaderas*. A double Scotch would be better, but that wasn't going to materialize. "What I could really murder is some food. Let's go out. My treat."

Her wallet was a little thin, but she'd feel better if she could get her visitor out of the flat. There was only so much priestessing Mrs. Addo could do over a menu.

———

Fee walked them to Bel Antalya, a little Turkish place that was normally too crowded to turn around in, but had thinned out in late afternoon. The choice was deliberate. It would be difficult for Mrs. Addo to dispense Ghanaian wisdom while figuring out what *mercimek köftesi* and *ezogolin corba* were. The moment they entered, one of the owners, a built-like-a-wall man in a suit whose short, graying beard ornamented a granite jaw, swiveled his attention to Abeni's mother and riveted it in place. Twice before their orders were in, he lumbered to their table like a purposeful bear and made suggestions from the menu, the whole while staring with dark, enraptured eyes at Mrs. Addo.

Mrs. Addo took the attention like a woman who was used to it. Handsome, exotic, and self-assured, she probably enraptured men the length and breadth of Britain. Abeni had never mentioned Mr. Addo. Had he died? Been left behind in Ghana? Maybe Mrs. Addo had always been a single mom, like Fee's mother before she'd flown through time to Paris in the—

"Not all ghosts become ancestors."

"Wha—? I'm sorry, I wasn't—*what?*" Fee's mouth and her brain jumped ship at the same time, leaving her floundering. Her eyes slewed wildly across the table to Abeni, who appeared deeply interested in her water glass. Or maybe she was used to her mother's nonsequiturs about the afterlife. With a priestess for a mom, who knew what dinner conversation in the Addo house consisted of?

Mercifully, their food arrived before any of them had to row the conversational boat back to shore. Over *gozleme,* flatbread stuffed with savory fillings, and glasses of Turkish tea, Fee and Abeni avoided looking directly at each other while Mrs. Addo serenely took in the restaurant and the food. Her Turkish bear continued to stare at her longingly from behind the small bar. As a waiter cleared their dishes, he came to their table again.

"I have ordered coffee and pastries," he rumbled like a

locomotive engine. "My gift to you." Since he really meant *my gift to the African goddess who has graced my café*, he made a little bow to Mrs. Addo.

"Teşekkür ederim, çok naziksiniz," she purred back. *"Yemek mükemmeldi."*

And they were off to the races, chattering in Turkish while Fee goggled and Abeni scowled.

Curiosity forced Fee past the invisible wall she'd built between herself and her flat mate. "Your mother speaks *Turkish*?" she whispered.

"One of her husbands was Turkish," Abeni whispered back.

Fee was too confused by the way the day was careening off-road to fully process a new detour. "One of —how many has she—"

"Three." Abeni glanced at Bel Antalya's owner and added mordantly, "At last count."

Maybe the fact that Fee and Abeni weren't enjoying the desserts and coffees a waiter had placed in front of them cued Mr. Orhan Erdik—who'd paused his Anatolian gabble with Abeni's mother long enough to introduce himself formally—to go away. Even after he went back to worshiping from afar, Fee left her fork on the table. Wrapping a hand around her warm coffee glass gave her a sense of reality, but she appreciated the irony of being preoccupied with thoughts of a man whom no one in the restaurant would believe was real at all.

Mrs. Addo sighed and took a last bite of *kadayif*, the honey-drenched phyllo roll her admirer had ordered, and followed it with a swallow of the strong, black Turkish coffee.

"Not all ghosts," she began as though a meal and a flirtation hadn't elapsed since she'd said it the first time, "become ancestors."

Fee's hand twitched so hard on her coffee glass she had to grab it with her other hand to keep it from upsetting onto the tablecloth. Despite the fact that Mrs. Addo had just said something along the lines of *six Clydesdales are now entering the room*, Abeni's face registered no emotion at all. She was staring at a clock mounted over the bar, probably wondering if it was late enough that she could plead a date with Sarah and make a break for it. *Oh, no, you don't*, Fee silently warned her flat mate's profile. *You are* not *leaving me here alone with your mother.*

She risked a swallow of the coffee. It was as bitter as it was dark. After a gulp of water to chase the flavor from her mouth, she asked as blandly as she could, "Is there a reason for you to mention ghosts, Mrs. Addo?"

Mrs. Addo smiled. It was a bit of a Cheshire Cat smile, white teeth fencing in secrets. "Oh, yes. My daughter reeks of one."

Before she could slap a gag order on her mouth, Fee burst out, "*Abeni?* How is that even—" At the same instant, Abeni's hand flew to her neck and Fee's eyes followed the motion.

The scarf. The two of them always hung their macs and scarves on pegs behind the flat door. In the scuffle of getting Mrs. Addo and themselves out of the flat and to the restaurant, Abeni had apparently grabbed Fee's blue UNC Chapel Hill scarf—the one her crafty Great-aunt Sophie had knitted when Fee was admitted to the university—instead of her own Sheffield F.C. scarf in the team's blue and white away colors. Abeni had shed her mac when they entered Bel Antalya, but the scarf was still wound around her neck.

The scarf. The one Fee had been wearing with her own mac when she'd gone directly to Gil after her abortive second meeting at MOLA. The one she'd then forgotten to take home from the Olympiad until today. Gil's lodging was redolent with his scent and now, apparently, the scarf was, too.

Abeni slowly and carefully unwound it and handed it across the table to Fee, like she was passing over a cobra. A panicked internal voice told Fee *don't don't don't*, but she brought it to her face, anyway, and inhaled. Ale, ginger, and the particular musk that was Gil.

Mrs. Addo let the scarf sniffing go by unremarked. For a bit, none of them said anything. Finally, as matter-of-factly as if she were ordering a second dessert from her new beau Mr. Erdik, Mrs. Addo offered, "It is a man ghost. A very randy fellow, him." She half-turned in her chair to look indulgently at Abeni. "For that reason, I don't think it is a ghost belonging to my daughter."

What an interesting choice of words. *A ghost belonging to.*

"All right, now," Mrs. Addo went on in the tone Fee had heard dozens of professors use when they began a lecture, "there are three types of ghosts, and each one has rules."

So, there *was* a Ministry of Phantoms, complete with rule-setting members and reams of regulations. Wherever the Ministry was, Abeni's mother had a key to the executive washroom.

"Some are the ghosts of people who died before they reached elderhood. Often, they met death violently, while defending another or fighting injustice. Their spirits are restless. They are trapped and cannot cross the waters that separate the living from the dead. They linger on the shore for the proper moment to return to complete their lifeline."

Mrs. Addo's lecture had been directed to a point somewhere above Fee's head. Abruptly, she dropped her fierce black eyes and locked them on Fee's. "I am speaking of the Asaman Twentwen, those who wait," she intoned gravely.

If Mrs. Addo had been advising her in Ashante, Fee couldn't have understood her any less. Tentatively, she said, "Okay. You're saying that not all people who die are really...dead?"

Mrs. Addo tranquilly sipped more coffee before she answered. "Miss Aoife, you are too intelligent to ask a foolish question like that."

Maybe Fee should have said "really *entirely* dead." Because some of them were between life and death. Neither dead nor alive. Half dead. She was becoming increasingly aware that death was a spectrum disorder.

Her headache was coming back. She felt it as pressure from inside her skull, pushing against her temples. It was as though everything Mrs. Addo was saying had somehow gotten into her brain and was too big for the space there. When she raised her eyes to Abeni's mother, they felt almost too heavy to lift.

The three of them—or maybe four, because Fee felt the uncomfortable presence of her witch-aunt Jana standing behind Mrs. Addo and nodding wisely—sat quietly at their table for a few more minutes. Fee and Abeni didn't look at each other. Mrs. Addo looked placidly into space. Mr. Erdik looked at Mrs. Addo. Unable to bear it anymore, Fee waved over a waiter and asked for the check. Mr. Erdik swept it grandly off the waiter's tray and crushed it in his huge fist. He brought Mrs. Addo's coat to the table himself, helping her into it as he muttered what sounded like sweet nothings in Turkish and Mrs. Addo laughed like a girl of fifteen.

Fee and Abeni were left to get their own coats off the rack. *Too much of this is happening in eateries*, Fee thought with disproportionate irritation. The conversation at the King's Café where Abeni browbeat her into the LUCIES expedition. The blind-date-gone-bad at New Young. Now this, at Bel Antalya. She'd never be able to eat Turkish food again without remembering Mrs. Addo passing down the ghost wisdom of Ghana over *kadayif* and coffee.

Leaving her mother to chat with Mr. Erdik, Abeni pushed open the café's door and held it while Fee plunged into the rainy London night, following close behind.

THIRTY-ONE

It was no shock that at some point in their foreign language courtship, Mr. Erdik had invited Abeni's mother to go to a gallery opening with him after dinner.

Outside Bel Antalya, with the owner hovering, Mrs. Addo embraced her daughter and patted Fee's cheek. "Orhan—" They were on a first-name basis, were they? "—will drop me off at my hotel later. You young ladies have a lovely evening." Mr. Erdik held out his arm, Mrs. Addo took it, and the pair strolled away, chattering. In Turkish, naturally. Perhaps, Mr. Erdik was telling Abeni's mother Turkish ghost stories.

The hastily arranged date night left Abeni and Fee to walk back to the flat alone. Wordlessly. It was only a few blocks, but Fee was pretty sure the walk would've been wordless if their destination had been Edinburgh.

Back at the flat, it was a marker of how long and well they knew each other that they didn't waste any breath on diversions. No "Think I'll shampoo my hair," or "I'm knackered; time for a nap." They plopped, almost simultaneously, into seats in the lounge, Abeni on the sofa where she usually sat with Sarah, Fee in the armchair.

After a long minute of subdued glaring, Abeni blurted, "I didn't ask her to come. And she didn't warn me. She just turned up at the door."

Fee felt her eyes narrowing. "Has she ever done that?"

"Not with me."

Not with her daughter. That left the question open about whether Mrs. Addo had done sneak-attack interventions with other people. "Have you been talking to her about me, Abeni?"

"No, no! Not a word, I swear." Abeni bent forward, then scratched her head hard, mussing the hairstyle that Sarah had probably spent hours creating. "It's...I told you, Fee. She *sees* things."

"Does she read Tarot cards?"

Abeni shook her head. "Nay, summat else." The degree of Abeni's discomfort was directly proportional to the amount of Yorkshire that crept into her speech. "Reads the bones, now and again. Pig knuckles, mostly."

Pig knuckles. First, the Three of Swords and the Two of Cups. Now, prophesying porcine phalanges.

Fee thought hard about her next question. She'd need to phrase it very carefully. "Abeni, do you think your mother can smell ghosts?"

Her flat mate let out a long, mirthless laugh and fell back on the sofa. She sighed and spoke to the ceiling. "Now you see what it was like livin' under the same roof with my mum for twenty-three years. I mean, I love her and respect her, truly I do. But one day to the next, I never knew...Anyway, that's why I came to London for grad school and never left." She heaved to a sitting position again. "Not far enough away, I guess." She fixed Fee with a baleful stare. "You're lucky your parents are in Paris."

Oh, Abeni. Paris was the apartment next door compared to where Fee's parents really were. She posed another question tentatively. "All those things your mother said. Crossing the waters and the Asam—Asama—"

"Asaman Twentwen. The spirits who must come back to earth to complete their lifelines."

"Yeah, those." Fee strove to mask her next words with scholarly detachment, as though she were asking, *Can DNA be successfully extracted from bog bodies? Does embalming residue affect the radiocarbon dating of Egyptian mummies?* "Do you believe all that?"

Abeni didn't answer at first. She pushed to her feet and went to the kitchen, banging cabinet doors until she found the lavender-mint tea she never put away in the same place twice, and switched on the kettle. "I'm not sure if I believe it or not. It's Akan culture, my mother's culture, and I guess it's mine. *Maame* believes it. The people who consult her believe it. You want tea, pet?" Abeni held up a mug questioningly. When Fee shook her head, Abeni went on talking.

"Putting aside all that stuff from Maame, I've got to say, there's something going on with you, Fee. It started with that old theatre on Drury Lane. It's probably just you feeling pressured to finish your book and all, but can

I lend you a hand? You know, hold the light, get on the excavation rota—"

"No, I don't need help." Fee said it too quickly, so she followed with, "Thanks, anyway." Her emotions vibrated with the choices Abeni's offer presented. Which of them was Fee reacting most strongly to? Introducing her flat mate to a man born in 1616? Or introducing the man to a woman he'd described as "most comely, that one"?

Abeni crossed back to the lounge, a steaming mug in her hand. Fee began to say, "I don't want any—" but the comment stalled as her flat mate used her free hand to pick up the fringed end of the scarf still around Fee's neck. Alarmingly, she brought it to her nose. Her dark eyes over the blue wool were large and perplexed.

"It does smell a bit funny, Fee," she said.

THIRTY-TWO

Because passing an entire day without Aoife would otherwise turn him into a gibbering madman, Gil used the time to sit on the stage and teach the mouse tricks. Aoife had left behind something she called "a protene bar." After unwrapping and giving it a sniff and a lick, Gil determined it was food, so he broke off tiny bits to praise the mouse for doing as it was bid. Making the creature spin around itself was simplicity itself. After a quarter hour, a single circle with his raised hand was enough to prompt the caper.

Aoife had already taught it to jump the hurdle of her thumbs, placed tip to tip. Gil dug out an aged embroidery hoop from his Cabinet of Curiosities and had the mouse leaping through it in the time it took to lace a doublet. Getting the creature to bow and offer its paw was a bit more challenging. But Gil was nothing if not persistent, and the mouse was uncommon clever for its kind. In the end, the gambit was a great success. Sitting on its haunches, the mouse ducked its head, then extended one little, long-toed paw like a gallant, placing it neatly on Gil's finger. For its manners, Gil handed over a fat chunk of the treat.

Summoning the mouse by its name was less of a triumph. The willful beast liked to govern its own comings and goings and sometimes answered Gil's call, sometimes not. Disappearing for long periods, it pretended to be deaf no matter how often, coaxingly, or loud it was hailed. Its return, Gil reckoned, was prompted by remembering the sweetmeat being offered.

Having exhausted his repertoire as mouse tamer, Gil trudged to his lodging. There, he leaned against the window overlooking the alley, watching the drear day and the drear people in it move through Covent Garden. Not one of them walked with the gait he loved, not one had the face he craved. The bells of nearby St. Paul's—the "actors' church," it was called, though churches and actors rarely rubbed shoulders—struck the hour of *none*, mid-afternoon, and still Aoife did not return to the Olympiad.

He knew where she was, and it was a mixed blessing. She'd come to him yesternight, all troubled and amaz'd. Crowning the unhelpfulness of the Society of Moles, some witch had dealt her lashings of equally unhelpful advice. Witches were ever wont to do that. Ask for a charm to fix a broken window and they'd tell you to build a house of elk turds from Scotland, then have it blessed by a Carthusian monk.

He'd gentled and cosseted her, as was *his* wont. They lost themselves in coupling—as was the wont of them both—and she slept. In early morning, she'd departed to spend the day "writing up my research." Careful as a monastic scribe, astute as any Oxford *dominus*, she was preparing a sheaf of arguments for that other august body of magisters, the National Trust. There, she would plead, again and as earnestly as before, the Olympiad's fate.

How she did it and kept on doing it in the face of failure, he'd no notion. He was no good at it, himself, had never been. The bowing and courtesies, the flattery and sops. The "Yes, your worships," and "As you please, your lordships." He'd as soon beg favor from a tree stump as from such puffed-up grandees as disposed of his beloved's most worthy, most hopeless cause.

Not that in his day *any* petition he dared to bring would have gained so much as a toe in the door. One look from London worthies at his 'Gyptian face and out he'd have gone, followed by curses, cuffs, or the bailiffs.

Aoife, his Dolkin…she was learned, she was fair, she was all he was not. But her curse was to be a woman, and he'd seen enough of the modern world to know that Eve's daughters were still yoked, in ways subtle and coarse, to men's caprice. By Heaven, was that why her suit was failing? He'd batter into pulp those apes to whom she humbled herself if that was the cause of her distress!

Having worked himself into a temper, his lodging closed around him like a fist. He'd seek relief atop the Olympiad, where he felt less confined. Climbing the steep stairs, he pushed open the dormer window and emerged onto the roof, where the limitless sky, even gray and heavy as London sky ever was, lightened his mood.

"Shakespeare!" he called on impulse to the air, and the mouse came gamboling cheerily across the slates as if he'd not ignored a dozen summons in the last hour. Gil settled against one of the chimney stacks, knees drawn up and spine against bricks that still held a touch of the day's warmth. The mouse scrambled up his thigh and perched on his knee. Sitting on its little arse, it extended its paw in a gentlemanly fashion, and Gil gave his finger to accept the featherlight brush.

"I've left your sweet below, my greedy friend," he told it. "And so you must content yourself with praise. You are a fine mouse, Shakespeare." He tweaked the creature's ear, quailing slightly when, for an instant, the ear dissolved completely at his touch.

"*Mors vincit omnia*," he told Shakespeare and himself. Death conquers all. He'd noticed the mouse was fading a day or so ago and hoped Aoife had not. She showed no sign. Mayhap she had convinced herself her pet was no less whole than it had been since it first appeared in its ghostly condition.

She was wrong, but Gil would not press the truth upon her. It would arrive in its own dreadful time. The truth about the mouse. About him. Truth was often a disagreeable visitor, but for it to arrive when so much between himself and the woman was yet unrealized— that was pain so sharp it made Earl Bandon's deadly stab seem like a pinprick.

He still wanted so many things. Some, he knew, were hopeless, leaden wants, that even a master alchemist could not turn to gold. He wanted them, anyway, as stupidly yearning as the parade of greedy fools in Ben

Jonson's play who paid real gold for the lead a trickster handed them.

Unlike the fools in *The Alchemist*, Gil wanted commonplace things. Should that not make a benevolent deity more inclined to bestow them? He would never ask his Maker for castles and carriages, for horses and rich equipage, for stacks of coin and titles and goods.

Only a home. He wanted that with fervor both genuine and despairing. Some simple place with a sound roof and gardens front and rear. A snug place, where he and Aoife could rise in the morning to kisses and laughter, then retire in the evening with their feet warmed by the fire and their hearts warmed by each other.

And a child. Or a few, if Aoife bore them easily and they thrived. To see her sit, aglow with love, and hold their babe to her breast...no man could want more and no more would he ask, except for—

Time. Most of all, he wanted time. Longer days, longer nights, more of both. Aoife was a land of marvels, and he the thrice-blessed pilgrim who wandered upon it. The continent of her mind, the terrain of her body: no explorer had been so entranced by far-off Cathay or bewitched by the realm of Faerie than was Gil when he crossed the sea of death and stepped onto her shores.

If he could but stay a little longer...

The deepening shadows called him back to the roof and the hour. The sun had dropped in the time he'd been sitting on the roof tiles, pondering impossibilities. Darkness was nothing to him, but he must make light for his darling when she arrived in the theatre. Flick on a lamp or two in the lower floors. Light a candle in his lodging.

Just as he'd done two days ago, when the tiny flame exposed the approaching wreck of his dreams.

'Twas but a candle. Such a trifling thing to make such a large misfortune. He had three candles in his lodging and a box of the sulfurous twigs Aoife called matches. He'd had some of the twigs decades ago—vestas, they'd been called by the stagehands who'd left them behind—but the damp had rendered them useless. Aoife's were fresh and sparked up instantly. Near sunset two days past, he'd turned up the sleeves of his fine new shirt, not wanting to besmirch it with soot or singe it in the flame. Then, he'd struck a match and put it to the wick of the candle on his desk.

Whereupon he saw the surface of the desk, as clear as a pebble at the bottom of a pond, through the transparent flesh of his forearm.

He'd dropped the match. It fell upon the desk and Gil was so dumbstruck he'd not even swept it to the floor, just let it burn down and go out in a wisp of smoke, leaving a small black scar on the oak. Hands shaking, he'd struck another, this time holding it up, his afflicted arm below it.

The grim spectacle repeated.

He let the second match die in his fingers, then released it and slumped unsteadily onto the four-legged chair to ponder what he'd just seen. What he'd seen once before, with the leech Phineas Gravely. His own words came back to damn him.

Old Phineas had been growing less substantial for weeks...he simply came apart before my eyes...like watching a handful of dust, blown away by a breath."

Gil stared at his arm, trusting and not trusting his eyes. To have been so long unchanging and then to be so swiftly changed was more than he could take in at once. Immutable to decay, he thought wryly, was not unchangeable. He had changed when he saw Aoife, and when she saw him. In an instant, he'd gone from being as unfeeling as a brick to every nerve bristling, every inch of skin on fire, his balls aching, his prick upstanding.

A man, in other words, afire for a woman. After three hundred years of death, he'd never felt more alive.

It might be that all men on the cusp of death—true death, not the half death in which he languished—felt the same aliveness. He'd heard it said that life passed like a play before one's eyes in those final moments. What cruel irony that his own edge-of-death play should be of a future he could never have, but only imagine with mingled fear and happiness until it was snatched away for good and all.

The chittering of the mouse called him back from dark reverie. From his knee, it ran down his leg and across the roof to the dormer window, into which it shot like a thrown dart. Better to be a mouse than a man, he considered, for mice were untroubled by philosophy. To be alive or dead, a mouse or a ghost, it was all the same to Shakespeare.

Perhaps, the creature would feel differently if he'd left behind a living mate, some sleek little paramour who mourned his loss. Would Gil be mourned when he left the shadow world in which he now existed? He could not say with certainty he'd been mourned when he left the sunlit world, the one of his time. Polly would have bemoaned his leaving, but she was dead six breaths before him. His tailor to whom he owed a few shillings might have spared a pang of loss. The actors who suffered inferior plays after Gil was no longer around to make better ones, and the plodding playwrights who had to write their own, for a change, and be shamed for the talentless lackwits they were...they'd have shed a tear or two.

Now, there was only Aoife. Aoife and him, the world entire. If he should disappear from it—

Not if, when. He lifted both arms and pushed back his sleeves, one at a time. He seemed whole today, his brown skin smooth over sinewy forearms. After the horrific interval with the candle, he'd stripped and examined his body like a man searching for plague spots. He'd repeated the inspection the day after, and again this day. The fading or thinning or transubstantiation, whatever it was, had not returned. Still, the awful specter of dispersal lurked like an eager creditor, ready to haul him away to satisfy the debt of his life.

Not now, not now. How often he had begged for annihilation in the past three hundred years! The void had seemed infinitely preferable to being jailed in a space between spaces, hopeless, friendless, loveless.

But now, each day was a wonder and a gift. He should not crave more, and yet he did. Oh, how he did.

He turned his head alertly to the dormer window. Sounds were rising from his lodging below. A thump and a curse. As the now-familiar tingle fired his limbs, he got to his feet, smiling. His woman had arrived, blaspheming as she dropped her sack on his desk. The mouse, who'd clearly known she was on her way, must have startled her, leaping as it liked to do from nowhere onto her bosom, laughing little mouse laughs.

Gil would go below to greet his lady love. They would kiss, exchanging the sweet touches that defied time and the Fates. He would discourage the lighting of candles. Into the bed they'd fall, letting their bodies have their way with each other. Gil would bare his nether parts but stay clothed in his shirt just in case his forearm—or his chest or his shoulder or his back—wandered again.

He and Aoife. They'd borrowed time from his sentence of eternal death, but the sand was running out of the glass. He must make every hour count.

THIRTY-THREE

"You can't let them destroy it, Marcus, you just *can't*." It wasn't in Fee's nature to beg, but she'd been begging Anthea Cookson and Marcus Bellwether for the past hour and wasn't ready to stop, even though her heart had done a suicide dive some minutes earlier, when she'd finally realized the futility of begging or anything else.

Would she have been more collected and persuasive this morning if she hadn't spent the night in Gil's bed? Possibly. She certainly would've been more rested. But she could no more stay away from Gil than stop breathing. She wasn't sure that eight hours of tossing and turning in her own bed would have eliminated the violet half-circles under her eyes or the ball of anxiety in her gut. And it certainly wouldn't have changed the outcome of this nine-in-the-morning meeting at the National Trust.

Nothing could move the Scheduling Officers across the conference table. Nothing would change Morsani-

Loeb Futura's plan for the Olympiad. For two months, she, Anthea, and Marcus—her leading the charge, and the other two reluctantly getting her six—had successfully protected the theatre—her theatre, and Gil's—from the investors who were weeks past their target date to raze the building, drive support piers into the earth, and pour a lake of concrete.

Now, her two allies in the fight for a work-halt order were preparing to cut and run.

"Please be assured, Aoife, I share your distress." Today, Marcus' plummy accent had a matching jam spot on his tie. "If it were up to me, every chimney pot in London would be Grade II listed. But..." He shrugged a tailored-in-tweed shoulder and brushed invisible dirt off the large London map on the table. Broken and solid lines criss-crossed it, and red circles dotted it like measles.

"That's exactly my point, Marcus! A lot of the neighborhood *is* listed."

"Not all of it. And not your theatre. Apart from it being an ugly bit of Victoriana, nothing historical happened there."

"That you know of. Nothing historical happened *that you know of.*"

"And you do?"

She decided not to drag out the Charles First coin and the collection boxes again. Nor her sketches of what she knew but couldn't prove was the footprint of the Coronet. They hadn't convinced the officers before, so why try again? She'd attack from a different angle. "I've shown you my perimeter drawings of the Jacobean theatre. The entrance had to have been on Wych Street."

Marcus sniffed. "There is no Wych Street."

"My project says there is! I know it was supposed to have disappeared completely in the early 1900s. Ripped apart, paved over, swallowed up by Aldwych Street and the Tube and Australia House and who knows what else. You've got to admit finding anything at all of Wych is a miracle."

Anthea leaned forward. Her smile was clement but deprecating. "Except you really haven't found it, Aoife. You've surmised it. Which, even if it can't be proven, is very good work. The miracle, if there is one, is *you*. You and your superlative scholarship."

The senior officer had never resorted to flattery, so Fee grudgingly admitted Anthea was giving her a compliment. Some other day, she might be pleased. Today, nothing could pry open the fist of panic and despair that had her in its grip. She barely registered Anthea's persistent kindness.

"Aoife, please hear me out. Your discovery didn't appear out of thin air because you waved a magic wand. You did the research no one else had done. You made the deductions only you were astute enough to make. And you followed them with fieldwork that was positively, well, brilliant."

Fee shook her head. "If it's so brilliant, why can't the Olympiad and the dig be protected from demolition?"

Anthea tapped the map on the table. "It's here in black and white, Aoife. The historic designation boundaries exclude your find because it wasn't discovered at the time the National Trust helped set those boundaries.

Chances of a redrawn designation at this late date…" Anthea trailed off, shaking her head.

"All right, I get it." Fee knew to stay calm in professional settings, but her voice wobbled. "What I don't understand is why raze a rare historical structure and pour concrete over a—" She clenched her jaw but said it, anyway, "—*surmised* Jacobean Era site just to lay the foundation for a new building? Why can't the investors restore the building? The alley could be another Neal's Yard." The Yard, a 17th century mews not even a quarter mile away, was a monument to restoration ingenuity and curb appeal.

Marcus spoke again, the drawling voice of implacable reason. "Neal's Yard started with reasonably sound buildings on both sides. Dusty and dirty, but not decrepit. And it had enough frontage to accommodate a dozen shops and cafes. The architectural scrap that is the Olympiad…well, can you see tourists breaking their necks in a fall down those stairs? I nearly did."

You were nearly pushed, Marcus. Doesn't count.

"Then, there's the cost of restoring that one building." Marcus shook his head sorrowfully, but Fee thought he probably relished bad tidings. "Hundreds of thousands of pounds, even a million. That's piled atop what the investors already have budgeted. And for what?" He took a moment to adjust his tie. Noticing the jam stain, he pulled a spotless linen handkerchief from his jacket pocket and scrubbed lightly at the stain, then put the handkerchief to one side.

Fee hadn't lost her place. "I found cobblestones, Marcus. *Cobblestones.*" She'd found them because Gil had told her where in the cellar to look. If she could've pried some of them up and brought them to the meeting in her backpack, she would have, but Marcus and Anthea would've had some rationale for their being unimportant, or undateable, or later additions to the site. It was an awkward fact that centuries of Londoners had robbed architectural components from even very ancient structures to shore up cellars, build cottages, and prop open scullery doors. The presence of a Corinthian column in a Victorian livery stable didn't mean Romans had been parking their horses there, just that the builder had scavenged the stone from somewhere else.

Marcus sighed like a man trying and failing to teach a chicken calculus. "Please listen, Aoife. The cobbled street that may and probably does run beneath the Olympiad is like all the Elizabethan paving in that part of the city. Three to four meters below the current London street levels. Three. To. Four. Meters. That pretty much precludes accessing it from any of the surrounding modern streets, unless you're suggesting the developers blast a giant hole in Drury Lane and create a sort of dug-up historical city? Knossos or Troy, but with twenty-five feet of cobbles?"

I can't give up. I won't give up. "Those cobbles led to a 17th century theatre, Marcus. In the most important decades of English drama, it sheltered poets and playwrights—"

"Who?" Marcus jabbed the question, sharp as the nib of the Waterman fountain pen he'd picked up and pointed in her direction. "I mean, you're the expert on

Jacobean and Carolean theatre, Aoife. Can you give us names?"

She sighed her own sigh of bone-deep frustration. Three years. She'd spent three years mapping the haunts of poets and playwrights from the era. She'd unearthed some hitherto unknown material, scribbled a few chapters, and promised more. But to date, the only definitive proof she'd found of undocumented poets, playwrights, and theatres around Drury Lane came from a dead man with whom she was having a burning hot affair. Not a citation she could envision seeing in a journal. Not one the National Trust—albeit wisely—would accept.

Struggling with emotion, she ignored Marcus' question and returned to the Olympiad's architectural glories. "I still suggest that the Victorian theatre is salvageable. The windows are intact—well, most of them. The gables are in place, the roof—" The roof where Gil first kissed her. Where they went to watch sunsets and moonrise. Where he'd first called her *chavi* and quoted Sappho and John Donne on the stars.

She bit her cheek to keep her voice from failing. "The roof is watertight, with all the original zinc shingles. The plasterwork inside is...is..." Furious that she couldn't finish the sentence without either shouting or crying, Fee clenched her fists. She planted them side by side on the table and stared at them.

"Aoife, Aoife, I've been there, remember?" Even Merciless Marcus softened his tone. "The plaster in the auditorium has fallen off in huge patches. There are spots where the lathing sticks out like the bones of a dead wildebeest by a water hole."

Anthea reached out to lay both her nicely manicured hands—no dirt under her nails from digging up a cellar—atop Aoife's fists. "The engineers from Morsani-Loeb have assessed it, dear, and their report landed on my desk a few days ago. I've just been waiting for this meeting to share it with you. The damage isn't only cosmetic, the theatre has structural weaknesses as well. I wouldn't like the Health and Safety Executive to get after the developers or us about it. You're not still spending time inside, are you?"

Because of Anthea's hands on hers, Fee couldn't cross her fingers, but they were crossed in her head. "No, I don't go inside anymore. I've made drawings and I try to document everything I can. From the outside."

The senior officer smiled again, patted Aoife's bunched fists, and took back her hands. Fee flexed her own and put them in her lap. "How much time do I have?" she asked, like a patient with a terminal disease.

Marcus had the answer on the tip of his tongue. He'd probably been watching the clock run down for months. "Three weeks, four days," he glanced at his wristwatch, "and twelve hours."

His precision made Anthea laugh, a tinkly sound like ice cubes in a glass of tea. Incongruously, it took Fee back to Savannah, to Bull Street and the big yellow house with the haint blue door. How long since she'd tasted her great-aunts' iced tea? With lime slices making it tart, and corn syrup making it sweet. Years, it had been years. She suddenly missed the four aging women keenly. Their sweet tea, their Sunday get-togethers with baked chicken and potato salad, and their nosey, chattering, unconditional love.

"Well," Anthea began stacking papers on the desk, telegraphing the end of the interview, "make the most of the time you have left. I can get you a few Archeology grad students to help you with drawings—"

Fee violently shook her head. "No. Thanks, but...no."

The chaos of a last-minute fieldwork team was the last thing she needed unless they were magicians and could somehow lift the cellar of the Olympiad up and out of the site. And what would be the point of that? Out of context, it would be just another sterile museum exhibit—if any museum wanted to undertake the enormous expense of acquiring and installing it, which was highly doubtful since her own fieldwork hadn't produced enough results to make it worth saving.

But much more problematic than the cellar was the old theatre above and the man inside. *Oh, God, Gil, my darling, my soul.* He wasn't just something worth saving, he was everything. When the Olympiad was razed, he'd have nowhere to be. He'd be dispersed, like the doctor he'd told her about. A man one second, a handful of dust the next.

She gathered up her laptop bag. No, and again, no. She didn't want any inquisitive, pen-scratching grad students poking around the Olympiad. She wanted every hour of the remaining time to herself. Just her and her theatres and her man and her mouse.

"Trust me when I say, Aoife," Anthea paused her paper stacking to direct a sympathetic look at Fee, "that no one will blame you for losing that building. We can't save them all, dear. I made my peace with that a long time ago."

Fee wondered if Anthea and Maybe Margaret from MOLA had Happy Hours together at the local pub, getting sloshed over G&Ts and lamenting the historic sites they'd been unable to save. Fee put on her good-soldier-in-the-heritage-army face and stood, nodding. "Of course," she told both officers. "Thank you for all you've done."

The grim facts she walked away from at the Trust got even grimmer when she returned to the Olympiad and saw the signs. They'd gone up while she'd been wasting everyone's time at Heelis. The signs were enormous, with bold red lettering on a charcoal background. One sign was affixed to the front of the theatre and one to the side wall, facing the alley.

Morsani-Loeb Futura
the U.K.'s premier development consortium
brings you
THE DRURY DIAMOND
Where today's Londoners will want to spend all their tomorrows

In a flash of angry insight, she got the picture. The big picture, not just the glimpses she'd been shown by the Trust's officers. By their lights, Marcus and Anthea had been martyrs to Fee's crackpot thesis. They'd stood between the developers and the Olympiad as long as they could, longer than they thought they should have. Absolutely no one wanted a repeat of the Rose Theatre, whose demolition was a media circus for many months. Celebrities got involved, demonstrations took place, and the site filled with placard-waving protestors and news cameras. Only, in the end, to produce a so-called compromise, consigning the ongoing dig to indefinite entombment under the huge new building that was allowed to be built, anyway.

The Trust, now under pressure from the investment-friendly City of London and the investors themselves, had washed its hands of Fee's project and her. Common sense told her she couldn't have expected anything else, but it didn't change her gut reaction. It felt like treason.

Into the icy paralysis of her rage came a badge-wearing, hard-hatted man, walking up the alley toward her from Arne Street. Stocky, with a weathered face, he wore workman's clothes with a bright yellow safety vest and carried a clipboard. When he was close enough, Fee read the laminated card on the lanyard around his neck. *R. Davies. Site Safety. Morsani-Loeb Futura.*

Not a man to waste his employers' time, Davies addressed her without preamble. "Ms. Gowdie."

Well, well, he knew who she was. Surprisingly, he pronounced her name correctly. Had he been coached?

"We should've taped up the building a month ago, you know." He gave Fee an up-and-down look. She was still wearing a stick-on badge from the Trust, but she doubted knowing she was only a dissertation away from a doctorate would alter the scorn in Davies' look.

"Three weeks, Ms. Gowdie. Three weeks and we'll remove the door handle and—" he waved his clipboard toward the stage door of the Olympiad, "—seal off that deathtrap."

Deathtrap. If he only knew. Death and life and love, all trapped together in a theatre within a theatre, like some ghastly Faberge egg.

Slapping his clipboard against his thigh, the Site Safety man nodded curtly, turned, and walked away, his thick legs carrying him back toward Arne Street.

And a very good day to you, too, Mr. Davies. Your math is wrong, though. You owe me four days and—Fee raised her eyes, noting that the sun had dropped behind the adjacent buildings—*nine hours, more or less.* She didn't know if she was grateful to Marcus Bellwether for computing exactly how much time she and Gil had left, or whether she despised him for planting the countdown in her brain. The hours and minutes ticked away like a bomb. *Three weeks, four days, nine hours. Eight, seven, six, five...*

She fumbled the blue key from the outer pocket of her laptop bag and put it to the lock in the stage door. The tremor in her hands was so pronounced it took her a couple of tries to insert and turn it. Tomorrow, when she left the Olympiad after the night and day she was planning to spend in Gil's arms, the tail end of the building's death sentence would be gone. There'd be only three weeks, three days, and zero hope.

Weeping with desperation, she went in the stage door, slammed it shut behind her, and threw the bolt.

THIRTY-FOUR

Without giving it a voice, she and Gil agreed to say nothing about the diminishing days before the Olympiad met its end. *As all things meet their end*, Fee reminded herself, *the theatre no more nor less than every tree and cat and mouse.*

Perhaps not every mouse. Shakespeare sat on Gil's desk, chewing the edges of a button he'd found. Fearing it might be plastic, Fee moved to extract it from his sharp little teeth, then realized the mouse could eat plastic all day and night and not get sick from it. She leaned in to examine the button more closely. Nicely carved. Genuine ivory, maybe. Heaven knew how old. Probably worth something to an antiques dealer. Worth more to her to see how happy it made her ghost mouse.

She decided not to return to the Bloomsbury flat at all for the time she had left with Gil. For some weeks, she'd been going back and forth to the Olympiad with a change of clothes in her backpack. A sink in one of the dressing rooms worked well enough, even though, when she first turned the squealing tap handle, the water ran rusty for a long while. When it cleared, she washed what she needed to and hung it to dry anywhere she could.

For clothes, there was also Gil's Cabinet of Curiosities. Apart from the green silk gown she'd worn for *The Alchemist*, it overflowed with a motley assortment of discarded costumes from the Olympiad's glory days. Gil insisted she try them all. Rosalind's breeches and doublet from *As You Like It* got him so worked up he nearly tore them off her.

She texted Abeni every other day. *Dig going well. Deadline nearing.* She always ended her texts with, *I'm fine.* It wasn't at all the closing she wanted to type, which was, *I'm with Gil.* She fired a few texts at Jana, telling her pretty much the same things she told Abeni. Transparent and useless lies, the Jana texts, since the Reverend Seer Nosey Tarot Witch could probably see in the cards what Fee and Gil were doing as clearly as if she were spying through the window in the attic.

Jana didn't return her texts. She was waiting, Fee guessed, for the other shoe to drop.

It was astounding how much she and Gil learned about each other in what he called the "three sennights" of grace they'd been given before the end of their world. He'd made a board for Fox and Geese and showed her how to play it, though it was such an unequal game and she was so bad at it she always lost, even when she was the greatly advantaged Fox. In a shop next to the kebab place up the block where she grabbed takeaway meals, she bought a simple folding chess board and plastic chess set. Gil went into raptures when he saw it. He'd been playing chess against himself on a board he drew, with cardboard pieces he'd illustrated in ink, the Queen looking very much like Elizabeth Tudor and the King a sour-faced James the First. Fee found a deck of playing cards in the same shop and it was good for endless entertainment. Gil not only taught her a half dozen 17th century games, he gave her all the fine points of cheating at them.

They rehearsed, not just *The Alchemist* and *Phaedre* but scenes and whole acts Gil pulled from his and the theatre's pasts. Fee had long suspected he had an eidetic memory or something like it. Certainly, she'd never known anyone who remembered so much, so clearly. Classic dramas from Sophocles and Aeschylus, popular plays of his own time—both those he'd written and those penned by others—plus some she'd never heard of. A few came from the Bard of Avon, but never *Romeo and Juliet*. That was too close to home.

He said he'd covered his ears when modern plays were being rehearsed in the Olympiad, but one day when they were both feeling silly, he walked her through the entire last act of Noel Coward's *Blithe Spirit*. The play had a stupefyingly long run at the Piccadilly Theatre in London from early 1941 to 1942. When it closed there, the Olympiad's management negotiated to stage it on the same boards where Gil had shown her the secret strengths of Dol Common. Jumping the gun at the start of 1942, the Olympiad started rehearsing *Blithe Spirit* and then stopped when the contract fell through, but by then, Gil had learned the whole script.

Blithe Spirit went to the Duchess and St. James Theatres instead of the Olympiad. Before the play was free again, the Germans dropped a bomb across Drury Lane and the Olympiad went dark, never to light up again.

In every hour between acting, rumpling the sheets, and gaming, they talked. Deeply, widely, in ways and for lengths of time they hadn't been able to before, when Fee was still distracted by what seemed now to be hills on a far distant horizon: her grant, her book, saving the theatre. They talked about all sorts of things, from the profound to the trivial. Polly Makepence, he related one day, had read in a broadsheet about a man named William Lithgow returning from a trip to the Holy Land with an elaborate tattoo on his right arm. Even though it was very old news at the time, Polly was besotted with the notion. For months, there was no peace in Covent Garden as she harried everyone from the lowest sweep to the highest player, asking where she might get such a mark for herself.

"At length, being told where an artist could be found, she dragged me to his hole of a workshop and bade me sit with her while her chosen design was inscribed—" Gil grazed his fingers along the upper swell of Fee's breast, "—there.

"The artist was a wizened fellow of dark and indeterminate mien. He might have come from Inverness or the Indies. By a rushlight, he laid out his tools, dipped a sharpened skewer into a pot of ink, and set it to Polly's breast.

"Before he so much as broke the skin, she cast up her dinner, including a full pint of ale, onto the man. I had to haul her away, the needler cursing us both from his doorstep until I tossed him a shilling to stop his clamor."

"What happened to her, to Polly?"

They were sitting on the roof, both of them wrapped in blankets against the chilly fog. Gil went very still at her question. Fee sensed him debating what and how much of something to tell her. In the end, he told her all.

"It was 1642, and the joy-throttling Puritans had closed the theatres. I was left alone in the Coronet, my pallet tolerated since the managers shook in their boots for fear of vandals, vagabonds, fire, and the like. I woke one night to the sounds of furious argument upon the stage.

"Taking up my dagger, I charged onto the boards to see Polly's protector of the hour, a noble varlet of drink-driven temper and vile tastes, in the very instant he ran her through with his rapier.

"The varlet and I engaged and, alas," his smile was wry, "the little prick did prick me a little."

Fee reached over and rested her hand on the whitened gash at Gil's throat. He covered her hand with his. They sat without moving or speaking for a time, while she silently cried.

One evening, as they lay side by side in his bed, happily emptied by sex, Fee finally found the nerve to ask again about the plays Gil had written. The ones branded under other playwrights' names.

"I know it must have been painful, so don't bother to say it wasn't."

"Labor of any sort is painful to a degree, is it not?"

To distract her, or because they weren't done with lovemaking yet, he slipped his tongue into her mouth. For a while, they kissed and nipped and plunged in delicious mimicry of what they'd just done, would do again, with and to every part of their bodies. Eventually, Gil pulled away and lay back with a sigh.

"I had no period of idleness in which I could attend to my own scribbling, Aoife. Certainly not when every scribble for another meant a few pence. Pence being unsociable coins, they could not be persuaded to keep together in sufficient masses to pay the landlord, the tavern keeper, and the tailor unless pressured by a great quantity of their peers."

He rolled on his side to face her, curling his hand around her hip and pulling her to him. "I penned but a single play of my own, by my own devices, of my own design."

"Where is it?" she whispered.

He shrugged, tugging her closer. "So many things were lost across the years." His hand trailed upward to cup her jaw. "One thing, only, was found." Lowering his head, he murmured into her lips. "You, my pearl, you."

Thirty-Five

Aoife slept curled like a leaf, and Gil stood next to the bed, watching her. He'd warrant she was dreaming of days wherein the sun never sank. Forsooth, it was what he, awake, was dreaming.

He'd claimed ignorance of the passing days, but doubted she believed him. In truth, every hour had clicked like a death watch beetle in his mind.

Today 'twas the last day.

He would not pretend to rue the final weeks of the sentence he had served in the prison of his body. However brief the blessing of Aoife and their union, he could not imagine anything more joyous, anything *more*.

And he was no coward, but still he hoped his ending would be quick as the rapier thrust that sent him from his first life. An ending more complete—he hoped for that as well. To go on in some form, aware of the ruin of his heart when she was ripped from it...

Had he been so wicked in life that he merited such a hell?

He'd stayed as long as he dared. Too long. Lifting one arm, he dragged back the sleeve with his other hand. A yawning gap in the flesh between wrist and shoulder displayed the bed, the blankets, and his beloved tucked beneath them. For weeks, he'd successfully hidden the evidence of his rot from her. Joined with her in his shirt, in the dark. Distracted her in the daylight, when her eyes strayed to some part of his body he knew to be transparent as rain. To stay even a day longer risked the unthinkable. He wanted with all his breaking heart for her to remember him as he had been, her hale and lively swain, his body strong and devoted to her pleasure and protection.

He would not, *could* not, let her see him as he was now, riddled with holes like a moth-eaten jerkin. Departing now would deprive him of the last few hours in her embrace, but he had his own last memories to preserve. The smooth, untroubled petals of her eyelids in sleep. The spill of her ebony hair upon the pillow. The cry of pleasure from her pretty mouth when he made her come.

His courage faltered when he considered such reflections of horror as would fill her eyes if she saw his present state.

Her fearless spirit would founder and break on the rocks of disbelief. She would resist the truth and vow to make him whole. Where would he find the strength to move her heart away from such desperate hope when his own was cleaved in twain?

Aye, she would fight it, his warrior queen, his Boudicca. She would say as she had when first they'd met a few months, a century, ago, "*No.*" She would stamp it away, all pride and fury, as she'd done, then. Gil stifled a small, sad sound of mirth, too low to wake Aoife, though the mouse sleeping in a ball at her feet lifted its head. "There's a grand and terrible symmetry to us, mouse," he murmured. "'Tis our play. We are naught but actors in it."

Stealthy as a shadow, he crossed to his desk and moved aside a stack of foolscap. Beneath, there was a thick folio, pages tightly bound by himself from unpicked twine he'd gathered through the years. Lifting it, he observed the stained calfskin covers through what had been, just days before, the flesh and bone of his fingers.

It had come to this. After this, there was nothing.

Cruel, some might say, for him to be given love at all, only for it to be snatched away. He did not see it so. He might have died, as most men did, without even the glimpse of Heaven he'd had with Aoife. Or lingered as half a man for all of time, with neither hope nor pleasure.

He remembered the way she spoke of her father. "*Papa thought dead and gone was better than what he'd been.*"

Her father was a wise man. So be it. He'd had his heavenly moment. Now, he'd be dead and gone. What a pretty poison they'd drunk, when first he and Aoife tasted each other! No remedy for their thirst, then, but to be with each other. No remedy for their ailing, now, but to be apart. At the last spark of his mind, though, he would recall the fatal nectar's sweetness. God would hear not a single complaint from him about the bitter dregs.

He hefted the folio in his once-strong, now wavering hands, assessing it, saying farewell. Compared to rings and vows and a home and babes, it was a trifle, but it was all he had to give her when she had given him the world.

The slightest of sounds from the bed stilled him. Aoife shifted, sighing, eyes still closed, and settled again. Gil listened for a count of twenty, but her breathing remained regular and slow. A smile hitched one corner of his mouth. He'd pleasured her witless last night. 'Twas no wonder she slept so deep.

The Charles First coin lay on the desk. That whoreson chip of silver...It had provoked Aoife's doomed battle to save the Olympiad and the bones of the Coronet beneath. Last eve, she had scrutinized the coin for an hour, as though looking for some hint of salvation in it that she had missed before. Finding none, she had tossed it onto the desk.

Gil deemed himself too educated for superstitions, but just on the odd chance he might need fare for the boatman of Hades, he picked up the coin and dropped it into the pocket of his breeches.

The folio, he brought to the bed. As carefully as depositing a cheepling into a nest, he placed it on the very spot where his body had lain minutes before. He allowed himself one final, longing look at Aoife, then made his silent way to the dormer window and eased onto the roof.

———

Icy air greeted him, and his breath escaped as a plume of mist. He walked to the very edge of the tiles and stood there, feeling suspended between earth and sky. 'Twas an hour yet until dawn, the night as thin as watered ink. One star alone still lingered. Venus, she who was dimmed only by the rising sun.

Pain as vast as the sea swallowed him, and for a time he lost the sense of being anywhere or anything at all. Loss clawed from his heart to his throat, where he trapped it lest it escape as the scream of a dying beast. He heard it in the cage of his chest, lamenting, remembering.

He'd seen men die, calling for their mothers. Perhaps that was why his own came to him, then. "*I know less of her than a flea knows of its dam,*" he'd told Aoife, a lie.

He'd been not quite four, he reckoned, and it was a night or two before his mother had left him on Baron Sorley's kitchen doorsteps. She'd held him in her lap as she sat in a circle of people—some young, some old, all dark—around a leaping fire. His mother's people, his people, in a camp, under the stars.

A man was singing. Gil, who bore some other name he'd long forgotten, hardly understood the words, but the sound was all knives. Raw hurt, raw pain...it poured like blood from the singer's throat. Gil had cried out and his mother swaddled him in her shawl, pressing him against her warm breast. "Be still, now, *chavo*. All is well."

But all was not well, not then, not now, not ever. He was parting from Aoife and would never see her face again.

As though called by his misery, the mouse appeared at his feet, squeaking. "Well met, mouse," he told it quietly. It shimmered one moment, dimmed the next, its light become as weak and changeable as moth wings. "Have you come to bid me a pleasant journey?"

He took his gaze away from the mouse and gave it to London, the city he'd known to its very bones for all the slow-marching years. The faint tang of the Thames, over-lain with modern fuels, made his nostrils twitch. He spared a few thoughts for All Hallows' Eve, this night. Three hundred years ago, Thameside would have been alight with a hundred bonfires, with feasting and ale. On the next day, All Saints', the air would still be thick with the smell of burned wood and roasted meat.

Covent Garden was rarely quiet in the modern age, but it was quietest now, just before dawn. Too quiet, the hour and the city. He'd never stopped missing the night watchmen. To lie abed as he'd done in life, or to sit on the roof as he'd done in death, and hear that voice floating upward from the street, "*Five of the clock and all is well.*" For so many years, it had made him feel less alone when, in truth, he was the loneliest man in the world.

Or had been, until her.

The mouse chirruped again, and Gil bent to scoop him into his hand. There was hardly anything left of the poor creature. It had faded like a small, pale moon on the brink of dawn.

"Nay, you'll not go with me, little friend. Your mistress has more need of you than I. Linger as long as you can, to ease her heart."

He lowered the mouse to the roof tiles. It scampered a small distance away and sat on its haunches, watching, paws crossed on its breast like a deacon at prayer. If Gil felt anything in the place where he was bound, he would miss the mouse, burr in his stocking that it had been. *Godspeed*, he thought toward it, and turned his face to the night again.

Surely, the moment called for verse. A couplet, at least, on farewell. But his heart was empty. After so many lifetimes of spouting words, he could think of nary a one.

The wind rose sharply. Gil squared his shoulders, took a single long step, and became one with the air.

A few seconds ticked by. The mouse gave a squeak, dashed to the edge of the roof, and leaped, becoming a tiny airborne smudge of fur.

The smudge vanished before it could fall.

Thirty-Six

She lay immobile, eyes shut, hoping she was still asleep and only dreaming of being awake. If she admitted she was awake, she'd have to acknowledge reality. She didn't think she could do it.

Gil was gone. She knew it in every particle of her being. She'd expected his departure to leave a gash in her the length of the Thames. To leave her a sobbing, shattered mess of grief and loss. Instead, she was completely numb.

Shock, she supposed. Under it, her heart was a severed blade of grass. It would blow away when she opened her eyes and so, for now, she'd keep them closed.

The past three weeks had flown by, but their last day, yesterday, had paradoxically seemed to go on forever. Mindful that nearly everything they were saying and doing was being said and done for the last time, Fee was keyed to a painfully high pitch of awareness from the minute the sun rose.

At the fading of daylight beyond the attic window,

she'd thrown herself into neatening the two rooms that held so much of Gil's life and all their love. She had no idea what impelled her to do it. Some hopeless fiction, maybe, that they were just going on a short trip—a few days in Majorca, a week tramping the Lake Country—and would want to come back to a tidy apartment.

She took everything from the Cabinet of Curiosities and put it all back, neatly, the green silk gown folded on top as though they'd be rehearsing *The Alchemist* later and he'd want her to dress the part. She dusted the furniture and the windowsills, then had a go at Gil's desk, but he pulled and pushed her away, herding her like an amorous sheepdog. Kissing, nipping, and dancing her toward the bed until, laughing, she let him tilt her onto the blankets. He followed her down and didn't let her rise again.

Their joining began tenderly and became a dark and desperate pagan rite. He made a deity of her body and worshiped every inch of it with the divine madness of a Viking berserker. She knelt at the heathen altar of his pleasure in return, experiencing it as intensely as her own. They bit each other, not gently. He slapped her buttocks as she crouched above him, cursing a blue streak, his cock buried in her to the hilt and her hair whipping his face.

"Foul-mouthed wench," he snarled.

"Fucking bastard," she hissed.

Without missing a thrust, he pressed his mouth against her jaw, his words a hot gust. "The Honorable Fucking Bastard, *sir.*" He locked her hips to his groin with implacable hands and released inside her, groaning.

At last, a few hours before daybreak, they were spent.

Depleted, ashamed, and exalted by what they'd done, they lay on their sides, facing each other, while their breath slowed. Methodically, she mapped his face with the pads of her fingers, taking into memory the planes and angles and textures of him. He did the same, careful with his callused fingertips, moving them lightly but thoroughly across her forehead, nose, and lips. Imprinting her. Keeping her.

Fatigue became her enemy. She fought it, minute by minute. There was so little time. Terrified to lose any scrap, she jerked herself awake each time she felt her eyelids droop.

"Hush, now, Dolkin," Gil lulled her, tucking her into the warmth and safety of his arms. "Bide in sleep for a while." Rocking her gently and rubbing her back, he whispered endearments, until she tumbled into the dreamless depths of exhaustion.

Or surrender, the torpor that finally overtook a bird hurling itself against a window in the room where it was trapped. When it fell to the floor, its eyes might still be fixed on the adamant pane, but they'd be dull with resignation. All done except the short, empty wait at the end of life.

It was a bird that finally made her open her eyes. A pigeon flapped noisily to the ledge of the window overlooking the alley and sat there, cooing. At least, she thought it was the cooing that woke her. Pushing herself to a sitting position on the sagging mattress, she scowled at other noises, both animal and mechanical, rising from the streets below. Heavy equipment, a tractor, maybe, grumbled in the alley. Men called to each other, broke out in laughter. A shout rose, clear and coarse, even through the closed window. "Oi! T'other way, you bloody wanker!"

They'd arrived, then, a crew of workmen to pull down the Olympiad. After all her efforts to keep it upright, the actual fall of the theatre seemed anticlimactic, a *ho hum, I knew this was coming* moment. Or maybe there were only so many scalpels in her emotional operating room and all of them were presently occupied, removing her heart.

He's gone. He's gone.

She untangled herself from the blankets and staggered into the First Room. Seeing it in daylight, she instantly understood why Gil had put a stop to her manic tidying. His desk was a skip of stacked papers, spilled ink, crow feather quills, gaming pieces, and the chess board. The four-legged chair was wonkily shoved back from the last time he'd risen from his work. Her hoodie was draped over the chair back and her backpack hung from one spindled corner.

The makeshift bookcase he'd built, tucked under the alley window, was just as it was when he'd last taken a book from those he'd pilfered over the years and the ones she'd brought him. Volumes tilted every which way. A dog-eared edition of *The Hobbit* was splayed open on top; they'd been reading chapters to each other. The page on which they'd stopped was marked by a ruler he'd made from a piece of notched lathing, the inches surmised from the end joint of his smallest finger.

The books, the desk, the chair, the bed—everything

was just as they'd left it in the final hours they'd had together. A painting, *Love Interrupted.*

It was all so, so Gil. He'd arranged for her to see it, to let it console and trick her into believing, even just for a few breaths, that he wasn't truly gone, that any second, he might return. He was merely...elsewhere.

Her half-awake brain ground into gear as she surveyed the rooms. Shakespeare was elsewhere, too. She might be mad as Miss Havisham, but not so mad she didn't acknowledge the futility of it when she called to them both.

"Shakespeare, where are you?" She swayed, feet curling against the cold floor. "Gil?" Her voice grew fainter and fainter until finally she could only whisper raggedly, "P-please answer me. Please..."

Brutal as it was, Gil had also arranged that. He could have left a note or said goodbye. But he understood her too well. Understood that the only way she'd ever really accept the truth was to call, and call, and call, until she proved it to herself.

A sharp tremor went through her. The morning air was frigid. She was wearing what she'd worn in bed, a long wooly pullover and thin socks. The cold seeped into her, filling her.

Like someone who'd gone suddenly blind, she fumbled back to the Second Room, feeling her way along the floor and walls to Gil's bed. Residual warmth would be there. His scent would be there. Grasping the edge of the blanket she'd flipped away when she lurched out of bed, she flipped it toward her, and froze.

What appeared to be a folio manuscript rested on the

blanket. She'd been so benumbed when she first woke that she hadn't even seen it, had just flung the edge of the covers over it in her haste to leave the bed and deny the awful reality of her future life.

Fee smoothed the blanket and sat on it, carefully, next to the folio. At first, she couldn't pick it up. Her hands shook violently from the cold and shock. She rubbed them roughly on her thighs, then blew on her fingers for warmth.

Tentatively, she ran a thumbnail along the folio's spine. Tiny cross-stitches of what looked like hemp or jute were spaced tightly along the edge; it must have been laborious work. There was no hard outer binding, just a mottled and creased leather cover. With quavering fingers, she turned it back and read the carefully hand-lettered page inside.

The Gyptian
By Gilbert Sorley of Kent
latterly of London and The Coronet Theatre
Anno Domine 1669

1669. But Gil had died in 1642. That meant he'd written the play in the twenty-seven years after his death. It had taken him the length of her whole life to write it, and he'd completed it over three hundred years before she'd been born.

The folio was thick. She could tell from the edges that the paper was very old and fine, cut by a sharp knife. The individual pages were a little larger than a modern sheet of printer paper. Folios were created to save paper.

A single large sheet was folded in half to make four usable pages, printed—in this case, hand-lettered—front and back. She riffled the pages to the last one. There were ninety-one numbered pages, each number neatly inked in the upper right corner. A respectable length for a play. The plays in William Shakespeare's First Folio averaged twenty-five pages, but those were printed on a hand press, in columned pages. The pages in this folio were covered with tightly-spaced lines of Gil's neat, forward-slanting writing.

He left this play for me.

A grinding howl from the alley distracted her and startled the flock of pigeons sheltering under the eaves. As the birds burst into flight, their shadows danced on the floor of the First Room; she could see them from where she sat.

She dropped the folio on the bed. Patting the floor, she found her jeans and struggled into them, stumbling over the hems and almost falling. Her body quaked so hard she could barely pull up the zipper. She wanted to wash sleep from her eyes and try to wake her brain, but, along with electricity, the water mains to the building had been cut off days ago. She snatched up a plastic bottle from the floor by the bed and poured water into one hand. Dashing the icy liquid against her face, she dried it on her pullover sleeve.

Hands, feet, brain, feelings...none of them were working, especially her feelings. They seemed distant, muffled, like they were wrapped in thick fleece. *He left the play for me. He left the play for me.* That one thing seemed important and immediate. She clung to it.

More and louder noises from the alley penetrated her insulating layer. Men's voices, punctuated by yelling and curses. Vehicular sounds. Something beeping like a forklift. Something so heavy landed on the pavement with a thud that it made the whole building quiver. The Olympiad was coming down.

Fee was suddenly frantic to get out, and it had nothing to do with safety. It was as though she'd had a dream of a terrible accident, a ship sinking or a car wreck. If she had to witness it actually happening, it would destroy her.

She careened from the bed into the First Room, bumping into walls. *I need more clothes.* Taking her hoodie from the back of the four-legged chair, she struggled into the zipped garment. *I'll put on my backpack.* She tried, but was too agitated, or too cold, or the straps didn't cooperate, or she'd forgotten how to operate a backpack.

Finally slinging it over one shoulder, she went back to Gil's bed and worked a pillowcase off one of the pillows, the one where he always lay his head, the one that held his scent. Carefully sliding the case over the folio, she folded under the edges. She pushed the bundle under the bottom edge of her hoodie and held it tight with an arm across her middle.

Her running shoes were next to the bed. She pushed her feet into them, not bothering with the laces since that would require loosening her hold on the folio and that was *not* happening.

She started to bolt from the room when a notion seized her. Whirling around, she returned to the bed, to the Cabinet of Curiosities at its foot. Snatching up the green silk gown, she crammed it, one-handed, into the outer pocket of her backpack.

Leave now, leave. Nearly at a run, she crossed the First Room, then skidded to a halt at the door to the attic stairs. One more step, and everything would change. One more step, and the fathoms-deep trench that had taken her parents and her brothers would swallow everything that had passed between Gil and her. History, it would all be history, as buried and unrecoverable as the Coronet and the Olympiad. No one but Fee would even know it had really happened.

Her fist flew to her mouth to block a howl of misery. A sob broke free, anyway, escaping into the room as a muffled, animalistic sound. It took all the control she had left, but she squeezed shut her eyes and locked the tears behind them. *Stay there*, she ordered the flood of grief. *Stay there.* Slowly, painfully, she rose above the crash scene of her life, watching as a thousand broken parts tumbled to a standstill.

Her hand fell to her side. On a cold-fogged and ragged breath, she gave the empty room the last two lines of the Christina Rossetti poem.

"And if thou wilt, remember,
And if thou wilt, forget."

She'd said them over Shakespeare's grave. Just words, but they brought a slight touch of comfort with them. Wherever her man and her mouse were, at least they were together.

I will always *remember*, she sent toward them both, *and I will* never *forget*.

Opening her eyes, she left Gil's lodging and pelted recklessly down the stairs, not looking back.

———

As she exited the Olympiad's stage door for the last time, the noises outside materialized as a line of vehicles clogging the alley. No wrecking ball in sight, yet, no heavy demolition equipment, just piles of planks and stacked plywood sheets. She assumed they were for building the fence that would hide the demo work from passersby, like the tent the police erected over a murder victim's body. At least thirty or forty men milled around—the Dead Building CSI team.

Outside the stage door, she dithered for a minute, not sure what to do with the blue key. Should she leave it in the lock? Pass it to someone in the demo crew? What was the point? She was sure they had keys of their own, for the little time they'd need them before they tore the doors off. No point giving the key back to Ben's husband, either. His part in the handoff of the theatre —*theatres*—was done even before the LUCIES had made their nocturnal visit. Fee dropped the key on the top step.

Walking stiffly along the alley to Drury Lane, she spotted Mr. R. Davies of Site Safety. He was minus his clipboard, but he held a big roll of bright yellow plastic tape, just like a uniformed cop tasked with taping off a homicide scene.

That's right, Mr. Davies, three dead. Two missing, one walking.

———

Fee somnambulated back to Bloomsbury, hardly noticing how she got there. When she opened the flat door, her attention momentarily sharpened. She wasn't even marginally astounded to see three people waiting for her in the lounge. Abeni, Mrs. Addo, and Auntie Jana.

Abeni's face was the one people wore to a funeral when they didn't know what to say but felt awkward saying nothing. The face spoke to Fee, however. *"I know stuff I wish I didn't."* Clearly, Auntie Jana and Mrs. Addo had been talking, both to each other and to Abeni.

Jana heaved off the sofa and opened her arms, but Fee didn't dare let herself be hugged. Her control was as thin as piano wire, twice as sharp, and coiled tight around her. If she let go of the end she was holding, she'd shatter like glass.

No one said anything at first. Fee used one arm to drop her backpack near the door. Still no comments as she pulled a mass of green silk from the pack and tucked it under her other arm. With both arms belted around the middle of her body, she gave six inflectionless words to the room at large. "Hello, everyone. I'm going to bed."

Fee went into her bedroom, latched the door behind her, and toed off her shoes. She lay the green dress tenderly across the foot of her bed. Then, fully dressed, she crawled under the duvet. The pillowcase holding the folio came with her.

Everything smelled like Gil.

THIRTY-SEVEN

When she woke the next day, Fee didn't bother to keep her eyes shut. She'd seen the worst and couldn't unsee it, no matter how long she pretended to be asleep. For an awful stretch of time, she lay open-eyed in bed, letting waves of grief roll over and through her.

When it was obvious that, even if she preferred death, she was stuck with a beating heart and a growling stomach, she sat up. Her cellphone was still in her backpack where she'd left it the night before, not on her bedside table. She guessed she'd overslept her usual seven o'clock wake-up time. Even with no window in her bedroom, it felt more like midday than morning.

She reached under the duvet and touched the pillowcase with Gil's folio, just to be sure it was there. Without it in her arms, she didn't think she could've slept at all. With it, she'd plunged into unconsciousness as though she'd taken knock-out drops. "A sleeping draught," Gil would have said, and her heart clenched. *It hurts, it hurts.*

She struggled out of the bed and stood uncertainly. A shiver raised goosebumps on her skin. She was sure the heat was on in the flat, but she felt cold, inside and out.

Leaving her bedroom, she stumbled a few steps into the kitchen of an empty flat. Abeni's bedroom door was open, the bed made and the room vacant. She didn't see any signs of Mrs. Addo, so maybe she and Abeni were off together somewhere. They might even be at Bel Antalya, if it served breakfast. No, they'd be eating lunch, since the retro wall clock in the kitchen read eleven-thirty. There was no sign of Jana, either, but the shower was running in the bathroom.

The kitchen table was clear of clutter, for a change, the only thing on it a sheet of white paper with a scrawled message.

Food. Icebox. Eat.

No signature, but the handwriting was Jana's. And only her witch-aunt still called it an icebox. Fee scratched at her stomach, where sleeping in her jeans had given her itchy creases, then shuffled to the refrigerator and opened it, her hand glancing off the handle on the first try.

A takeaway box sat on the middle shelf. Fee took it to the table and examined the receipt taped on top. Bel Antalya, dated yesterday at six o'clock.

Six o'clock yesterday evening. Fee had come back to the flat in the early morning. She'd apparently slept away the rest of that day, all night, and half of today. She supposed she ought to be alarmed, but her feelings were still far, far away, in a place she needed them to stay. Maybe forever.

Prying open the takeaway box, she stared at the meal inside. *Gozleme*, Turkish stuffed flatbread. The meal they'd had on the evening Mrs. Addo told her about good ghosts. Fee pressed the lid back on the box and returned it to the fridge. Green tea would do, if Abeni had restocked the flat with it. Fee certainly hadn't been around to do the shopping. She'd been in the attic of the Olympiad, saying a long goodbye to—

It hurts, it hurts. Fire ants of panic skittered up her spine and Fee stamped on them.

She got through tea-making without botching it and took her mug into the garden. Two rarely used wood and metal folding chairs leaned against the wall outside the French doors, but Fee didn't feel up to dealing with them. The morning dew had evaporated, and the patch of lawn looked reasonably dry. She went to the climbing roses and sat —deflated might be a better word—next to Shakespeare's grave. Surprisingly practical thoughts streamed through her mind, like a moving banner. *Grass is overgrowing. Find some small stones. Pile them on the grave. Don't let it disappear.*

Jana's unmistakable Liverpudlian accent, wrapped around some lavish swearing, alerted Fee that her witch-aunt had come outside. Fee turned to watch Jana wrestling, left-handed, with one of the folding chairs, her right hand occupied with a steaming mug. She was draped in a vintage kimono in explosive colors, like a bomb had gone off in a 70s paint store.

Before Fee's sluggish brain got the order to her legs to

get up and help, Jana managed to shake the chair open. Kimono billowing, she towed it to Fee's side. There was no paving in the garden, but just the *scrwaach thump thump* of the chair being dragged across the grass made Fee's frayed nerves flinch.

The chair gave a rusty squeal when Jana sank into it. With a sigh, she put her mug to her lips and drank. Her face crumpled in every direction.

"Keemun green," Fee said hoarsely. Her voice sounded like she hadn't used it in a year. "We're out of Earl Gray. Probably no coffee, either. I've been—"

"Gone for a bit." Her witch-aunt said it matter-of-factly, as though Fee had been on a holiday jaunt. "No worries. I should develop global tastes." She took a cautious second gulp from her mug and forced a smile.

Silence settled. Fee wasn't even close to being ready to talk about what she'd been doing and with whom for the past three weeks. She asked, "Did you sleep in Abeni's room?"

"I did. She kipped with her mum at a hotel."

"Who's minding Rumpelstiltskin?"

"Poppy Norris."

"Poppy." Fee flipped through her memory files. "Is she still a docent at St. Rhydian's?" St. Rhydian's Castle in Wales, where Mom had met Papa, a leathling, like Gil. Where Papa had vanished, leaving Mom a wasteland of grief, like Fee.

Jana shook her head, her messily pinned-up, blue-streaked hair flopping. With a twinge at the ravages of time, Fee noted there was a lot more white in her witch-aunt's hair than the last time she'd seen her, only a year before.

"Poppy hasn't been a docent for a long time," Jana explained. "She said all the fun went out of it when your mother left. The Castle took her on as a paid guide in the Gardens for a few years, enough to feather her nest as her late husband didn't leave her much. Now, she works at the Broom & Bottle four days a week and helps Morgana make powders and potions one weekend a month."

The silence came back. The little Bloomsbury garden was singularly quiet in fall and winter, considering it was in the heart of the city. When it got really cold, Fee worried about the birds, but they were descendants of countless generations of London sparrows and pigeons and starlings and crows, all of them experts at finding warm nooks where they could survive. She and Abeni always put out breadcrumbs and fat balls for them, starting in November.

Wait. It was already November. She'd slept through Halloween and All Saints' Day.

Jana broke into her musing on urban wildlife and the calendar. "Your leathling—"

"He has a name," Fee snapped, then felt guilty. She'd never shared his name, so she had no business being irritated if people didn't know it. "Sorry," she mumbled. "His name is Gil. Gilbert Sorley." She'd never said it aloud to anyone but him. Just for a few seconds, it brought him back. Warm recollection, icy regret. *Oh, Gil, my Gil.*

Jana nodded and drank more tea. "Good name,

Sorley. Very old, very English. Norse origins, or maybe—"

"The name was his father's. He was a terrible man and a worse father."

"Yes, well, fathers can be like that."

Guilt prodded Fee again. Did Jana have first-hand experience of bad fathering? Fee had never asked, even once, about her upbringing. She knew she was from Liverpool, came from a long line of witches, and made a mean scouse, the local stew, but nothing personal beyond that.

Fee coughed, trying to clear the rustiness from her speech. "Jana, I've been a bad student and a worse niece. I mean, I know I'm not really your niece, but you're the best aunt I could ever have asked for. And I haven't always—"

"Oh, reel it in, Aoife," Jana huffed. "You're a good girl. Hard-headed as a nanny goat and flighty as a kite, but you never need to apologize to me. Get on with it, say what you need to say about your—about Gilbert Sorley. You'll be better for it."

Fee swallowed painfully. In addition to the raspy voice, her throat felt tight and sore. If she hadn't gotten sick from the stress of the past few weeks, it wasn't because she hadn't tried.

"In Paris, Mom explained to me about the fading that happened to her in Wales."

"After she and your father had been, um, *close* for some months."

"Right. I expected it might happen to me, since Gil and I were also...close."

"And did it?"

"No." Fee uncrossed her legs and recrossed them. She was pretty sure dampness had soaked into the seat of her jeans, but they were going into the wash, anyway. "It happened to *him*."

"Well." That was all Jana said for a quarter minute, then, "Well, well." Another quarter minute and she added, "What did you say to him about it?"

"Nothing. He didn't know I knew. He was hiding it from me, I'm sure, and it felt wrong to...anyway, one morning he lifted his arm to lower a window sash and his sleeve slipped down. His back was to me and he pushed the sleeve up right away, but I'd already seen." She tilted her head wistfully, remembering how she'd dropped her eyes as he'd turned, pretending to be absorbed in losing another game of Fox and Geese. "We never spoke of it. What I want to ask," she finished, her voice cracking, "is if you...I mean, you said there are a lot of unknowns about soulers and leathlings, but have you ever heard of that?"

Jana laughed her whiskey-deep laugh, the broad bosom of her kimono jiggling. "A lot of unknowns? Oh, Aoife, child! There are a *thousand* more unknowns than knowns about what you are, and what your Gilbert Sorley is."

Fee took comfort wherever she could. In what Jana said, it was the verb. What her Gilbert Sorley *is*.

Jana finished her tea and put the mug on the grass next to her chair, then rearranged her formidable physique, chair yelps accompanying her actions. With a last wriggle and squeal, she folded her hands in her lap and ordered, "Tell me what your intention was. You had one, I presume. What was it?"

Fee wasn't sure in her present state that she could tell Jana what her surname was, much less come up with an answer to Question One on a witchy pop quiz. Jana read her dropped jaw as *None of the Above.*

"Come on, Aoife. What's the First Rule?"

Rule, rule, back in school. "Intention is at the heart of all ritual, and all ritual is a journey."

"Um hm. And the Second Rule?"

"There's a second rule?"

"I refuse to accept that your very detail-oriented mum didn't give you the Second Rule!"

"She may have, but..." *I probably wiped it as soon as I heard it.* There'd been so many distractions in Paris. The new bonnet with violet silk ribbons. The young dandy in the Rue Royale who'd smiled and bowed to her.

With a huge sigh, Jana recited what was apparently the Second Rule of Intention. "Intention manifests when it is freed."

"Okay, that's—what does that mean?"

"It means you must release your intention into the world of actions, not just of desires." Mrs. Addo's lilting Ghanaian voice arrived in the garden, followed by the ancestor priestess herself. "Am I correct, Jana?"

"You most certainly are, Kate."

Mrs. Addo grabbed the second of the two folding chairs, neatly shook it open, and dragged it across the grass. *Scrwaach thump thump.* The sound wasn't any easier on Fee's nerves the second time.

When she reached Fee's other side, Mrs. Addo sat.

Being as slim as Abeni and almost as athletic, she sank gracefully into the chair. She had a navy wool suit jacket over her *kente* cloth blouse, and dressy trousers instead of a skirt.

Fee's sigh sounded pathetic even to her. An ancestor priestess to her left, a Reverend Tarot Clairvoyant Spy Witch to her right. She was hopelessly outflanked.

Jana hadn't lost her place in the conversation when Mrs. Addo entered it. "On second thought, it's not entirely surprising that your mum left out the Second Rule of Intention when she was coaching you. She didn't have the best grasp on it when she dealt with her leathling in Wales. And it's also possible—" Jana squirmed a bit, "—that we didn't explain it well." She brushed a toast crumb off her lap. "Or at all."

Jana leaned forward and patted Fee's head like she was placating the four-year-old she'd been when they first met. "I'm sorry, Aoife. None of my sisters in the Craft had ever seen anything like your mum and you. Oh, we'd read about soulers and leathlings, learned all the folklore and history, and studied the old grimoires. We knew the *canon*, you might say. But if we missed a few points, well, that was our fault."

"It is impossible to prepare for every eventuality," Mrs. Addo told Jana sympathetically.

Of course, Abeni's mother and Auntie Jana were backing each other up. Did everyone have an old school tie except Fee?

Let's just move on, please. "Back to my intention. It was to rescue my soul."

Jana shook her head. "That's not an intention.

That's your identity. You're a souler. Soulers rescue souls. It's not an elective."

Yeah, she got that, now. "I *intended* that Gil would—"

"Gil?" Mrs. Addo asked Jana over Fee's head.

"Gilbert Sorley, a fine old English name," Jana editorialized, also over Fee's head.

"My *intention*," Fee began again, loudly, "was that Gil would be restored to life. He was taken away before he really had a chance to be the man he could have, *should* have been."

"How did he die?" Mrs. Addo leaned toward Fee as she asked it, her dark eyes sharp. Fee didn't see what difference the circumstances of Gil's death made, but maybe an ancestor priestess saw it differently.

"He was avenging the murder of someone he cared for. A dear friend, who was helpless to defend herself and had done no wrong." Polly Makepence, poor feckless doxy, dying in Gil's arms.

"Ah, well, then," said Mrs. Addo, standing, "*ne sunsum ye duro*. His spirit is strong. Let us ask the ancestors to give your ghost some help. I know it will be hard, but you must go now and wash the scent of him off your body. Make yourself very clean." She looked around the garden, then pointed at Shakespeare's tiny, half grown-over plot. "Is this place important to you, or to your ghost?"

Fee's next words were ones she could never have imagined saying. "It's the grave of someone we both loved." The three of them, one living and two dead, had all loved each other.

Mrs. Addo nodded at Fee's witch-aunt. "We will do this together, will we not, Jana?"

Jana struggled to her feet, the chair complaining. "We will indeed."

"Good." Mrs. Addo spoke to Fee again. "Go inside. Abeni is there. Send her to me."

Numbly, Fee got to her feet. Her jeans were as damp as she'd feared, she was cross-eyed with exhaustion, and her limbs were stiff from sitting in the cold. She limped toward the French doors.

"Stop!" Mrs. Addo called, and Fee turned tiredly to face her.

"What drink does your ghost take?"

The man or the mouse? she almost asked. Instead, she thought for a few seconds and answered, "Pale ale. Malted, if you can find it." Because that was the norm in the 1600s. The ale that Gil's skin—and now her hoodie, her jeans, and her own skin—smelled of. That, and ginger.

"Abeni will purchase it. Go, now. We will call you when it's time."

Time time time...

As she plodded into the flat, the word thudded in Fee's chest like a second heart. Or maybe the only heart she had. Gil Sorley took the other with him when he left.

THIRTY-EIGHT

By the time she'd showered—*and yes, Mrs. Addo, it was incredibly hard to wash Gil from my body*—the tiniest spark of hope had started to glow inside Fee. Reason, that steely and unwelcome hall monitor, said she should stamp it out. That she was being delusional if she imagined she'd ever see Gil again.

Still, she thought as she dressed in clean jeans and a cashmere pullover a little grayer than Gil's eyes, Jana and Mrs. Addo were the two people in her life who knew the most about what she and her leathling were. Neither of them had said the words "Forget him," not even once. They hadn't inflicted the tired old platitudes on her, "Plenty of fish in the sea," or "Leave the past behind," or even "Every time a door closes, another opens."

Most heartening of all, they hadn't said, "He's dead." The two women in the garden knew that dead was a relative term.

"Miss Aoife!"

Mrs. Addo was calling her. It was time to go out there and do whatever was necessary, whatever was *possible*, to restore Gil to her arms.

———

The garden, when Fee went outside, certainly looked like some sort of ceremony was going to happen. White tea towels were laid on the ground in a half circle around Shakespeare's grave, and the coffee table had been brought from the lounge and placed to one side. Mrs. Addo, Abeni, and Aunt Jana stood on the tea towels, barefoot. Jana had changed to street clothes, a 60s-style, two-piece pantsuit in brilliant pomegranate.

There were things on the coffee table: a brown bottle, and a clear drinking glass.

As Fee got closer, she saw the brown bottle was an opened pint of Adnam's Ghost Ship Ale. That was either Abeni's idea of a joke or really appropriate. Fee raised her eyebrows at Abeni, who waggled her head with a half smile. A joke, then, and Fee felt a surge of warmth for her flat mate, who'd been with her at the start. On the day that they'd buried Shakespeare on the spot where they were now doing...whatever they were doing.

Mrs. Addo pointed at Fee's running shoes. Fee tugged them off. Mrs. Addo nodded at her own tea towel, edging over to make room, and Fee stepped onto it.

"Here's where we are." Jana, on Fee's other side, began the ritual—if that's what it was—with a sitrep.

"Because you didn't enact the Second Rule of Intention, you motored off into the universe without programming the SatNav."

A day for wonders, then. Auntie Jana, who didn't have a driving permit, was terrified of airplanes, and insisted on buying rail tickets at the station window rather than online, was using a tech savvy transportation metaphor.

"Just wanting your leathling to complete his lifeline could send him anywhere. Any *when*."

And that was Auntie Jana explaining why Fee's mother should have paid more attention to the Second Rule. "Is that why Papa ended up in Paris in the 1700s, so Mom and I had to rejoin him there?"

Jana's face was grave. "Probably."

That's not what I want to hear, Jana. "We can fix it with Gil, though, right? Isn't that what this is all about?"

Mrs. Addo chimed in with a chuckle. "Oh, you are like some of my clients, Miss Aoife. They want a money-back guarantee. No such thing in the ghost world."

"If we are successful in freeing your intention," Jana added, "it could still take a long time to actualize. Leathling time isn't our time."

"*Ne sunsum ye duro,*" Mrs. Addo said again, grasping Fee's shoulder and giving it a little shake. "His spirit is strong and his desire very great. If he can come to you, he will."

Jana nodded her assent. "Just be prepared, Aoife. It might take years and—"

Fee held up her hand to stop the words. "I'll wait," she told the two women. When they looked unconvinced, she repeated firmly, "I'll. Wait."

"Let us begin," said the ancestor priestess.

———

The next half hour was a blur. Mrs. Addo poured ale from the bottle into the glass and held it up in her right hand. She started singing something low and rhythmic in a language Fee didn't recognize. With a jolt of surprise, she realized Abeni was singing along with her mother, or at least making responses at intervals in the same tongue. Fee hadn't known Abeni spoke any of what she guessed was Twi, the Ashante language group.

Just as the melodic call and response was lulling Fee into a near trance, Mrs. Addo switched to English. "I call upon Mother Earth, whose power embraces and changes all. I give you this drink." She tilted the glass, spilling a little ale onto the ground next to Shakespeare's grave. "Come and receive this drink."

Eyes half-closed, Mrs. Addo continued. "I call the ancestors whose names I do not know. I call the mother of Gilbert Sorley."

Fee gave a startled twitch. Gil had told her he didn't remember his mother, but, evidently, not being remembered wasn't the same as not existing.

"It is your son's..." The ancestor priestess hesitated. "The bride of your son calls you."

Was Fee Gil's bride? Would she be any more joined to him if they were married? She couldn't see how. Weeks ago, she'd relinquished any claim she might have had to a future with another man. For the rest of her life, Gil would be the only one, the mate of her heart.

"Your son is between worlds," Mrs. Addo went on, "and must return to the shores of the living to complete his destiny. Let his soul pass. I give you this drink," Mrs. Addo spilled ale onto the ground. "Come and receive it."

The glass was nearly empty. Mrs. Addo opened her eyes. "We thank you for your help and blessings—"

"Wait." At the word from Fee, three pairs of eyes locked on her. Fee straightened her spine and went on decisively. Even if she was told to butt out, she had to say it. "My mouse," she pointed at the shoe-length mound at the center of the half-circle, "is with my—with Gil, wherever he—they are. Shakespeare is a good mouse. He also has a strong spirit and desire."

In a different context, it would have been comical to see the way Mrs. Addo's and Abeni's eyebrows rose to exactly the same height. Fee glanced at Jana, who looked perfectly unruffled. Of course, Jana had owned a series of color-changing cats, so asking for help with the afterlife condition of a mouse probably seemed like a day at the office for her.

Mrs. Addo cleared her throat. "It is the..." her eyes flicked to Fee, who said, "friend." "The friend of the mouse Shakespeare asks for the release of its spirit, so it may also fulfill its destiny. She asks this of the..." Mrs. Addo's brow creased, she pursed her lips, and finally finished, "...ancestors of the mouse, Shakespeare, and we give you this drink." With a sigh of relief, she dribbled the last few drops from the glass onto the grave. "*Now* we thank you for your help and blessings."

There was more singing in the language Mrs. Addo and Abeni shared, and then it was over. Dazed, Fee stood where she was, still staring at Shakespeare's grave. Mrs. Addo and Abeni moved away, chatting in low voices. Jana came to Fee's side, patting her back to get her attention.

"Come to Wales, Aoife. You can work there as well as anywhere and everyone will be happy to see you."

Wales. Why not? Fleetingly, Fee considered Savannah, but that felt too far. Not only too far from London, but too far from the most recent place she'd seen Gil. How illogical was that? Gil wasn't like a pet who'd strayed off and would be returning to its last home.

In Wales, she wouldn't have to hand out creative fictions about what had happened. No "gone to Paris" stories for the neighbors. She would stay among the witches and the witches all knew the score, or they would when Jana filled them in. If Gil never came back and Fee turned into Miss Havisham before the Welsh witches' eyes, hair gone gray, arthritic limbs clad in shredded green silk, shambling around as she moaned Gil's name...well, at least she wouldn't have to explain herself.

"All right," she told Jana, "Wales it is."

Mrs. Addo came back to gather the tea towels and the empty glass. Jana swept up the Ghost Ship Ale bottle just before Abeni hefted the coffee table and carried it back into the flat, followed by her mother.

Left behind with Jana, Fee couldn't stiff arm the tension and fatigue any longer. As she started to sag, Jana shot out her hand and grabbed Fee's elbow. "None of that," her witch-aunt ordered. She raised the bottle and intoned, "To those on the other side." After a long drink, she handed the bottle to Fee.

Mom. Papa. Her brothers. Wise elder witch Selene. Shakespeare. Gil. "The other side," Fee said, and she drained the ale.

————

"So, Fee, about a month back," Abeni spoke as she put plates and cutlery on the kitchen table, "when you were talking in your sleep..."

"Sleep talking. Yeah, I guess I was, after all." Fee took the box of Turkish food out of the fridge and transferred it to a platter for microwaving. Abeni's mother and Auntie Jana had gone off to New Young, but Fee and Abeni both announced they'd have lunch at the flat. Thankfully, Mrs. Addo's new Turkish beau had sent home enough takeaway the night before to feed Genghis Khan's army.

"Right, then. You *were* sayin' a man's name."

Fee put the platter in the microwave and punched buttons. "A reasonable deduction." She took the water pitcher from the fridge, filled two glasses, and set them on the table. "Abeni, I'm sorry about all this. I thought a hundred times about telling you everything, but it's not —I just couldn't be sure you'd—that I could..." She trailed off.

There wasn't any good way to say she hadn't trusted her friend enough to blurt, *"Hey, I'm a souler! I'm fated to rescue a person trapped between life and death! And my flight to the U.K. didn't originate in North Carolina. I had a connecting flight from France in the 1770s!"*

Abeni waved a hand dismissively. "No worries, hen.

I'd hoped the ghost business would stay behind in Doncaster when I came to London. But I suppose if it's in your blood, then there's nowt you can do about it."

Not a damn thing, Abeni. I tried. The microwave chimed and Fee removed the platter, placing it in the middle of the table. She and Abeni sat but didn't immediately serve themselves. Fee wasn't sure if they were waiting for the food or their feelings to cool.

"Mind if I ask you something?" Abeni's mouth shaped a smile, but her voice was tense.

"Yeah, sure. Shoot."

"Are your parents really in Paris?"

Bloody fucking hell. Everything her flat mate had heard in the past couple of days, and she was asking *that*?

One way or another, Fee would have to tell Abeni. Buying time, she unfolded the paper napkin she'd just balled up. She smoothed it on the table while a short and unsettling video streamed in her brain. Her, at seventeen, just back from "Paris." The living room of the Bull Street house in Savannah. Her four great-aunts, sitting on the long sofa across from her. Great-aunt Hélène saying softly, sadly, *"I'm sorry, sweetheart. They're all gone, now."*

"My parents are dead, Abeni. Before that, they were in Paris. I grew up there."

Abeni nodded once and picked up her fork and knife. Fee did the same. The quiet lengthened while they ate. When they finished, Fee took their plates to the sink.

Abeni, still sitting, asked, "Will you go to Wales straight away?"

Fee ran water until it was hot, then put the drain plug

in the sink. "Not right away," she said over the splashing, "I want to wrap things up with my grantors first."

"Will they be arsed because you don't have a book for them?"

Fee turned off the tap. "But I do have a book, Abeni. A really, really good one."

Thirty-Nine

One year later, November 2, All Souls Day

Gil shook with cold, ached from head to foot, was wet to the skin, and was perishing from thirst. Added together, his discomforts yielded a sum so shatteringly fine that he felt himself to be floating in bliss above the mucky field whereon he lay, face to the sky.

He was alive.

How had the impossible happened? He had no sense of where he had been or for how long, only an impression of emptiness so vast his mind could not encircle it. The last thing he remembered was standing atop the Olympiad Theatre, his hole-marred ghostly form leaning into the wind on a moonless night.

He must have fallen but had no memory of it. A darkness darker than the night had swallowed him. Now, apparently, it had spit him up like something the cat didn't care for.

To be sure, lying in the mud while rain pelted him, he was much like a puddle of vomit. The thought made him happy anew. He'd forgotten what a buggering bother life could be. Short, hard, full of pain and—

Hunger. It was surpassing odd to hear the rumble from his stomach.

Gil rolled over and got to his hands and knees with more effort than he would have thought necessary for a man of not yet thirty years. He held the pose for a bit, his head hanging between his shoulders. The whirl of his senses suggested he stay thus, even though icy rivulets ran off his hair into his face and every gasping breath sucked water into his nose and mouth.

He'd try standing. Eventually. For the moment, it pleased him inordinately just to watch the rain pooling between his fingers and to feel the grit of what he hoped was Britain's soil under his palms.

On a ragged breath and a cough—God in Heaven, the catch in his lungs sent another jolt of joy through him!—he heaved to his feet. Swaying as though he'd been at the drink for a day and a night, he turned cautiously around himself to survey his surroundings.

A field, then, as he'd surmised. It stretched on all sides save one, where a copse of brown, autumn-bare trees filled an acre or two. A dozen yards to his rear, a circle of jagged stones, such as people said were erected by giants in the distant past, embraced the charred remains of a fire.

Gil dropped his eyes to his feet. His shoes were splashed with red-brown clay and his stockings were so drenched they sagged in rings around his ankles. But he was relieved to see his feet were planted, however unsteadily, on a well-trodden path. Tracking it with his sight, he saw it began at the center of the stones. There, it met another track, a faint one, hardly more than a scratch in the stubble of the field.

He turned again, wiping rain from his eyes. In the direction opposite its origin, the well-trodden path unspooled toward the horizon, where the rising sun painted rose onto the undersides of rain clouds. The path led to uncertainty, perhaps to danger, but at least it led through fields. Where there were fields, there were beasts and barns. Where there were barns, there were people. Where there were people, there were warm hearths and fresh clothing.

And food.

With a hand so chilled he could barely work it, Gil reached into his sodden breeches pocket. The cold disc of the silver pence piece in his fingers heartened him. He was alive. He was a man. He had coin.

And he was standing on the Earth whereon his woman also, God willing, stood. He would walk until he found her. If he encountered dragons, he would slay them. If a mountain blocked his way, he would scale it. If he tumbled off the mountain into an ocean, he would swim it. And if the searing deserts of Arabia stretched before him, he would trek across them until the last drop of moisture dried from his bones. No distance too far, no obstacle too fearsome. He would find Aoife Gowdie and claim her, as she had claimed him.

Gil raised his head, shook the rain from his hair, and began striding along the path.

FORTY

"It's wonderful, Hugh, *diolch yn fawr iawn*." Fee tried out her latest Welsh phrase, *thank you very much*. She stepped back a few feet to see the whole, freshly-painted marquee on the façade of what had been, until the 1980s, the Wesleyan United Methodist Chapel.

Hugh Bevan's paint picked up the colors of the rectangular stained glass window over the double doors. Red lettering on the sign's cobalt blue ground read, *The Coronet Playhouse*.

"Glad to help, Miss Gowdie," Hugh said warmly as he began packing up his gear. "It's fine to see some use bein' made of the old church, though what those Methody would think of actors in the nave..." The Welshman grinned wickedly.

"'*The most dangerousest people in the world*;' that's what one Oxford preacher called them in the 1500s."

"That so? Well, we survived the Vikings and the English. I reckon we'll survive a few actors." Hugh slung his work bag over his shoulder, grabbed the handles of two paint cans in one broad fist, and walked toward his panel truck. "*Pob lwc,*" he called cheerily over his shoulder.

"Thanks!" Fee shouted back.

Yeah, Hugh, I could use some good luck with this insane venture. She entered the building, leaving one of the double doors open behind her. The night had been all about rain and wind, but near daybreak the clouds broke. A clear fall day brought cool air and a distant scent of woodsmoke. Breezes through the open door would help banish the lingering odors of paint and sawn boards in the church's foyer.

It amused her that a building designed for no-nonsense worship had converted so easily and well to a theatre. Standing on the checkerboard tiles of the foyer, she blessed the Victorian aesthetics of the chapel's builders. The red and white floor tiles had mellowed with age and use from the 1894 date of the chapel's construction, becoming a rich maroon and cream. The oak wainscoting and stark white walls above were probably intended to invoke reverence. Now, they were stylish and inviting.

Fee pushed through a second set of double doors from the foyer into a modest-sized nave, once filled with pews, now filled with rows of iron-and-wood theatre seats. As she did every day, she made her way down the center aisle and chose a seat. Today's was No. 12, aisle end, stage left, front row. It gave her an unobstructed view of the altar, now a completely modern stage with rigging, lights, and velvet curtains in a maroon that matched the floor tiles of the foyer.

Settling in, she reached over and ran her hand across the seat next to her. The touch of satiny wood filled her with satisfaction, since the seating was one of the things she'd done best when she converted the church.

The original pews, oak like the wainscoting, had been sold off years ago, when the church dissolved. Diving headfirst into the salvage marketplace, Fee tracked down the seats from the Olympiad Theatre on Drury Lane. It took months. In the end, she'd paid a reclamation warehouse more than the wood-and-iron folding seats were worth, but she bought them all. After discarding the hopeless ones, she ended up with 243 perfectly operational seats, now bolted to the floor, for audiences to park their bums. Over the last few months, she'd sat in every one.

It was delusional behavior, she knew, but she thought perhaps if Gil had sat in one, as she knew he might have when they were still in the Olympiad, she could sense some trace of him. It never happened, but hope didn't die completely for a long time.

It had taken nearly as long for her to give up on Gil's recorded voice in her cellphone. She'd heard it at the time; they both had. But that was in the Olympiad. It wasn't until a few days after she fled the site, after Gil had vanished and the theatre was on its way to a rubbish heap, that she'd tried to find the recording again.

Dead and gone, like the rest of her life with Gil. Her panic was like electrocution. Senseless rage followed. For the first time in her life, she threw things. Only a few IKEA plates from the Bloomsbury flat, but she'd wanted to shatter the whole set and her cellphone, too.

When she got herself under control, she understood the frustration of ghosthunters, with their failed photographs, videos, and sound recordings. What she didn't understand was *why* the recording vanished with Gil. As Jana said, there were thousands of unknowns about leathlings.

At least Gil had given her something she could hold in her hands: the folio. She didn't need to read it anymore, since she'd memorized the most important part. Gil's poem, inscribed in crisp new ink on the very last page.

"If e'er I pas't an hour fair,
Or knew the sweet surcease of care,
Or happy was, that time did slow,
Her velvet touch did make it so.
When mountains fall and kingdoms fail,
This iron truth shall yet prevail;
If e'er a man I was at all,
'Twas for my own Beloved Dol."

Below the poem, he'd penned one additional line. Four words that cradled the whole world in them.

"To A.G. from G.S."

The tears welled and burned in her eyes, as they always did. She resolutely blinked them away, as she always did. She hadn't cried in the entire twelve months since Gil left her.

Why didn't she weep? According to what Mom had

told her so long ago, hysterical tear shedding had been such a fixture of her loss of Papa that she hadn't been able to leave her apartment for weeks. When she did, she had to duck into lavatories, empty hallways, and behind trees for a blubber.

Was Fee's refusal to cry just another form of the rebellion that she'd enacted all her life?

Or was she afraid that if she once let go, she'd never be able to stop?

The answer scared her into a violent shudder, like a wasp had just landed on her shoulder. She jumped to her feet and began her meaningless, habitual task of flipping up all the seats in the nave. *Thwack thwack thwack.* The slap of oak against oak, row after row, was calming in a mindless way, like kneading dough or shooting hoops, neither of which she did.

Auntie Jana, she was pretty sure, knew about her dry-eyes resolve. She didn't badger Fee, not in so many words. But she regularly pointed to signposts of recovery, stopping just short of Great-aunt Nikki's woo-woo dictums; "*There is only Now,*" or "*Don't get so attached to anything that you can't let it go,*" and "*Life moves on, and so must we.*"

Jana's advice was practical, involving the social life of a small Welsh town. "I know it's old-fashioned, Fee, but there's an active Women's Institute here."

Really, Jana, the WI? It wasn't old-fashioned, it was World War II. Jam-making and knitting and singing "*O Jerusalem*" at meetings.

"Poppy's friend Mairead told her, and Poppy told

me, there's a jive dancing class on Wednesday and Saturday nights at the Scout Hut."

A few hours of Lindy hop on aging linoleum floors twice a week. Sure, that would turn Fee's depression into bliss. Or knee problems, whichever came first.

"The bell ringers at St. Bodwen's are looking for another person."

"The ashram up the mountain offers yoga three mornings a week."

"Your mum used to help out at the library."

It exasperated Jana that Fee consistently turned down the local diversions. Her witch-aunt didn't say it, but her unspoken question was, *What* do *you want, Fee?*

Him. She wanted him beside her every hour. Within sight, within the reach of her outstretched hand. At dawn. At dusk. At two in the morning, when she woke from the tired old dream where she wandered between one time and another. One day in Paris, wearing a *robe a l'anglaise* with lace at the elbows. The next in Savannah, wearing jeans, her feet in new sandals of orange and green leather.

Gil was the only one who could stop the clock. He was her time, her era of being. Without him, she was nowhen at all.

Thwack thwack thwack. Last row of seats gone bottoms up, Fee headed toward Part Two of her daily ritual: the transepts, the "arms" of the cross that constituted church design.

One arm had the original baptismal font in it, and she'd decided to leave it in place. It was a handsome thing, carved marble, lidded, with motifs of acanthus leaves symbolizing eternal life.

In the other arm, she'd constructed what Jana would call a not-moving-on exhibit, one devoted to the original —risen, fallen, and erased—Coronet Theatre. Today, as every day, the sight of the two long tables gave her a warm rush of pleasure. Above the tables, a stained-glass window depicting Christ among the lilies of the field rose nearly to the ceiling, admitting light and rainbow stripes of color.

Her first chore was straightening the poster on the first table's easel, whether or not it was crooked. The image was an enlarged, color version of Gil's drawing of the exterior of the Coronet in its day. An inset image was her own work, a cross-section of the Coronet's interior. She'd relied on projected or documented interiors of other period theatres—the Rose, the Hope, the first Globe—and was fairly confident she'd got it right. The legend below the images read:

The presumed Coronet Theatre, built in 1603 between Drury Lane and Arne Street

She'd hoped to display the Charles First silver penny with the poster, but after her final departure from the Olympiad, when she'd recovered enough to look in her backpack, the coin was gone. Into some Morsani-Loeb workman's pocket, she assumed bitterly. Or back into hiding, like millions of other vestiges of old London. Beneath the rubble of a demolished building. Tucked into the earth under concrete.

Next to the easel was a stack of printed paper stapled together in sheaves of five two-sided sheets. Her monograph about the Coronet was a masterpiece of informed guesswork and comparative data. It hadn't been easy to leave out everything Gil had told her and still make a convincing argument. She'd made a speculative leap and identified the theatre on the strength of a single evidentiary crumb, a 1612 reference by Richard Burbage, leading actor of the day, to *"that rucktious house, Coronet, near th' Holy Well."* The spring-fed basin of the Well was now in the basement of the Australian embassy; she'd seen it with the LUCIES. In Burbage's—and Gil's— time, it was a local source of drinking water. Holy Well Street ran parallel (so period maps said) to Wych Street, and the spring was close enough to the Coronet that actors (so her period ghost said) drew water from it.

Before she left London, she'd paid a small fortune to send a courier to the National Trust with her notes and the remains of the two Coronet coin boxes. The second was doomed, anyway, and Gil had helped her extract it from the cellar. If Marcus and Anthea had responded to the parcel, Fee hadn't gotten the message.

She ran her hands over the top of the two locked glass display cases on the table. She checked them every day for dust and was especially careful with the first. It pleased her sense of irony that visitors had a crystal-clear view of the most outrageous literary smokescreen of the 21st century.

Gil's play made such a pretty book. The novelty had worn off a bit, so Fee didn't unlock the case to handle the glossy paper cover and thumb the pages, as she'd done when it was new.

After the libation ritual orchestrated by Mrs. Addo

in the Bloomsbury garden, Fee had spent a manic week typing up *The 'Gyptian* from Gil's hand-penned folio. Abeni—wrongly and rightly deducing that her flat mate was finally writing her grant-funded book—brought her mugs of tea and sandwiches, reminding her to shower and sleep.

Abeni never gave the antique document at Fee's side a second look. Just another of the "old books" between whose pages she'd accused Fee of crawling when Abeni was trying to talk her out of her grant obsession and into a LUCIES expedition.

The morning she finished the manuscript, Fee called Dr. Gretchen Hyde. By ten-thirty, she was in Dr. Hyde's office, manuscript in hand. "My book," she said tersely to the AHRC staffer. "I think it should be published."

Dr. Hyde's eyebrows lofted so high they nearly disappeared. There were any number of replies she could've fired at Fee. *Don't you want to give this to the NEH? Shouldn't you be looking for a literary agent? Why are you here?* But she took the manuscript from Fee's hands, saying, "I'll take a look tonight." With a nod, Fee left her office.

The ensuing months were like the out-of-control coach and four Fee had seen one day in Paris. Pedestrians screaming and jumping out of the way. Horses thundering, wild-eyed, mouths splaying foam. The driver at the reins, straining and shouting.

In the middle of her own runaway event, Fee was surprisingly tranquil.

And stubborn. Dr. Hyde, once she'd read the manuscript, scented a sensation. She pressed it into the hands of an old friend, the director of a prestigious but withering academic publishing house called Perseus Press. In their first meeting, Fee insisted that the author was Gilbert Sorley, late of the King's Men. Both Dr. Hyde and Perseus probably thought Fee was what Gil would have called "addle-pated."

A junior staffer at the press thought differently. Seeing *viral sensation* in invisible ink on the manuscript's title page, he lobbied until he got it pushed at warp speed into print. Fee's name appeared only in a very tiny font on the copyright page.

The cyclonic spin started with the tech-savvy staffer's aggressive campaign on social media. By the time pre-orders were up, reports of a hitherto undiscovered, controversial, wickedly sexy, and falling-down-funny 17th century play were burning up the Internet.

Advance copies went to noted actors and directors. Perseus was swamped by requests from celebrity agents to acquire reading copies. A half-dozen movie producers fought each other like wildcats for film rights. By the time print and digital copies of *The 'Gyptian* were online, it had been translated into nine languages, ranging from French to Tamil. An audio version, like a radio play, was grabbed by PBS, with name actors reading the parts. A fashion designer used the play for a season's worth of clothing inspired by Jacobean and Carolean dress. Haute couture hadn't seen anything like it since *The Three Musketeers* film of 1993 put lace jabots and thigh-high boots on runways for a while.

Sales of the book skyrocketed. People who had previously never read a play debated the fine points of

Jacobean stagecraft at cocktail parties. In academe, discussion about *The 'Gyptian* raged with less alcohol but more big words. Fee was offered a fellowship and several grants for additional study and publication in theatre history of the Jacobean and Carolean Ages. She turned them down. The offers kept coming.

The more she protested that she hadn't written the play, the more rumors spread that she had. One noted scholar of 17th century literature called her "an intuitive savant of period prose." Months afterward, Fee still had no idea what that meant.

Apart from not telling the world that she was a souler and Gil was her leathling, Fee told not a single lie. All her honesty did was convince absolutely *everyone* that she was playing a part, that she was a consummate actor-academic who'd found a way to make scholarship sexy, a fusion of Red Carpet Hottie and Stodgy Librarian.

Fee sighed and checked again for dust on the book's display case. Even as she adjusted the relative positions of the cases by half an inch, she recalled that she needed to email Perseus. BBC Television was still negotiating rights to "*The 'Gyptian:* A Series."

Once 'Gyptian Mania was well underway, Fee had given herself permission to slowly and surely fall apart. She disappeared into the tiny Welsh town where Jana's Broom & Bottle sat snugly on a street called Puzzle Lane. Where stood St. Rhydian's, the castle where Papa had once lived-not lived and met Mom. Where the Irish Sea rolled up to a rocky beach a mile from the town.

And where we'll stay, just me and the big bank account Gil's play gave me. But that, she mused as she stared at her Coronet exhibit, was the lesser of the two enormous gifts Gil had given her.

She was an actor, now. The real thing, the thing she'd yearned for, given up on, then recaptured in those arduous and delicious sessions with Gil on the stage of the Olympiad. The poor, sad Olympiad, now only a memory.

Thoughts of the Olympiad brought her to the second glass display case on the table. In a transparent version of the box a wedding dress might arrive in, lay the green silk dress in which she'd rehearsed *The Alchemist*. A printed card was affixed to one corner of the case.

Theatrical costume, n.d. From the Olympiad Theatre, built 1881, Drury Lane

Recovered by A. Gowdie prior to the Theatre's demolition

As though called by the twinge she always felt at the thought of her London life and losses, her cellphone chirped out a notification, *Light 'Em Up*. Abeni. Fee plucked her cell from the pocket of her blue-green lambswool jacket—she dressed in skirts, knee-high socks, and local woolens these days, not jeans and UNC Lacrosse hoodies—and swiped open the text. It was a long one for her usually laconic friend.

Sarah's chum at Lloyd's says Morsani-Loeb had no Unexpected Archeological Discovery Insurance. A verified find would have buggered their project. Cash always wins, yeah? Some good news attached. Fee scrolled to the two photos.

The first was of the imposing, aggressively modern entrance of The Drury Diamond. To the right of the steel and glass doors, a bright blue, dinner plate-sized English Heritage plaque was just visible. The second photo was a close-up of the plaque and the white enameled lettering on it.

A Jacobean Era theatre stood here
circa 1603 to 1881.

Now that she had some distance from everything that led up to it, Fee had to admit the plaque was a nice reward for the by-courier package she'd sent to the Trust. Not as nice as an ongoing archeological investigation would have been.

It was kind of Abeni to follow up on the fate of the Coronet. She'd moved in with Sarah a month after Fee left the Bloomsbury flat but was lowkey about the upgrade in her relationship and the happiness it brought. That was kind, too.

Fee sensed that Abeni felt a little guilty about dragging Fee into the LUCIES expedition that ultimately connected her with Gil. It was too complicated to explain that there was nothing Abeni could have done differently that would've affected the outcome. As Papa liked to say, "Fate goes as she will."

She dropped her cellphone into her pocket and turned away from the Coronet exhibit, toward the nave aisle. The exhibit had seemed necessary and consoling at the time she'd installed it. Now, she wondered if it was becoming a shrine, like those ancestor altars that some people erected in their homes. If so, Mrs. Addo might approve. On the other hand, Auntie Jana might—

"Aoife! Are you in there?"

Damn. For the second time in five minutes, thinking of something had manifested it.

"I'm in the auditorium, Jana!" she hollered back. "I'll come to the front."

"Good. I've got a little something for you."

Oh, no, Fee thought as she moved up the aisle toward the foyer. Jana's gifts were always well-intentioned, but sometimes bizarre. A few weeks ago, her witch-aunt had given her a protection charm made from fox teeth she'd pried out of a carcass. All very sanitized and ritualized, but dead teeth were still dead teeth. Fee had hung the charm inside the small box office she'd built in the foyer. It couldn't hurt to have a fox guarding the credit card transactions.

The amulet seemed trivial compared to what Jana shoved at Fee when she got to the foyer.

"It's a mouse." Fee peered into the antique birdcage her witch-aunt was proffering.

"See now," Jana replied drily, "that's your expensive education at work."

Fee took the birdcage by its ring at the top, examining the sleek rodent inside. It was a small mouse, hardly more than an adolescent, black as ink with a pink nose and comically large ears. The cage was also small, budgie scaled. Not the huge iron Victorian contraption in which Rumpelstiltskin lay on a puffy pillow when he wasn't terrorizing visitors to the Broom & Bottle.

Fee didn't even try to mask her suspicion. "Where did you find it?"

"*It* is a him, as I think you'll spot when he gives you a rear view. And I didn't find him, he found me. I was just sitting down to a reading for a customer when out of nowhere popped His Lordship. Ran across the table while the customer was screaming the shop down, Rumpel in hot pursuit."

Jana pointed at the mouse. "He's a fast'un, or he'd have been lunch for the cat, but between customer and me, we got them both corralled."

Fee wished she'd witnessed the corralling. Jana's hair —she was dyeing it hot pink these days—was a disordered haystack, and the jacket of her two-piece 60's caramel bouclé wool suit was awry, one of the buttons gone.

"Jana," Fee began, "I understand housing a mouse and a cat under the same roof isn't a good idea, but are you suggesting I should *keep* this little guy?" She lifted the cage a few inches and the mouse, who'd been staring fixedly at her in an unnerving way, squeaked as loudly as a mouse twice its size. "I mean, I used to have a mouse, but he died, and..."

Became a ghost mouse. Friend and companion of my ghost lover.

"Well, keep him for a few days, then. Blayney Pets is shut for the week as Cavan's missus had a hysterectomy. He's only got the daughter, who's not all there, if you ask me, coming in to feed the animals. We can sort it later." That was apparently Jana's last word on the subject, as she turned on her stiletto heels and marched out the open half of the double front doors.

That's what Fee got for leaving the door open. It was a mouth yelling, *Come right in, everyone! Bring me your stray animals and any other inconvenient thing you need to offload!*

"You," she told the mouse, "are just visiting. Don't start picking paint colors."

She placed the cage on the scarred old oak table just inside the doors where, in the chapel's heyday, parish bulletins, missionary appeals, and spiritual pamphlets had waited to ambush churchgoers when they arrived. For now, it was empty and out of the wind. Just to be sure neither wind nor more unexpected visitors entered, she pushed the front door shut, though she didn't bother to throw the old-fashioned bolt. After London, it was nice to live in a place where not every entrance had to be secured like the vault at Fort Knox.

There were carrots and celery in her small fridge in the rectory kitchen. She might have some old newspapers for bedding, too. She'd packed her treasured V&A mug in a copy of *The Times* when she moved to Wales, and she bought the local rag now and then. A jar lid for water, a scrap of flannel in a box for a napping place, and she'd be able to make a cozy bed and breakfast out of the birdcage for the few days the mouse would be bunking there.

———

Invariably, the simplest tasks took the most time. It was a

half hour before she put together a mouse Welcome Wagon and returned to the foyer.

Where there was a man.

He was facing away, bent slightly forward, his head bowed over the birdcage on the foyer table. At first glance, he was simply a tall man in a gray tweed suit jacket, a little strained across shoulders that were obviously too wide for it, wearing dark trousers and shoes. At the sound of her heels on the tiled floor, he straightened, and his hair spilled over his collar.

"I have my mother's hair." Gil's hair caught bursts of colored light from the stained-glass window over the chapel door. For a tortured instant, the light was all Fee could see, transparent brushstrokes of red and blue on hair that was blacker than brown but browner than black.

Everything she held in her hands dropped to the floor with an echoing crash. Shock played a hot arpeggio up her spine to the back of her neck and her eyes rolled up.

She fell.

FORTY-ONE

He caught her before she touched the floor, then lowered them both to the coldly magnificent tiles of the chapel with the improbable name *Coronet Playhouse* over the door.

She was senseless in his arms for mere moments, while his heart leapt and bounded like a frightened hare. When her eyes fluttered open, Gil fell straight into their depths and entirely forgot the things he'd instructed himself to say during the six miles of walking it had taken to get him from the muddy field to the town.

The eyes he loved filled with tears. The body he loved shook in his embrace. Long-denied sorrow and joy and fear and disbelief—they were fighting their way out of her. He knew, because they were fighting their way out of him.

She wept. No words, no restraint, she simply clung with both hands to his new and ill-fitting doublet and convulsed with grief. Sobs racked her slender frame. She'd lost weight, he could feel the bones of her shoulders and spine under his hands. The salt tide from her eyes ran down her cheeks, soaking the black ringlets that gathered around her pretty face.

Ah, she's cut her hair. The thought pained him. Had she suffered a fever? Her glorious, curling, silken hair was half the length he remembered from when it fell against his face as she rode his thighs. The small change pierced him sharp as a blade. How long had he been absent? What else had he missed? Gil brought his face down to hers, kissing her forehead, her eyes, and her tears.

And then, he was fighting his own tears, fighting them the way a boy does when weeping shamed him. It had been that long since he'd let grief overmaster him. Now it did, a beast that clawed its way to his eyes and took his pride with it. He wept silently, harshly, his shoulders hunched as if waiting for a blow. *A man does not weep*, the baron had said, his fists adding bruises to a boy's pain at the loss of his mother.

But Gil was a boy no longer. He was a man, and he wept. Torn from life, from love, both things lost and found again. Alive at last, with Aoife held against his beating, living heart. There were no words for such a state, only tears.

Their clothing came away as though peeled from their bodies by invisible agents. Angels, perhaps, or demons, he'd cared not which. In seconds they were flesh to flesh. At the touch of Aoife's skin, finer than velvet, warmer than the sun on his face at Midsummer, Gil gave a shout. Her name, he thought, but it might have been God's or some other deity's, hidden inside his lost soul until it woke with his new life.

She uttered one word alone, *Gil*. He took fire at the sound and his cock, already stiff, surged and flexed against his belly. He tossed their clothing into a rough pile and lifted Aoife upon it. He'd not let her wasted frame touch the frigid floor.

Her arms encircled his neck, her knees came up, and in one fierce motion he was inside her. She made another sound, a wordless, hungry cry, and madness overtook him.

Coarse and lewd and savage. Fine and pure and sweet. It was all those things and more. As he plowed her deep, she rose to meet him, tight and wet, gripping him with her sex and raking his shoulders with her nails. His body roared him toward his ending almost before he had started. He shoved his hand between them and stroked the trigger at her cleft, once, twice.

She came apart, screaming. He gave his own hoarse cry and loosed a flood of seed into her body.

Sound and sight deserted him. He clung to Aoife, stunned deaf and blind by joy. Some small rustlings finally intruded: her breath, in whimpers, his own, rough and sawing. Even though his entire body quivered from the force of his release, Gil could not withdraw. He was still solid as a tree limb and Aoife, beneath him, continued to clutch and shudder around his undiminished length.

Slowly, he moved again inside her, curling his hips and delving the spend-slick tunnel that gripped him close as a fist. He felt her climbing, trying, for a second peak. He knew she would not want control or finesse, only the coin of steady stroking for what she needed. And by

God, he'd pay for her body's pleasure with everything left in his.

The wordless slapping of their skin and their hitching breaths were the only sound in the cold church. They rutted like beasts in a field, but their hearts soared so high they left the earth behind. Up there, in the stars, Gil wanted to tell her that he loved her, that he'd always loved her, that he would never stop loving her. He wanted to return to the hidden fastness of their love, that dear, dead theatre on Drury Lane, if only to pull forth the moments of their story, gifting them to her like jewels.

Do you remember the night we met without meeting? How you danced upon the stage and I, yearning, watched you from the shadows? The first time I bowed to you and brushed my lips against your hand? The rooftop, silvered by moonlight, and a kiss that seemed to go on forever? The first time we coupled, how the bed fell, and we laughed and laughed and laughed?

I remember all, her body seemed to answer. She arched and held, tight and taut, against his groin. Her mouth, incomparably soft, opened in a low moan as completion took her. The sight and sound unstitched him. With a final violent plunge, he collapsed upon the saddle of her hips, sensation flooding his own limbs while he trembled from head to toe. A tide of velvet darkness took them both away.

———

"I should have come to you with gifts. Yellow gloves. A bracelet of coral. Cheese."

Even considering their boneless, brainless condition, Fee had hoped to hear something different from Gil when they both returned to their senses. Maybe she hadn't understood him correctly.

"Cheese?" She considered the noun, shifting on the rumpled heap of their clothes. "What kind?"

"Suffolk Bang, I think. Or Cheshire."

A bubble of laughter rose in Fee's throat and burst from her lips. "What, no *queso* and chips?"

"I don't know what took me, *chavi*. At the very least, I should have handed over a wheel of Wensleydale."

"Stop, stop!" She rolled atop him, laughing so hard she couldn't breathe.

"A basket of fruit wouldn't have gone amiss, or a—"

Unable to speak, she grabbed his shoulders and hung on, guffawing.

"Instead, I leapt upon you like—"

She touched his mouth and he went silent, smiling behind her fingers. If she kept laughing, she'd start crying again. With all the moments she planned to devote to happiness, she wouldn't waste a single one on tears.

Splaying across his chest, she tucked her head beneath his chin, inhaling his scent. It was different than before, not ginger and ale. Now, it was Welsh clay. Sweet dried grass. Autumn rain. English rose, from her soap.

They'd both have new scents from now on. Mingled, from the merging of two into one.

She made a complaining noise as he bucked their two bodies up to pull his shirt from underneath, but when he spread it over her bare back and anchored it with a protective arm, she was glad of both. "Where did you get those clothes?" she asked sleepily.

"I had the coin."

Not just any coin, *the* coin. "The Charles First penny?"

"The very one. On the way here, I passed a shop with gold and silver in the window. The shopkeeper was all amaz'd to see the penny. He gave me fine goods in trade. The clothes from his very back, in fact."

Fee was sure Arwel Simms, the High Street jeweler who lived above his shop, didn't hesitate to swap whatever he'd been wearing for that particular historic coin. When Fee had researched it after plucking it from the cellar floor of the Olympiad, the penny was worth over 400 pounds sterling.

"He also, very kindly, methought, gave me a handful of ready money." Gil kissed the top of Fee's head and she nuzzled closer. God, how she'd missed his touch. "From a man in a cart, I purchased a bacon bop."

She laughed again, absurdly happy. "Bacon *bap*. It's a...oh, never mind. Good, was it?"

"Exceedingly. The swine did not die for naught." His stomach growled in approval.

Her man was hungry. They would rise from the floor and go to the kitchen in the rectory. They'd eat bacon sandwiches together, now and always. "The pig probably died up the road, at Gilroy's Farm."

"Ah, a Welsh pig. My first." Gil lifted his head to look around the foyer, settling on the cross still affixed to the wall over the front doors. "First time having carnal relations in a church, as well."

Fee knuckled his arm, then kissed the spot. "It's not a church, anymore. It's a theatre."

"Whatever you say, dear one."

There'd be a lot of firsts for Gil in the coming months. Fee warmed at the thought of bringing him up to speed in her world, now theirs. She'd start slowly, but knowing Gil's insatiable curiosity and quick mind, her 17th century lover would have social media accounts in a month.

A series of squeaks from the oak table snapped her attention to the birdcage sitting on it. If she weren't still brain-scrambled from shock and sex, she might have come up with a better way to phrase her next remark. As it was, it just burbled out.

"You stole my mouse."

Gil's response was a deep, amused rumble. "The mouse left of its own accord, and I knew nothing of its defection. I knew nothing at all until the dawn of this very day, when I woke, flat on my back in a pissing rain, next to a circle of stones in a field." He waved toward the door of the theatre. "About six miles to the east."

A stone circle six miles away. That would be Sol Helod, on Rowan and Wren's Basil and Bee Farm. How Gil had gotten from there to the town would be a story. How he'd found the theatre and her, another. *The 'Gyptian,* and how Gil had given the two of them a future with a book he'd authored when he was technically dead...

The air around them was thick with stories that

needed to be told, shimmering with words that wanted to be said. Fee was terrified to even begin sorting them out. It seemed safest to stick with the mouse for a while.

"At about the same time you were walking from the country to the town, I acquired a new mouse."

"And a fine mouse, it is."

"True. But it's not Shakespeare."

"Are you so sure?"

Of course, Fee was sure. Wasn't she? She was debating how to answer Gil when a dark ball of fur, squeaking, launched itself at them. Fee yelped.

"Oh, it's like that, is it?" Gil seemed unsurprised that the rodent he'd seen in a birdcage a short while before was burrowing between him and Fee. "Shall we never have an hour to ourselves, mouse?"

"How did he get out of the cage?" Fee rolled off Gil and struggled to a sitting position. She scooped the small intruder into her hand. It was a relief that he felt as solid as any living mouse could feel.

"You remember how clever he is."

"I remember how clever *Shakespeare* was."

"Shakespeare." Gil looked meaningfully at the mouse, who lifted his head attentively. "Dance." Gil made a rotating motion with his hand and the mouse chased its tail several times.

Gil smirked as he extended his forefinger to the mouse. "Shakespeare, are you a gentleman?"

Fee's jaw fell as the mouse sat on its haunches, bobbed its upper body, and then delicately placed one forepaw on Gil's finger. Speechless, all Fee could do was gently stroke her new-old pet, rubbing lightly behind his ears as Shakespeare used to like.

"God's hat," she finally choked out, "it *is* the Bard."

"A bit more mannerly than the last edition, I hope." Gil took the mouse from her hand and placed him on the floor with the celery and carrots she'd dropped. "Dine, ratling. My lady and I have things to discuss, and you should not impose your hairy self upon the private affairs of your betters."

She didn't think they were quite done discussing the mouse, but she let Gil pull her down to their makeshift pallet. Something still trembled inside her; it had to be settled before they slid into sleep or coupling again.

"Gil, are you...are you really..."

For answer, he took her fingers, laying them on the spot where the wound that killed him was gone, nothing but smooth bronze skin in its place. She smiled, but her eyes flooded. Before she knew it and despite her prohibition against more tears, she was crying again, laughing at the same time.

Gil, because he was Gil, just laughed. "Ah, you're giddy as a windmill now, woman, as you've only known me in my prime. But when my hair goes gray and my back aches, when I rise to piddle six times a night and fart under the covers, then you'll be whistling another tune."

"I'm not getting any younger, Old Man Sorley," she told him in a thick voice, "and I'll want you just the same. I'll waggle my septuagenarian tits at you and, achy back or not, you'll make a grab for them."

He made a grab for them, then, and she giggled. The grab became tender stroking and squeezing, and her giggles turned to sighs. Shakespeare the Second chittered and gnawed carrots for a bit, then scrambled up their bodies to Fee's bosom, where he dodged Gil's hand and dove into her cleavage.

Fee yelped. "Behave yourself, S2! When the babies come, you'll have competition for your favorite spot."

Gil's hand froze on Fee's nipple. "B-babies?"

"I'm not on the pill, anymore, Gil." It was the moment when a lesser man might have found a reason to snatch up his clothes and head for the hills. But this was Gil, her Gil.

His face brightened as he kissed her lightly. "Then, let us flout the proverb and marry in haste, my love. Our house shall have but one bastard in it."

"The Honorable Fucking Bastard, sir?"

"The very one." He looked over his shoulder at the doors leading out of the foyer, and Fee read his mind.

"I have a lodging." She pointed toward the door that led to the Rectory. "Eight rooms and a number of chairs, all with four legs."

"Have you a bed?"

"A sturdy one. The last pastor and his wife had seven children."

"Then, my beauty," he lifted her into his arms, mouse and all, "exeunt, the players."

FORTY-TWO

FOUR YEARS LATER

"Jana, what's wrong? Is it Lee-lee? Is she—"

"Félice is fine. She's playing with Rumpel, and Poppy's keeping an eye on them both."

Fear whooshed out of Fee on an exhalation. Her three-year-old loved sleeping over with Auntie Jana, because who else had a color-changing cat? But kids that age could get into trouble anywhere.

"It's just that your text was..."

Alarming, Fee had thought when she read the three words, all caps. *RING ME NOW.* She and Gil were in rehearsal with the cast of *As You Like It*. As soon as her cellphone pinged and she read Jana's text, she caught Gil's eye. He was onstage, coaching the hapless young man cast as Le Beau. Fee pointed at her cell and rushed into the foyer so she could call her witch-aunt in private.

True to form, Jana picked up and dove in. "Last night, we had the Samhain ritual at Sol Helod."

"Sure. Sorry I missed it. I'm in bed early these days." Because the first trimester of pregnancy with twins did that to a person. When Fee wasn't directing or acting, she was asleep. Or vomiting.

"We were all early to bed last night. Félice was yawning, Morgana's got a head cold, and I was expecting a delivery at the shop first thing this morning. Anyway, we all went home before nine. About three hours after I got back to town, Wren and Rowan rang me. They said I needed to drive back to the farm right away, which I did. Poppy stayed with Félice and—"

"Jana, I can hardly hear you. Is that *singing* behind you?"

"Oh, right, it's definitely that."

Fee stilled, listening. "I'm not sure I—do you—"

"I hope you're not going to ask me if I recognize the song, Aoife, because I don't."

Definitely singing, though. She couldn't make out the words, but the music was martial, even aggressive. In the next minute, either the singer moved away or Jana did, since her witch-aunt's voice was more audible.

"Singer says it's the uh guh fight song."

"Uh guh—what?" Fee's brain did a few pirouettes and a back flip before it finally nailed the phonetics. Uh. Guh. UGA.

God's beard, as Gil might say. "Okay, Jana. I think it's a sports song from an American school, University of Georgia."

Jana grunted. "That would explain the accent."

"Uh, right, I guess it would. Pretty odd, but I'm not sure what a trespassing American with a song in their heart has to do with Wren phoning you in the middle of the—"

"Wren sounded very rattled on her mobile, which isn't like her. You know how she is. Placid, serene, What Would Buddha Do. I finally got through the babbling and she told me she'd counted the goat kids when she put them to bed in the barn, and she was one short. She went out to the fields, looking. That's when she heard singing up on Sol Helod.

"When she got there, she saw not one kid, but two. One was the goat variety. The other was a young woman —a teenager, really, as near as we can figure out. Sixteen or seventeen, maybe."

Gil entered the foyer. Her Tyger of the stage, lean and powerful. He wrapped his arms around her, and she leaned back into his chest. His hands rested protectively on her belly, and Fee put her free hand over his.

"This girl," Jana went on, "had built up the fire at the crossroads, dropped her clothes on the ground, and was dancing around the fire and yodeling like a drunk on karaoke night at the Anchor and Bell. In the nude, Aoife. In. The. Nude."

Probably something Fee should comment on, but for the life of her she couldn't think what to say. Jana went on without her.

"And the goat kid was leaping around with her, having the time of its baby goat life."

"Well, Jana, that's...strange, to say the least."

"Oh, I'm not done with strange, yet. The girl's got hair like a house on fire and a ring in her nose and a tattoo the size of a dinner plate on her backside."

"Okay." Fee decided not to mention Jana's hair, which roamed the color wheel, nor her love for earrings the size of cellphones. "Why did you call me, Jana?"

"This outdoor ballerina, as near as we can make out through the accent, says she's your great-aunt Helen's namesake."

"*Hélène*?" Fee's mind whirled, trying to make sense of what Jana was telling her. "Is the girl from Savannah? How does she know my great-aunt?"

"'No' to the first, and 'how would I know' to the second. Her name is Helen Catherine, but according to her, and I believe it, everyone calls her Hell Cat.

"Listen, Aoife." Fee could almost see Jana's broad bosom release the sigh she sent over the connection. "The little goat dancer says she's your *cousin*."

Cousin? To say Fee barely knew her cousins was an understatement. She'd always thought the whole pack of them lived in Moniac, Georgia, on the St. Mary's River. She certainly hadn't seen any of them since she was what her great-aunts called "*p'tit p'tit*," little little. Great-aunt Nikki, whose longtime partner Leonora was from one of the Barrier Islands off the coast, mentioned some distant Gowdie kin in her part of the state. Nothing else.

Her attempt to say just that to Jana was lost in a confused mélange of voices at the other end. Jana's, forceful and Liverpudlian, and another, high-pitched and very Southern. Suddenly, excited words blared in Fee's ear from a mouth apparently pressed to the other phone. "Well, *dang*, cuz, how you doin'? It's me, Hell Cat! I'm a souler an' I'm finally *here*!"

The girl's accent was sun sparkling on coastal waters,

the flash of mullet leaping on a hot day, and the smells of marsh grass and mud. It also reminded Fee of Leonora's soft island speech.

More confusing squawks from the phone ended with her witch-aunt's voice again. "She spent the night on the couch in the Broom & Bottle, Aoife, and I gave her breakfast this morning. I'll put her outside the shop and point her toward the theatre. Best of British luck." Jana ended the call.

"All well, *chavi*?" Behind Fee, Gil's voice reassured her warmly, but with an edge of concern.

Fee tilted back her head and looked up into Gil's smoky blue eyes. She wished she could hide in them. Then she wouldn't have to investigate why an unknown, Southern drawling, inked and pierced, teenaged souler cousin named Hell Cat was found dancing naked in a Welsh field on Halloween.

There was a muffled pounding at the theatre's double doors, latched to keep interruptions out of rehearsals. The girl must have run the block from Jana's shop like a cheetah.

"Sweetheart," Fee said as calmly as she could, "I hadn't planned for it to happen this way, but I think you're about to meet my family."

Acknowledgments

My deep thanks go to the teachers in my life who led me to appreciate English literature. They opened doors to joy, grandeur, and a career in writing.

Thanks, as well, to Mrs. T, my long-ago Scout troop leader. She made sure every campfire had a good ghost story.

About the Author

A career historian, Annie R McEwen has lived in six countries and under every roof from a canvas tent to a Georgian Era manor house. Annie is published by Harbor Lane Books (US), Bloodhound Books (UK), The Wild Rose Press, and Rowan Prose Publishing. When she's not in her 1920s bungalow in Florida, Annie lives, writes, and explores castles in Wales.

Winner of the 2022 Page Turners Writing Award (Romance Category), Annie garnered both a First and Second Place 2022 RTTA (Romance Through the Ages Award), the 2023 MAGGIE Award, and the 2023 Daphne du Maurier Award. Annie's short fiction appears in numerous anthologies.

Find Annie online at www.anniermcewen.com

facebook.com/Quillist

instagram.com/anniermcewen

bookbub.com/profile/annie-r-mcewen

About the Publisher

Harbor Lane Books, LLC is a US-based independent digital publisher of commercial fiction, non-fiction, and poetry.

Connect with Harbor Lane Books on their website (www.harborlanebooks.com) and social media.

facebook.com/harborlanebooks

x.com/harborlanebooks

instagram.com/harborlanebooks

bsky.app/profile/harborlanebooks.bsky.social

tiktok.com/@harborlanebooks

threads.net/harborlanebooks

youtube.com/harborlanebooks

pinterest.com/harborlanebooks

If You Enjoyed Bound Across Time and Bound to Happen, Then You Might Enjoy

9 781963 705072